SWEET ROME

AUDREY STAINTON

Sweet Rome

A NOVEL

Holt, Rinehart and Winston
New York

Copyright © 1982 by Audrey Stainton
All rights reserved, including the right to reproduce
this book or portions thereof in any form.
Published by Holt, Rinehart and Winston,
383 Madison Avenue, New York, New York 10017.
Published simultaneously in Canada by Holt, Rinehart
and Winston of Canada, Limited.

Library of Congress Cataloging in Publication Data
Stainton, Audrey.
Sweet Rome.
I. Title.
PR6069.T186S9   823′.914   81-7026   AACR2
ISBN: 0-03-059579-7

First Edition

Designer: Amy Hill
Printed in the United States of America
1 3 5 7 9 10 8 6 4 2

ISBN 0-03-059579-7

For Anis

"And, after all, what is a lie? 'Tis but
The truth in masquerade"
　　　—Lord Byron, *Don Juan* XI, 37

Part 1

ONE

Mike took his time getting off the train; he was afraid of being knocked down. When everyone else had gone and he stepped out carefully on to the platform, it was like getting out of bed after a long illness, when the floor comes up and hits you and the shortest distance is immensely far to walk.

It was almost dark and oddly quiet, except for the muffled footsteps and soft voices common to all railway stations, and a sporadic whistle, a shout, and the sudden hiss of an engine, like a sigh. But as he made his way slowly towards the barrier, he became aware of a faint reverberation, which for a moment he took to be the pounding of his own brain.

By the time he reached the glare of the arcade, he wished he had let Avvocato Sora come to meet him. He had dreaded being patted on the shoulder and asked how he felt, but he had not anticipated being as frightened as this.

People kept jostling him as they hurried past, absorbed in their own lives. A seedy little fellow in a garish tie, who had been hanging round all day, looking for someone raw enough to make a profit out of, stared at him uncertainly, pondered his once-smart, long-outdated suit, his expensive shoes, his haircut, his pasty face, and instinctively decided to leave him alone. An old man with a hungry smile and desperate eyes sidled up to him and ventured, without much conviction: "Hotel, mister?" Nobody recognized him. Nobody at all.

In a way this was a relief. He had expected to be waylaid by at least one reporter. It was one of the things he was afraid of. All the same, it hurt a little to discover that his release was of no interest to anyone.

3

A slim, dark-eyed girl with long, flowing hair swept past, intent on making an impression, not on Mike, whom she did not notice, but perhaps on Fellini, if he should happen to be lurking somewhere on the lookout for a new star. Mike stopped to watch her go and noted that she was only about eighteen. She must have been born *afterwards*, and had all the time since then to grow up and leave school. There was a whole new generation like her, that had never heard of him.

He walked unsteadily on, past the benches in the ticket hall, a vast gray limbo where shadow-people huddled over cardboard suitcases, waiting for trains to Chiasso and Domodossola. On towards the great glass façade, clouded over by a fog of human breath. Out into the deep blue twilight of Rome.

The square was empty, unnaturally empty and silent, except for that dull reverberation, which was louder now and more sinister, like a gathering earthquake. The barrier all round that kept out the cars made the square an eerie, unreal place. It seemed to reflect his own state of numbness, the feeling that he was shut off from the world, like a man who was no longer a man, but a ghost.

His plan had been to take a taxi to Trinità dei Monti and enjoy his first half hour in Rome sitting quietly on the Spanish Steps. But he had not expected to find a queue for taxis, headed by a policeman. He decided to walk.

As he stepped past the barrier into the street, the noise hit him instantly in all its violence. That dull reverberation became a roar. It was the traffic.

The first impact was shattering. The sight of all those headlights and wheels, that impenetrable mass of metal and glass, made him feel sick. He could see no way of ever crossing the road, for even when the cars came to a halt and he saw other people squeezing nonchalantly between the fenders, he could not find it in himself to do the same. Finally he darted forward just as the lights changed. A motorbike lurched ahead; Mike leaped out of its way, almost under a bus.

He plunged into a bar and asked for whiskey, which he swallowed with shaking hands and a racing heart. He could easily telephone Sora and ask to be rescued, even now; but the thought of

Sora's little smile was too much for him. He could not let himself be defeated so soon.

When he felt calm enough to set off again, he cut through the back streets by the Opera House and headed for Via Quattro Fontane. He found he had to walk very slowly, keeping close to the walls, and it proved to be much farther than he had thought. If there was one thing he had dreamed of and longed for all these years, it was to stroll through Rome again in the sweet spring twilight. And now all he could feel was panic. His eyes, dazzled by the lights of the shops, seemed unable to focus, and from time to time he had to stop and put down his case because he was too dizzy to go on. He was even tempted to dive into any hotel, and take refuge in some cell-like room. But he had to get away from the station area, where the buildings were grimy and hotels tended to be sordid. He braved himself to cross Via Nazionale.

The sight of the four fountains at the crossroads made his spirits rise again. Those peacefully reclining figures had not changed. Nor had Bernini's stubborn old Triton, still blowing his seashell in Piazza Barberini, impervious to the roaring bedlam that had been loosed all around.

At the corner of Via Francesco Crispi he stopped again, and instead of going straight ahead, he turned left down the hill, and then sharp right.

There it was. Via Gregoriana. For the first time he felt something stir in him—the feeling that he was back in the world again. There were cars parked nose to tail the whole length of the street, but nothing else had changed. He knew each house, each door. These ageless stones were friendlier than people, warm to the touch, placid and comforting. There was his own doorway, Number 49. He stepped into the dark, narrow hall and stood there, seething with memories, poised between delight and despair.

The only discordant note in what might otherwise still have been the past was the name Gordon where his own name used to be: the sight of it all at once made him fume. It was idiotic of him, he realized that. The flat had no part in his plans; it was a corner of the past, no more. He did not know what had made him head straight for it like this, but it infuriated him to think there was someone up there able to enjoy it at this present moment. Impulsively he jabbed the bell with his finger. An unmistakably American voice said: "Yes?"

"Is Mike Donato there?" asked Mike.

"Who?"

"You never heard of Mike Donato?"

"What? Who *is* that?"

"A ghost!" Mike cupped his hands to give the word a spooky sound. Then he darted off up the road, feeling more like himself, even chuckling a little at the thought of Mr. Gordon dangling over the balustrade, trying to see the ghost. From that terrace no one could see the street.

It was probably the most unpractical flat in the world, an impossible attempt to turn the two rambling top floors of a narrow and decrepit old Roman building into a luxurious modern penthouse. To reach it—except on the rare occasions when the lift was working—you had to climb up three flights of steep, dark stairs. If the hall light was not broken, as it usually was, and if you succeeded, with the help of its wan, pinkish glow, in fitting your key into the lock, then you walked straight into the bedroom.

"It may look like a bedsit from this angle," he had said to Robin the first time he took her there. "But that's only to make seduction easier—and the flat more expensive. There's a proper living room upstairs if you're interested."

"I'm not."

She must be forty-five now. She could not still be the slim, laughing girl he had loved. His mother was not much more than that when he had left England, and she was already an old woman, shapeless and hopeless. He could not bear to think that Robin might have aged like that.

She was never exactly beautiful, not in the conventional sense. What he remembered best were her faults: the way her nose used to go bright red in the sun, and the unmanageably straight, vaporous hair she was always grumbling about and threatening to have permanently waved, but which had highlights the color of copper when it was newly washed and electrified by brushing.

They had made love in front of the fire that first night in Via Gregoriana, and the image of the flames dancing in her eyes had remained with him ever since. Over the years it had become one of his favorite daydreams, especially in the early mornings. He used to try to fend off the moment when the rusty bolt would grate back and the cell door would open on another grim day by burying himself under the blanket and leafing through sweet memories such as this, word by word, sensation by sensation, embroidering them with new erotic fantasies each time, till the sweetness turned to scorching pain and he had to bite his pillow to stop himself from crying out.

But now he could open his eyes without seeing one of the guards peering in through the Judas hole to make sure he was still alive, without having to lie and stare at the moisture on the stone ceiling and wait for it to shed its next melancholy tear. He was in Rome, looking down at Piazza di Spagna from the top of the steps, a free man. Only he was still too dazed to feel happy he was there, still too frightened to emerge from the shell of his dreams and reach out for reality.

The only joy he had felt so far that day was when he first stepped out through the prison gates and saw unlimited space in front of him. He had inhaled a great lungful of fresh sea air and taken one step forward, then another. "This is it!" he had said to himself. "No one can stop me now." But before he had walked a few yards he was in a cold sweat, paralyzed with terror at the thought of what lay ahead.

It was getting late. If he was to book into a hotel, he would have to produce a document of some sort, and the brand-new identity card that had been issued to him upon his release was liable to attract attention. His passport would be less conspicuous, but it was with the rest of his things in Sora's hands. There was nothing for it, he must find a telephone and call Sora, whether he wanted to or not.

Mario Sora was a neat little man who smelled of talcum powder and cologne, and that fine evening in March, as he steered his

7

white Mercedes into Piazza del Popolo, he was boiling with self-righteous irritation.

"I was worried," he told Mike, leaning over to open the car door for him. It was an understatement. Sora was always parsimonious with words, but his tone of accusation took Mike by surprise almost as much as did the luxury of his car.

"I told you I'd take my time," Mike retorted, bristling. The mere sight of the man stirred up feelings of resentment, though Mike knew that, ultimately, he had no one to blame for what had happened but himself. He had been so naïve at the time as to think that in a court of justice the obvious truth could be trusted to speak for itself. If he had only known. He would have engaged the best lawyer in the country to defend him, instead of the only one whose name he chanced to know. He would have put up a proper fight, instead of sitting there letting them all talk, if he had ever thought their nonsense could be believed. But by the time he realized what was happening, it was suddenly, incredibly, too late. A handful of people who knew nothing about him had gravely decided to pulverize his life.

Sora was full of excuses and justifications; his letters continued for years to be optimistic, each offering some new scheme for putting everything right, or explaining away the legal quirk that had invalidated the previous scheme. And every time he came to visit Mike in prison, Mike found him a little older and a little more pathetic, fussing for points and paragraphs among his papers and waiting with a tentative little smile of triumph for Mike's reaction to each new flicker of salvation he unearthed. And as plea after plea was quashed, Mike, who had witnessed so much pain in prison that he had grown exceptionally sensitive to other men's anguish, at times felt almost sorrier for Sora than for himself.

There was no need. Sora was far from being the poor wretch that Mike took him for, prematurely aged by the burden of his failure. If this was the impression he had been apt to give when visiting the prison, it was largely on account of a queasiness of his stomach that invariably affected him at the first whiff of prison stench. He certainly did not blame himself for Mike's misfortune. On the

8

contrary, with the passing of years he had gradually adjusted the facts in his mind until he was no longer sure that Mike was not guilty. Oh, he would not voice such a thought aloud to anyone, but he did occasionally display a little secretive smile, as if to convey that, heaven knows, he had done his best but there are some cases no advocate can or ought to win. For the rest, he had done very well with his career, having wisely escaped from the pitfalls of penal law and turned his attention to the entertainment industry, where he was now comfortably established as legal adviser to several film companies. As far as he was concerned, what Mike represented now was a tattered and disproportionately bulky file he would be very glad to relegate to the cellar.

No one, however, could accuse him of being unconscientious. He would certainly not have shirked his professional duty to travel to Elba and meet Mike at the prison gate if Mike had not insisted on being left alone. Failing that, it would have been proper, at least, to go and meet him at Stazione Termini, but no, Mike stubbornly refused to be met.

"I'll call you if I need you," Mike had added by way of a postscript to his last note, and although Sora found this peremptory, not to say insolent, he had felt obliged to sit in his office all day in case the telephone rang with an S.O.S. He had continued to wait long after Mike's train had arrived and his secretary had gone home. When the phone finally rang, his stomach was rumbling and he was completely out of patience with Mike Donato.

But he had come at once to pick Mike up, heavily conscious of doing his duty and more than his duty, not only as a lawyer, but also as a Christian. On top of everything else, it was a Thursday and he was missing a television quiz program of which he was particularly fond.

"Have you eaten?" he asked Mike, as he drove across the river towards Prati.

"No, but—"

"We can go to Micci's. It's quiet in the evenings."

It was more than quiet, it was deserted, but that suited Mike very well. He was not really hungry. The emotions of the day had drained him of all desire except to find a bed and go to sleep. He suspected he had a slight fever. He watched Sora confabulate eagerly with the waiter about the various virtues of each dish and felt not the slightest curiosity about what they decided he was to eat. When he had finished ordering the meal, Sora turned back to Mike and said: "I haven't found your passport."

"What do you mean? Where is it?"

"Sssh! Don't get excited!" Sora glanced uneasily at the only other occupied table, at the far end of the room. "Nothing that was in your flat has been lost. It was all packed away and no one's touched it since. But we couldn't look for your passport without unpacking the lot, and I think you should be the one to do that. In the meantime I brought you this, for the hotel." He placed an Italian driving license on the table.

"Hello, Michele Donadio," said Mike, opening it and staring at the photograph. "You were a handsome bastard once." He placed his new identity card beside it and added: "This other one's less flattering, but more realistic. They're a callous lot, these prison photographers. What worries me is the place of issue, but a driving license twenty years out of date—that's worse."

"Your passport, too, is twenty years old."

"Yes, but it's British. More anonymous. I need it badly, as a matter of fact."

"Very well. Tomorrow you can look for it yourself."

It was then that Mike noticed how sure of himself Sora was. The little flickering smile that Mike had always taken as a sign of the poor man's shamefaced inadequacy was in fact, he suddenly realized, quite the opposite. It was a smile of self-satisfaction.

The waiter arrived with two handsome portions of cannelloni and Sora picked up his fork and said, *"Buon appetito!"* as he jauntily dug in. Mike started eating more slowly, savoring the first mouthful like a new experience.

After a minute or two, Sora said, "My advice to you is to go back to London right away. Nobody knows this story of yours over there. You can start afresh—make a new career."

"At forty-eight? You must be joking."

"Well, here it will be impossible." Sora said this with some irritation. He was determined that Mike should leave the country without delay, and he had not anticipated any serious opposition to what was so obviously the wisest plan.

"I daresay. But I'm staying here anyway. There's something I've got to do."

"Do? What?"

"Find Beppe Palazzo."

"But he's—" Sora was about to say "dead," and though he quickly changed this in midsentence to: "—he's never been heard of since," by then it was too late. He lowered his head and became intensely interested in his food to try and cover up his gaffe, but Mike simply went on staring at him, every pore in his body tingling with the shock of that unpronounced word. To have sprung so spontaneously to Sora's lips, it must have been completely at home in Sora's mind. Here's the man who pleaded my case, Mike thought, the man who knows more than anyone else about the facts, and all the time he's been convinced that Beppe Palazzo is dead. Well, of course, it's so obvious. He's never been heard of since. Since the night I killed him.

Sora blushed and added lamely, "He's not in Rome, anyway."

"He must be somewhere."

"Listen. What's done is done. Even if you find him, what can you do?"

"Kill him."

Sora stopped eating abruptly, and looked up. Mike was not joking. After a moment, Sora made an awkward attempt to laugh it off.

"Perfect! So you can go back to jail for another twenty years!"

"Oh, no. I've served my full sentence for killing Beppe Palazzo. Now I've got the right to kill him."

TWO

When Mike came to Rome as a young man, the words *dolce vita* had yet to be pronounced. There were very few cars even on weekdays, and on Sundays in August there was not a soul in the streets. In the evenings there was singing in the trattorias, and in the daytime any shady, cobbled alley might lead to a quiet fountain playing in a sunlit square. Films were being made, however; hope was already being pinned on the studio called Cinecittà, "the city of cinema." That was why he had come. In England there had seemed no end to the tours of the provinces and the cheap bed-and-breakfast world of theatrical digs. When an article caught his eye about filming in Rome, he knew at once that that was where he belonged.

He had always had a feeling, an almost magical feeling, that Rome was his place, from the time he first set foot there as a boy of twelve. He was with his mother then, on the way to his grandfather's funeral, and she had hurried him straight from the station to the bus. Then they were off again, in the old blue *corriera* bulging with passengers and piled high with boxes and bundles, rumbling through the ugliest of Rome's nether regions, past the cemetery and out along Via Tiburtina towards Anticoli Corrado, his mother's village. That was all he was allowed to see of Rome that time, nothing but hideous tenement buildings and factories. And yet he had gazed out at it entranced, as if he were seeing Piazza Navona and Trinità dei Monti and the Forum. *Ecco Roma*, he had muttered to himself—this is Rome, this is Rome, this is Rome.

But all his mother could say was *"Ecco Anticoli!"*—with a light in her eyes that he had never seen before or since. She had been pining for her precious *paese* for thirteen years, ever since she ran away in the middle of the night with Mike's father. "Is *that* it?" Mike had asked, when the *corriera* turned off the main road and he caught his first glimpse of the jagged hill, with its crest of stark little houses that seemed to have erupted out of the rock and trickled down one side. "*Sì,*" she had sighed, with a proud little smile, not catching the disappointment in his tone.

When he returned to Rome alone, a man of twenty-five, Anticoli was as far removed as anything could be from his immediate plans for taking Cinecittà by storm, but his mother had begged him to go back there as soon as he arrived and kiss all her brothers for her and send her their news. So for her sake he boarded the old blue bus again, and this time, as before, when it made its triumphal entry into the dusty piazza and stopped by the fountain with the four frogs that was the best Anticoli could offer in the way of art, the whole village clamored round to welcome it. All sorts of people flung their arms round Mike's neck and wept and kissed him again and again with shrieks of "*Michele! Michele!*" Who they all were, he had no idea—some were uncles and aunts and cousins of his, but he did not sort them out until later, and it never seemed to matter very much. Mike's arrival concerned everyone in Anticoli, just as it had when he was a boy. Out of all the images and voices and smells that were still pungent in his memory in later years, he hardly knew which belonged to the first time and which to the second; nor could he remember which tears had been for his grandfather's death and which for joy. Probably they were all mixed up even then, like the smells and the tastes and the sounds. The acrid perfume of poverty that exuded from every stone of Anticoli mingled in his mind with the flavor of boiled goat's milk and sour black bread, and with the swishing and tinkling of a herd of goats being driven past the house, up the stony path before daybreak, and the *clop-clop* of a mule, and the quiet footsteps of peasants on their way to the fields.

The second time, in any case, nothing had changed. The women still cooked, incredibly, in a cauldron over an open wood fire; they still carried water in from the fountain in great copper jugs balanced on their heads. The hens still darted here and there inside the house. And everything smelled exactly as it had before.

It was certainly the most unlikely place to meet anyone who could launch him on a film career. And yet, this time, that was exactly the extraordinary thing that happened. At the height of the festa, when the men had finished their pasta and the women had served them each a small piece of hedgehog, stewed as a special delicacy in Mike's honor, when Uncle Gino's wife, Rosa, was walking round the table, filling their glasses with the acidulous wine they made themselves, and Uncle Vito's wife, Pasqualina, was cutting more bread, and the other women were fussing between the table and the fire as they always did at mealtimes, without ever sitting down, a voice in the doorway said, *"Permesso?"* and a young man walked in.

"Forgive the intrusion," he said, when all eyes turned on him in surprise. "I am a film director, and I have come to see if I can shoot my film in Anticoli."

If he had announced that he was God, he could not have created a greater effect. They fell over one another to pour him a glass of wine, already counting the millions in their heads.

As for Mike, he knew in his heart the minute he heard those words that such a chance could only have been arranged by fate. Sure enough, later on, when he drove Mike back to Rome, Nicola D'Angelo confessed that the only reason he had walked in and made that announcement was that the commotion over Mike's arrival in the village had so intrigued him that he had felt impelled to find out more. It was true that he was location-hunting, but he had found little to appeal to him in Anticoli until the *corriera* came rumbling into the piazza and Mike stepped out. "An Englishman talking like a peasant of Anticoli? That's more than curious," he said, "it's an idea."

It became the central idea of Nicola's film, *Corriera*, in which Mike played the part of himself. But what a mess that film turned out to be.

Nicola was small and wiry, with intense brown eyes and infectious verve—and what struck one first was that his hair was completely white, although he was only thirty-one. At that time, to tell the truth, he was not a film director at all, but a journalist who felt he had it in him to make films. He had belonged to all the film clubs in Rome that ever projected *The Battleship Potemkin* on a Sunday morning; he had read a number of large volumes about the Art of the Cinema; but he was not on intimate terms with the technicalities of real filmmaking, and was constantly inspired by brilliant ideas that did not work.

"Now here the camera whizzes round in a circle," he would tell the cameraman. "Circular pan. Very fast. *Whirrrr!*"

The cameraman would look blank for a moment and then point out patiently, "All you'll see on the screen will be a blur."

"No, no!" Nicola would insist, convinced that he could defy the rules of photography by the sheer force of his zest. "It will be a marvelous effect, believe me!"

It was nothing but a blur.

Nicola carried on undaunted, making wilder and wilder decisions and disregarding the crew's looks of dismay. In the end they all began to get lightheaded, infected by Nicola's own certainty that he was making a masterpiece. The only person who looked more and more unhappy every time he went to see what they had shot was the poor fool who had put up the money, a prosperous builder who had decided to try his hand at film-producing under the misguided impression that all films made profits.

In fact, *Corriera* was such a disaster that it was never released. But it was the making of Mike all the same, because Oscar Lorenzi, the owner of one of Italy's biggest film companies, was among the many people to whom it was offered for distribution. He walked out after ten minutes like everyone else, but in those ten minutes he was so taken with Mike that he came back later with some of his staff to screen a bit more. He was casting a comedy called *Un Bel Pasticcio*, and he chose Mike to play the lead.

Mike was Nicola's guest at that time, in a large, old-fashioned flat on the Aventino, which Nicola had inherited from his mother, along with an elderly housekeeper and a number of dark paintings in gold frames. At first sight all this had seemed unlike Nicola, but it wasn't, not when you found out that he wore striped flannel

15

pajamas and was not above putting on long woolen underpants when the weather got cold. He had invited Mike to stay with him soon after they met. "Till you find a place of your own," he had said. Only Mike was paid so little for his part in *Corriera* that he could not afford a place of his own. Not that this bothered him too much. Sharing digs and being broke were part of the trade, as he knew it. It was not until later that any embarrassment crept in, when Nicola began telling him he was writing a new script specially for him. Fun as it had all been, Mike had no wish to make another *Corriera*; by now he was itching to move on.

He was busy hanging silver balls on the Christmas tree when the telephone rang. Nicola answered it and appeared a moment later, looking stunned. "That was Oscar Lorenzi," he said.

"What did he want?"

"You."

Mike tried to hide his excitement. He knew Nicola well enough by then to guess he would be a little peeved, and so he was. But he was a good enough sport, all the same, to have pretended impulsively to be the butler, in order to boost Mike's status.

"I said you were not in, and I would give you the message. That's what they want, these people. You must be difficult to find. In fact it's better you don't talk to them at all."

Mike laughed. "Fantastic! And supposing they want to give me a part?"

"They do. That's why you must have an agent to talk for you."

Nicola made it his business to find Mike the right agent, too. Franco Bernabei, the man people said was the best, was fresh back from a long spell in the States, and remarkably high-powered. The fee he managed to squeeze out of Lorenzi seemed like immeasurable wealth.

Things changed for Mike after that. He was able to find an apartment at last, and it was *the* apartment, the one he loved, in Via Gregoriana, as romantic and impractical as a castle in the air; just living there made him feel effervescent. In any case, it would have been impossible now to go on living under Nicola's roof, with all the phoning and photographing and interviewing that went on. It was all phony, of course, all part of the game to make sure

Lorenzi got his money's worth. They had changed his name to Mike Donato and were plugging it for all they were worth. In those days of blessed anonymity, it tickled Mike to find his photograph in every other magazine and read news about himself that was news to him as well—even if he did know it was all being organized at a desk inside Lorenzi Film. There was no unpleasantness attached to it at that stage, no sign yet of the malice that real fame provokes.

Oscar Lorenzi was a thickset, unremittingly dynamic man, who slept very little and expected everyone else to do the same. Not content with changing Mike's name, his next scheme was to change his nationality too.

"You could be Italian just like that," he told Mike with an imperious click of his fingers. "Then you'd qualify for quota. Know what that means? A premium of eighteen percent on the box office gross."

"For me? Or for you?"

Lorenzi flashed him a winning smile. "For people who produce Italian films, with the right quota of Italian actors and technicians. But think what an asset for your career, now that everyone's starting to shoot films in English. An English actor with Italian nationality. You'd be in demand like no one else."

Franco said of course he should do it; he had everything to gain and nothing to lose, since he could keep his British passport as well. All he needed was his parents' birth certificates, to prove they were Italian born. If nothing else, it was as good an excuse as any to fly home and surprise them with a load of presents.

His father was overjoyed with everything he brought, but what interested him most were Mike's photographs in a pile of magazines.

"Look, Elsa, look!" he cried out. *"E' famoso! Hai capito?"* He kissed Mike on both cheeks and held him at arm's length and laughed for joy. "I knew it!" he said. "It's in your blood. Didn't I always say you'd be a famous actor one day?" As if it were Mike, not himself, he had been talking about all those years when he said, "You'll see—a little patience and you'll see." As if he had planned it all this way from the start.

17

Salvatore was the most hopeful man alive. When he had whisked Elsa away from Anticoli, it was to go in pursuit of a traveling circus whose brief appearance in the neighborhood had opened up glittering visions of himself as a clown, a dream he had clung to all across Europe, gladly doing all the dirty work and the odd jobs, until the circus owner, always short of cash, eventually vanished, leaving them high and dry in Hove. "Didn't I tell you we were lucky?" said Salvatore. "God's brought us to England. You wait and see if this isn't where I'll get rich." Elsa was nine months pregnant by then, and exhausted after nearly a year on the road. When they reached London, she loathed it at first sight, but even a bedsit over the Eel and Pie House in Seaton Place was better than the circus wagon next door to the lions; and they were just in time to get married before Mike was born. Salvatore started washing dishes for a living, and after a while this led to a job as a waiter. "One of these days I'll get back to the circus," he used to say from time to time. And little by little he transferred his dreams to his boy.

Mike had been dying to see his father's face when he turned up in one of his Battistoni shirts and a suit made by Caraceni, but now, sitting in the dark little kitchen with the two wretched rooms beyond, the pride in those glistening eyes filled him with guilt.

His mother reached out and touched his shirt. "Silk," she said, and nodded thoughtfully. "Who does your washing?" she asked.

"A woman," he told her. "A woman I pay." She mulled that over in her mind for a while, and gave a kind of grunt to show that she doubted the woman knew how to iron his shirts. Then she stood up abruptly and started putting on her hat. *"Vado un momento in chiesa,"* she said.

"What, more burnt offerings?" said Salvatore.

She was going to light a candle, naturally. She was lighting candles all the time. "Bargaining with God," Salvatore called it. Mike could remember when he was quite tiny, staring at the melting wax and thinking that God's mercy must be very precarious if it depended on that little spattering flame. "What happens when it goes out?" he had asked her once. She never did reply.

18

THREE

Beppe Palazzo began his career in a modest way, as an employee of *seconda categoria* in the publicity department of Alba Films, where he spent his days pasting press cuttings into large scrapbooks. After proving his mettle with the pot of paste, he was promoted to sticking typewritten captions on the backs of photographs and eventually to typing addresses on envelopes from an interminably long and, it turned out, inaccurate mailing list, which he took the opportunity to type a copy of for his own use. He was rather small and plain, the kind of man of whom no one takes any notice, and these humble tasks enabled him to sit all day in an obscure corner of the one big room that contained the entire department, learning a great deal about what went on, not only there but in all the other departments as well, since the publicity department was on the ground floor, and when the door was open, as it usually was, it commanded an excellent view of the lobby and the stairs.

It was after three or four months of this, when he was just thinking it was time to start edging his way upward, that Robin appeared one morning in the doorway.

"Excuse me," she said, in English. "Signor Mannino?"

Before anyone else could open his mouth, Beppe was out of the room, leading her towards the stairs. "Mr. Mannino's office is up above," he told her. "I will show you."

Joe Mannino, the man who owned Alba films, was looking for a secretary, and Robin had obviously come to apply for the post. What was more, she had the detached, unflustered air of the girl who knows she is equal to the job, an attitude easily mistaken for *sangue freddo inglese*, which Italians tend to find challengingly attractive, like a sand castle they cannot wait to batter with their spades. She was a girl whom it would be amusing to seduce in any case, but as the boss's secretary she opened up new vistas in Beppe's quicksilver mind.

As a matter of fact, Robin felt anything but calm and collected that morning. The advertisement in *The Rome Daily American* called for an experienced executive secretary. All she had behind her was a three-month course in shorthand and typing and a few weeks' clumsy work as a temporary in various London offices, all of which she was glad she would never have to face again. On impulse, she had bought a ticket to Rome, where at least she would possess the qualification of being English, a valuable one in those days, when English secretaries were rare in Rome and were supposed to be the most efficient in the world. In fact, Joe Mannino took it for granted the minute he saw her that she was the perfect English secretary of his dreams. Besides, he liked the look of her.

He picked up a letter and rattled it off at about two hundred words a minute. Robin's speed was only sixty at the best of times, and just then she was too nervous to catch more than one word in ten. But she sat scribbling without a pause until he had finished, then calmly walked to the typewriter, inserted two sheets of paper and a carbon (backwards), and typed at a fantastic pace a page of total gibberish. Signor Mannino stood watching her with enthusiasm. He took the page, read it from beginning to end, and said:

"Wonderful! When can you start?"

He was in his early forties, an Italian-American whose family must originally have come from the North, to judge from his fair hair and mustache and the light blue eyes that rarely missed a thing. Later, when Robin found out how hard he was to fool, she suspected him of giving her the job because he admired her nerve. True, he did boast about her speed to his sales manager, but that was probably because he liked people to think he dictated letters, whereas in fact he had no gift for correspondence and considered it

20

a useless bore. In other words, he had no use for a truly efficient stenographer. Robin looked efficient; that was enough.

She had not been at Alba films more than a week before one of the envelopes Beppe had typed came back with "not known at this address" scrawled across it. It was the stroke of luck he had been waiting for. As soon as he saw Joe Mannino leave the office, he stood up, announced to the room at large, "I'm going to check this mailing list," and sprinted upstairs to see Robin.

She happened to be the person least qualified to check anything of the sort, but she was also the person least qualified to know that in any case it was not her job. Having no idea what Beppe's position might be, she began amiably—with his help—to ransack her office for a similar list, which he said her predecessor must have left somewhere, since it was as indispensable to her work as to his. The search took more than an hour, during which time Beppe got a good look at some very interesting papers in Mannino's private files. When it proved fruitless, he had no trouble in persuading her to keep the list and check all the addresses herself.

"By telephone," he explained.

"Yes, of course," she agreed, wondering how, with her poor knowledge of Italian, she would ever manage to cope with such a task. Beppe grinned, as well he might; he had found a perfect excuse to come upstairs every day and see how she was getting on.

His next brainstorm smote him when he was typing envelopes for the invitations to a gala film opening and pondering whether he dared send one to himself. Instead he addressed one to Miss Robin Lane and took it with him when he went upstairs to deliver Mannino's.

"Invitations for the premiere," he told her. "For Mr. Mannino." She nodded and went on typing. "I wondered if you also would wish to come," he said, producing the envelope addressed to her. She looked up, surprised and pleased. "With me," he added firmly. Which spoiled everything.

"Oh," she said, without a trace of enthusiasm, and then, politely, "thank you."

That was how Beppe came to make his first appearance in

society, and to discover that no one questioned his right to be there. From that day on, he made a point of never missing a cocktail party or a premiere or an official dinner to which he could possibly procure an invitation, and people soon learned to take his presence at these things for granted.

The night he escorted Robin to his first gala premiere, he was still distinctly gauche. His dinner jacket looked as if it might not be his own, and his bow tie was askew, but Robin was too ill at ease herself to notice the difference. It was her first experience of flashbulbs and limelight, and she was painfully conscious of her inelegant dress and unsuitable shoes, amid the jewels and satins and furs of the film-starry crowd. Afterwards, Beppe took her back to her *pensione* in a taxi and, to her acute embarrassment, tried to kiss her. It was one of those lip-dodging, nose-bumping bungles that leave a certain coolness in the air. In fact, for two or three months after that, he made no more advances; instead he gave all his attention to self-aggrandizement.

He took to walking in and out of the office carrying sets of stills or mysterious rolls of paper that may or may not have been poster designs; and nobody ever asked him where he was going or how he had acquired this new air of importance, because it was assumed that he had been promoted. The only person who knew he had not was the head of the department, who took the line of least resistance and got a new junior to handle the scissors and glue.

Beppe's next move was to acquire a secondhand Alfa Romeo. From then on, if a sketch was to be delivered to the printer, Beppe took it; but he would make it clear that he had come to check the quality of the printer's work. If stills had to be collected from a photographer, Beppe fetched them; but to be sure no one mistook him for an errand boy, he always made a point of examining them on the spot and turning some of them down. It was not long before he demanded—and obtained—a petrol allowance, after which he spent less and less time in the office, and more and more driving round Rome.

In June, when the car was still a novelty, he managed to lure Robin into it and drive her home from work. By that time he had taken to smoking a pipe and sporting an open-necked shirt and a silk foulard, which gave him a certain air of distinction, if not charm.

"Do you still live in that *pensione*?" he asked in a lofty tone, as he eased his foot carefully off the clutch, anxious not to start with a jolt.

"Yes. Do you mind?"

"Why don't you take an apartment?"

"Can't afford it yet."

"But you must spend to earn, don't you know that? Look at me, I have a car now. And not a Fiat, not a cinquecento, but an Alfa Romeo. Immediately I am more important."

"Really?"

"You are too innocent. You do not know these things. I tell you, the more you have, the more you get."

"Have you got an apartment, Beppe?"

"No, I live with my mother. That is different. My father was killed, you know, in Eritrea, when I was only a little boy. And if it wasn't for her, I would have been killed too, ten times, during the war. She has done everything for me, everything. I could not leave her to live alone. But soon she is getting married and then you will see—I will have a very beautiful apartment."

"Your mother's getting married?"

"Yes. To the Conte De Cleris. Why so surprised?"

"Well, surely—I mean, isn't she—?"

"She is fifty-two. She is not beautiful. But she is very clever, very interesting. She has always had many admirers. I'll invite you to the wedding and you will see."

He was driving through the Villa Borghese gardens. It was not the shortest route to the *pensione*, but not so far out of the way as to have attracted Robin's attention. She did not object, either, when he turned off the main thoroughfare and into a small, dark lane, which she took to be a shortcut. When he abruptly stopped the car, she was taken by surprise, and by using the tactic of the sudden swoop, he managed to grab one of her breasts and kiss her quite savagely before she slammed her fist hard into the middle of his

23

forehead. He gave a shout of pain and let go, after which she made him drive her straight home and refused to say another word, not even goodbye.

From then on, when she encountered him in the office, she avoided looking at him; but she could not help feeling unpleasantly aware of him. About the beginning of August she condescended to let him drive her home again and, with some show of reluctance, accepted his invitation to eat a pizza. By then he had made great progress as a man of the world. He took her to a working-class pizzeria—a barnlike place in Trastevere, with marble-topped tables and paper napkins—and behaved as if he were entertaining her at La Tour d'Argent.

"Now you will eat a pizza like you never ate before," he told her, pouring the coarse white wine into a not-very-clean tumbler and sipping it as if to test the vintage, before filling another tumbler and handing it delicately to his guest. "You must come here to the real Rome to eat the best. With the *popolo*." He waved at the crowded tables all round them, where inordinately numerous families were lustily cutting up pizzas, elbow to elbow, and chewing them and shouting at one another all at the same time, trying in vain to compete with the impossible din of clattering plates and yelling waiters and squealing children chasing one another round the tables. Robin stared in fascination at an immensely fat woman who was trying to stop up the mouth of her bawling infant by stuffing bits of pizza into it.

Beppe greeted the arrival of their own pizzas with exaggerated joy, and for a while they ate in silence. Then he asked, "What do you think of Mannino?"

"I don't really know him all that well. He's got a brain, though. I do know that."

"But where did he get all that money?"

"All what money?"

"To start Alba Films. He spent millions. Hundreds of millions."

"He's a rich man."

Beppe laughed. "Oh, you are sweet. And so naïve. No one is just rich for nothing."

"It's no business of mine. Or yours."

"But I like to understand people, don't you?"

"Understanding people is one thing. Prying into their private affairs is something else."

"You are so English! If I don't know people's private affairs, what do I understand?"

Robin said nothing. She was thinking uneasily of the day when Beppe had spent an hour peering over her shoulder as she went through every folder in Mannino's filing cabinet, looking for a nonexistent list.

"I think I'll go home now," she said.

"So soon? Don't you want an ice cream, a coffee?"

"No, thank you, really."

He shrugged and smiled. But instead of driving her home the shortest way, he made a wide detour over the Gianicolo hill and stopped between two plane trees, where they could see the whole of Rome without getting out of the car.

"What a view!" he sighed.

"Beppe, do you really expect the view of Rome to make me collapse into your arms with emotion?"

"No. Because you are a cold Englishwoman and you have no emotion."

"If by emotion you mean the desire to be kissed by you—"

"I mean warmth—*spontaneità*. You are always so controlled, so careful."

"I don't find you attractive. It's as simple as that."

Beppe turned to look at her without replying. In a sudden rage he backed the car onto the road and started driving downhill, much too fast for an inexperienced driver on such a steep, winding road. He reached the bottom of the hill and headed straight for the bridge over the Tiber, completely ignoring a tram, which was trundling round the corner right in his path and which he missed by about half an inch.

"You think I am nobody," he snarled, "a little employee not important enough to kiss. Well, we'll see about that, Signorina Lane. One day you may have a surprise."

25

FOUR

Un Bel Pasticcio was released at the beginning of October and Mike was immediately acclaimed as an extraordinary new star. It was not exactly a surprise. There had been many private screenings of the film before then, and all the people who were supposed to know had predicted a huge success, not the least among them Oscar Lorenzi himself, who, in the meantime, had hustled Mike straight into making another film. But before *Pasticcio* came out, no one could tell for sure, and it had dawned on Mike towards the end of September that until the magic night of the premiere he would be floating on a big cloud of hot air.

It was a sobering thought, and it had a good deal to do with why he promised Nicola he would play the lead in *Povero Valentino*, because Nicola chose that delicate moment to present him with the script he had been writing for the past nine months. To turn it down at that point would have been like saying, "I'm too big for you now," and he despised himself for so much as thinking that. He didn't want to be like everyone else and let success change him. Besides, the script really was good, surprisingly good, with none of the limp dialogue and nonsensical trickery that had made *Corriera* such a fiasco. It would have been unfair to turn it down.

When Franco, his agent, heard about it, he groaned at first and said, "Oh, no! Not Nicola again, not now!" Later he admitted grudgingly that it was not a bad script and handed it on to Joe Mannino, who pricked up his ears at the mention of Mike's name, because by that time *Un Bel Pasticcio* was breaking box-office records in a dozen Italian towns.

Robin remained curiously unaware of all this, although she was so close at hand. It was she who announced Franco's visit to Mannino, and she who put Mike himself through when he phoned, as he did several times in the weeks that followed. But Mike's name meant nothing to her yet; she had not even seen his film. And it was not until she met Nicola, at a dinner party at Mannino's towards the end of October, that she learned what all the phone calls and discussions had been about.

Mannino had invited Nicola to meet a man called Abe Schulbach, whom he was trying to coax into providing American backing for the film, and since he happened to need an extra English-speaking female whose discretion could be guaranteed, he had asked Robin to come along too. That was the first she heard of *Povero Valentino*, and what they were saying about it was mostly above her head. She certainly could never have guessed then what an effect the making of that film was going to have on her life.

Schulbach was a gross, bulky man with a rasping voice and a shrill, sequin-spattered wife called Dolly. He was supposed to have awesome quantities of money behind him, but he showed no inclination to give it away. He was not impressed by Nicola, nor by Joe's smooth talk about the project, and at the mention of Mike's name he pursed his lips and shook his head.

"Without a star, forget it," he said. And when he said "a star," he meant Gregory Peck.

Nicola did not even flinch. He set very little store by what Mr. Schulbach thought, primarily because Joe had assured him that he would make the picture anyway, and that the only reason he wanted Schulbach in on the deal was that American money would make all the difference between a small budget and a nice fat one. Nicola explained all this to Robin afterwards. He had taken it for granted that he was driving her home.

"You want we go around a little? Rome by night?" he asked her as he started the car.

"Yes, let's," she said.

They drove round the Piazza del Campidoglio and looked down at the Forum in the moonlight. They inspected the Colosseum and the Via Appia Antica, and ended up in bed in Nicola's flat because it seemed the natural thing to do.

Next morning he leaped out of bed and did a few frenzied exercises before singing his head off in the shower and reappearing, aglow with energy, vigorously rubbing himself dry. Robin, drowsily watching him, came to the conclusion that he expended so much vitality on everything he did during the day that there was none left for the refinements of bed, where he had proved unexpectedly dull. She liked him, though. In fact she liked him so much that it was a relief to have sex out of the way, so that she could enjoy him as a friend.

She saw a lot of him in the weeks that followed. He took her to the theater and to private screenings and to a party or two. Sometimes he would pick her up at the office in the evening and drive like a madman down to the sea with her, to walk along the windy beach hand in hand in the darkness, or lie on the damp sand in their overcoats and listen to the waves. The one thing they never did was make love—except once more, when they might as well not have bothered. It was uninspired.

"Can I tell you something?" she asked him afterwards. He had his face buried in the pillow.

"No," he said. "I know it already."

"I love you all the same. You know that."

"No. You like me. It is different."

"I like you so much it's as good as loving you."

"Yes. As you like spaghetti *alla carbonara*! I think you do not know English well. The verb 'to love' is a serious thing."

"How about *ti amo*?"

"No, no! *Per carità! Ti amo* is so serious that it is funny. We never use such words except in songs. Horrible songs."

"So what do you say? You must say something. Don't tell me Italians are more undemonstrative than the English."

"I think we are more afraid of being ridiculous. In desperate cases we say *ti voglio bene*: 'I wish you well.' "

"Can I say that to you, Nicola? *Ti voglio bene?*"

"Yes, this I allow. *Anch'io ti voglio bene.* We are friends for the skin, always."

"What on earth does that mean?"

"*Amici per la pelle!* Real friends. Your skin is your life, no? So—friends for the skin."

Beppe had a number of useful assets, and one of them was girls. He had collected a whole address book full of them, with a code mark beside each name, denoting status. There were starlets and would-be starlets, extras and would-be extras, girls-ready-to-strip and girls-not-ready-to-strip, professional whores, semiprofessional whores, and—the largest category of all—the nonprofessional-whores-craving-the-limelight. These were the ones who continually leaped into bed with all the wrong people, people who would promise them anything from a screen test to instant stardom, when the most they had the power to produce was a free movie ticket—people like Beppe himself, who afterwards handed their phone numbers on to anyone whose gratitude might oil a few wheels. They were pathetic girls who eagerly let themselves be passed on from bed to bed, until most of them forgot it was fame they had been dreaming of, and settled for a square meal from time to time. The others quietly swallowed a tube or two of sleeping pills.

Poor girls, they never knew to what extent Beppe owed it to them if he went so far so fast—particularly with Abe Schulbach, whom he cornered at one of Alba Films' cocktail parties and clung to for dear life.

"In Italy nobody understands public relations," he informed Schulbach confidentially.

"Nobody but yourself, I presume you mean," Abe replied.

"That may be so," said Beppe. "I have made a profound study of the question. What is needed here is an agency in the American style."

Abe said nothing, but the last two words brought an encouraging gleam to his eye.

Considering how hard Abe Schulbach was to please, it was amazing what a liking he took to Beppe Palazzo. Not that this did not cost Beppe a lot of hard work and the very liberal use of his little address book. During the whole of November he ran round in circles, not only providing for Abe's private pleasures, but also taking him to the tailor and the shirtmaker, helping his wife buy gloves and shoes, and escorting them both to all the best restaurants in Rome. On one occasion he even picked up the check. When he saw the amount, he nearly put it down again; but he braced himself and paid up without so much as a wince. It proved an excellent investment. By the time Schulbach returned to the States in December, the two of them had formed a company to handle public relations in the American style. Not even Beppe had expected such a coup as this.

Just before Schulbach left, Joe Mannino threw a dazzling party in his honor—at least it was meant to be dazzling; in fact, it was one of those overcrowded parties nobody enjoys, where producers huddle together discussing multimillion-dollar deals that will never be signed, where girls flash their sexiest smiles at tired directors whose main interest is the *maccheroni al forno*, where all the anxious people who came hoping this might be their lucky night stand about pretending to talk, their eyes darting here and there in search of bigger game than whoever it is they happen to be stuck with.

"I think I hate parties," Nicola muttered in Robin's ear. He had spent a good hour trying to buttonhole Joe, who kept slipping out of his way.

"Don't look so embarrassed," she said. "I know you're with Luisa."

"You are jealous!"

"Not at all."

"So why you want that I am embarrassed? I must make love to *someone*, no? Here, let me introduce my friend Mike Donato."

Mike had his back to them, but he turned when Nicola prodded him, and gave Robin an absentminded smile. They might have started talking and even fallen in love that night, if Joe Mannino had not hailed him from the other side of the room, so that all he said was, "Excuse me," before hurrying away.

"So that's the famous Mike Donato," Robin said.

"Yes," said Nicola, "and look at our friend Mr. Schulbach

now." Abe was patting Mike heartily on the back. "He did not want to put money into my film because Mike was in it, but he puts money immediately into another film just *because* Mike is in it. Do you understand that?"

Robin neither understood nor cared where Mr. Schulbach put his money, as long as he kept away from her. He had been spending hours closed in with Joe lately, and he always expected her to call him a taxi afterwards, and breathed repulsively over her till it came. She knew nothing about *Showdown*, the film Mike had just started shooting, which was one of those weird co-productions that materialize out of nowhere, backed by companies formed in Liechtenstein the week before. It had not been mentioned in the office and Joe did not figure as the producer, but Nicola knew from Mike that he certainly was involved, and it smelled very much like the kind of *combinazione* where someone like Joe makes a bundle before the shooting begins, simply by raising more money than the film can possibly cost. Joe was a master at that kind of thing—or so they said. And the proof of it was that he had wheedled all this money out of Abe Schulbach, of all people, by persuading him that an action picture like *Showdown* was a cinch, provided it was shot in English, with Mike Donato in the lead.

"I wish I could know what is in Mannino's mind," Nicola said, frowning at the corner where Joe, with his arm round Mike, was now chatting up Oscar Lorenzi.

"Now you're asking too much."

"I think maybe he will never make *Povero Valentino*. It was just an excuse to get his hands on Mike." He turned back to Robin and said, "You want to come home with me now and we leave Luisa here?"

"No." She laughed. "Go back to Luisa. She's looking pretty sulky at the moment." She nodded towards a sleek and strikingly beautiful dark-haired girl, who was sitting by the fire, pouting into her drink.

Nicola shrugged. "All right," he said. "I'll see you later, yes?"

"Yes, of course." She watched Nicola walk away. And Beppe chose that moment to devote himself to getting her drunk.

For someone unaccustomed to drinking even wine, Robin swallowed a great deal that evening of whatever Beppe kept pouring into her glass. At some indefinable hour of the night she began to hear statements pouring out of her mouth that had no relation to what she was trying to say. At the same time she felt extremely well disposed towards everybody around her—even Beppe, who kept kissing her hand and murmuring something that sounded like a poem in Italian.

Somebody was helping her into her coat and guiding her gently down the stairs. A car door was opened for her and she got in. Somewhere in the distance, as the car started gliding down Via Archimede, she heard Beppe's voice saying he was going to show her a very beautiful thing.

The car stopped in a tiny square in Trastevere, a few steps from the Tiber.

"There," said Beppe. He was pointing at a miniature, two-story house. It had a tiled roof and a chimney, and three steps leading up to the front door.

"What's that?"

"Come and see." He helped her out of the car and guided her across the little piazza to the door marked Number 2. Still dazed, she watched him fit the key into the lock and let him steer her through a narrow entrance hall into a newly painted, empty room with a red-tiled floor and a big stone fireplace. A lightbulb had been attached to some wires sticking out of the wall.

"My house," he announced. "Isn't it beautiful?"

She did not reply. The place seemed to her peculiarly unreal, and she could not quite grasp what she was doing there.

"I have still to buy furniture," he said.

"Oh," said Robin. A light began to dawn. "Do you mean you live here?"

"For three days now."

"Oh," she said again, battling with the unpleasant thought that this was Beppe's house and she was in it. "What's out there?" she asked, more to gain time than anything else, waving at the black panes of a large, uncurtained French window.

"My garden." He walked over to press a switch, and a lamp outside lit up an attractive courtyard with an old fountain, an orange tree, and a high wall covered with jasmine and ivy.

"Good Lord!" she gasped. "It must cost a fortune!"

"I can pay for it."

"How?"

Beppe laughed. "The more you spend, the more you get."

He steered her towards a spiral staircase in one corner. Their footsteps clinked noisily on the open ironwork.

"I don't think I want to go upstairs," she said, and stopped dead with her eyes on a level with the upstairs floor. There it was, of course, big and white and unmistakable, a double bed with the covers turned down and a pair of rather fancy male pajamas spread out on it. She tried to back down the stairs again, which was difficult with Beppe holding her firmly in place from behind.

"I am *not* going to bed with you, Beppe," she said.

"Don't worry," he purred. "I'm just showing you the house."

"I think I've seen it."

"Why are you like a virgin suddenly?"

"You bring out the worst in me."

"If you want, I'll go away."

"That's right, you go downstairs."

"I will make you some coffee."

She heard him retreating, *ping-pong-pang* down the iron stairs. Oh, well, she thought, at least there's no chance of being pounced on unawares with a staircase like that. She clambered up the last few steps and headed for the bed.

The next thing she knew, Beppe was bending over her with a glass.

"I brought you some whisky," he said.

"I thought you said coffee."

"I'm sorry, there is no coffee. I have only some whisky and some wine."

"I must go home now, anyway."

"In a minute," he said silkily. "Don't worry. Rest a little and then I'll take you home."

She was shielding her eyes from the naked lightbulb overhead.

"Does the light hurt your eyes?" he asked.

"Yes, but if you turn it off we'll be in the dark."

"Yes," he agreed, and switched it off.

It was not completely dark, because he had left the lamp on in the courtyard outside and its flickering, sensuous glow turned them both into shadows in a weird, nowhere world.

"What are you doing?" she mumbled sleepily.

"Nothing," he said.

"Oh." If it was nothing, she need not bother to stop it, which was a good thing because just now she felt no compulsion to resist the soft pleasure of expert hands exploring her body. They could not possibly be Beppe's hands. She did not know whose hands they were, and she felt too weak to care.

She woke up with a head like a bomb left over from the last war, an aching but superlatively satisfied feeling between her legs, and not the faintest recollection of where she was. Then she turned in the bed and found Beppe's face on the pillow beside her, framed in a black hairnet. For a moment she thought she was going to vomit. It can't be true, she thought. I couldn't have. But unfortunately there was absolutely no doubt that she had. What was more, as she remembered, she couldn't help thinking: Why the hell can't Nicola learn to make love like that? Then she forced herself to take another look at Beppe. In his hairnet and his purple paisley pajamas, he was a sight.

She snatched up her scattered clothes and started putting them on.

"Good morning, my darling," Beppe said, opening his eyes.

"Your darling, my foot!" she growled, retreating into the bathroom to finish struggling into her dress.

"Well?" he called out. "How was it, eh?"

How was it? Damn it, it was unbelievably fantastic. Anybody'd think he'd been taking lessons in sex.

"I am good, no?" he said complacently, folding his hands across his chest and smiling at her when she reappeared. "You didn't expect that, did you? I am naturally gifted. And you are not so cold after all."

"Thank you very much," she said. "But I'm sorry to say I really can't stand men in hairnets." She started down the stairs, *clink-clonk-clank*—quite good for an exit noise.

"Don't bother to take me home," she called out. "I'll find a taxi."

"Where are you going?" he shouted, startled. "You don't want breakfast?"

"There's no coffee, remember? And what I want most now is a bath! Goodbye."

The front door slammed. Her high heels tinkled over the cobblestones towards the river.

FIVE

Opening an office was easy, Beppe discovered, especially with Schulbach behind him, wanting nothing but the best, and a fat bank account in his own name to pay for it. He chose an apartment in Via Veneto, opposite Doney's, carpeted all the floors with thick red moquette, and covered the walls with floor-to-ceiling blowups of Piranesi's Rome. Then he asked Robin to be his secretary.

He had been phoning her nearly every day for a month—ever since that night which he continued to think had turned out well, in spite of her unfriendliness the next morning. He had sent her roses, orchids, a basket of exotic fruit, and a large bottle of Femme, with no result whatsoever. When he topped it all by offering her a job, she snapped back at him over the telephone, *"Va all'inferno!"* Why she chose to use Italian to send him to hell was as mysterious to him as why she should feel insulted by the offer of a job. But her thick English accent made it sound childish and rather sweet. He laughed.

"Why are you angry if I offer you a job?"

"I don't happen to want a job. Will you please get it into your thick, greasy head that I don't want anything to do with you!"

The line went dead.

Beppe went and looked in a mirror. His hair was shiny, but not greasy; it upset him that Robin should think it was. He went out at once and bought an expensive shampoo, and took to washing his hair with it every day. He also had it cut in a new style, by the best barber in Rome.

Next he turned his attention to getting some clients. The problem was how to make himself known to the world so that no one

36

would suspect he had never been heard of before, and the solution he found was ingeniously neat. He invented a film festival—only a small one, but remarkably successful in its way. The Tivoli Festival of Promise, he called it. Putting the accent on "promise" was a good ruse for a start—calculated to attract people on the way up, the ones most in need of the publicity he knew so well how to provide; it also saved him the embarrassment of trying to procure any important films. Instead he rounded up a number of obscure, unreleased pictures by more or less promising and mostly unheard-of directors, who were all overjoyed to take part. He chose Tivoli for three reasons: it was only twenty miles away from Rome; he found a theater there that he could use for the screenings at no great cost; and above all, he had obtained permission, by heaven knows what miracle of persuasion and luck, to hold a preliminary reception in Villa d'Este. If there was one way to be sure the festival was taken seriously, it was to announce it in a setting as impressive as that.

Sure enough, his invitations brought a throng of elegant people to Villa d'Este that cold winter evening, and when he stood up in the painted Renaissance room to address them, Beppe was struck by the realization that the hoax was no longer a hoax; the festival was real. At the same moment he discovered that men who organize festivals wield real power.

Look at the jury he had put together, for instance. They were all highly reputable people, and all eating out of his hand: three critics, a once-famous star of silent film days, an elderly director who specialized in costume pictures, and a well-known producer-distributor in the shape of Joe Mannino. As a finishing touch he had appointed Mike Donato to preside. Mike was, after all, the most promising personality of the year, as Beppe never lost an opportunity to point out to the press.

It was surprising how many people fell for all this. One of them was Mike Donato himself.

Mike was battling hard at that time to retain his sense of perspective. He kept telling himself that nothing had changed but his luck. But sudden success is an insidious thing. It was getting easier and easier to take the adulation for granted, and harder and harder to distinguish the flatterers from the friends.

Then there were the girls, any number of girls intent on going to bed with him. Very pleasant it was too, at first; very gratifying, for a while. But they all turned out to be obsessed with themselves, and in the end it got to be a bore. There was one in particular, an Austrian girl, who dogged him for months.

She came up to him at the party at Villa d'Este and said her name was Maria Rose Aron. "But they call me Mitzi," she told him.

"*Piacere,*" said Mike.

"Let's go out to see the fountains," she said, "and dance naked in the moon."

"Let's," he said. "When the weather's warmer."

She looked anemic and unhealthily thin. With her wispy hair and big, baleful eyes, she was no sexier than a stray puppy. In any case, just then he was busy being president of the jury. He gave her a little pat on the cheek and turned away.

She hung about in Tivoli all week. He saw her at the cinema every night, and she always seemed to have her eyes on him, ready to smile and wave if he looked her way. Once, when he was having dinner with Joe Mannino before the show, she pounced on him from behind with a shriek of "Mike!" and kissed him on the mouth. The photograph came out in a magazine called *Fandango*, with the caption: "Who is Mike's new friend?" He was used to that kind of thing; it was only when she did it again that he began to smell a rat. But by then it was obvious she was simply enacting a scheme that Beppe had been trying to talk him into all the time they were in Tivoli.

It was a week after the festival when it happened the second time. He was strolling down Via Veneto late at night when Mitzi came dashing out of Doney's and grabbed his arm. He turned in surprise and she reached up and gave him a passionate kiss; needless to say, there was more than one photographer outside Doney's at that hour, ready to immortalize such cut-and-dried evidence of romance.

"Now look here," Mike told her, "you don't mean any harm, I'm sure, but if you do this once more, I'll be very angry indeed."

She gazed up at him with her liquid eyes and said, "Don't you want to make love with me?"

"Mitzi, Mitzi, what a poor, silly girl you are." He stroked back her straggly blonde hair. "It was Beppe Palazzo who put you up to this nonsense, wasn't it?"

She frowned—of course.

"I thought I said no," Mike told Beppe over the phone the next day.

"No what?" Beppe asked him sweetly.

"No kissing mystery girls. No dirt!"

"My dear Mike, it's you that does the kissing, not me."

"**W**hat kind of man is this Beppe Palazzo?" Mike asked one night, when Nicola dropped in at his place for a drink.

"What do I know?" said Nicola. "I never heard of him till now."

"You never *heard* of him? What about this festival?"

"*Caro mio*, anyone can make a festival. Whoever heard of the Festival of Tivoli?"

"There were an awful lot of people there."

"Who? Was Visconti there? Or De Sica? Or Anna Magnani?"

"Anna Magnani's shooting."

"Oh, yes, and Visconti's rehearsing. And De Sica's still crying because nobody likes *Umberto D.* Come on, Mike, don't be funny! What films were there? Rubbish, no? Nothing but rubbish."

"Well, thanks! Why didn't you say this before?"

"You didn't ask me before."

It was true. He was so damned tickled at being president of the jury that he had leaped up and gone without asking a thing. Of course, it could also be a case of sour grapes. Nicola must have felt a bit hurt about *Corriera*'s not being invited. But how could it have been, with Mike on the jury? Even if, goodness knows, it had as much right to be shown as some of the things he had been obliged to sit through—most of them, actually. Nicola was right. Mike suddenly saw himself up on the platform handing out prizes. There were photos of him doing it in all this week's magazines. A fine fool he must have looked, bestowing statuettes of the "Sibyl" on a bunch of untalented pipsqueaks as solemnly as if they were Oscars.

He remembered the letter he had written to his father, boasting about being the most promising personality of the year, and his father's reply, in his buoyantly artless hand: "*Figlio mio*, I always knew you would do it. This pays me back for what I never did myself."

"I could strangle that Beppe Palazzo," Mike said.

"Why? It's all good publicity."

"Publicity! So that's what it was, is it? Like this muck here." He pushed a pile of magazines towards Nicola.

"The more photographs the better, no?"

"But I told him not to do this, don't you see? He had a whole plan worked out for plastering my name round the world by inventing a nasty little love affair and making it come true. Beginning like this—look—with me kissing some girl."

"But Mike, if you—"

"Oh, I know. I behaved like an idiot that time. The photographers could hardly believe their luck. The girl was so pathetic—I even drove her home. No, I didn't go in, but what difference does that make? Here's a picture of us heading straight for a door marked 'Hotel.' Trust her to live in a place called Hotel Arcobaleno—what else could that be but a love nest? And sure enough, that's what it says: '*Il nido d'amore segreto*'—which I swear were Beppe's very own words. See what I mean? It *has* to be Beppe who did this."

"Why? It can also be the girl—making publicity for herself."

"Doing exactly what Beppe planned?"

"Then perhaps he is helping her."

"What, using *me* to advertise *her*? Oh, great! And mind you, this was only the beginning. What he had in mind next was a nice juicy scandal, complete with drugs, orgies, the lot. In the end, the girl would try to kill herself. I told him I had a better idea: I could kill the girl."

Nicola shrugged. "Why you make so much fuss out of it? Photographs, scandals—it is all a part of the game."

"Look, we all need publicity, I know—but not this kind. It makes me feel dirty, as if I'm being used in some sort of slimy intrigue."

"But *Fandango* is full of this stuff all the time. Nobody cares."

"Well, I do. And I've told Beppe's secretary straight out that if there's any more, I'll wring his neck."

Nicola laughed. "I hope he is not found dead one day. Everybody will know who did it."

Mike laughed too.

Beppe's plan, or whatever it was, forged steadily ahead, regardless of Mike's foul language, indignation, and threats. The next phase began with the publication in *Fandango* of a photo of Mike punching an unidentified man on the corner outside Doney's, while Mitzi stood by, covering her face with her hands, under the title, "Jealousy!" It was faked, naturally, with the help of a picture taken the previous October. The man getting punched was a photographer called Leo Santi, whom Mike had impulsively knocked flat in the gutter for pestering a *principessa* who happened to be a nymphomaniac, but who had no wish to be photographed with some boxer character she had taken a fancy to. It was a damned stupid thing to do, granted. The poor photographer was only trying to make a living, and he wasn't the only one. Several others had popped up in time to catch the scene, which had found its way into several newspapers. In this hitherto unpublished version, Leo Santi had his back to the camera and Mitzi had been added to the background by means of a simple paste-up.

Mitzi phoned him and asked, "Are you angry with me now?"

"Not with you. With Beppe."

"Me too. I hate him."

"So why do you do what he tells you?"

"Do you know the why of everything?"

"I suppose he pays you." There was a silence. "What else do you do for a living?" Mike asked dryly.

"Sometimes I work a little, as a model. But is difficult. I have no *permesso di lavoro*, nothing."

"So how do you live?"

"The hotel manager is nice. When I have nothing, he waits. Sometimes I borrow. Sometimes—"

"People like Beppe take advantage of all that. Right?"

"Mike, I am so much alone." She burst into tears.

Mike's heart sank. He said, "Have you eaten today?"

"No."

"Where are you?"

"In the hotel."

"Go downstairs. I'll be there in ten minutes."

He took her to a restaurant near her hotel, and chose a table in the basement, which was deserted. He ordered a substantial meal for her and listened to the dismal tale of her efforts to make good. It was a tale he had heard before, from other girls who had come to Rome in pursuit of egocentric dreams. As usual, it made him feel guilty.

"Listen, Mitzi, why don't you go back to—wherever you came from?"

"I can't. I write my mother I am success already. I say I made two, three films with big part."

Mike knew what this meant. He remembered his father's proud little note.

"So she'll be disappointed. What's that, compared with the mess you're in here?"

"She will ask me how I live then, these three years. What will I tell her, huh?" She shook her head. "I can't go back. What to do? Marry a nice boy from Lienz?"

"Why not?"

"I am different now. I want another life, not this one and not that one. Is a mess, everything."

"You want fame and money and real love too, I suppose." She turned quickly to see if he was making fun of her. "Mitzi, Mitzi, these are all silly dreams. Why should you be famous? Famous for what? You know what your trouble is? You're greedy and vain. Yes, you are—it's no use looking at me like that. If you weren't, you'd have stayed at home and been content with much, much less, instead of thinking the world owed you all the things you want—and ending up here, starving and weeping and expecting me to help you. Why should I?"

She put down her fork and turned her head away. "Do not disturb yourself," she said. "Beppe will help me."

"Oh, for Christ's sake! Above all, keep away from Beppe!"

"He's my only hope now."

"Then you have no hope."

She broke down completely then, and cried uncontrollably. He put his arms round her and patted her like a child and told her he was sorry and he did not mean it. He did not hear the footsteps coming softly down the stairs. But he saw the blaze of the flashbulb.

He dropped Mitzi and flung himself at the photographer, who tossed his camera to a second man who appeared under the arch at the bottom of the stairs and caught it just in time to get a shot of Mike knocking his colleague back against the table and pinioning his arms as he roared, "Who told you I was here?"

"No one. I followed you. From Via Gregoriana."

It might have been true.

The picture of him holding Mitzi in his arms in a cellar was published in several magazines. The one of him attacking the photographer was front-page news. And what made him even more furious with himself afterwards was that he continued to worry about Mitzi, and wonder if she was getting enough to eat.

S I X

In the meantime, Robin had found a place of her own. It was not much of a place, just one room and a tiny bathroom, with a cavity large enough to take a gas ring in the wall by the front door, and a tiled floor with an ugly pattern on it in dark red and gray; but once she had typed her name on a card and pinned it up on the brown paint of the front door, she got a thrill every time she fitted her key into the lock.

It was not exactly chic, but it was hers and she loved it. The only bad thing about it was coming home alone at night. Once inside, with the light on, the door bolted, and the shutters secured, she felt relatively safe. But stepping through the big street door into the shadowy hallway and walking up five flights of dark stairs was an ordeal. The last flight was the worst. She always stopped and peeped round the corner at it from the top of the last flight but one, in expectation of some indefinable horror; and when, one night towards the end of March, she found a man lurking on her doorstep, she was back on the landing below so fast that she could not be sure if she had run or jumped. A voice behind her said, "*Ciao*, Robin." It was Beppe.

"Oh, it's *you*," she said. The blood rushed back into her cheeks, but her heart went on pounding.

He shrugged. "You won't talk to me on the phone, so—"

She was so relieved, she could have hugged him. He was someone she knew, someone safe. All that mattered to her at that moment was that for once she would not mind stepping into her dark flat, because he would be there beside her while she opened the door. As for Beppe, the last thing he had expected was to be greeted with a smile; but he had no intention of going away.

She pushed the door open and went in, groping along the wall of the narrow passage for the switch. Beppe stepped in after her and shut the door before she could think of stopping him. When she switched on the light she found him standing very close to her.

"Now look here—" she started to say. But before she had reached the final consonant, Beppe had grabbed her and thrust his tongue deep into her mouth.

Beppe was not an attractive man to look at. He had improved his hair and smartened up his clothes, but they were still a bit too loud for such a nondescript face; and he still had blackheads, and a tendency to pimples too. But the chemistry that draws one body to another has practically nothing to do with the beauty of a face, and Robin had felt some kind of morbid attraction to him—attraction and revulsion at the same time—ever since he first kissed her, in the car in Villa Borghese, the previous June. When she looked at him coldly, she refused to admit this even to herself. But when she could no longer see him, only feel the effect his body had on hers, that was a different matter. When he took off his clothes, there was nothing wrong with the body underneath; it was smooth and golden, like most Italian bodies, vigorously sexed and surprisingly sweet in contact with her skin. Moreover, he was a lover of exceptional skill. The minute those fingers of his began to probe, she was no longer answerable for what she did.

Ages later, when she came to her senses lying face-down on the bed, she thought: Why on earth did I do that? But those were only words, formed in her mind to soothe her conscience. The truth was that she felt fantastic, it was no use pretending she didn't; it appalled her that anyone so awful should have this unique effect on her. If only he could have vanished afterwards, it might not have been so bad. But no, he was sitting there, fully dressed, contemplating her from the armchair.

"Will you marry me?" he asked.

"Oh, don't be silly!"

"I have money now. I am successful." She didn't bother to answer this because she was busy thinking she would have liked to remove the indecency of her scattered clothes, if she hadn't felt too limp to move. Beppe stood up and did the job for her, placing the

45

garments carefully on the chest of drawers. It embarrassed her intensely to see him examining her underwear.

"Can I keep these?" he asked.

"No, you can't! Put them down!"

"As a souvenir."

"Beppe, you're mad! One minute you ask me to marry you, and the next you want my—" She broke off, unable to say it.

"This is love too," he said, still holding them. She turned her head away. "Why are you like a puritan suddenly? You just made love with me for two hours like crazy." He was walking about, surveying the tiny flat. She had nailed straw matting round the walls, which she thought made it look quite attractive, but to judge from the expression on Beppe's face, he did not share her taste. "You deserve a better house than this," he said.

"I happen to like this one."

"You are a funny girl. *Testarda da morire*. What is the word? Stubborn?"

"It's you that's stubborn. I just mean what I say."

"I am in love with you. I have discovered that I am in love with you."

"Well, I'm not in love with you. I can't think why you keep cropping up."

"It's no use to say no. You cannot resist me." He waved a lofty arm at her nakedness. "Will you come to my mother's wedding?"

"Your *mother's* wedding?"

"Yes. I told you, no? It's at Santa Francesca Romana, on April tenth, at eleven o'clock. It will be interesting for you. The Conte De Cleris has important friends."

"Good for him."

"Also good for me." He came and sat on the edge of the bed and stroked her naked back and said, "I will go away now."

"Goodbye," she said, already stirring under his hand again.

"*Amore mio!*" he whispered, and then, thank goodness, "*Buona notte.*" After which he went.

Heaven knows what made her go to the wedding. Curiosity, perhaps. Or some demon. Certainly, if she could have foreseen

46

what would come of it, she would have tossed the invitation card into the wastebasket, instead of making the frivolous decision to go and see what Beppe's mother was like.

In a last-minute panic she even bought herself a hat, which made her feel ridiculous the second she put it on, and prevented her from moving freely, for fear that it might fall off. When she got to the church, she saw that it was not the proper kind of feathery hat that the other women had on, and halfway through the interminable service she snatched it off and kicked it behind a pillar, which made the woman next to her turn and eye her with distrust. By this time, Robin was so heartily sick of the incense and the lilies and the mumbled gibberish that she decided to slink away. By coming in late, she had avoided Beppe so far, and with any luck she might get away without being caught.

She edged her way out of the pew without much trouble and was just about to tiptoe down the side aisle when she tripped on a loose flagstone, clutched at something to save herself, and dropped her handbag, scattering its contents over the resonant marble floor. Everybody in the church turned to look, and when Robin staggered to her feet after retrieving the last ten-lire coin, she found Beppe standing over her. *"Ciao, amore!"* he whispered, and gripped her wrist.

After that, there was no escape. He dragged her firmly to his own pew at the front and kept her by him to the end. When at last the ceremony was over, he introduced her to his mother, who was a small, upright, shrewd-looking blonde, carefully made up to look, yes, a little less than her fifty-two years, and pretending to flutter a little, as any bride should, although she was patently not the fluttering type. The Conte Gastone De Cleris (a born flutterer) looked faintly surprised at what had just befallen him. Robin sympathized with his bewilderment. The Palazzo family, it seemed, had a gift for making people do whatever suited *them*—as Beppe did with Robin now, sweeping her along with him to the luncheon that followed, introducing her as his fiancée, and seeing to it that she drank glass after glass of champagne, until she was one big smile and so confused that she scarcely knew where she was or how she came to be there. At that stage, with all the kissing

47

and embracing and weeping and photographing that was going on, there seemed to be nothing wrong with letting Beppe kiss her in public, or being photographed with him arm in arm, hand in hand, and cheek to cheek.

The next day, however, when Beppe phoned her and said, "Tonight we will have dinner at my house," she said, "No, we won't. Thanks very much all the same." She was sober again by then, and she had a bad headache.

"Why?" he asked in an affronted tone.

"I don't happen to want to, that's all."

"But you're my fiancée."

"I most certainly am not."

"I told my mother."

"I can't help that."

"Well, you can come to dinner anyway. I want to show you the house."

"You did that once before."

"There was no furniture then."

"There was a bed."

"Oh, sorry! I forgot you are a virgin."

"What's that supposed to be? Sarcastic?"

"You are making me mad!"

"Well, then, leave me in peace!"

It was no use. The next day he called again and said, *"Ciao, amore,"* as amiably as if they had parted with a kiss. This time he had two seats in the stalls for the opening night of Visconti's new production, and she turned down that invitation too, without stopping to reflect that it was an attractive one, and that it would have done no harm to accept.

She heard no more from him until two weeks later, when he breezed into her office on a Saturday morning and informed her that Joe Mannino was expecting him. He was, too. Beppe remained in Joe's office for more than an hour and came out looking pleased with himself. She had no idea why.

"Shall we go to Passetto's tonight?" he asked, sitting on the edge of her desk and reaching for her hand.

"Beppe, why do you insist? You know I don't want to."

"Not at all. I know you want to, and you will." He laughed and ran a finger lightly up her arm. "I think I'll buy a big cage and put you in it." She looked up, startled, and he grinned. "Yes, that way you'll have no choice and no obligation to feel guilt. I'll keep you in a cage and take you out when I want you. And you will like it, you'll see." Robin was silent, unaccountably stirred and subdued. That night she accepted his invitation.

There were flowers scattered over the table at Passetto's. It looked very expensive. Beppe ordered dry martinis to begin with, which quickly disposed of her self-control.

"So now," he said, about halfway through the meal, "why do you keep pretending you don't like making love, when you do— especially with me?"

She stared at him and made no attempt to reply. She was not sure herself why the thought of him was so distasteful when her mind was clear enough to think. Perhaps the pleasure of making love with him was too intense, too physical; like an orgy of masturbation, it produced all kinds of orgasmic spasms but no kind of love, not even that vague friendliness that less successful couplings almost always generated for a while. When she was lucid, her mind rebelled against Beppe's skillful manipulation of her body. At the moment she was not lucid enough. She had drunk two glasses of wine after the dry martini.

Still smiling at her embarrassment, he asked, "Have you ever done it to the music of Bach?"

"No!" she said, too loudly. She was losing ground.

"I have a new record player and some good records. A prelude and fugue is the most exciting. And lights that change color."

His eyes turned darker as he stared at her. She felt a treacherous twinge at her navel. That night she went back to Beppe's place again, drawn by the incongruous appeal of Bach.

The little house was elegant inside now, with a blue carpet and a white sofa and a lot of bright cushions and modern paintings and lamps.

"What do you think?" he asked proudly, as he took her coat.

"Oh," she said, "Very nice." The effect of the drink was wearing off. He had a large pimple on his cheek. The idea of Bach began to pall.

"Sit down," he said. "Don't be shy."

He was walking across the room. She stood and watched him in acute discomfort and saw quite clearly that he was slimy and small. At that moment she knew for certain that she must on no account go through with this. He switched on the light in the courtyard and then turned off the lamps in the room, ceremoniously, one by one. She could see that if she was going to get out she had better move fast, and like a fool she went on standing there all the same.

"I don't know why I came," she said.

"I do." He flicked a knob on the radio and got music. It was not Bach, because that meant a record and it would have taken too long; just then what mattered most was timing, and Beppe's timing was perfect. The next thing Robin knew, she was on the floor.

Then, what? The smell of the new carpet, a pimple under her fingers on his back, a moment of revulsion, the vestige of a thought battling somewhere to survive the softness—then a void of pure pleasure.

The telephone rang and everything stopped.

The darkness turned pale as he switched on the light. She heard him say *"pronto,"* but her slip was over her head and she could not see. When she pulled it off, she found herself under the table, with her clothes half off and half on. Beppe was standing at the telephone in his underpants, which were pale blue.

It was ugly.

She began surreptitiously collecting her garments, pulling on stockings, struggling into her bra. When Beppe finished talking and turned round, he was surprised to find her fully dressed.

"What's wrong?" he said.

"Everything," she told him. "Pale blue underpants make me sick."

For a moment he just gaped. It was an exit line, and if she had walked out then, she would have won. Unfortunately, to her chagrin, she was defeated by an irresistible urge to pee. The bathroom was upstairs. There was nothing for it but to dash up that absurd spiral staircase—*cling-clong-clang-cling-clong.*

When she came out of the bathroom a few moments later, he was standing in her way, stark naked. The bedroom was dark except for the tremulous glow that filtered in from outside. He unzipped her dress.

"Pink is depressing too," he said. "You should wear black."

SEVEN

At ten o'clock on a Sunday night Mitzi suddenly turned up on Mike's doorstep, looking distraught. It was more than five weeks since the photographers had caught them at supper, and he had heard nothing from her since.

"Mike, please, I am in bad trouble," she said. "If you do not to help me, I kill myself."

Here we go again, thought Mike. "Come in," he said. What else could he do?

She poured out a tangled tale about a screen test that Beppe had arranged for her to have, not in a studio, but in somebody's home. "I think it is funny," she told him, "but I say maybe a test it is like this."

"Go on."

"Then there is a man who tell me take off my clothes. You know, sometimes, when you are not famous yet, it is difficult to say no."

"So you took off your clothes."

"Then suddenly a young man takes off his clothes too, and they tell me, now we shoot love scene. Well, one thing I know is that if you shoot love scene in films, you do not make really love. So I shout and say, 'No—this is not possible! What you doing?' And Beppe, he say, 'Don't make such fuss. You want this part or no?' What am I to do?"

"So you made a pornographic film."

"How can I be so stupid?"

"I don't know."

The rest of her story was dismally banal. Having made one piece of pornography, she was soon blackmailed into making another, for fear that if she didn't, they would show the first one to heaven knows whom. And after that there was no end to it; they made her make film after film, until now it was not only films she was in, but other things too, terrible things, she said, at parties where people—

Mike cut her short. "I don't believe it," he told her. "This is Grand Guignol."

"But is true!" she insisted. "There are people who do bad things, really. You know the girl who was dead on the beach last week?"

"The case of the missing clothes? The one who drowned herself with her jacket on and no skirt?"

"She never drowned. They give her too much drugs—at a party."

"How do you know?"

"I was there—I see it. And after, everyone was so afraid—they all try to put her clothes on her again and it is a mess and half the things they forget, and then quickly they take her and put her on the beach so people will think she drowned."

"In two inches of water. Yes, I read all about it. And the police keep insisting it was suicide. A sillier tale I never heard."

"But she is dead, Mike. And now I am afraid to go there again and I say I will not, I will not any more. But Beppe say I must go tonight to this—this house—" She fumbled in her handbag and pulled out a scrap of paper with an address and a phone number on it.

"What is it, an orgy?"

She nodded, unaware, it seemed, of the skepticism in his tone. "Beppe say is better for me to be nice, because these people are very important and powerful people. They can help me a lot and hurt me too. If they get angry, they can report me to the police, he say, and the police will send me away from Italy, or maybe arrest me for *oscenità*, or—or—"

"Or what?"

"I don't know!" she moaned.

Mike knew he would be a fool to believe this tale. It tallied too precisely with Beppe's project for a publicity hoax. The fact that the case of the girl on the beach had been given a good deal of space in all the newspapers was no proof that Mitzi's version of it was true. All the same, he had a sick feeling somewhere about the middle of his stomach. Unless she was a first-class actress, Mitzi was in genuine distress. And if it *was* true, if she really had been a witness to this mysterious death, about which some very curious things were being whispered around Rome, if she knew who or what was behind this sordid little enigma and the haste and authority with which it was so firmly being hushed up, then to say she was in trouble was an understatement.

"Oh, Mike, what I will do?" she whined.

"Nothing," he said. "Just don't go."

"But he is waiting there for me to phone." She waved the scrap of paper at him. "He say I must think about it quick and decide."

"Mitzi, now listen—" He leaned forward and took the paper from her and put it aside, then clasped her two pale, thin hands in his. "What you've just told me is no joke. Is it really true?" She stared back at him and nodded. "It's not some made-up yarn that Beppe told you to tell me?"

"No, no. Beppe will be angry if he know I tell you."

"And all that other nonsense—those photographers that pop up whenever I meet you—was it Beppe that fixed that?"

She shook her head.

"Who was it, then—you?"

"Me?"

"Are they friends of yours or not, all those photographers?"

"Friends," she murmured with a helpless shrug, as if the word itself were imbued with sarcasm.

"All right, we'll skip that. Do you promise me it's not Beppe who sent you here now?"

"Yes, yes, promise!"

"What you've told me has nothing to do with any publicity stunt?"

"No!"

"You really saw that girl die and you know who dumped her on the beach?"

She nodded again, with wide-open, anxious eyes.

"Then if you want my advice, there's only one thing you can do. Call a taxi, go to the station, and get on the first train out of Rome."

"To where?"

"Anywhere but here."

"But is impossible."

"Why? Is it money? You must have been earning quite a bit."

"Yes, but Beppe has it."

"*Beppe* has it! For Christ's sake, why?"

"He give me little at a time, when I need it. He say like that is better for me."

"The bastard! My God, he's a real pimp!"

Mike stood up in a sudden fury and pointed at the telephone. "Phone him," he told her. "Phone him and say you want to meet him at"—he looked at the address on the scrap of paper—"Piazza Mattei." Mitzi's eyes opened wide with alarm. "Don't worry, I'm coming with you," Mike told her. "But don't tell him that. Just say you don't want to go to the party. He's to come down and meet you by the Fountain of the Tortoises. In twenty minutes. And if he's not there by then, you'll call the police."

Beppe did not look angry—far from it; he was all smiles when he came round the corner from Via dei Funari and saw the two of them waiting for him in the piazza.

"Hello, Mike!" he said. "What a nice surprise! But what's going on? Why don't you come up to the party, both of you?"

"No, thank you. I don't like that kind of party—if what Mitzi says is true."

"Oh, *Mitzi*. You mustn't listen to her—*è mitomane*. How do you say that in English? She makes up stories all the time."

"Is a lie!" said Mitzi, clutching Mike's arm.

"She tells me you've got all her money. Is that a story or is it true?"

"My dear Mike, forgive me—but what has Mitzi's money to do with you?"

"So it *is* true."

"True—not true—what does it mean? Mitzi, what have you been telling him?"

"She wants her money back. All of it. Tonight."

"You must be crazy."

"Now look here, I've had all I can take out of you. Just wipe that silly grin off your face and give her back her money. Now."

"Oh *basta*! Now it is me that has had enough. Who are you, anyway? Mitzi's protector?"

Mike lost his head then, and shot out his fist. Beppe dodged and toppled backwards over the iron guardrail round the Fountain of the Tortoises. Mike dived after him and sent him splashing into the water. Mitzi let out a squeal.

The shuttered windows of the little piazza were thrown back, one by one; tousled heads started craning out to see what was going on. There was also a flash, but Mike was too enraged to notice.

He waded into the water, hoisted Beppe to his feet, and forced his face down into one of the four shell-shaped bowls at the base of the fountain.

"There," he said. "There, you dirty bastard. You filthy little insect, you!"

"Oh! Oh!" Mitzi moaned. "What are you doing?"

"Washing his face. What does it look like?" said Mike. As he jerked Beppe's head out of the water to let him catch his breath, there was another flash. This time he turned, startled. It was Pino Fieroni, the same photographer who had caught him with Mitzi in the restaurant and received a punch in the nose for his pains. Come to think of it, Pino had been in Via Veneto, too, the time he drove Mitzi back to the Hotel Arcobaleno. "How did *you* get here?" Mike snapped.

"Same way as you," Pino told him, coolly clicking another shot, while Beppe went on spluttering and gurgling and wriggling in Mike's grip.

"*You* brought him," Mike said, turning on Mitzi, who was biting her fingers and darting anguished looks at Pino, torn between the urge to get her picture taken by jumping into the fountain and her nervousness lest the commotion attract the attention of the police.

"No, Mike!" she protested. "I promise, no!"

"I followed you, for God's sake," Pino told him. "I follow you all the time. That's my job."

"Who pays you for it? Him?" He pushed Beppe's head back under the surface.

"Why him?" said Pino. "I take photographs. Period."

"Photographs! I'll give you photographs! Here, how's this?" Mike wrenched Beppe out of the water by the scruff of his neck and posed for a picture like Cellini's *Perseus with the Head of Medusa*. "Behold!" he said, "the famous Beppe Palazzo! Whom I hereby baptize Beppe Bacherozzo!" He thrust Beppe's head down into the water one last time and then, his anger assuaged, abruptly let him go.

"What is *bacherozzo*?" Mitzi asked.

"A disgusting black insect with a smooth hard skin that feeds on filth—otherwise known as a cockroach. Don't you think the name suits him? Beppe Bacherozzo?"

Beppe had staggered blindly out of the fountain, shaking the water out of his hair. He stumbled against the guardrail and sat down on it in a daze, trying to open his smarting eyes.

"Hey, Beppe—are you all right?" said Pino, bending over him. Beppe's reply was obscene.

"What happened, Signor Donato?" someone called out from the little crowd that had gathered to watch. "What's it all about?"

"Ask *him*," Mike said. "He knows." With that, he took Mitzi by the hand and led her firmly back to his car, without allowing himself to be ruffled by the incessant, malicious clicking of Pino's camera. Maddening as it was to know he was being reduced to scandal-fodder again, this time he refused to lose his temper, either with Pino or this silly Mitzi, busily preening herself at his side as if she had quite forgotten the squalid tale of woe she had poured out to him only an hour before.

"We'll stop at your hotel so you can fetch your things," he told her as he started the car. "Then I'm taking you to the station."

"Oh, no, Mike, please. What I will do at the station?"

"Catch a train."

"But is late now. I cannot just go."

"You can, Mitzi. I'll give you some money, don't worry. Even if you only get as far as Florence, it's better than staying here."

"Mike, I am afraid," she said, suddenly wan. "Now Beppe will be so angry with me! And more than him, the other people. They will know that I tell you."

"What kind of people are they? Gangsters?"

She shook her head.

"Politicians?"

"I don't know. Maybe."

"Rich, important, influential people, eh?" She nodded. "And you know something that could put one or two of them in jail for life. Can't you see that it's silly to hang around?"

"But what I can do?"

"Go home! I told you that before."

"And I tell you before that I cannot."

"Well, there's only one other thing you can do—go to the police."

"The police! No, no! Impossible."

"Then I give up. I don't know how to help you."

"Let me come with you to your house."

"What do you want me to do, adopt you?"

"Please, Mike. Just tonight. Tomorrow I will go."

"Away?"

"Away from you. Promise."

He took her back with him in the end to Via Gregoriana and let her sleep beside him in his big double bed: a thin, sad creature whom he felt no desire to touch and whose tentative effort to seduce him during the night aroused nothing more in him than sickly pity.

The next morning, though she accepted a little money, she stubbornly refused to let him hustle her out of town, and after breakfast she went away looking wispier than ever, stepping carefully down the steep stairs in her precariously high heels, with her black cocktail dress all crumpled and her hair unbrushed.

"Look after yourself," he called after her, knowing well how futile such words were.

"Yes," she called back. "I will telephone—soon."

Three days later, she was found dead.

Mike was in his agent's office when he heard. Franco Bernabei pushed the evening paper across his desk and asked "Isn't this that Mitzi girl you've been running around with?"

Mike stared at the two laconic sentences that were all Mitzi's death was deemed to deserve. He read them again and again without lifting his eyes from the page. "Maria Rose Aron, aged 23, committed suicide by slashing the veins of her wrists in her room at the Hotel Arcobaleno in Piazza del Paradiso. The body was found at 12 noon today . . ." He thought of Mitzi's thin, pale wrists and her plaintive voice saying, "Mike, I am afraid." Far away in the distance, he heard Franco say, "Were you in love with her?" and he muttered, "Of course not. I hardly knew her." She was so frail and helpless, half drained of life already.

He stood up, suddenly angry. "She never killed herself," he said.

"What makes you say that?"

"Why should she?"

"Drugs, probably. Wasn't she one of Beppe Palazzo's little girls?"

"You mean drugs and Beppe Palazzo are two things that go together?"

"I didn't say that."

"What is he, a crook or what?"

"No more than a lot of other people we know. He's a damn good publicity man, I'll tell you that."

"Depends what you mean by publicity. Mitzi said that other girl was drugged too, by the way. The one they found on the beach."

"Oh, that one. God knows what was behind that."

"Mitzi knew. And all of a sudden she's dead. And Beppe's

mixed up in it somewhere. That could make him a murderer."

"Now you're going too far. I know you hate his guts, but there are limits. Suppose we change the subject and talk about that script I sent you."

"All right. It's not bad, but if it starts next month it'll clash with Nicola's film."

"Mike, you think I ought to have warned you about Beppe. Let me warn you about Nicola. He's a wonderful guy. I love him. But his film will never be made."

"He told me it's all set."

"It's always all set, except not quite. That American money he keeps talking about is pretty hard to get. The Americans aren't such fools."

"Oh, I know. And I'm not Gregory Peck."

"It's not you that's the trouble, it's him. He's third-rate, don't you see? Always will be. But no one's got the guts to look him in the eye and say, 'We don't trust you to make a film.' So they pull out the old, old story—'The Americans won't do it without Clark Gable.' It's the easy way out."

"All the same, I can't let him down. I owe it to him that I'm where I am now."

"Okay, he's your friend and you're grateful to him and you'll never forget it. But don't fool around with your own career out of kindness. Mike, you're on top now—you've got offers pouring in on all sides—and you've been sitting on your ass for three months. One day you'll wake up and find you're forgotten. Success is a flimsy thing."

"So's life."

There had not been a paper that had failed to print the ignominious picture of Beppe with tightly shut eyes, being held up, dripping and spluttering, by the scruff of his neck in the fountain.

For most people it was merely the source of some hilarity, but Beppe himself—who heard giggles wherever he went—was convinced he had been done irreparable harm. All his months of hard work to forge an impressive identity for himself had gone down the drain; he was the laughingstock of Rome.

Robin had seen the picture the very next day, in the lobby at Alba Films, where it was being passed round from hand to hand with gloating remarks. She had spent the previous Saturday night in Beppe's bed, and here was someone reading aloud that he was "a cockroach that feeds on filth." She heard herself asking vaguely, "What does it mean?" But their malevolent gossip turned to a buzzing in her ears as she grappled with the shock of it, and all she caught were snatches like, "Didn't you know?" and "It *may* not be true . . ." and "Well, I *did* hear . . ." and then, in a whisper, the awesome new word: *"Drugs."*

She recalled various enigmatic phone calls she had overheard at Beppe's, and his evasive answers to her questions; she thought of the money that had come so fast to the little employee with the one cheap suit who now had a red Ferrari and piles of Cucci shirts; and the blood rushed to her head as she perceived that in some horrible way this unpleasantness was connected with her. She managed to stroll away as if it were no concern of hers, and to pay no attention to the whispering behind her back; but when Beppe phoned her that night, she asked him point-blank:

"What did they mean by 'a cockroach that feeds on filth'?"

He was silent for a moment; then he asked, "Who said that?"

"I read it in the paper. Under a picture of you."

Once more, Beppe paused before saying, "You should not believe such things. You are my girl."

"I am not your girl. Let's get that straight."

"In bed you seemed to be."

"Well, that was the last time. And you still haven't told me what it means."

"It means nothing!" he shouted.

"Why should anyone say a thing like that for nothing? Or throw you in a fountain, for that matter."

"Some people do stupid things. But they pay for them, don't worry."

"I'm not worried. I'm not even interested. Just keep away from me from now on."

"Why?"

"Because you make me vomit!"

61

"But I love you!"

"Goodbye."

She replaced the receiver and took a deep breath. She was rid of him. That day she blanked him clean out of her mind.

"What's wrong with Rome?" Mike said to Nicola. "This piazza is such a calm and comforting place; and all the time terrible things are going on." They were in Piazza del Popolo, sitting outside Rosati's before lunch, enjoying the gentle sunshine of early May. Nicola was enjoying it, at any rate. Mike was still haunted by the echo of Mitzi's voice saying, "Mike, I am afraid," and by other things that her death had magnified into horrors he did not want to believe.

"Perhaps it is the demons," said Nicola.

"The what?"

"There is a legend that Nero was buried there." Nicola pointed to the church in the far corner of the piazza. "And on the tomb grew a—how do you say, *albero di noce*?"

"A walnut tree."

"Yes, a gigantic walnut tree, full of crows, so many crows that they were a pestilence to the people, who believed they were demons. One night Pope Pasquale II dreamed that the Madonna commanded him to cut down the tree, the *albero malnato*, and build a church in its place. So he came with an axe and cut it himself."

"And built Santa Maria del Popolo?"

"No, that was later, another Pope. This one made only a *santuario* to send the demons away."

"Did they fly away then, those demons? Or hang around?"

"That is the question. Sometimes I think they fly around all the time. All over Rome."

"Beppe does look a bit like a crow."

Nicola laughed. "You see what I mean?"

Mike sighed and stretched. "Who can believe in evil, sitting here in the sun?"

"Sitting here always makes me think of Queen Christina. See the date up there on the gate? 1655—the year she arrived in

Rome. That would be a film to make. Remember Greta Garbo? Can't you see her riding in on a black horse, with all the cardinals and the princes in the piazza to welcome her? With trumpets!"

"I suppose it's the same gate where Luther walked out in disgust. He's the one, isn't he, who said, 'Goodbye, Rome! Where everything is allowed except to be an honest man!' "

"Poor Luther, he wanted perfection—perfect Christianity. Rome is pagan. Look around you. These are the same Romans that went to the Colosseum to watch the gladiators. Thumbs up, thumbs down. You can be Jesus Christ, and they will say, *'Ma chi sei?'* Who do you think you are?"

"But they've a smile for everyone."

"Oh, yes, plenty of smiles. If you're *simpatico*. But if you're the King of England and you think that makes you somebody important, they say, *'ma chi sei?'* Who are you? Nobody. When she arrives, Christina gets a big welcome from everybody. *Evviva* Christina! Thumbs up for *la svedese*. Then they got bored with her, like everything else. When she died, she was almost alone. Look, there's a demon!" Nicola pointed at a sparrow hopping about on the cobbles.

"Idiot! That's not a crow."

"Perhaps they have changed to sparrows now."

"No, they're invisible. Ghosts. Like Queen Christina and Luther and Nero."

And Mitzi.

Mike shuddered suddenly. "What I hate is this feeling there's someone pulling mysterious strings. As if it's all part of a plan, and I don't even know whose."

Whoever may or may not have been pulling the strings, Mitzi's death did not stop *Fandango* from printing stories about her and Mike. On the contrary, they became nastier; the innuendoes acquired an air of menace. One of the worst, entitled "Suicide or Something Else?" suggested that *if* Mitzi's death remained a mystery and *if* the police wanted to find out more, they might be advised to interrogate a certain "M.D.," who had had, it was rumored, an affectionate friendship with the poor girl, and whose white Alfa Romeo had been seen more than once outside her hotel.

"This is libel!" Mike shouted, bursting into Franco Bernabei's office with the magazine in his hand.

Franco calmly read the article through before replying, "There's no mention of your name."

"Well, who's 'M.D.,' for Christ's sake? And there are photographs!"

"Yes, of you in your car. So what?"

"But it makes it look as if I killed the girl! God! If I get my hands on Beppe, I'll reduce him to pulp."

"I wouldn't say things like that if I were you," Franco told him sternly.

"But this is all his doing, don't you see?"

"We've been through this before. You don't *know* it's Beppe. It's only a hunch."

"Well, whoever it is, I'm going to sue their heads off."

"God knows what you'll stir up if you do. It's not worth it, believe me. No one pays any attention to *Fandango*. Let it go, and it'll soon fizzle out like all their other yarns. People have short memories, especially in Rome."

"Too short, if you ask me. I've got a good mind to go to the police."

"For heaven's sake!"

"When there's been a crime, aren't you supposed to tell them what you know?"

"You don't even know if there's been a crime. You don't know anything. You only imagine."

"I know what Mitzi said. And I know she's dead."

"Girls like Mitzi will say anything to attract attention. She was a poor lost soul who ran out of hope and killed herself. If the police say so, that's it."

"And the girl on the beach?"

"That's none of your business."

"Ah, that's different, eh? That scares even you."

"I've heard rumors I don't like. Listen, Mike, do me a favor, will you? Clean all this out of your head. Forget it. Okay?"

But Mike's doubts about Mitzi continued to haunt him for a very long time, and it was not easy to forget the girl on the beach, either, because while the press, for once, had fallen strangely silent, most people were talking of nothing else. The police had decided, now, that it was not suicide after all. The girl must have fainted while she was paddling, they said, and fallen down with her face in the water and drowned. A simple case of accidental death, they said. And that was that; the case was closed.

Everywhere one went in Rome those days, the most outrageous conjectures were being made, the most unlikely names tossed around; no prominent personality was immune from the suspicion of having had a hand in what some went so far as to insist could only have been murder.

Fandango took the opportunity to publish an article entitled "Was the Man in the Alfa Romeo Mike Donato?" in which, without saying anything definite at all except that a white Alfa Romeo was believed to have been seen near the beach where the girl was found, they managed somehow to insinuate that Mike was involved in that business too.

"This time it's too much," Mike said, tossing the magazine to Nicola and turning away to pour him a drink. "If I didn't have that film starting in June, I really think I'd go away."

"Away from Rome? Are you crazy? Just because of this stupid *Fandango*?"

"It's not only *Fandango*, it's the whole thing. All these sinister secrets, this anonymous nastiness. It's odious. Take no notice, says Franco. Get it out of your mind. But how can I, with these bastards baiting me all the time, when there's nothing I can do to stop them. I'm not even supposed to go and spit in their eye. Forget it, says Franco. I'd like to see him forget it, in my place."

"He's right, you know. It is not so important."

"Not so important? Have you read that one there?"

Nicola sat down with his drink and finished reading the article. "But Mike, it doesn't say a thing."

"It hints plenty, though, doesn't it? Beppe's obviously out to get my skin."

"How can you be sure it's Beppe?"

"Who else could it be?"

"These things happen. I'll tell you how. At the beginning, it was an idea for publicity. Beppe's idea, right? Then perhaps two, three times it was Mitzi who fixed it—to make publicity for herself. But also, do not forget, those photographers have to live from these things. They follow you always, and invent any story they can to get more money. So? That is part of being famous. Sometimes it is not nice for you. *Pazienza*. But then one day—look what *you* did to Beppe. You threw him in a fountain and made him look stupid. *Then* he got mad with you and tried perhaps to have his revenge. Perhaps. Perhaps not. You will never be sure. For me, this Beppe is not so wicked as you believe. I think he is just a *povero diavolo*, trying to be somebody—and succeeding too. Look, how long is it since that silly festival in Tivoli? Three months? Four? Before that, no one ever heard of him—and now everyone knows who he is. Maybe, at first, he *pretended* you were his client, to do publicity for himself. Maybe *he* needed money also, like the photographers. Maybe he had a deal with them to split fifty-fifty on the stories they could sell. Who knows? There is no precise truth in such things. These poor people live out of dirt. Let them live. What do you care?"

"A lot. Nico, did it ever occur to you what effect all this might have on my father?"

Salvatore had said in one of his letters that he often went to a shop that sold Italian newspapers and magazines, and leafed through them to see if he could find anything about Mike. He had never mentioned *Fandango*, and Mike could only hope that it was not on sale in London, because it hurt to think of him puzzling his amiable mind over some of their "revelations" and insinuations. Mike hoped against hope that even if he had seen them, Salvatore would not for one moment believe any of their lies, that he would simply mutter to himself, "Oh, well, that's success—the higher you go, the more envy and malice you'll run up against—that's life." Yes, surely that is what he would say. But still, Mike was tormented by the thought that the vicious smear published this week might be too much for him to take.

To judge from his letters, Salvatore was more cheerful these days than he had ever been. And there was a reason: at Christmas, Mike had sent his parents the money to open a café of their own. "See what it means to have a son?" Salvatore had written. "I always did dream of seeing my name up in lights. Now I've got it painted up in gold." But at the end of May he suddenly died. Heart failure, they said.

Mike was shattered by the news. He flew home at once, only to find himself faced with the problem of his mother, left all alone in the gray desert of Clerkenwell to cope with Salvatore's café.

"Michele mio," she moaned. *"Che faccio adesso?"*

She had never taken to England, never managed to speak proper English, and never quite understood what she was doing there, living hand to mouth in a foreign slum, with a son who had grown up more cockney than Italian and a husband always chasing rainbows. What could she do now but go back to Anticoli, where she belonged? But when Mike said this, she shook her head. After twenty-eight years? When the café had cost Mike all that money? He tried to make her see that that didn't matter; they could sell it or give it away, for all he cared. But if they sold it, someone would come and paint out Salvatore's name. She could not let them do that.

The fact was that she had no idea how to set about the task of transplanting herself from one country to another; how to dispose of the contents of her modest flat and tackle a new life on different terms. Mike knew it was up to him to handle all these problems for her, but he was starting a new picture in June and he simply did not have the time. He promised himself that once he was back in Rome he would drive out to Anticoli and see where she could be fitted in, but he knew this was easier said than done. Once the shooting began, with all the tension and fatigue that filmmaking involved, he was more than likely to put it off and put it off. In the meantime there was nothing he could do but leave her there, forlornly rinsing cups.

EIGHT

The gateway to Cinecittà is a rectangular chunk of peeling yellow masonry, like a derelict façade without a building. When Robin drove through it for the first time, one morning in September, squeezed into the back seat of a production car between the sound man and the dialogue coach, it looked as unfriendly a place as she had ever seen.

Joe Mannino had at last found a backer for *Povero Valentino*, and Nicola, in his excitement, had offered her the job of script girl. Mannino had had no objection to letting her make the switch, and she had jumped at the chance, though she knew nothing about making films. Nicola had patiently rehearsed with her all the things she would have to do. "Just use your good sense and your Polaroid," he had told her. "Photograph every shot, write everything down. Then you cannot be wrong." Except that "everything" comprised a series of sacramental mysteries into which she had not been initiated, and when she stepped through the padded door into the darkness of the sound stage and turned a plywood corner straight into a blaze of arc lights, she felt a powerful urge to turn round and run away.

Nicola was a different man that day; she had never seen him so edgy and morose. He took very little notice of her all morning, and when they stopped for lunch he ignored her and went off with Mike Donato. She did not blame him. It was enough to make anyone nervous, having all those people hanging on his words, after a year of broken promises and dashed hopes.

She was so tense herself with the effort of doing her job right that for the first two days Mike meant no more to her than a character marked "Valentino" in her script, capable of ruffling his hair the wrong way or varying his lines. After photographing him with her Polaroid at the end of each shot and making a note in her script of the exact words he had used, she dismissed him utterly from her mind and rushed back to her typewriter to battle with her progress reports.

On the third day, Nicola began to relax and invited her to have lunch with him and Mike. But no sooner had they placed their order than Nicola was hauled away for some urgent confabulation, so that Mike and Robin found themselves eating *pomodori al riso* together alone. To break the awkward silence that descended on them, Mike asked her the first thing that came into his head.

"Been a script girl long?"

"Two days."

"What?" He laughed. "You mean it's the first time?"

"Does it show?"

"Not a bit. You look disgustingly efficient."

"People always say that, but I'm not really—I'm a phony."

"Aren't we all? But how did you—?"

"Get the job?" She shrugged. "Nicola just said, 'Do you want to be the script girl?' When I said I didn't know how, he told me everyone starts sometime. And here I am. He must have been mad."

"Did he have a—personal reason?"

She glanced up quickly and said, "Not the kind you mean." And Mike was aware of being illogically pleased to hear it.

He said, "If you're such a friend of Nicola's, how come we never met before?"

"We did once, actually, at a party, just for a second. And I've often talked to you on the phone. I used to be Joe Mannino's secretary."

"No! That sweet little voice that said, *'chi parla, per favore?'* " He mimicked her English accent and they laughed. "Which reminds me. I didn't catch your name."

"Robin. Robin Lane."

He already had his address book out. "Phone number?"

69

She laughed. "My goodness, you *are* fast!"

"No. Psychic. I know we'll be seeing a lot of each other. Don't you?"

She looked at him in a strange way, half excited and half scared. But the lunch break was over—and they had forgotten to order a second course. The assistant director was standing over them, saying, "We're ready when you are, Mike."

"Coming," he said, as he pushed the address book over to Robin and handed her the pencil. He had already written down her name. She filled in the number.

That was on Wednesday. On Thursday he took her out to supper, at the little trattoria near the Porta San Pancrazio that afterwards became "their place" and, for a little while, their secret.

"Hello, Robin," he said, leaning forward with his arms crossed on the table.

"Hello, Mike," she answered, doing the same. They sat there grinning at each other for a while.

"Tell me all about you."

"No, you start."

"No, you."

The waiter was hanging over them with the menu.

"Do you care what you eat?" Mike asked her, and she shook her head. "Give us anything you want," he told the waiter, turning back at once to Robin. "Let's begin when you were little," he said. "Where did you live?"

"In London. Holland Park. And you?"

"Lots of places. All scruffy. Round Clerkenwell and Euston Road."

"I thought you were Italian."

"My parents are. I'm just me. I don't believe in nationality, do you? Other things, maybe. The sun, the stars. Fate. Like running into you—in Rome."

Even then she felt a pang of apprehension, as one does when something is too good to be true. Perhaps he felt it too. They bombarded each other with questions and answers, impatient to get under each other's skin, as if they both sensed from the start that their time was short. Only when the waiter began flicking off tablecloths and pointedly upturning chairs did they get up at last, reluctantly, to go. On their way out, Mike stopped at the table of the only other customer left, an American student from the Academy nearby.

"You may not know it," he told him, "but this is a very important and historic place."

"It is?" said the young man eagerly.

"*Certo!*" chipped in the waiter. "Here is the gate which Garibaldi defended from the French!"

They burst out laughing and dived for the door. On the way to Mike's car, Robin paused to look at the gateway.

"That's funny," she said. "Why is there a gap in the wall on either side?"

"So the French can get in without knocking it down next time. And cars can drive round it without waking up whoever lives inside."

"Yes—look! It's a house."

Whoever had built the Porta San Pancrazio may have meant it to look like the Arch of Titus, but it had turned out too square and homely for a glorious gate, and now it was certainly somebody's house, quite an ordinary house at that. There were flowerpots on the windowsills and a clothesline attached to the flagpole.

"I wonder who lives there," Robin said.

"Garibaldi's ghost, I expect."

They got into the car and drove round the gateway, and Mike shouted, "*Viva Garibaldi!*" Then he pressed his foot down on the accelerator and went round again, faster. "Imitation of a circular pan!" he said—he had been telling her about Nicola's antics on *Corriera*. They started to laugh again, lightheadedly, and he drove faster still. "Imitation of a man turning into a blur!" he said. The tires screeched and Robin shut her eyes and cried out:

"Mike! Don't!" Round he went again. "Mike!" she moaned. "Please!"

He swerved off to the right, through the gate into the Gianicolo gardens, round the statue of Garibaldi, and down the hill, to the place where you could see all of Rome without getting out of the car. He swung the car off the road between two plane trees, braked, switched off the ignition, and turned to kiss her all in one movement. He could not have waited another second.

"Aren't we old-fashioned?" he said finally, smoothing her hair back off her forehead.

"Yes," she said.

"You know this is the most hackneyed spot in Rome?"

"Yes."

"I suppose you've been here before, with somebody else."

"Yes."

"Don't ever tell me who." He kissed her again. "Let's go home," he said, and started the car.

Suddenly they were both very serious and thoughtful. Neither of them spoke until they reached her door in Via della Scrofa. He pocketed the car key and started to get out. She stopped him, with a hand on his arm.

"I have to type my reports," she said. He turned back towards her in surprise. She grinned. "You *are* pretty fast, aren't you?"

"No. Realistic. Why waste precious time?"

"I only met you on Monday."

"You see? Four days wasted already."

She laughed and got out of the car. "See you at the studio in the morning."

He was by her side before she could get her key into the lock. He took it from her and opened the door and handed the key back.

"You don't want me to come in?"

"No."

"I thought I was irresistible."

"I can resist you at least once."

They were standing just inside the door. He pushed it shut with his foot and took her into his arms. She slipped away. "Good night," she said.

He stood at the bottom of the stairs and watched her hand on the banister, all the way to the top. At the fourth-floor landing, she leaned over and blew him a kiss.

"Ciao!" she whispered.

"Buona notte!" he whispered back. He waited till he heard her close her door.

As she was getting into bed, the telephone rang.

"Ciao." It was Mike. "Finished typing those reports?"

"Yes." She had forgotten all about them.

"Shall I come back?"

"No. Mike—don't let's rush it."

"You mean you have doubts?"

"I'm so afraid of finding out it's—nothing."

"It's not nothing. You know that."

"Not for me. But for you, maybe it's just, you know, the usual thing."

"If you think it's usual for me to be packed off to bed alone—"

"Oh, Mike, can't you be serious?"

"I'll show you tomorrow how serious I can be. Get a good night's sleep while you can!"

Some instinct made them keep their secret to themselves at first, as if what they had found was so precious that it must be guarded, as if only by keeping it hidden could they keep it safe. They were as friendly with each other on the set as with all the rest of the crew. Sometimes they had lunch together, but usually not alone. Occasionally, if he thought no one was looking, Mike gave her a wink or formed his lips into a kiss. But they left the set in separate production cars. Then whoever got home first started dialing the other one's number. Within an hour, Mike's car would be outside Robin's door, and they would be off and away, across the river and up the hill to Porta San Pancrazio.

For two whole weeks they did nothing but talk and talk and talk. Childhood memories, likes and dislikes, disjointed episodes of their life stories, all came tumbling out at random night after night. She could easily have told him about Beppe too; it would have made no difference then. But she could not bring herself to mention that. She had almost persuaded herself it had never happened. The trouble was, it had.

The first time a photographer caught them in the little trattoria,

Mike looked ready to kill. He leaped up from the table and was out of the room before Robin knew what had happened. The photographer was faster still; he was whisked away by a friend on a Vespa as Mike reached the door.

"Damn!" said Mike, sitting down again.

"What happened?"

"They've found us. Now they'll never let us alone."

"Someone took a photograph?" Robin could not grasp why he was so angry. She felt proud to be photographed with Mike.

"I can see you don't know what it means, that little flash just now."

She shrugged. "A picture of us having supper in a trattoria?"

"Ah. You think they'll be content with that? From now on they'll hound us everywhere we go. They'll make up some filthy tale about us. The filthier it is, the more it's worth."

"What filthy tale can they make up about us?"

He looked at her clear, bright eyes and thought of Mitzi.

"You'd be surprised," he said.

"Does it matter?"

"Oh, not to me—I'm used to it. But I'm not having them hurling dirt at you."

"We'll dodge them."

"Some hopes. Where can we go?"

"What about my place?"

She had held him off for two weeks, and it had been quite hard. Now it seemed silly: she was so sure of herself and of him.

"Your place?"

"Yes."

"You mean—?"

"Yes."

"Now?"

"Yes."

He forgot the photographer, the coffee he had ordered—he almost forgot to pay the bill. They were in the car and down the hill so fast that it was a wonder nobody got killed, especially since he turned his head to look at her from time to time, and took one hand off the wheel to seize hers and kiss it when she touched the nape of his neck.

By the time they reached her street door, every tiny thing stirred her: his smile, his touch, even his hand thrusting her key into the lock; and when they had run, gasping and laughing like children, up the five flights of stairs to her flat, they could hardly wait to get inside. By then they were out of touch with details like putting lights on or closing shutters or locking doors. They simply melted together, and it was so perfect and so true that afterwards they could not imagine how they had lived two separate lives.

" 'That's the wise thrush,' " he murmured, stroking her hair at some point during the night. " 'He sings each song twice over, lest you should think he never could recapture the first fine careless rapture!' "

"Twice!" She laughed. "I've lost count."

"I told you I could be serious."

"Mmmm. It feels so smooth and comfortable. How many times did you say he sang that song?"

"Want to bet on it?"

"It would save trouble if he just didn't stop."

"Who's stopping?"

He was lying on the floor when she woke, at dawn. She reached out to touch his naked chest and he smiled without opening his eyes and said, *"Buon giorno."*

"What are you doing down there?"

"I was squashing you."

"Come back and squash me again, quick!"

She breathed in his fragrant male warmth as he squeezed back in under the bedclothes beside her and pressed his vigorous thighs against hers.

"Why don't you try squashing *me* for a change?"

"Like this? Mmmm—that feels good. Oh, Mike, I love you!"

It was lucky it was a Sunday morning.

Later, while she was having her bath, he ransacked the cupboard under the gas ring for a saucepan to boil the milk in.

"What do you do?" he asked. "Drink it cold?"

"If it hasn't gone bad."

"Got anything eatable, at least?" He started poking about in the cupboard again as she came out of the bathroom with a towel knotted round her freshly powdered body.

"There's some jam and some sort of rusks."

She pulled out a mangled lump of something crumpled up in greasy paper, which she sniffed at without much hope. "Italian butter smells awful," she said.

Mike sniffed it too, and made a face. "Especially when it's six months old." He smelled the bottle of milk and put it down. "*You* smell good, anyway," he said, pulling her to him and sniffing her neck. He untied the towel and tossed it away as he kissed her. "I see I'm going to have to take you in hand."

NINE

That same Saturday night, while they were lost to the world in Robin's little narrow bed, telephones had been ringing all over Rome. At two o'clock in the morning, Nicola had called Joe Mannino and announced that he was rewriting the script. The immediate result was that on the following Monday, instead of rolling into Cinecittà with the usual early-morning cordiality, the crew found themselves in a state of some confusion, on the top of a mountain at Manziana.

The production manager was pacing about, rubbing his face with his hands. "What does he say about the set?" he asked the assistant director. "Will he use it?"

"He doesn't know."

"It cost millions!"

It was a huge set of a section of the Colosseum, which Nicola had insisted he could not do without. The production manager had worn himself out with cursing and coaxing to get it ready by Saturday night, and by the time he had crawled home from Cinecittà, it was a quarter to twelve. He had taken two pills to make sure he slept till noon, and at a quarter past two in the morning, there was Nicola on the phone, saying he wanted a mountain with a ruin on top instead.

Luckily, that was not hard to find; the mountain at Manziana had come in handy many times before. It was a small, spiky, picturesque mountain with a grassy space on top, in front of a cave so romantically gnarled and overgrown that it looked as if nature had copied it from Piranesi for the benefit of people who made films. Here Nicola calmly set up his first shot with the camera crew, impervious to the disgruntled looks of those whose Sunday afternoon had been spoiled by the need to mimeograph the new pages and make arrangements for the cars, food, and complications that they entailed.

Luisa, who had managed to cajole out of Nicola a sizeable part for herself, was in tears at the prospect of having to learn her lines in English all over again, and the dialogue coach looked equally unhappy about starting from scratch on the struggle with her mispronunciation.

Only the grips were their usual cheerful selves. They thought nothing of trekking up and down a mountain in single file, laden with cameras, lamps, tripods, tracks, tables, and chairs. The rest of the crew looked baffled and depressed. It was not the extra work or the unexpected change of plan that they resented—such things were the essence of making films. It was the fact that Nicola himself had changed. It was unlike him to be off in the clouds, acting the genius. Till then, they had been a loyal and united team; all at once it was his private game.

As a result, the general mood was so black that Robin and Mike felt impelled to hide their personal state of bliss. They would certainly have told Nicola their secret that day, if he had not been blind and deaf to everything but his work. As it was, Robin simply made the effort from time to time to wipe the smile off her face, and settled back quite quickly into the habit of keeping her happiness to herself.

Mike was the only one on the set who never stopped smiling. Apart from everything else, he was truly excited about the change in the script. He had let himself be inveigled, on Sunday afternoon, into trying to stop Nicola from disrupting everybody's peace of mind; instead, Nicola converted him.

"Listen, Mike," Nicola said. "I know I am more a writer than a director. But this time I decided there would be no more circular pans. I drew pictures in the margin of every set-up, every camera movement, every frame. Like that, I thought, I cannot go wrong. But it's no use. You can't keep your nose on the page and do what it says in the recipe. A film is not a pudding. And even good cooks invent. You have to break the rules. Throw yourself off a cliff and hope you can fly."

"And if you can't?"

"Why be a pessimist? Listen, it's no use to talk. Let's try the scene."

When they had worked on it for an hour, Mike saw what he meant. It had a dimension that the rest of the script lacked. He felt his character come to life at last, and he went back to Robin exuberant. Far from taking leave of his senses, he told her, Nicola had found his key.

Joe Mannino was less than enchanted with Nicola's sudden fit of inspiration. He had had trouble enough on *Showdown* with a director who decided not to stick to the script, and when he realized that *Povero Valentino*, which he had sold to his backers as an inexpensive, safe comedy, was liable to be less comic, less safe, and a great deal more expensive than he had foreseen, he cursed the day he had let Nicola loose on the set. When, three or four days after they started shooting at Manziana, he read in the paper that Mike had broken his leg, he began to think he himself had been hit by the worst calamity in show business: bad luck.

"What the hell's going on?" he shouted, bursting into the publicity office with the newspaper in his hand.

"Nothing's going on. That's the trouble," said Silvana, who was in charge of the publicity. She was a large, plain woman of forty or thereabouts, with a rasping, masculine voice and the aggressive joviality that comes of having had to fight tooth and nail for more years than was fair to get anyone to give her credit for her competence.

"It says here Mike slipped and fell halfway down the mountain!" he insisted. "Why, for Christ's sake, wasn't I told?"

"Joe, my love! Don't say you believe the things you read in the papers."

Joe threw down the paper and laughed. "Oh, no! One of yours, is it? Jesus! I've started believing my own publicity department. This film's getting me jittery."

"You're not the only one."

"Well, if there's nothing wrong with Mike, at least that's one headache less."

"There's something wrong with him, all right, but I don't know what." She started riffling through a pile of newspapers and magazines that her secretary had just dumped on her desk. "He used to be up to his neck in scandals from morning to night. Orgies, dead girls, never a dull moment. These days he doesn't even punch anyone in the nose."

"I wish he'd punch Nicola in the nose once in a while. Stop him fooling around."

"Fooling around?" said Silvana, raising her eyes with a gleam of new hope.

"With the script. All this chopping and changing. He's driving me crazy."

"Scripts always get changed, don't they?" said Silvana, going back to her reading.

"It's a damn pity. It was good."

"Was it?"

"Didn't you read it?"

"Oh, I never read the script. I'm supposed to tell the world it's a masterpiece. What if it's not?"

Joe stared at her, shocked. Then he smiled and patted her cheek. "Silvana, you're great," he said, and departed, chuckling and shaking his head. Silvana shrugged and handed a magazine to her secretary, tapping a photograph in it with her pencil.

"That's not the still we sent them, is it?"

The girl shook her head. "Never saw it before."

It was the photograph of Robin and Mike having supper at their little trattoria.

"Mmm. Robin, eh? Well, it's an idea."

Mike had stopped losing his temper with photographers and turned the art of dodging them into a game. There was always at least one hanging around his place, so he avoided taking Robin back there in the evenings; and for a while it was fun, roughing it in the little secretive room that was so peculiarly hers.

One night when her doorbell rang in Mike's usual playful style, Robin opened the door and screamed. The man facing her looked like Cyrano de Bergerac in a Humphrey Bogart hat and coat. But the laughter she heard outside as she slammed the door shut was unmistakably Mike's.

"Hey, you silly chump," he called out. "It's me."

When she peeped out again, he swept off his hat and declaimed: *"Je t'aime, je suis fou, je n'en peux plus, c'est trop!"*

"What in the world—?"

"Ever been raped by a man with a nose like this?" he asked, grabbing her suddenly and pushing her inside.

"Ooh, you're all prickly!" she squealed, laughing as she pulled loose.

"Sorry—that's the worst of disguises." He peeled off his little false beard and mustache. "Don't you like my Cyrano nose?" he asked her, turning sideways to show it to her before heading for the bathroom to remove it. "I've got a whole collection of them at home: Oedipus, Shylock, Mr. Puff. I never could get anyone to give me those parts, but I love the noses. Thought I'd give this one a try tonight—see if I could fool the photographers. It worked, too. Old Pino was sitting bang in front of the house and I walked past him cool as a frog; he didn't even bother to look. I'm getting fed up with sprinting down side alleys and dashing in the front door of Passetto's and out the back. Besides, they're onto all those tricks by now. And do you know what? Who cares? We must be mad, sleeping here. When I think of the gorgeous great bed I've got at my place."

"Don't you like my bed?"

He came out of the bathroom with a clean, undisguised face and said, "Well, it does tend to squeak, doesn't it? And you might call it a bit of a tight squeeze."

"That's what I like about it."

"You're definitely cuckoo, you know that? Completely bonkers, that's what you are." He crushed her in his arms and kissed her nose and eyes and ears. "What with a hot water thingamabob that blows up every time you light it and—"

"It doesn't blow up, it only goes bang."

"Whatever it does, it's not safe. If you don't get blown up, you'll get gassed. And no pillows. Not even a saucepan till I came along. Listen, tomorrow we're going to sleep at Via Gregoriana."

"**O**h, my goodness!" she said. "It's gorgeous!"

"I told you so."

The room they had stepped into was L-shaped, laid out on three levels, with a couple of steps up to each one and a big open fireplace facing the recess with the double bed in it. A staircase by the front door led up to the living room on the floor above, and a door by the bed led into the bathroom, which was vast, all blue and gold tiles of Renaissance design, with the tub at the far end, and above it, stuck to the wall with adhesive tape, a big poster of a clown.

Mike arranged some bits of wood in the grate and sprinkled them with Courvoisier—"for luck," he explained, when she gasped at his extravagance. Then he lifted the bottle and said, "To us!" and took a swig before passing it on to her. While she sipped at it and made a face—she hated cognac—he threw a lighted match into the grate and watched the flare. Then he put the bottle out of the way and pulled her down onto the carpet.

" 'How fair and how pleasant art thou, O love, for delights!' " he quoted, gently unbuttoning her blouse.

"I wish I knew some poetry to quote," she said, smiling up at him as she reached out to unbutton his shirt. "All I can do is go, 'Mmmm.' It's not fair." She ran her hand over his smooth golden chest with its discreet crop of dark hair down the center. "Mmmm."

" 'Thy navel is like a round goblet, which wanteth not liquor: thy belly is like an heap of wheat set about with lilies. Thy two breasts are like two young roes that are twins.' " He kissed them slowly, one after the other, and laughed when the nipples turned hard.

"Mmmm," she murmured. "Recite some more, please."

"Later. I'm too busy just now."

When his impetus was spent and their bodies stilled at last, he remained where he was, with his head resting on her shoulder, and she clung to him, marveling at the sense of completion his body gave to hers. "Mike," she breathed, stroking his hair. "Let's stay like this for ever."

"Don't you want to see the rest of the flat?"

"No. Don't move. Later on I'll see it, when the fire burns down. Not now."

They were silent for a while, perfectly tranquil. Then Robin said, "Mike, what's that clown you've got up on the wall in your bathroom?"

"That's Dad." He sighed and pulled himself up and away from her, turning to reach for a log and throw it onto the fire, before lying down again on the carpet beside her. "Well, it isn't really, but I like to think it is. He wanted to be a clown, you know. In a way, I suppose it's an itch I've got myself. But for Dad it was his one dream, all his life. He used to dress up as one sometimes, when I was little, to make me laugh. He had a costume he'd filched from the circus to make up for some of the money he never got. Used to put it on myself when I got bigger, or we'd each wear half and paint our faces white and do an act. Mamma wasn't much of an audience, though. She'd just sit there shaking her head at us over her sewing. If she ever so much as smiled, we knew we were great."

"He must have been very proud of you, your father."

"Oh, yes, ridiculously. I remember when I got my very first part on the stage, at the 'Q' Theatre, he put on his best black suit and rode all the way to Kew on the bus. I only had about three words to say, but I was so nervous, anybody'd think I was playing King Lear. I could just picture him perched on his seat out there, chuckling with pride, and sure enough, when I stepped through the rather wobbly door into the limelight, he clapped."

"And now you're a star."

"Yes. And he's dead. God, why did I say that? I can't lie here with you and be sad."

"You're not sad, just peaceful. From what you've told me, I'd say there's nothing sad about your father."

"No. No, you're right. He used to say heaven is what's left over

83

of a person after he dies. That's how you get judged, he said—you get remembered for what you were."

She reached out for his hand and pressed it against her cheek. "What comes after 'the first fine careless rapture'?" she asked, after a moment.

"The second and the third and the fourth and the—"

"No, no, come on," she laughed. "I want to hear the next bit."

" 'And though the fields look rough with hoary dew,
All will be gay when moontide wakes anew
The buttercups—' "

"Oh, Mike, say that again—buttercups!"

"Buttercups. What's wrong?"

"Nothing. It's the way you say it. Go on."

" 'The buttercups, the little children's dower—' "

" '—Far brighter than this gaudy melon-flower!' That's the only line I remember, that, and 'Oh, to be in England now that April's there,' " She paused, fondling his hand. "Do you ever miss it? England, I mean."

"No. It's not where you're born, it's where you belong, my father used to say."

"Don't you miss talking English, though, a bit?"

"We *are* talking English, aren't we?"

"I know. That's what I love—your voice talking English."

"Only my voice?"

"Oh, no, no." she propped herself up on her elbow and stroked his strong young body. "I love this too, all of it, every little bit, even the smell of it—mmm!" She pressed her nose to his chest and inhaled his sweet male odor, slightly tinged with soap. "And this," she said, touching his sex, which leaped to life again under her fingers. "This is the most beautiful thing I've ever seen." She ran her nose down past his navel and snuggled into the crisp, black curls that smelled of love. "Mmmm," she murmured, "you taste so good."

"Here, two can play at that game," he laughed, reaching down and gripping her shoulders to pull her back onto the floor. "Just you come here." He ran his tongue round her mouth and up over the tip of her nose to her eyes. "You taste good too," he said. "Delicious, in fact. But most of all, you feel good. Oh, God, you feel good." He had slipped into her again so naturally that it was as if they could never stay apart.

Povero Valentino was what is known as a tough picture, and on the last day of shooting, nerves were frayed. Nicola had reserved till the very end an entirely superfluous scene for which there was neither time nor money left, but which, nevertheless, he had insisted on shooting with an obstinacy that very nearly caused a revolt, since it meant working late, after the light had gone—a thing the crew would have done with better grace if they had known what sense it made.

Unfortunately, Nicola had been growing increasingly bad-tempered as the weeks went by, tending more and more to shout as he strained every nerve in the effort to make his film a prizewinner, and creating a state of tension that had, in turn, been reflected on the crew. There had been constant friction, and in some curious way the love affair between Robin and Mike had served as a focus for the vague feeling of discontent for which only Nicola was to blame. Budding romances are part of the filmmaking routine, and Robin's and Mike's would not normally have caused so much as a titter. But secrecy is unpopular on the set, and these two had kept their secret so well that when it got out, as it inevitably did after the photograph of them having supper at their little trattoria was published, a lot of petty spitefulness was unleashed with it.

They were immune to it all. Nothing could touch them, not even the photographers, who, having once tracked them down, began hounding them everywhere they went, just as Mike had foreseen.

But at the end of that last, difficult day, the minute Nicola shouted "Cut!" Mike strode straight past the arc lamps that were being switched off, over the cables and the tracks that the grips were collecting up for loading, past the camera, to Robin, who was closing her typewriter and sorting out her notes. As if finally to put an end to all the paltry sneers and gossip, he gathered her into his arms and gave her a long, theatrically passionate kiss. After a brief, startled hush, someone cheered; immediately, a round of enthusiastic applause broke out. Nicola turned and stared, shocked—not by the kiss, which meant nothing, but by the fact that this was evidently a joke that everyone was in on except him. And in fact he was the only one still in the dark. He had been too absorbed in his work to notice what was going on between Robin and Mike, and too touchy to make them feel like going out of their way to tell him.

They were taking a bow now, laughing happily at the change of mood their little performance had provoked in the crew, who were suddenly all on their side, smiling and clapping and cheering and demanding an encore. All except Nicola, who, having taken it all in at a glance, remained sullenly silent, visibly offended at finding himself the odd man out.

Seeing the look on his face, Mike quickly held up his hand for some quiet before saying, "Now how about a cheer for our director—the man who brought us together."

Nothing happened for a moment, then everyone politely clapped. One solitary voice called out, "Bravo, Nicola!"

"Thank you," Nicola said tartly. "I'll remember that."

He turned and left, like a man inexplicably betrayed.

TEN

Not long after they finished shooting *Povero Valentino*, she told him about the baby. She was sitting up in bed in the hotel on top of a cliff at Ansedonia, where they had come for the weekend. It was December. The sea was dark and turbulent and there were magnetic forces in the air. The hotel was deserted, shut off from the world, with a high wall round it and no access to the sea but an iron ladder down the cliff.

The waiter had just put down the breakfast tray and gone out when Robin said, "I think I'm pregnant."

Mike was standing near the window when she said it; the shock of her words froze that moment in his mind. Years later he still recalled the faint aroma of coffee and the grayness of the sky, the swishing of the waves on the rocks below, and the anxiety in her eyes when he turned to look at her.

"I'm not *sure*," she said.

"How sure?"

"I've missed two months."

"Two months!"

"Didn't you notice?"

It had never entered his head to count the days or query the continuity of his happiness.

"Why didn't you tell me?"

"I was afraid."

"What of?"

"I don't know."

He pondered that for a moment. Perhaps she was afraid he would want her to get rid of it, which would have gone without

87

saying if she had been anyone else. He thought of himself at eighteen, frantically boiling up pounds of parsley in the middle of the night and forcing some unfortunate girl to drink the foul brew, which someone had told him was infallible. But this was Robin. He only grinned.

"So diaphragms aren't so safe after all," he said, just for the sake of saying something while he came to grips with the amazing fact that he felt no panic, nothing but elation. He heard her say:

"I think it was that Sunday we went to Sabaudia. Remember?"

They had made love among the dunes, with the long pale grass swaying in the breeze. She had fluttered a little when he pulled off her bathing suit: "Suppose someone comes." But no one did. Her body smelled of salt and sand, and the tip of her nose was pink from basking all day in the October sun. Feeling the soft sea air on their naked skin had made it all the more poignant for that one brief moment before they forgot the danger of discovery, forgot everything but themselves. He started to laugh.

"You mean you don't mind?" she asked.

"*Mind?*" The child of that day would be a creature of the sun. "I feel like diving into the sea and blowing bubbles like a dolphin. Do dolphins blow bubbles?"

"I don't know."

"Look at it out there, chuckling and rolling about."

"What?" She knelt up on the bed to look out of the window.

"The sea! The strength of it, look!"

"It's rough. Frightening."

"Frightening? It's the force of life."

"But what shall we do?"

"Get married, of course." He started pouring the coffee. "Here, this is getting cold."

"Imagine forgetting it, right in the middle of the month."

"Fate," he said, and leaned forward to kiss her. "Let's get married at Santa Maria in Cosmedin."

"In *church*?"

"Well, we can't go and take an oath to Apollo on the Palatine, because the baby wouldn't be legitimate."

"But I hate all that pomp and gilt."

88

"Santa Maria in Cosmedin isn't like that. It's incredibly ancient and beautiful—and pure, like you."

"Pure!" She laughed.

"Yes, it's a gift you have. Didn't I ever tell you? Whatever you do is—clean."

"Oh." She laughed again, a little uncomfortably. "Anyway, I'm not a Catholic."

"That doesn't matter. It's a lovers' church. It's where they used to show Saint Valentine's skull on Saint Valentine's day. Crowned with roses."

"How revolting!"

"Well, it's not there now. There's the 'mouth of truth' instead. *La bocca della verità.* You know, that round stone face?"

"Oh, that. Yes, Nicola once took me there. He told me if I put my hand in the mouth, I was liable to get it bitten off."

"Only if you tell lies. We'll go and try, shall we? Tomorrow?"

"All right," she said, without much warmth.

"In the Middle Ages they used to take corn merchants there to test their honesty. Did he tell you that? He says it's a millstone, actually, carved with the face of a man. And in Roman times the church itself was the temple of the wheat goddess. That's what I love, this mix-up of Christian and pagan and garbled history and human confusion. You never can tell what's true and what isn't, but that's Rome, don't you see?"

In the end they opted for a civil wedding at the Campidoglio, Rome's town hall. Unfortunately he presented himself as an Italian citizen, and that was a mistake, because an Italian who wants to get married must first prove that he has been born, a fact nobody is prepared to take his word for. Mike soon discovered that nobody was prepared to take his word for anything. He had to produce a whole series of certificates, one for each of the many things that the representatives of the law were disinclined to believe. Even so, he approached the General Register, called the Anagrafe, with a light heart and brushed aside the man at the top of the steps who offered to get him his certificates fast, for a modest fee.

Inside, a burly fellow sat like Cerberus, surveying the turmoil in the entrance hall, and assured Mike with a smile that all certificates could be obtained "immediately." Mike believed him. That, too, was a mistake. It turned out to be an enterprise as arduous as Jason's quest for the Golden Fleece.

The Anagrafe was a cheerless place, grandiose but dusty, spacious and yet dark, a kind of inferno for lost souls in pursuit of their identity. The minute Mike crossed the threshold he saw that his dark glasses were superfluous. The people inside were far too frantic to take any notice of each other as they milled to and fro, fighting a losing battle against some dark, malignant powers that seemed to have doomed them never to attain what was theirs.

Among other things, Cerberus had neglected to tell Mike that everything stopped at noon. So, having arrived optimistically late in the morning, he stood for three-quarters of an hour in a slow-moving and disconsolate queue before it came to a total halt. There was a moan of protest.

"What's happened?" Mike asked the man in front of him.

"Midday!" the man snapped, and walked away with a wide gesture of contempt that embraced the entire building and all its occupants.

Mike went storming back to give Cerberus a piece of his mind. But he could not get a word in edgewise because of all the wild-eyed citizens who kept dashing up to beg for help, carrying lists of certificates and half-filled-in forms, or with nothing but empty hands and tales of woe. Cerberus listened to them with the composure of one who knows it all, and Mike thought he detected a sort of grim satisfaction in his smile.

"**D**o you *have* to do all this queuing?" Robin asked that night, in bed. "Aren't there agencies that do it for you?"

"Oh, yes. And shady little men as well. When I got my Italian nationality, I never lifted a finger. But that wasn't a secret. I don't want this story to get splashed all over the scandal rags, my sweet. That's why I'm doing it myself, if it's the last thing I do."

Robin lay staring at the ceiling for a moment, in silence. Then she said, "Mike, do you think there's really going to be a baby? I mean, can you honestly picture a cot over there in six months' time?"

Mike peered over towards the window. A cot with a baby in it, squealing. True, that was not precisely what he had had in mind. He had imagined, if anything, a golden boy about seven years old. "Does it have to be *there*?" he said.

"See what I mean?"

"Now come on, don't be silly. We don't have to have the cot in our bedroom. We'll have a nursery."

"In this flat? Where?"

It was not the ideal flat for a baby, with all that unusable space, and silly steps up and down everywhere, and not one small room. But he certainly would hate to have to move.

"Nappies, bottles, prams—oh, Mike, I just can't see it. I can't see what's going to happen."

"Well, I'll tell you. To start with, I'm going to get back into that bloody queue tomorrow and stand there till I've got every certificate anybody can name. Then we'll fix the date. Then we'll live happily ever after. And in the meantime, if the doctor says yes, we'll get cracking on the geography of this flat."

The doctor did say yes; a few days before Christmas he confirmed that Robin was in her tenth week of pregnancy.

"He says it may not show for about another month," she told Mike rather nervously that evening.

"We'll be married by then, I promise you," he said. "I mean, how long can it take?"

But how long bureaucracy can take in Italy is a question to which not many people would care to hazard a reply. In any case, Mike had forgotten that he was going to be busy with the dubbing, which kept him fully occupied throughout the week before Christmas and during the fortnight that followed on all the days—and there were not many—that were neither public holidays nor weekends. It was the second week in January before he could get back to the Anagrafe, and then the queues were longer than ever; it took him an hour and twenty minutes to reach the counter, by which time his spirits were low. When he saw the man shaking his head again, he growled, "Now what?"

"You were born in London," said the man, staring at the form.

"Yes," said Mike. "But I'm Italian."

"Yes, but the birth certificate's English. It won't do. Not for marriage. You'll have to go to the Pretura and make an *atto notorio.*"

"A what?" It was not a question, only dismay. An *atto notorio* was a kind of affidavit, sworn in front of a notary public. He had to swear he was him, in other words.

"With four witnesses," said the man. A British birth certificate was not proof enough.

"But it's all here," Mike protested. "I'm an Italian citizen. And you've got it all registered here in your files."

The man looked up at him with new curiosity, perhaps wondering what species of animal this was, to have such blind faith in files.

"Mm," he grunted noncommittally. "You want to leave me the form?" It was like saying, "You want to bet?" He made a vague gesture behind him, towards the tables stacked high with piles of thick, dusty folders. Mike saw what he meant; the precious facts of his life lay buried somewhere at the bottom of a pile like that.

The man's patience was exhausted. He tossed the form into a tray and said, "All right. Come back in ten days and we'll see."

Mike felt the rage well up inside him, and strained to suppress it. It struck him that he must be looking as distraught as everyone else.

In the entrance hall, a hefty man of about thirty-five was spluttering obscenities.

"What's up with him?" Mike asked the man's wife, who was doing her best to hold on to four boisterous children.

"They've got him down as dead," she said.

"I've been dead three years!" the man yelled. "How about that? I came here to get a Certificate of Residence and they told me I was dead!"

"Now he's got to get a Certificate of Existence," said his wife.

"A *what?*"

92

"A Certificate of Existence!" the man bellowed. "To prove I'm alive and not dead!"

Mike turned very calmly and headed for the door. He walked down the steps and crossed the road and got into his car. I'll give them two weeks, he told himself. Two weeks, that's all. After that, I'll tell them I'm British and they can go to hell. We'll go and get married in London.

If only they had.

ELEVEN

It was when Beppe turned up at the Grand Hotel that the trouble began.

"If this party's for the crew," Mike was saying, "what the devil is Beppe Palazzo doing here?"

If Robin blanched, as she surely must have, it passed unnoticed in the discreet light of the elegant room, full of soft talk and vacuous smiles and careful ripples of laughter. All she had to do was say something harmless like, "Goodness knows." Instead, like an idiot, she said, "Who?"

"Don't you know our Beppe? There he is, look, over there. The *bacherozzo* that squelched."

She turned and let Mike point Beppe out to her, as if she had never seen him before in her life. She had been dreading something of this kind. Even so, she could easily have said, "Oh, Beppe—yes of course"; or simply, "Oh, *him!*" or, best of all, "Oh, yes, we used to work together." But no, she said not a word. Her face remained a blank.

"Just look at him, slavering all over Joe, the skunk. Well, it serves Joe right for inviting him here. I mean, how tactless can you be?"

She did not know what he meant by that, and she attempted to say so, but in a voice too faint to be heard. Mike was intent only on preserving his smile no matter what, and keeping up a barrage of words, any words, while he concentrated on ignoring the flash-bulbs and exuding charm. He was the center of attraction and it was awful for Robin to have to stand there with him, pretending to make cocktail talk, with Beppe's nearness like a load of mud on her mind.

94

"You see," Mike was saying, "there's only one reason for giving a party at the end of a film, and that's because when the director says 'cut' for the last time and you see the crew walking away with a piece of your life, you suddenly love them all, even the ones you've wanted to murder a dozen times; and there's nothing you can do about it but sit down and eat a *spaghettata* and drink everybody's health in bad *spumante*, and smile and kiss and cry. Even if you're so tired you can't wait to get home and creep into bed, you need a party then, to stop you feeling like a burst balloon. But now? This? Only half the crew's here anyway—the ones who are still out of work. What do they care about making small talk with all these phonies?"

He waved to three grips who were coming down the steps, looking self-conscious in their best suits and ties. "*Ciao, ragazzi!*" he called out, and they grinned and waved back. "See what I mean?" he said. "Three cheerful goldfish in a sea full of sharks."

To Joe Mannino it had probably seemed like a bright idea to combine some lucrative publicity for the film with the party he had omitted to give the crew at the end of the shooting, when they were two weeks behind schedule and so much over budget that he was in no mood to throw money away on celebrations. Only now, two months later, was it beginning to look as if Joe might possibly, accidentally, have produced a remarkable film. Several people had reacted with enthusiasm to the bits of it they had seen, and Joe had confessed to Mike that this made him feel a little ashamed of having packed off his hard-working crew without so much as a farewell drink. Hence this hodgepodge of bored people thrown together at the Grand Hotel, this smooth, well-organized waste of money and time.

"*Ciao, belli!*" Nicola placed a paternal hand on each of their shoulders.

"Hello!" Robin exclaimed, rather too squeakily.

"*Salve!*" said Mike.

Their effusive tone of voice rang false; they knew it did. Mike tried to cover it up by asking, "How's it going?" It was the most natural thing to ask, but it sounded strained.

Nicola shrugged and made a face. He was tired and depressed

after spending days and nights in a dark, airless room, staring at the miniature screen on the moviola and arguing himself sick with the English editor, who kept throwing out his favorite bits. By now Nicola hated him. That afternoon he and the editor and the composer had sat through a rough cut of the film, and he had hated that too. Just then he hated everything and everyone—especially Robin and Mike, with their unnatural smiles and shifty eyes, too embarrassed to look him straight in the face. He was not jealous, only hurt, very deeply hurt by the way they had fallen into each other's arms behind his back and not let him into their secret until everyone else in the crew had found out. The two dear friends that he had wanted with him on the film at all costs. It would have been so much easier to get a script girl who knew the job; so much more profitable to let Schulbach go and sign up Gregory Peck. By now he had convinced himself that he could have had Gregory Peck just by choosing to give in; but no, it had to be Mike and no one else, with the result that he had been kept hanging about for a whole year while Mannino scraped together the money to make it. And if there was one person he hated with all his heart, it was Joe Mannino, who was bearing down on him now with outstretched arms, booming across the room, "Nicola! I hear it's fantastic!"

"Who says so?" Nicola growled.

"My spies. When are you going to let me see it?"

"When I'm ready."

His ungracious tone visibly ruffled Joe, who looked as if he thought he had been patient long enough. Robin said quickly, "You look tired, Nicola."

"I am."

"*Tesoro!*" Luisa flung her arms round Nicola with such passion that she neatly ousted all the others in one move. "I'm not talking to *you*, and you know why," she tossed over her shoulder at Joe, adding, as an afterthought, "*Ciao*, Mike," as she linked her arm possessively through Nicola's and led him away, whispering into his ear.

"What have you done to *her*?" Mike asked Joe, who shrugged and shook his head, turning at the same moment to greet the general manager of Cinecittà.

Mike picked up a *fiasco* of wine. "I'm going over there to have a proper drink with the boys," he told Robin. "Why don't you round up some of the others and bring them along."

She nodded and set off in search of familiar faces. Beppe barred her way. *"Ciao, amore,"* he said.

"Leave me alone, will you?"

"Why? I'm not your *amore* any more?"

"No! And I can't think what you're doing here."

"The star of the picture is a client of mine."

"What, *Mike*?"

"Luisa Lenzi."

"Luisa? The *star*?"

"Certainly—if *I* say so."

"Certainly not! She's just one of the girls."

"Like you, eh? Mike Donato's latest. Headline: 'How Long Will This One Last?' "

"Oh, go to hell!"

"Poor Robin. Everyone knows he's a Don Giovanni. Even Luisa had a flirt with him once."

"She's had what you call a 'flirt' with every man I know."

"And how about you, *tesoro*? Does Mike know you have made love with me?"

For a moment Robin stood and stared at him. Then she walked away and subsided into the nearest chair, overcome by an indefinable malaise, which she decided must be the weakness of an empty stomach; whatever it was, when Beppe loomed up in front of her again, she could not find the strength to get away.

"Ti voglio bene, sai," he said, eyeing her with apparent regret. "It makes me sad to see you hurt."

"Oh, you wish me well, do you?"

"Ti voglio bene means I love you."

With that he strolled away, leaving her with a bad taste in her mouth. Impetuously she stumbled towards the table, seized with an illogical urge to eat something. She took a sandwich from the nearest plate and felt sick the minute she tasted it.

"Ciao, Robin," said Silvana, the publicity woman, who appeared to be simmering with rage. She spiked a stuffed olive and

97

popped it viciously into her mouth. As she did so, she turned, and her eyes opened dangerously wide. "Ah!" she exclaimed, "Beppe Palazzo! So *you're* looking after our dear Luisa now."

"That is so," said Beppe, spiking a stuffed olive himself, as if accepting a challenge.

"I hear she complains of getting no publicity. But what can I do if no one wants her photograph? *You* try, Beppe dear! If you can get them published, you're a genius."

"I am," said Beppe. "I always get what I want." He turned his insolent grin on Robin and added, "No?" She knew then that she was going to faint, and that she must not do it there. She managed to squeeze past a mountainous gentleman who was too important to move out of her way, and Mike caught her in his arms, not a moment too soon.

No one saw her faint. He eased her quickly into an armchair, and she came round almost instantly. Through the ringing in her ears she heard Mike say, "Undo your belt!"

She groped for the buckle and discovered for the first time that her belt was a good deal too tight. Then she saw Beppe watching her loosen it.

"Better?" asked Mike. She nodded.

"She feels faint," said Beppe, coming up behind his back. "That is normal, I think. No?"

"Think what you like," Mike snapped. "Just clear off."

"Sorry. At parties one always tries to be nice."

"Go and be nice to somebody else."

Beppe smiled at Robin. "This man does not like me," he said. "I wonder why."

He went on standing there, his eyes fixed on Robin's waist.

A few days later the telephone rang when Mike was out.

"You're pregnant, aren't you?" said Beppe's voice. Robin slammed down the receiver, but it rang and rang until she picked it up again. "It's no use hanging up," he said. "It shows."

"Why can't you leave me alone?"

"You are in trouble, I think. It must be three months at least. Why doesn't he marry you?"

"Look, it's none of your bloody business."

"No? I think yes. I am willing to marry you if he is not."

"Don't be ridiculous."

"Why is it ridiculous? You need a father for your child. So—I am here. Remember that. I am always here. *Arrivederci.*"

Click went the receiver. She stared at it, cursing herself for ever picking it up. It sickened her to think that Beppe would always be there. Naturally she never mentioned that telephone call to Mike.

He had gone back to the Anagrafe that morning, to see if they had found his file. They hadn't. They never did, in spite of all the forms he filled in and the waiting in line he put up with and the innumerable witnesses he raked together to countersign his affidavits. And all the time Robin's belly continued to swell. It made a difference to her now, seeing that there really was something inside there, determined to grow, while Mike plowed helplessly back and forth between the Anagrafe and the Pretura and the Prefettura, and time went rambling on and on from one *domani* to the next. Soon, none of her skirts would fasten any more, and she knew she ought to be thinking about maternity clothes and knitting little woolly cardigans, neither of which appealed to her in the least.

Her mother would have been knitting tiny garments by the score, if she had had the slightest suspicion they were going to be needed. The trouble was, her reactions were so unpredictable that Robin had not even broken the news to her about Mike, let alone about being pregnant, and she had left it so late now that she did not know where to start. Dear Mother, I'm expecting a baby and hope to get married soon. Would you knit some little cardigans for me, please? She remembered her mother fussing over the tea things at Norland Square, and knew that a letter of that kind would not go down well.

Mike also had his mother very much on his conscience. He had not been out to Anticoli as he had promised, to work out some plan for her with Uncle Gino, and when he pictured her walking up Clerkenwell Road all alone, a small, lumpy figure in a skimpy dress that had shrunk when she dyed it black, he felt so bad about the way he had neglected her that he didn't have the heart to write

99

her a joyful letter about his own astonishing new happiness. How could he make her understand? After several false starts, he had given up trying and been brutally brief: "*Cara Mamma,*" he had written. "*Mi sposo.*" And as he slipped it into the mailbox he had thought to himself: Now she'll go straight out and light a candle. He hated those candles. It scared him still to think that they always burned out.

It was nearly the end of February before Robin found out that as two British subjects all they had to do was put up the banns in the Consulate and in three weeks, without a single complication, they would get a *nulla osta* for the wedding.

"With any luck, we'll beat the baby to it yet," she told Mike when she came home, kicking off her shoes and putting her feet up on the bed. The Consulate in Piazza di Spagna was only five minutes' walk away, but coming back up the Spanish Steps had proved more strenuous than she had anticipated. Mike went off to make her a cup of tea, and just then something extraordinary happened. She felt a movement inside her, an almost imperceptible stirring in her womb.

"Mike!" she shrieked. "Mike! It's moving!"

"What?" He came leaping back down the stairs, thinking something terrible had happened.

"The baby," she told him. "It's alive!" And for no reason at all, her eyes began to smart with tears.

"What's the matter? What are you crying for?" he asked, throwing himself down on the bed beside her.

"I don't know. I don't know." She held on to him and sobbed.

"Come on, don't be silly." He pushed her down and patted her big round belly. "Pancrazio, your mother's daft."

"Pancrazio?" She laughed, through her tears.

"Well, he must have a name, mustn't he? Let's make it Pan for short."

"Mike, shall we risk flying and just go home?" she said suddenly. "It might solve everything."

"But it's all solved," he said. "We'll be married in no time now."

And so they doubtless would have been, had Beppe Palazzo not reared his pimply head again a few weeks later, just when they had forgotten his existence. Coming when it did, the announcement he made in one of the March issues of *Fandango* drove Mike wild with rage.

No one blamed him, not even the police. How else could he have been expected to behave when he saw a picture of the pregnant Robin beside one of Beppe, who was quoted as saying, "Mike Donato is a born Don Quixote. Too bad the father of the child is me."

TWELVE

The night everything fell to pieces, Mike had been out to dinner with Joe Mannino, who was after him again for another film. It was the twenty-first of March. That was one date in her life Robin would never forget.

It had been a particularly happy day. They had been down to the Consulate to pick up the *nulla osta*, which meant that at last there was no further impediment to their wedding. Robin was suddenly much bigger. The Spanish Steps were now quite difficult for her to negotiate even on the way down, and Mike had tucked her under his wing for support, his wing being the flap of his English riding mac, which still had a new, rubbery smell. She was proud of her *pancia* now. She actually liked having to lean back to support the weight and roll a bit as she walked. Mike said she overdid it on purpose, to give the photographers their money's worth—as if she took any notice of *them* any more.

Joe Mannino was a different matter. The idea of seeing him did embarrass her a bit, and since, by suppertime, she was really tired, she had asked Mike to go without her.

She was sitting up in bed, trying to keep awake with a book, when she heard his key in the lock at last.

"Mike?" she called out. "Quick, come and look! Pan's turning somersaults."

She was smiling expectantly, eager to show him the little bulges that kept protruding here and there in her now enormous belly. But he didn't call back as he usually did from the door. He just appeared at the foot of the bed and stood there without a word. When she saw the look on his face, she froze. He threw down the magazine he had in his hand and walked away, leaving her staring numbly at the cover, which had a stark yellow title down one side: "The Child with Two Fathers." And a great big photograph of herself and Beppe, cheek to cheek.

There were more photographs inside, three pages of them, including the one of her looking even bigger than she was and the smirking face of Beppe making his outrageous claim. The rest were the ones taken at Beppe's mother's wedding, she could see that at a glance. But they had been tampered with to make it look as if she and Beppe were hugging and kissing for sentimental reasons of their own.

Mike came back with a glass in his hand. "How about it?" he said.

"They're faked," she told him. "There was a whole roomful of people there. They've made it look as if we were alone. Anyway, I won't have you storming in like this and going for me over some silly photos that were taken ages before I knew you. For heaven's sake! Do you think I never kissed anyone but you?"

"Oh, I know you did. But not Beppe Palazzo. That's new."

He was staring at her very hard and his eyes were cold. Disenchanted. She couldn't bear it.

"I know it must look awful," she said, "but it wasn't like that at all, honestly. They were taken at Beppe's mother's wedding, as a matter of fact. Everyone was kissing everyone else and I'd drunk a lot of champagne."

"What the hell were you doing at Beppe's mother's wedding?"

"God knows. Look, it's a long story and—"

"How come you pretended not to know him?"

"I suppose I preferred to think I didn't."

"That's one way of looking at it."

"Listen, if you must know, he once tried to get me to marry him."

"Ah! Now we're getting somewhere."

"Mike, please! What's the matter with you? I feel as sick as you do about this. Sicker, probably, considering it's me who's been made to look like a bitch." She bit her lip and put her hand over her belly as a violent kick took her breath away. Mike rushed to her side, instantly solicitous.

"What is it?"

"Only Pan. He's been kicking me black and blue."

Mike melted then. He sat on the edge of the bed and put his arms round her. "Oh, my love, I'm sorry! This bastard made me lose my head." He flung the magazine across the room, in the direction of the grate.

She winced again. "Look," she said, pushing aside the blanket. He was just in time to see a little bump appear and then subside. "The doctor says he's a *bimbo vivace*. He's kicking more than he should."

"With fury, probably." Mike got to his feet, his own fury rising again. "That bastard! I'm going to go out and smash his face in! He's not getting away with it, not this time." He drained his glass and put it down. "You go to sleep. I don't know how long I'll be."

"But it's midnight!"

"Beppe's a night bird."

"What are you going to do?"

"I don't know. Kill him, probably."

"Oh, Mike, don't be silly."

"It'd be silly not to. I ought to have done it long ago."

He picked up his mac, blew her a kiss, and was gone. She looked at the clock beside the bed. It was ten past twelve.

She should have stopped him, calmed him down, even tried somehow to explain—anything but let him go off like that, looking for trouble in the middle of the night. What kind of trouble he might run into she had no precise idea—only a clammy sense of dread. Only a feeling that she ought to try to prevent it, even if it meant getting dressed and going out in search of Beppe herself. On impulse, she reached for the telephone. If by any chance he was at home, she could tell him to stay there. Bolt the door and not let anyone in. That was the best thing. Give Mike time to cool down.

"*Pronto*," said Beppe's voice. Her relief turned instantly to rage as she remembered what he had done.

"It's Robin," she said, in a tone so grim that he must have guessed straight off what it was about.

"Ah? *Come stai?*"

"How could you *do* such a thing?"

"Do what?"

"You know perfectly well. This thing in *Fandango*. How could you be so foul?"

"*Tesoro mio*, is it my fault if Mike Donato lets you walk about Rome getting bigger and bigger so that everybody can see your shame?"

"But you've proclaimed you're the father!"

"Do you believe what they write in magazines? They invent things all the time, to sell more copies."

"Well, what about the photos, then? No one could have dug those up but you."

"Madonna! What is wrong with you people? Every time your Mike sees his picture in the paper, he accuses me of putting it there—as if I would waste my time to make him famous for nothing. And now *you* start."

"You're just dodging my question."

"What question? You don't ask a question. You don't ask, 'Beppe, do you know something about this?' No, you accuse me, like him. I am foul. I am bad. But what have I done? Nothing. I fell in love. I sent you flowers, poems, little gifts. Is that bad? I asked you to marry me. If you want, I will marry you even now."

"Are you mad, or what?"

"No. I am coherent, more than you. But you don't want to understand. *Peccato! Ciao.*"

He hung up quickly—a favorite trick of his—and that was the last time Robin spoke to him. She was left with the dead receiver in her hand, and in her mind all at once appeared the image of him standing discomfited by the telephone in his pale blue underwear and black socks. It was true she had always treated him like dirt, and after all, what *had* he done? She remembered him in bed with his purple paisley pajamas and black hairnet. She remembered the pimple on his cheek. For one incredible moment she felt sorry for

105

him. Then she realized she had forgotten to warn him that Mike had just set out to smash his face in. She dialed the number again. This time there was no reply.

Mike was angry, exceedingly angry, anyone could see that. They made a lot of it at the trial. In a *processo indiziario*, a trial based on presumptive evidence, cause and effect, at least, are supposed to be clear; and according to the prosecution, in Mike's case they could not have been clearer. The cause of his anger was common knowledge; the effect was the willful murder of Beppe that night. His anger was plain to everybody he met as he strode up one side of Via Veneto and down the other, in and out of Doney's and Rosati's, the Caffè Strega and the Excelsior Bar, answering greetings with no more than a grunt, if at all. They all came to give evidence, the people he had grunted at or ignored, all those stale, half-familiar faces from the cafés and clubs; the crowd that was always there, embedded in the couches at Rosati's, or on the prowl from the Strega to Doney's, hunting for luck. A little limelight in court was more luck than they ever dared to expect. They gave evidence eagerly, all of them, even some who, on the night of March twenty-first, were tucked up in bed. Among them they proved how long it took him to track Beppe down—a detail that, according to the prosecution, ruled out provocation and proved malice aforethought.

It was about half past one by the time he reached the Diavolo Blu, a melancholy place, almost totally dark except for the spotlights on a small patch of floor where a few bored couples swayed to the strumming of a lackluster band while a plump-faced youth in a red satin suit crooned "Smoke Gets in Your Eyes" in what purported to be the English tongue.

As Mike walked in, there was a burst of ribald laughter, and it was Beppe who had cracked the joke. He was sitting by the dance floor, surrounded by his little court, and Mike saw, when he strode across to their table, that, for all his chuckling, he had red eyes and a sweaty nose. The people with him, the people who flattered him and drank exorbitant booze at his expense, were a sad, hungry lot. Mike glanced round the table at the girls, pathetically dolled up to titillate, with bare shoulders and wretched bits of glitter and self-conscious mouths—Beppe's girls. Some were on the way up, others on the way down; mostly they were just down, like Mitzi, grasping at straws—never real, never a real woman like Robin. Beppe might have tried, but he never could have touched Robin, no matter what he said.

"Funny little chap, aren't you?" Mike told him. "Make a lot of people laugh, one way and another. But not me! I've had enough of you and your little jokes. Understand? I want a public statement. There's a microphone over there. I want you to get up and walk over to it and solemnly declare that all these stories you've been telling are a lot of filthy lies."

"What stories?"

"Come on, get up!" Mike walked over to the microphone, dislodged the singer from it, and addressed the room with a commanding but pleasant *"Buona sera."*

The band stopped playing, the dancers stopped dancing. The waiters stood still, balancing their trays in midair, when they saw who he was. A ripple of whispers went round the tables, and heads rose in surprise. Mike acknowledged all this with a professional smile.

"Forgive the interruption," he said, "but our friend Beppe Palazzo here has something important he wants to say. Right, Beppe, it's all yours!"

Beppe did not move. No one at his table moved. All heads turned in his direction, and he only grinned.

"Come along now," said Mike. He walked over and gripped Beppe by the scruff of the neck, jerking him to his feet. "Don't keep everybody waiting."

Formidable opponent as he was in any battle of wits, Beppe was helpless against physical aggression. He dangled from Mike's hand, his neck sunk into his collar, his face dead white, as Mike half dragged, half marched him to the microphone. He made one attempt to dart away, while Mike loosened his hold to lower the microphone to his level; when Mike grabbed hold of him again he let out an obscenity, which was greeted with a short burst of awkward laughter, and then silence, chillier than before.

"If you fight this, you'll only make a fool of yourself," Mike breathed into his ear. "So give them a smile and say *buona sera* to start with."

"Buona sera," Beppe said.

"Say 'I'm a liar,' " Mike told him. " '*Sono un bugiardo schifoso.*' " Beppe said nothing. "Go on," Mike hissed. "Say '*dichiaro di aver calunniato* Robin Lane.' "

"I will not say that!"

"You will, you know." Mike twisted his arm. The manager was hovering nearby, looking embarrassed.

"Signor Donato," he said. *"Mi scusi, ma—"*

"Cos'è questa storia?" someone called out. It was Carlo Rolli, a journalist Mike knew well.

"Carlo! Just the man I need."

"So explain at least, no?"

"It's so simple," said Beppe. "His girlfriend is pregnant. Did you ever hear anything more banal?"

He had scored. You could feel it.

"You don't understand!" shouted Mike, enraged. "This worm goes round saying he's the father. Which is a lie!"

"What do *you* say, Beppe?" Carlo asked.

"I say nothing. I am a gentleman. I will not be forced to say things."

"Giusto!" someone called out.

"He's right!" said someone else.

"Well, stop him, then!" shouted Beppe. "Make him let me go."

There were shouts of *"Lo lasci stare!"* Mike realized that, incredible as it seemed, they were on Beppe's side, not his. He let go of Beppe then, and turned to face the room.

"How can you all sit there and take his side against me?" he said. "He's not just a liar, he's a pimp—a cheap crook—"

"That's a slander!" cried Beppe. "I'll sue you for that."

"Go ahead, sue! Let's have it all out in court. How you got rich so fast. And what you had to do with Mitzi Aron and that other girl they found dead—the one on the beach."

There was an instant hush. Beppe's face turned white. Mike had everyone's attention at last.

"Aha!" he said. "You all know about that one, don't you? But I'll bet Beppe knows more. I'll bet he knows *all* about it—just like Mitzi did, poor girl. And do you know what happened to her? She ended up dead too, in a squalid hotel room. Twenty-three years old." Beppe began to sidle away. "That's not so funny, is it, Beppe, eh? Look at him trying to sneak away. He knew Mitzi very well, you see—and a lot of other girls like her. He makes money out of that kind of misery—that's the sort of man he is. But what's worse, much worse, is that he knows why Mitzi's dead."

Beppe turned back and made a rush at the microphone, howling, "Lies! It's all lies! Every word! This man's out of his mind. He doesn't know what he's saying. And you know why? He's lost his head over this girl called Robin Lane. And today a magazine came out with a lot of pictures of her kissing *me*."

At that point Mike lost all control. He punched Beppe so hard that he knocked him out.

There was a gasp.

"Mike!" said Carlo. "That wasn't very wise."

"No, it wasn't was it? But just you put it in tomorrow's paper—all of it, especially the bit about those poor dead girls."

The manager bent down and peered into Beppe's eyes. Beppe's friends were creeping forward, uncertain what, if anything, they ought to do.

"And the bit about Robin?" Carlo asked.

Mike hauled Beppe up from the floor and slung him over his shoulder. "He's going to apologize for that. In writing. If I have to skin him alive." He headed for the door. Beppe's friends tried rather feebly to bar the way. Mike barged straight through them, using Beppe's body as a shield.

The manager took a deep breath and dialed the police.

"Mike, wait!" Carlo called out. "Don't be a fool!" Mike took no notice. "What are you going to do?"

"I don't know—yet."

109

THIRTEEN

Mike and Robin were still asleep when the doorbell rang early the next morning, and it rang again before Mike could find the sleeves of his dressing gown and shuffle to the door. There were two men standing outside.

"Michele Donadio?"

He must have said yes—or some noise that sounded like it— because they then announced simultaneously, *"Polizia."*

"Would you mind coming along with us for a moment?" said one of them.

"To help with a few inquiries," said the other.

"What about?"

Instead of answering, they stepped forward into the flat and one of them suggested, with a courteous smile, that Mike might care to get dressed.

Still half asleep, Mike headed for the wardrobe and started groping blearily for socks. He did not notice that the police officers had mounted the steps behind him until it was too late to prevent one of them from reaching the recess where Robin was sitting up in bed with the blankets hoisted to her chin, trying to catch what was going on.

"Oh! Excuse me!" the man said, with a little bow. "I didn't know there was a lady here." As he spoke, his practiced eye spotted *Fandango* on the floor; he stepped forward to pick it up and place it politely on the bed. When he had withdrawn, Mike and Robin exchanged looks of dismay.

"Am I allowed to have a shower?" Mike called out.

"Take your time!"

Robin followed Mike into the bathroom. "What is it?" she whispered. "What do they want?"

"Some inquiries, they said," he whispered back. "I think I did make a bit of a rumpus last night."

He had come in at five minutes to three and gone straight to sleep, like a man worn out but satisfied that he has done a good job.

"Oh, Mike!" Robin said. "What did you do?"

Mike plugged in his electric razor and started to shave. "Nothing. They want to ask me about Beppe, I expect. I seem to remember shouting out a thing or two that would have made them sit up and take notice."

They both felt uneasier than they dared to say. But Mike emerged with a cheerful smile when he was ready to go. He even hazarded, "How about a cup of coffee?"

To which the officer in charge replied, rather sharply, "Afterwards." He picked Mike's mac up off the chair by the door and handed it to him.

Still, the very word "afterwards" did help to ease their minds, implying—they allowed themselves to hope—that he would be back for breakfast.

"You have yours," he told Robin, turning back at the door to blow her a kiss.

Down in the street there were three policemen searching his car. A hand on his elbow steered him firmly towards a police car parked in front of it.

"Here, what's going on?" Mike asked. It was no use. They made him get into the back of the police car with the plainclothesmen, one on either side. Two of the uniformed men took their places in front, and the third got into Mike's Alfa Romeo.

"He's bringing it along," they told him, hastily forestalling his indignation, "so it'll be there for you to drive home in."

"Don't you think you might explain?" Mike asked, infuriated by their air of silent mystification.

"Don't worry, it's only a formality."

As always, the corridors of the Questura, Rome's central police station, were crowded with photographers. When Mike was escorted in, they bombarded him, running backwards ahead of him, clicking and flashing all along the corridor.

"Is he under arrest?" one asked.

"Of course not," said Mike.

"Did he do it?" asked another.

"Do what?" said Mike, and laughed.

He knew most of the bunch by name and would have offered any one of them a drink if he had chanced on them in a bar. Poor devils, they had a hard time scraping a living out of other people's lives. But today they smelled blood, and there was money in it, and they were thirsty for a kill.

A door was opened; it closed behind him. He was alone in a small, empty room. All at once he stopped smiling and felt the anger brimming over at the way they had dragged him out of bed and coerced him, and above all at the way he had allowed himself to be pushed in here and left to stew.

There was nothing to look at: no papers on the desk, no coats on the coat stand, no books on the shelf; only a calendar on the wall, nothing else. The door opened. Two policemen brought in a typing table and set it down against the wall beside the window.

"Listen," said Mike. "I refuse to wait here like this!"

"Sit down," one of them said on his way out. "They won't be long." And Mike, to his own astonishment, sat down.

After a while another one came in, carrying an antiquated black typewriter, which he put on the typing table.

"For God's sake!" Mike burst out. "What's going on?"

"Nothing, nothing. don't worry." The door closed again.

After that he waited and waited, how long he could not be sure; he had forgotten his watch. Keeping people waiting was an old trick, he knew that. He had often been kept waiting when he first came to Rome, and it had always maddened him. But Mike Donato was never kept waiting any more. They seemed not to know who he was.

He was just toying with the idea of getting up and walking out when the door opened again and a man came in who clearly possessed some authority, for he was followed by a train of under-lings. They were all in plain clothes except one, who came armed with a chair, on which he sat down in front of the typewriter.

The man in charge of the proceedings was fiftyish and rather heavily built, with keen eyes under thick black brows. He seated himself behind the desk and examined the file he had brought in with him. "Michele Donadio?" he said.

"Yes," said Mike. The question was enough in itself to chasten him.

"Would you kindly describe in detail what you did yesterday?"

Mike felt his first pang of apprehension then. The only word that sprang to his lips was "Why?"

"Never mind why. Just describe what you did."

Behind his back, Mike heard a slow tap-tapping as the police-man at the typewriter laboriously recorded each letter of the words already said. *Il verbale.* Everything you say will be taken down and used as evidence against you. Except that in Italy no such cautions are administered. No explanations, either.

An extraordinary blankness took hold of him. It was the class-ical nightmare situation of finding yourself onstage and not know-ing your lines. But it was worse than that; he had no idea what part he was supposed to be playing, or even what play he was in. And they were all staring at him, waiting for him to give an account of himself, the man behind the desk and the four or five others standing round. It took him a full minute to pull himself together sufficiently to say, "Look, if it's about Beppe—"

"Yes?"

"Well, I know I went a bit berserk last night. God, I think I even pinched a megaphone. But surely it can't be that?"

The megaphone belonged to an assistant director called Massimo Fabbri, who was standing holding it in his hand in a blaze of light in the middle of the road when Mike's car came round the corner from the Diavolo Blu and turned into Via Veneto at Porta Pin-ciana. There was a whole film crew with him, shooting a night sequence, but Mike had not recognized anyone else he knew, nor, as far as he could see at the speed he was going, had anyone else recognized him. He had snatched the megaphone from Massimo as he swept past, leaving him stunned, with his hands outstretched as if to grab it back. Mike meant to return it right away, but it was just the thing for a loud public apology, and he said so over his shoulder to Beppe, in the back seat. There was no reply. "Don't tell me you're still out," Mike said. "Come on, take this and do your stuff." But Beppe showed no sign of life. "All right, you asked for it," Mike told him, and as he swooped on down via Veneto, he leaned out of the window and bellowed through the megaphone himself.

"*Attenzione! Polizia! Attenzione!* Investigate Beppe Palazzo! *Con urgenza!* Ask Beppe Palazzo about Mitzi Aron and the girl found dead on the beach! *Attenzione! Polizia! Attenzione!*"

"**W**hat time was it then?" asked the man behind the desk, whose name was Maselli.

"Too late to be shouting in the streets. I know. I made a terrible racket and I'm sorry. I suppose there've been complaints."

There was an icy silence. Maselli contemplated him thoughtfully.

"Well, *is* it that?" Mike snapped. "Or do you want the lowdown on Beppe Palazzo?"

"I want to begin at the beginning," Maselli said quietly. "With what you did yesterday afternoon."

After that it went on and on, for an hour or two hours or three, an endless rigmarole of questions and answers, until Mike lost all sense of reality. The men who were standing round went in and out of the room from time to time, and he was not sure if they were the same ones who came back. He could not say how many there were, or what they looked like. He was aware only of a fluctuating, indeterminate, obsessive presence, watching him, listening, weighing his words, waiting to catch him out. Where did he have dinner? How much did he drink? Where did he park his car? *Tap-tap, tap-tap,* letter by letter, it all went down in the *verbale,* without so much as a flicker of an eyelash to indicate whether what he was saying had anything to do with what it was all about. Finally the phone rang, and after listening for a moment, Maselli stood up, as if that clinched it, whatever it might be. He then swept out of the room, only to return a few minutes later, holding out at arm's length a bloodstained handkerchief. "This was found on the floor in the back of your car," he announced.

Mike felt an inappropriate urge to laugh, but he did his best to look respectfully serious as he stared at the handkerchief.

"I expect it's Beppe's," he said.

"Ah! And the blood?"

"Also Beppe's, I suppose. His nose must have been bleeding from the punch I gave him."

"So you admit you punched him in the nose?"

"Yes, I admit that too. I lost my head for a moment. Who wouldn't, after what he said?"

"What did he say?"

"Oh, a lot of stuff about—about a girl I'm fond of."

"This girl?"

Maselli snapped his fingers and a copy of *Fandango* was placed on the desk, the one with Robin on the cover. Mike felt a little sick at the sight of it there. "Yes," he said.

"Right. So now what did Giuseppe Palazzo say about the girl?"

"Does it matter? I don't want to remember."

"It matters. You must remember. What, when, and where."

The whole sordid scene in the Diavolo Blu had to be hauled out and dissected—all he recollected of what he had said and what Beppe had said, leading up to the punch that laid Beppe flat on the floor.

"And then?"

"And then what?" His mind was a blank.

"Did you examine him at least, to see if he was dead?"

"Of course he wasn't dead." Mike laughed.

"He was on the floor. Motionless. What did you do?"

"All right, I give up. You tell me."

Maselli placed a copy of *Il Messaggero* in front of Mike. "This may refresh your memory," he said.

115

There was a large photograph of him leaving the nightclub with Beppe slung over his shoulder. Funny, he had no recollection of being photographed. Some friend, that Carlo Rolli.

"What do you say now?" said Maselli.

"All right, so I lugged him out and put him in my car. If you knew it all along, why didn't you say so? Now you've got the whole story."

"Except what you did after you left the nightclub."

"I told you that. About the megaphone. I do feel rather guilty about that, but I'll—"

"You neglected to mention that Beppe Palazzo was lying unconscious in the back of your car."

"He wasn't unconscious. Not by the time we got to Via Veneto. He sat up and made a dive for the megaphone. That's when I flung it out of the window. We had a bit of a tussle, actually."

"Ah. You drove with one hand and tussled with the other, did you? And naturally there were people in Via Veneto who saw that too?"

"I don't know. We were past the cafés by then. About level with the Hotel Regina."

"And you were driving fast?"

"Oh, no, not at that point. But I think I did jam my foot down on the gas a bit when I turned off left up Via Bissolati and headed for Trastevere."

"You headed for Trastevere? Why was that?"

"Well, I'd let off enough steam by then, and I'd kind of cooled down. Besides, I couldn't do any more yelling because I'd lost the megaphone. So I said to Beppe, 'All right, I think I've made myself clear. Now I'll take you home.' "

Maselli eyed him coldly, without bothering to comment. "What did Palazzo say?" he asked.

"I don't remember."

"Ah. And then?"

"Then I drove him home."

"You drove him all the way to his home, did you?"

"Well, not right to the door. He lives in Piazza dei Ponziani, you know, and it's a bit awkward to get to. He told me to drop him off at the Isola Tiberina to save me going round."

Maselli raised his eyes and gave Mike a long, infinitely skeptical look. "Signor Donadio, I think I ought to inform you that there are footprints on the back seat of your car, and traces of blood."

"If his nose was bleeding, of course there are traces of blood."

Maselli drummed his fingers on the desk and stared reflectively at Mike. "So you drove him to the Isola Tiberina and left him there. Did anyone see him get out of your car?"

"There aren't many people round there at that time of night."

"Exactly."

"Now listen, this is getting ridiculous. Why don't you ring him up and ask *him*?"

"Palazzo did not go home last night. Nor this morning."

"Who says so? He lives alone."

"His bed has not been slept in. His charwoman found everything untouched."

Mike shrugged. "All I can say is I saw him set off across the bridge. He was making straight for Piazza dei Ponziani, and it's not more than a hundred yards away."

"Unfortunately no one else has seen or heard from Palazzo since you carried him out of the Diavolo Blu last night. At which time, according to this report, you said you were going to skin him alive."

"I was joking."

"You didn't seem to be joking."

"You don't think I did skin him alive, do you?"

Maselli shrugged and stood up. He did not bother to reply.

FOURTEEN

The narrow steps leading down to the riverbank were fetid with stale urine and littered with refuse and the leftovers of furtive sex. At the bottom there were cobblestones and dust and broken glass, and the starkness of a place that most people shun by instinct. It was uncannily quiet and distant from the street above.

Mike was escorted down the steps between two policemen and made to stand waiting while Maselli paced up and down, scanning the prospects, pointing here and there and peering into the Tiber as if he expected to see Beppe floating in its turbid green water amid the bits of wood and cigarette packs and scum. The other men bent down and examined the cobbles inch by inch, while the parapet of the little bridge overhead grew more and more crowded with onlookers. The sight of policemen on a riverbank always suggests the likelihood of a free drama of some kind. Mike could not tell whether anyone had spotted him, but he felt embarrassingly conspicuous standing there like a prisoner, even if they had had the good grace not to handcuff him, and the tact—if you could call it that—not to tell him yet that he was under arrest.

"Here's something!" shouted one of the men, and the others all hurried to join him in a huddle, practically sniffing at the cobblestones. They walked up and down the steps, studying each one with minute care, until they picked up the trail they wanted and followed it in a straight line to the edge of the bank. Mike's guards, no longer able to restrain their curiosity, steered Mike across to have a look.

A short stretch of earth, thickly overgrown with nettles, led down from the brick-faced riverbank to a clutter of cement blocks that had been dumped in the water. Where the men were standing, a gap in the nettles left bare a steep slope of dusty ground between the stone bank and the water. Mike stared down at it. There were scrape marks in the dust, as if a heavy object had recently been dragged down the slope to the water's edge.

"Well, now," said Maselli, turning to Mike with a look of intense satisfaction. "So you stopped your car up there by the bridge, did you?"

"That's what I said."

"And Palazzo got out and walked across the bridge."

"That's right."

"Signor Donadio! If you wanted me to swallow a tale like that, you should have said you left him somewhere else. How could you be so naïve as to bring me here?"

Mike felt a little dizzy suddenly. "Why don't you tell me what I'm supposed to have done?" he said.

"Very well. You say you stopped your car up there? I believe you. But I don't believe Palazzo got out and walked across the bridge. I think he was dead by then. Unconscious, anyway. I think you dragged his body out of the car, across the pavement, and down those steps. There are scratches in the stone all the way down."

"But that's ridiculous! What would I do that for?"

"The river is deep here and the current is strong."

There was a shout from farther along the bank: "Dottor Maselli! Look at this!"

Maselli moved instantly, and all the others followed him. One of the men had found a bundle, half hidden in a clump of nettles. When they laid it out on the bank and unrolled the piece of sacking it was wrapped in, they found that it contained the suit Beppe was wearing the night before, together with a shirt and a crocodile belt and a pink and purple tie. There was a bunch of keys in the coat pocket, a cigarette lighter with the initials "B.P." on it, and a letter with Beppe's full name and address.

"Oh, come on!" Mike burst out. "You can't honestly believe I'd chuck Beppe into the river and hide his stuff three steps away."

Unfortunately they did.

It was almost funny. One part of him felt a definite urge to giggle at the sight of them gloating over Beppe's suit, with all those bits and pieces left in the pockets in case anybody missed the point. Hello! he thought, what's this supposed to be—the *corpus delicti*? It was hard to take it all seriously. Still, he felt less and less inclined to laugh at the solemnity with which they photographed and measured and noted every detail down, as if a rolled-up suit in a clump of weeds were proof, beyond a shadow of a doubt, that the owner of the suit had been done in. By him. Steady on, he told himself. It isn't a corpse. It isn't even a clue. All it proves is that Beppe wants to be presumed dead.

"What floors me," he remarked on the way back to the Questura, "is why I should have taken the trouble to undress him." But that was one mystery that did not bother them in the least.

When they put a card in his hand with a number on it and made him hold it up while he was photographed from the front and then from the side, he wanted to say, "Oh, look now, come off it!" It was too silly—him, of all people, being photographed like that.

Then someone grabbed his left hand and pressed it down on an inkpad, and all at once he was crushed, annihilated. They could have told him to do it himself, but no, they did it for him and he had to let them do it, as if he had no control over his own body any more. They lifted his hand off the inkpad and lowered it onto a card that already had his name filled in at the top; they pressed each finger down on the card and let it go, first the left hand, then the right. He watched them do it, as if his two hands were objects that no longer belonged to him. When they had finished, he stood there looking down at his ink-stained fingers in shocked amazement, until one of the men thrust a bit of soap into his hand and told him to wash himself; he blundered over to the washbasin and did as he was told. The ink would not come off, rub as he would, and since there was no towel, he scrubbed his fingers with his handkerchief until that was black too: but the fingers were just as stained as before.

That was the moment they chose to tell him he was under arrest.

When he found himself alone in the cell, his first reaction was rage at the utter nerve of it, sticking him in there and going away like that, without telling him what was going to happen next; it was not knowing where he stood that was the worst thing of all. It amazed him afterwards that he had let them go on, from one stage to the next, without putting up any real resistance or offering any serious argument. It was all so far removed from what he thought was reality that his brain had rejected the possibility of its being true.

When he had recovered from the shock of hearing them say he was to be imprisoned, he began telling himself it must be a trick to make him tell them more. If they had had the decency to say, "You'll have to talk to so-and-so, and we must ask you to wait in here till he comes," it would have been, if not all right, at least better than this, better than being hurled into nothingness without knowing why. To be cut off without warning from every form of human intercourse was violence of a kind he never suspected could exist. They can't do this, he thought. The outrage of those four walls was intolerable. And then he thought: How can I stop them? And he was overwhelmed with fear.

At first he kept expecting someone to open the door and say they were terribly sorry, it was all a dreadful mistake. When this failed to happen the first day, the second, or the third, he rang the bell on the wall. The peephole in the door slid back. "What do you want?" said a voice.

"When is someone going to come?" he asked.

"I don't know," said the guard. "You just keep calm." He shut the peephole and disappeared. After that, no one ever came when Mike rang the bell. He was alone in absolute silence.

The words *habeas corpus* came into his mind. But what the hell did they mean? You must have a corpse. Was that it? If so, they didn't have one. No, it couldn't be that. It was something to do with the Magna Carta, and they didn't talk about corpses in those days. It was something to do with justice and human rights, one of those things you think you know as a matter of course, until you find yourself face to face with it like this and your mind's a blank. And yet he felt sure it was the key to his salvation.

Habeas corpus. There was nobody to ask, no way to find out. He scratched it on the wall with his thumbnail and stared at it, day in and day out. A spider walked across the wall and looked at him, listening gravely, it seemed, to the way he was muttering to himself, locked in with his ignorance and the tantalizing feeling that it might be a matter of his own life or death. Nicola would know. So would his lawyer. But they had not let him speak to his lawyer yet. They would not let him read the newspapers or write a letter or smoke or take a shower. Nothing. Only walk up and down the narrow space between his bed and the wall and think and think and think.

"They can't do this to me," he told the spider, who seemed to blink as if it had heard that said before. "If they haven't got a corpse and there hasn't been a crime, they've got to let me out of here. Or have they? That's the point. Maybe *habeas corpus*, whatever it means, doesn't exist in Italian law."

The spider looked thoughtful, and infinitely wise.

"**R**oberta Lane?" said the man behind the desk, studying the paper in front of him. She nodded, though it sounded strange; she had never been called anything but Robin since she was born. "Signorina?" the man asked.

"*Sì.*"

He raised his eyes pointedly to her waist.

"Mike Donato and I are getting married, as soon as we can."

"Mmmm," said the man. "I understand." But it was obvious that he did not. He had announced with some pride that he intended to conduct the interrogation in English, and she had not wished to offend him by pointing out that she could have managed quite well in Italian without the help of the interpreter, who now explained, "*E' la fidanzata.*"

"*Sì, sì,*" she said impatiently. She thought the whole world knew by now that she was Mike's fiancée. "I live with him. *Come sua moglie.*"

He refused to understand her Italian. "*Donadio ha una moglie?*" he asked the interpreter.

"No," Robin chipped in before the interpreter could supply his own interpretation of the facts. Enunciating each word with exag-

122

gerated clarity, she explained, "I live with him as if I were his wife."

He did not like that. He cast his eyes down sternly at the paper in front of him. *"Qui dice che la sua residenza a Roma è a Via della Scrofa novantuno."*

"That's my—official residence."

"Insomma, dove abita?" He was irritated now.

"Where you live?" asked the interpreter, getting it in fast.

"In Via Gregoriana."

"Allora questo è un indirizzo falso."

"Why you make false declaration?" asked the interpreter.

"What false declaration? I've kept the flat at Via della Scrofa too."

The man behind the desk frowned. *"Lei è in stato interessante?"*

"What?"

"E' incinta?"

"Pregnant," the interpreter popped in triumphantly.

"Yes."

"And the father is Donadio, eh? You are sure?"

"Of course I'm sure!"

Oh, they had her classified all right. She was a foreign, unmarried, pregnant woman, who might euphemistically be termed *la fidanzata* or, when they felt less kindly disposed towards her, *l'amica.* Apart from that, by law she was no one, neither a relative of Mike's nor his wife. The fact that she lived with him meant nothing, except that she was immoral. Whether or not he was the father of her child remained to be seen. When she asked to see him she was told it was impossible—he was in solitary confinement. When she asked why, she was told it was the law. She could apply for permission to see him if she wanted to; if she was eligible, in due course she would be informed. When? That would depend. On what? A number of things. When she begged to be told what was going on, what in the name of God it was all about, the most she could get out of any of them was a shrug.

It was a secret: *il segreto istruttorio.* That was the law.

They would supply no answers, but their questions went on and on, without mercy. When they sent her away, mortified and prostrate, she was dazzled by flashbulbs and chased by reporters, who continued to pester and beleaguer her until they had squeezed the news of her misfortune dry.

Nicola tried to help. When she called him he told her to pack up her things, and he came and fetched her away from Via Gregoriana, back to his own place.

She had always liked the austerity of Nicola's flat, with its bare parquet floors and spacious white walls. It felt funny walking in there again now, but there was something soothing about the placid familiarity of the big Deruta vase on the chest in the hall. Nicola had sober taste. Everything he possessed, each carefully chosen piece of antique furniture, was, like him, a sturdy and Spartan friend.

"What was it we were?" she said, "friends for the skin?"

"Not were, are. Always. *Amici per la pelle.*" He poured her a glass of red wine.

"Yes." She sat down in the wing chair by the window. "It's good to be back here again."

It was not, really. Everything was too different now. Her friendship with Nicola was all mixed up, all twisted with various sorts of jealousy and doubt.

She took the glass of wine he handed her and stared out of the window at the terrace, which was cluttered with soggy leaves. The March sunlight glistened on a solitary daffodil, and the unkempt privet shrubs were in bud. In her head she could hear Mike's voice reciting Browning:

> . . . the lowest boughs and the brushwood sheaf
> Round the elm-tree bole are in tiny leaf.

"What a disaster, all this," Nicola said. "I wanted Mike with me in Cannes next month."

"Oh, Cannes." That was what was on his mind. "Is *Valentino* going to the festival, then?"

"I am fighting for that. I am afraid this story will be bad for it."

"It will be bad for me too," she said bitterly. He turned sharply to look at her, as if struck for the first time by her predicament, and she thought: How funny, he doesn't care about me and Mike, he's just afraid of being involved. He's got all these problems of his own—screenings to sit through and critics to woo and all sorts of fools to fight. He had told them all about it the last time they saw him, when they had invited him to supper at Via Gregoriana to make their peace. She had remarked to Mike then on how Nicola had changed, and Mike had said it was only normal, it happened to everyone, or almost everyone, when they saw the first glimmer of success shining out there at the end of the long black tunnel. They nearly all lost their heads, and their friends as well. It seemed a pity, though, when she remembered the person Nicola used to be, with those deep brown eyes of his phosphorescent with excitement—like that time he took her to lunch, and leaned forward over the table to tell her the story of *Povero Valentino*. That was less than a year ago, and now, with the film all ready for release, here he was with no more fervor in his eyes, only egocentric anxiety, as he asked, "When will the child be born?"

"In July. What's the matter? Afraid I'll dump it on you?"

"I was thinking, 'Poor Robin—with a *bastardo*.' "

"There's four months."

"The trial can take a year—or two."

"It can't!"

"Unfortunately, yes."

She could not believe it. This implausible temporary emptiness could not go on for a year—or two.

"How can they do this?" she burst out, getting up and moving restlessly round the room. "How can they take a man like Mike and just put him in prison?"

"What if Mike is a murderer?"

"Oh, don't be silly!"

"Can you be sure he is not?"

"Of course I'm sure!"

"How? Beppe is gone. And many people say—"

"People will say anything, specially in Rome—you told me that yourself. Specially about their idols, that's what you said. I see now what you meant."

"Yes. It's true. First they put them up on pedestals, then they get tired of them and pull them down. You see, the ones up on the pedestals soon start thinking they are big. Specially actors. They forget the people who helped them, the people who made them what they are. They think the success is all theirs by right."

"Mike is not like that."

"He thinks he is not. But if *Povero Valentino* is a success, he will think it is because of him. In his heart, he thinks now he is big and I am small. Because I have had no luck and he has."

"You seem to hate him."

"Of course not. He is my friend."

"You hate his success. And if he falls on his face, you'll be glad."

"That is not at all what I said."

"But it's the truth. It's thumbs up or thumbs down in Rome. Right? And as far as you're concerned, it's thumbs down for Mike now. Oh, Nicola, you're not the same person anymore."

"No one is the same as before. What about you—and Mike? I killed myself to have you both on the film, and then you treated me like a stranger."

"We didn't mean to. We wanted to tell you—about us. But you were so busy—we put it off, that's all. You were rather horrid, actually, on the film. Nothing like the old Nicola I remember."

"Well, you know, when you and I were—"

"Friends for the skin?"

"If you like."

"Were?" asked Robin.

"I meant when we were more than friends. Anyway, you know when I mean. It was easy to be nice then—I had nothing to do then but be nice. But now—if you knew what a fight it has been. Your nerves get destroyed. Fighting, fighting all the time. For success."

"So they can put you on a pedestal? And then pull you down?"

"Oh, no, I don't want to be an idol, not even a genius. Just . . . not a failure. That is difficult enough."

She watched his profile as he poured himself another glass of wine, and noticed how tense he was. His whole body was taut with determination—yes, that was it, determination to get what he wanted, to get where he wanted, to succeed even in doing things he did not know how to do. As he was pouring his wine, she could see him clenching his jaw with the effort of thinking, It's hard to succeed, but I'll do it and no one will stop me. He was not thinking about Mike, or her.

She turned abruptly away and started dialing a number.

"Supposing he's there all the time," she said, "laughing his head off."

"Who?"

"Beppe, of course!" She stood listening to the telephone ringing and ringing in Beppe's empty flat. "Answer, you pig!" she muttered. "Answer, do you hear?"

"So you know his number by memory," Nicola said. "You know him well." It was only then that she saw how he was watching her, judging her in a way it had never occurred to her she could be judged.

"I used to work with him," she said quickly; but she refused to hang up for another five minutes, as if sheer persistence would force Beppe's voice to say *pronto* in the end. And meanwhile, Nicola said:

"You've been to bed with him."

"Oh, God! What's the matter with you Italians? You've got one-track minds, all of you. Yes, I've been to bed with him. What difference does it make?"

"A big difference."

"Since when were you a puritan?"

"It is not a question of puritan or not puritan. What counts is that Mike was sure you did not know Beppe, and you did not tell him different. You did not say to him that you met Beppe, you had an adventure with him, and finish. I saw you, *Robina mia.* When we talked about Beppe you were very ashamed—you did not want that Mike should know. And you were wrong. If you told him the truth, you see, he would not like it, maybe, but he would say, 'All right, is finished now, to hell with Beppe and *basta.*' Instead, the reason Mike was so angry with Beppe was because he was sure Beppe was telling a lie."

"Well, look who's preaching. What about you and me, then? Should I have told him about that too?"

"That was different. He knows we are old friends."

"What's so different about it? The fact that you're a nice chap and Beppe isn't?"

"Also."

"Oh, come off it. You're you and he's him, that's what you mean. I never thought you were a hypocrite." She slammed down the receiver and said, "Oh, God! I think I'll go home."

She could not stay there; it made no sense. Nicola argued a bit, but she could see he was glad, really. He had done his duty; he had offered to take care of her; but when he had driven her back to Via della Scrofa and helped her up the stairs with her cases and seen her safely inside her own front door, he sprinted back down to the street as if he felt several tons lighter for having her off his back.

As for her, if she felt anything just then, it was disbelief in the entire situation. It was seven o'clock in the evening. Her little room smelled dank and dusty, and there was nothing to eat. There were no sheets on the bed, either, and she felt too weak to do anything about it, too weak to do anything about anything, too weak all at once to do anything whatsoever except lie down just as she was, with her cases unopened on the floor beside her, and let herself fade away into a void.

FIFTEEN

More than a month went by before she heard from Mike, and she spent the first two weeks of it in a state of torpidity, lying on her bed most of the time, waiting for news that never came.

Her landlady, who lived on the floor below, invited her down for a meal from time to time, so that she could cross-examine her about her family while plying her with food. Signora Filippini found nothing shocking about her being pregnant by a man who had been arrested for murder—"Such things do happen," she said, nodding wisely—but she was shattered by the fact that Robin's mother had not been informed. How could Robin convey to this voluminous, determined Italian *mamma* that her own mother was flimsy and unpractical and would only fret and dither if she knew. In Rome she would be no use at all. The very idea of her in Via della Scrofa was unthinkable, though it was true that Robin did think of it occasionally, when she caught sight of the two cushions she had sent, two silly satin cushions with frilly borders and sedately stitched patterning, so touchingly reminiscent of her mother that Robin would sit and hug them when she felt more than usually homesick and depressed.

A lot of people felt the urge to call her during those first weeks: all the people who had some kind of vested interest in Mike, and others she hardly knew, like the switchboard girl from Alba Films; ghoulish voices fishing for morsels about Mike while effusing sham concern about her health. There were anonymous phone calls too. Often, when she picked up the receiver, she heard someone hang up. Some mysterious enemy—the police, perhaps, checking up on her, or a hostile reporter. Even Beppe. It was just the sort of thing that Beppe would do, and it gave her the creeps.

The big surprise was Joe Mannino, who called to invite her to lunch at his place.

"I wanted to talk to you about Mike," he said, pouring her a glass of grapefruit juice. She seated herself tentatively on the edge of the sofa and glanced through the glass doors into the dining room, where a manservant was putting the finishing touches to the table. She had never felt at ease with Joe Mannino, and this unaccustomed courtesy of his struck her as weird. "He means a lot to me, you know," he was saying. "I'm proud to think I was the first to believe in him. Remember how hard I tried to sell him to Abe Schulbach that night we all had dinner right there at that table?" She nodded. It was the night she had met Nicola—it seemed like a hundred years ago. "And now," Mannino went on, "if *Povero Valentino* goes to Cannes, I wouldn't be surprised if he won the best-actor award." He paused as if distracted by an uneasy thought, and then quickly went on, in a tone of slightly forced joviality, "Abe thought he knew everything, didn't he? Comical, really—when you think he turned down *Valentino* and put his money on *Showdown* instead. He thought that one was 'safe' if we shot it in English, which just shows how wrong you can be. My God! Did you ever see it?"

She shook her head. "I don't think I ever heard of it."

He smiled. "Why should you? It was the bomb of the century. Your friend Mike was in it, but not even he could prevent it from going right off the rails. And Abe blamed it all on me. He just couldn't understand that in Italy the director is God. If he loses his mind and starts making up a new script as he goes along, there's nothing anyone can do to stop him; and when he makes it up in Italian and gets his girlfriend to translate it line by line—oh, boy! The rats may escape but the producer sinks with the ship. Anyway, Abe dropped me after that and, as you know, in the end I found another way to finance *Povero Valentino*."

So all this was before *Povero Valentino*, Robin was thinking; it was in the days when Mike was only a voice on the phone. "You mean you produced a film with Mike in it, and I didn't even know?"

130

He leaned over and patted her hand. "My dear, if you knew the things I did without your knowing. Most of it wasn't on paper, you know. The only reason I'm telling you about it now is that all this unpleasantness round Mike, this rumpus between him and Beppe, did start at about that time, and I can't help feeling—well, not guilty, but to some extent indirectly responsible for—well, you know, Abe was hand in glove with Beppe, and God knows what they may have cooked up together, maybe to try and boost the film—how do I know?"

"What do you mean? What unpleasantness?"

"Oh, you know, all that business of the girl on the beach—and that other one who ended up with her wrists slashed."

He broke off, seeing the expression on Robin's face. "Don't say you never heard about that, either?"

"I didn't know Mike then."

"But the papers were full of it."

"Full of what? I don't understand. What did it have to do with Mike?"

"Who knows? Probably nothing. But you know, those things stick."

"*What* things?"

"Dead girls." Robin was staring at him in horror. "My dear, I don't mean he killed them. They probably killed themselves. But there were some pretty unsavory insinuations, which won't do him any good now, if you get my meaning.'

"No, I don't."

"Look, you do realize, I suppose, that a lot of people think Mike is guilty."

"They can't."

"My dear, they do. Which brings me to what I set out to say in the first place. You see, it's not enough to be innocent; you need a lawyer who can *prove* you are. And I'm afraid the one he's got—"

"Has he got one? How do you know?"

"Because unfortunately it was I who introduced him to Mike, and he phoned me to brag about how he'd been called. Which leaves me holding the baby."

"You mean he isn't any good?"

"He may be. I've no idea. But you know the sort of crap you come up with when you introduce people. You don't expect to be taken at your word."

That evening at the restaurant, when he introduced Avvocato Sora to Mike, what Joe had actually said was, "Allow me to present one of the luminaries of Italian law." At the time, he had thought it sounded too ironic to be polite—though not, it seemed, to the so-called luminary himself, who had small, greedy eyes in his pinkish, plump face, and a way of smoothing his little mustache with one finger when he felt particularly pleased with himself. In fact, Joe had only the vaguest notion who Sora was, other than a self-important little man who had once sat next to him at some film-company lunch and bored him to death. And when, at a crucial point of the deal he was cooking with Mike, he had been cut off in midsentence by Sora's bumptious *"Buona sera!"*, he had lashed out at the intruder with the kind of venomous joviality that no one but an upstart like Sora could have taken to be sincere.

As for Mike, he was so busy trying to sort out the snags in what Joe was glibly about to talk him into that he hardly heard what he said about Sora then. It was only the next day that he registered it fully, when they told him at the Questura to name a lawyer, and he realized that this Sora was the only one whose name he knew.

It was easy to curse himself for his flippancy, later on. If he had realized how vital the choice of a lawyer was, he would of course have taken pains to get the best; but there and then, in his innocence—*because* of his innocence—he thought *any* lawyer would be able to disentangle him from the mistake that had led to his arrest. Besides, when they tell you to name a lawyer, they don't let you call up your friends and ask for advice.

True, when at last they allowed him to see the "luminary" in whom alone he had placed his trust, he was a good deal more frightened than he had been at first. He found he had forgotten how unimpressive young Sora looked, and he did have some serious doubts about his choice. A whole month had gone by then, since his arrest, a month spent in solitary confinement to prevent him from being polluted by outside information before the examining magistrate was in full possession of his version of the facts. *Habeas corpus* had faded to a clumsy scribble on the wall, and he had learned that human beings do not necessarily have any rights. His old self was already as remote as the objects they had stripped him of and shut away in a box: the coins, the comb, the ink-stained handkerchief, and the key to his flat. Only the key had not been shut away; it had been used. They had been in there, nosing about among his things. The examining magistrate had dropped hints about "material" they had "discovered"—hints that were supposed to intimidate him, presumably, but merely aggravated him; for what could they possibly have found, except a few bad scripts and the poster of a clown? What worried him most was that the things they did made no sense. When Mike asked what steps they had taken to try and find Beppe, the examining magistrate gave him a long, ponderous look, as if carefully weighing in his mind the significance of such a futile question. And of course he said nothing. He was efficient and honest, no doubt of that; he just happened to have started along the wrong road and could not be persuaded to look left or right.

In the end, Mike gave up trying to make him listen to reason and pinned all his hopes on the judge, who would obviously look the facts in the face and say, "Where is the proof that Beppe Palazzo is dead?" And the prosecutor would stand dumbfounded and the examining magistrate would blush with shame. In a court of law, the truth was bound to come to light, and he would have Robin back in his arms again, in Via Gregoriana. They would make love for hours, and afterwards they would go upstairs on the terrace and talk, lying side by side in their two deck chairs beneath the soft indigo sky.

If the weather was still warm.

But of course it would be. Why shouldn't it? There were six full months of warm summer weather ahead.

Dearest love,
I'm so dreadfully worried. . . .

No, that would make it worse. She must try not to worry *him*.

My love,
I can't believe you won't be back with me before this
ever arrives. But all the same, I thought I'd better tell
you that Joe Mannino phoned yesterday and insisted on
having me to lunch. . . .

No, that might give him altogether the wrong idea.

My darling,
What can I say? Every day, every night without you
seems more incredible than the one before. I've tried
and tried to make them let me come and see you; they
just say no and no and no. They won't even let me leave
you a parcel or a letter or anything. I only hope that this
will reach you by post. Or better still, that it won't reach
you ever at all, because long before it gets to Regina
Coeli, you'll be back home again with me, laughing the
whole thing off. Oh, won't that be marvelous?

I've walked all round that ghastly place several times,
wondering which, out of all those boarded-up windows,
you're hidden behind. I thought of shouting out your
name, to see if you would hear me and shout back. I
know that's what some of the relatives do, and I wanted
to try, I really did. But I couldn't, I just couldn't open
my mouth and yell. Not yet, anyway. Perhaps one of
these days I might.

People keep phoning and asking for news, and all I
can tell them is that I wish I had some myself. I can't
understand what's going on. How can they be keeping
you so long without telling anyone anything?

Joe Mannino called to say he wants to help you get the
best lawyer there is. He told me he's not sure this
Avvocato Sora he introduced to you is the best man for
your case. He seems worried about it and pretends this

is because he feels guilty, but actually I think he badly wants you out in time for Cannes. Anyway, I'm worried too, now, so please do let him help you. If you say you agree, he'll do the rest. I think you ought to let him. I mean, if somebody brilliant can get you out faster, why not?

By the way, I had lunch with Mannino and he says I look splendid. Don't worry, he didn't make any passes—who would, with a tummy my size? But it's true I look well. I feel well too. So don't worry about me.

It was true. She did look well, and considering everything, her health was not too bad. Considering. At least she didn't feel sick any more. But what she took care not to mention in her letter was that for the last day or two there had been something funny about the baby's movements. Today, in particular, there was a marked lack of verve about the little kicks and punches to which by now she was accustomed. There. There was another one. She put down her pen and lifted up her skirt to study her belly in consternation. No doubt about it—the movements were tremulous, as if the little fists were quivering and growing frailer from hour to hour. Now come on, Robin, she told herself. There's enough trouble as it is, without getting silly ideas like that into your head. The movements had always been sporadic, after all. How could she tell the difference between one day and the next?

She finished the letter off and took it out at once to mail. But in the street the noise of the traffic irritated her, as if it prevented her from listening to her baby's infinitesimal sounds.

So she went on, for ten days. She would lie breathlessly still for hours at a time, promising herself after each little kick that the next would be stronger, and explaining to herself again and again that there had always been small kicks as well as big ones, and besides, some of it was only gas.

And all the time she was searching the previous days for the cause. She had lifted her suitcase onto the bed. Perhaps the effort had torn some vital cord, or dislodged the baby from the right position; she ought to have considered how delicate he was. Or perhaps he was sensitive, more than she, to the shock she had had; perhaps he possessed some form of magnetic awareness and knew what was happening to Mike. No, that was too farfetched. Above all she was aware that before it began, whatever it was, she had been lying about in a stupor, hardly bothering to eat, for the best part of two weeks; perhaps, like an animal in hibernation, she had lowered her body temperature and slowed down her heart and starved her unborn child to death. No, he was not dead yet. But he was dying. She could feel him dying inside her, from day to day.

Eventually the little feet stopped kicking and merely fidgeted from time to time. Eleven days after the movements started weakening, there was just one feeble little kick; on the twelfth day, an imperceptible flutter; then nothing moved inside her any more.

She waited another five days before making up her mind to see the doctor, who stared at her gravely and said she had lost weight. He was a tall, thin man with a stoop and slow, deliberate movements. When he had her on her back with her feet in the steel loops, he ran his stethoscope all over her belly, and grunted and pursed his lips and went "Mmmm." Then he said:

"Can't seem to—no, I can't hear the heartbeat. But I don't think . . ." He broke off and tried again. "Mmmm. In itself that's not . . . Now there's no cause for alarm." He walked back to his desk and wrote out a prescription for a sedative. "Come back in two days," he told her.

She found herself out in the street again without having dared to ask how, if he could not hear the baby's heartbeat, there could be "no cause for alarm." He had heard the heartbeat the other times, she was sure of it. He had smiled too, the other times, and complimented her on the *bimbo vivace* and the *bellissima gravidanza*. This time he had not smiled once. But she could not find it in herself to ask outright, *Is the baby dead?*

Not that she had any need to ask. Her breasts were no longer tender and her belly had shrunk. Though the next time she saw the doctor he put up a show of hemming and hawing when he prodded her, she knew it was no use. Two days after that she said to him, "I don't feel pregnant anymore."

136

He looked up and met her eyes that time and said, "That means more than any doctor's diagnosis."

It was five weeks then since Mike's arrest. When she got home she found his first letter.

. . . Oh, my sweet love, how are you? I'm going out of my mind about the way time is going by. It can't go on, it can't! They've got to stop this madness and let me out. The fact is they don't give a damn. They've decided I killed Beppe and that's that. When it turns out he's alive and kicking, someone's going to look silly, and they don't like looking silly one bit. But in the meantime your body's growing. Pan's body's growing. And my body's shut up in here, cut off from you, from Pan, from everything that's real. What goes on in here can't be real. If it was, it could drive you insane.

I got your letter today. It's taken two weeks to reach me. But that's because till now I've been in isolation, or whatever it's called in English. Oh, yes, solitary confinement. That's why I didn't write before. They wouldn't even let me see the papers.

That reminds me. I'm worried about my mother and I daren't write to her from here—imagine the shock she'd get. But God knows what she'll think if she reads about it in the newspapers. I shudder to think what mincemeat they'll have made of it all. And what about Zio Gino in Anticoli and all those aunts and nieces and nephews and cousins—they'll have lapped up every word! Supposing they write to Mamma and tell it to her all wrong? That's why I want you to drop her a tactful note and tell her it's all a silly mistake and not to worry.

Oh, Robin, Robin, you're so far away and the lawyer says that short of a miracle I'll never be out of here before the baby's born. I can't believe it's that bad. Beppe has to be somewhere. If only we could find him, they'd be *forced* to let me out.

As for what Joe says about the lawyer, it's not so easy

137

to change now. Let's see how it goes. I can't believe I need a genius just to point out that no one's been hurt. Besides, why should I be obliged to Joe Mannino?

By the way, I asked Sora if I couldn't get bail, but he says they don't grant it when the charge is murder. He says *habeas corpus* doesn't mean anything here. You can ask Joe to ask someone about that, if you like.

I don't know if they'll let you come and see me, but please keep trying! Now that I'm out of solitary, they might say yes. Look after little Pan for me, and above all, look after yourself, my love!

> *Ti abbraccio forte!*
> Mike

Little Pan. What a stupid name. It was supposed to mean so much, and now it was nothing but a lifeless lump that went *plop-plop-plop*, a dead weight going *plop-plop* at every step she took, going *flomp* in the night when she turned over restlessly in her narrow bed, without Mike. She could not wait to get rid of it now.

They should never have given it a name. It was like buying a cradle. She had not even bought a pair of booties, not so much as a rattle. Don't run on ahead, she had told herself. Don't tempt Providence! The only things she had allowed herself were a pair of knitting needles and some pale blue wool to knit a small cardigan, which, because she hated knitting and could never get the stitches even, had not progressed beyond the fifth row. It was easy to get rid of that. She stuffed it into the dustbin along with the whole bag of soft, hopeful blue wool and the magazine with the pattern in it and the photograph of that cozy, smug, synthetic baby.

But she could not tell Mike. It would be one thing less for him to worry about, and he might be relieved not to have to be obsessed with that particular race against time, but little Pan was more than a baby. He was a creature of the sun. And he was dead.

She had always been frightened of hospitals and the smell of sick bodies in beds. But her room at Salvator Mundi had green-and-

138

brown curtains that billowed in the breeze, and walls colored orange, green, and cream. Facing her bed there was a Cézanne still life: apples, onions, and a sturdy bottle to soothe her eyes.

Smiling nuns floated crisply in and out with syringes and thermometers and pills, and felt her pulse and stroked her forehead and patted her cheek. And if at night she heard the peacocks cry, in the day all was well, all was reasonably well.

"There," they said comfortingly as they hooked up a bottle of liquid over her bed and plugged a tube into her vein so that it could seep into her, drop by drop.

"*Che cos'è?*" she asked drowsily. They had given her an injection first.

"*L'infusione,*" they said; and almost at once the pains began.

"*Bene,*" said the doctor. And a nun held her hand as her body became possessed by the contractions.

I'm giving birth, she thought. And in a passing flash of unreality she dared to hope absurdly that the baby might be born alive. Then something was happening to her vagina and they were wheeling her, bed and all, out of the room, rushing her down the corridor to the labor room. She felt them doing things to her legs, and all at once she was terrified that she might see the baby dead. She started shouting "No!" and "Please!" and "Mike!" and "*Per favore!*" and "Oh! Oh, no!" And someone said to her, "Count!" and she thought: What a stupid thing to ask anyone to do just now. "*Americana?*" someone asked. "No!" she cried out. She could feel it, she could feel it coming; why couldn't they be quick? "I want an anesthetic!" she sobbed, and they said, "*Ma sì! Conta!*" And she gave in and murmured, "One, two . . ." And that was all.

When she came round, she was back in her room and her body was at peace. All she felt was an immense relief, a sense of physical satisfaction, as if she had made love and was fulfilled.

She lay back and basked in the colors of her room in the gentle light of afternoon, and thought: It's all over. And marveled at how well she felt. The dead thing was gone and she was free. Not until an hour or two later, when the sedatives wore off, did she begin to realize the extent to which she was now alone.

The other things came later: the milk oozing from her swollen breasts, which the nuns bound tightly with long strips of white cotton cloth until they dried up. The sudden, unexpected longing for a child in her arms that made her burst into noisy torrents of tears in the night and brought the nun on night duty scuttling in to bend over her and cluck sympathetically in German. And then the dreams, the terrible dreams about a bundle wrapped in newspaper that she left somewhere and forgot—or threw out of the window or stuffed into the fridge—only to remember with horror that it was the baby, when it was too late to save its life.

She had called Nicola in the evening. He was shocked to hear that she was alone and came at once, with a huge bunch of multicolored gladioli and a copy of his new script for her to read. He was kind, she had to admit that. He was always kind. He came to see her every day as long as she was in the hospital. But he was embarrassed too, especially when the nuns took him for the father and, without exactly frowning, displayed their disapproval by wiping off their smiles when he appeared.

The sister in charge of the maternity ward asked him, rather than Robin, "What name shall we give the child?"

"What name?" Nicola was trapped and disconcerted. "I don't know."

"She must have a name. To be buried, you know."

"Pan," Robin said, when the sister came and asked her.

"Pan? But it must be a Christian name."

"Pancrazio, then." Why should a thing that went *plop* have a Christian name?

"It's a girl."

"A girl?" She was sure it was a boy. If it was anything, it was a boy. "You decide, then," she told the sister. "I don't honestly care."

They must have had a consultation about it, all the nuns on the third floor, because after a while the sister came back and said that it was true it was San Pancrazio's day—Is it really? How curious! Robin thought—but there was no such name for a girl as Pancrazia, so if she agreed, they would call her Grazia. She did. It was as good a name as any other, and a girl by the name of Grazia had nothing, she felt, to do with her—which was all to the good. As long as they didn't expect her to see it, or take it to the cemetery herself, in a small white coffin. What do they do with babies that die in the womb? she wondered. No one ever told her and she never dared to ask.

SIXTEEN

Six months went by, and then another three; the weather turned bitterly cold and the cell was damp. For Christmas each prisoner got five packs of cigarettes and a book about the saints, and chicken at the midday meal. On New Year's Day they each got a glass of wine. Then January plodded monotonously on into February, the highlight of each day being the two hours in the open air, with a glimpse of the Roman sky up there above the gray walls of the yard, and sometimes the flutter of warm feathers, when a sparrow was coaxed down to earth by a patient old prisoner with a handful of crumbs. Above all, those two hours out in the yard represented a chance to communicate with other men, if only to hold forth about the iniquities of Italian law, or let off steam about sex.

When March came round again, Mike still had no idea when his trial would be. That was the worst of it, not knowing. That was where they had him by the balls. They kept him waiting from day to day, waiting and hoping. Hoping till he could smash out his brains against the walls, as some men did, when their hopes went down. Hopes had a way of going down all the time, down and up, up and down. When they were up, he didn't even mind sweeping out the cell under the indolent eye of the guard. It's not his fault, he could say to himself; he doesn't know. When his hopes were down, he got this terrible feeling that they had crossed him off, or forgotten him altogether; and he saw himself sweeping out the cell for the rest of his life, because nobody out there would take the trouble to have a look at his file. Then he felt like picking up that filthy slop pail and hurling it, piss and shit and all, into somebody's face. The *bugliolo*, they called it. It served all three of them in the cell as a chamberpot and was emptied once a day, when they let them out six at a time—all fifty or sixty of them—to go to the one and only toilet on that floor. Mike kept a bottle of bleach, which he used every night to try and kill the smell. Sometimes it worked, more or less, and sometimes not. But they still had to live with it there in the corner, their own communal excreta. They still had to use it and do their best, bit by bit, to shut their minds to the shame.

When his hopes were high, Mike would count the days—and the weeks and the months—he had been inside, and say, "Oh, well, it can't be much longer now." When his hopes were low, he began to sweat and pace up and down in the night, two steps each way—that was all there was room for between the bunk and the door. Then he felt that he knew what a tiger must feel like, incomprehensibly caged in for people to look at when it suited their whim; and when that feeling came over him, it was all he could do not to open his mouth and roar. But he was liable to end up in a punishment cell if he did that, strapped to a bed with a hole in it. That was worse, a lot worse, than the *bugliolo*—a hole in the bed for his excreta. So he gritted his teeth and buried his head under the blanket and said, "Tomorrow. Tomorrow they'll tell me. Tomorrow they'll tell me when it's going to be." Next morning, every morning, when he opened his eyes and saw the slop pail standing there, near the greasy jug of water that was all they had, all three of them, to wash in, he would tell himself, "This can't go on. They've got to fix the date today."

And in between "today" and "tomorrow" he answered questions, again and again and always the same ones, circling round and round a story that had nothing to do with the truth. All that remained was to count the days and wait for the trial.

"Don't kid yourself," his cellmates told him. "Justice is a dirty joke." But Mike's case was not the same as theirs, even if they did both claim to be as innocent as he was. Mauro had been caught driving without a license, but that was only a quibble, according to him, because they never could catch him smuggling cigarettes.

Ettore had been in other times for burglary, but he swore that this time they'd caught him for a job he didn't do.

"But in my case there was nothing. It didn't happen!"

"That'll take some proving."

They all said the same: It was no use thinking they'd let him off just because he was innocent.

Mike refused to be depressed by their melancholy forecasts, but after Joe's offer to help, he did suggest that Sora might get one of the big penal lawyers to assist him. Sora only shook his head and, with a knowing little smile, said, *"Non si preoccupi—ci penso io."* Don't worry—I'll handle it. These are terrible words in the Italian language, more often than not the preface to disaster. But what could Mike do, other than ditch Sora and start again? He had no motive for ditching him at that stage, and what was more, Sora was not about to be ditched. Mike's trial was headline stuff; it would go down in history, and so would Sora. It was the chance of his career.

Twenty-two months went by before the trial began, and Sora started straight off with a flourish by pulling out his trump card at the first hearing.

Tucking his thumbs into his gown and puffing out his chest, he claimed that Robin was virtually the defendant's wife, and that therefore she had as much right as a legal wife to refuse to give evidence for the prosecution. He tossed this argument at the court with such an air of triumph that one would have thought the outcome of the trial depended on it. When it was quashed, after the court had withdrawn for an hour to consider it, Mike felt a kind of dread creep over his skin, as if, inexplicably, his case were already lost.

To begin with, it antagonized the judge, whose irritable eyes betrayed a gleam of panic, Mike thought, in the face of Sora's opening thrust. He seemed to be ransacking his brain for the bit about this in the *Codice Penale*, and failing to find it, he raised his eyebrows and gave Sora a blatantly unfriendly look. Then he stood up and announced, "The court will retire to deliberate," and

144

hurried away into the Camera di Consiglio, causing a fluster among the six *giudici popolari*, or members of the jury, who had barely settled into some degree of comfort on the dais and still felt self-conscious about the red, green, and white ribbons they wore across their chests. They stumbled uncertainly to their feet and trailed after him, four men and two women, all solidly middle-aged and middle class; plus another man and a woman who were there as substitutes, without ribbons, in case one of the six was taken ill; plus a second judge in a gown, called the *giudice a latere*, to assist the main judge, who was called the President of the Court. That's an awful lot of judges, Mike reflected as he watched them go traipsing out. It was unnerving to think that they had his life in their hands.

The moment the door had shut behind them, the four *carabinieri* guarding him handcuffed his wrists again and led him away to wait in an adjacent room. Robin caught his eye as he passed, and bit her lip. He saw her eyes flicker down to the handcuffs and up again, and he could not bring himself even to smile. He had been half planning, half dreaming of walking right up to her and kissing her, but he had reckoned without these terrible handcuffs. They were heavy black irons, like medieval instruments of torture, square in shape and separated by a bar with notches for tightening so as to prevent movement of any kind, and a long chain attached for added security. They made him feel degraded, trapped, unworthy to face up to his fellow men.

It was an hour before they brought him back, and a murmur went round when he appeared; there were craned necks and a fresh outburst of flashbulbs. The courtroom was packed now; people were standing all round the doorway at the back and along the walls on both sides. When they took off the handcuffs, he turned and mouthed a kiss at Robin, who gave him a pallid smile.

He had been waiting twenty-two months for that day, waiting with feverish impatience to appear before the judge and be set free. In all those six hundred and sixty-nine days, in spite of his lack of confidence in Sora and the warnings he had received from the other men, he had never seriously doubted that, when the time came, justice would be done. Yet when they came for him at eight o'clock that morning, and he walked out of his cell, freshly shaven and elegantly dressed in the suit and shirt that Robin had brought for him, he had felt his hands turn ice cold, as they do in an acute attack of stage fright. The streets he had been longing to see whizzed past the windows of the van and receded out of focus and out of reach. By the time he sighted the Palazzo di Giustizia, all his confidence was gone. The crowds made him feel faint. He could sense the hostility of those craning necks, those inquisitive eyes. And he entered the courtroom with the wrong expression on his face, not smiling as he had thought he would, not greeting the friends who had come to back him up, but looking as dazed and bewildered as he felt, letting the *carabinieri* guide him into the dock, and taking a long, long time to pick the faces he knew out of the blur that started just behind his lawyers' heads.

He had two lawyers now. The second one, Avvocato Mellini, was a most distinguished member of the legal profession, and so acutely aware of it that by deigning to put in an appearance the first day and lending his sacred name to Mike Donato's cause, he evidently considered that he had done very nearly enough. Or he may have opted out after a shrewd assessment of the odds as he sat, sphinxlike, his eyes half closed to dissociate himself from Sora's opening gaffe. Whatever the reason, although he turned up at the end to deliver a sonorous but, by then, superfluous harangue, during the rest of the trial he was rarely seen.

Mike disliked Avvocato Mellini at first sight, almost as much as he did the President of the Court, who was nothing like the judge he had had in mind, the sort with a curly white wig and a look of ineffable wisdom, who would have been shocked to learn how long Mike had been in prison without just cause. The President of the Court, on the contrary, eyed Mike from the start with undisguised antipathy, and when the court reconvened after deliberating about Robin, he declared testily that only near relatives were entitled to abstain from giving evidence, and that the meaning of "near relatives," as defined in the Penal Code, did not include relationships of the kind alleged to exist between the defendant and Signorina Lane.

Mike threw a bewildered glance at Sora, who patted the air as if to say, "Don't worry—I'll fix it." *Non si preoccupi—ci penso io.* He had fixed it already, no doubt about that. By laying all this emphasis on Robin's testimony, he had managed to make it appear as if what she had to say were conclusive proof of Mike's guilt.

Avvocato Mellini had shut his eyes completely now, and was drumming lightly on the table with his fingertips, as if engrossed in some intensely pertinent thought.

Non si preoccupi—ci penso io.

Mike shook his head in frustration and buried his face in his hands. As he did so, he heard a rustling among the public benches. A ripple of pleasure. They were interpreting this gesture of his as despair at the prospect of being incriminated by the testimony of the woman he loved. That was the kind of drama they had come to watch.

Beppe's mother, the Contessa De Cleris, sat in the front row, straight-backed and still, the picture of solemnity and controlled grief. Mike scrutinized her often during the trial, trying to make out whether she knew the truth. But she never blinked once, not even during the indictment, when the voice of the *giudice a latere* droned on and on with the list of crimes of which Mike stood accused. Causing the death of Giuseppe Palazzo was only the first. He was also charged with knocking him unconscious at the Diavolo Blu *(percosse)*—well, he didn't mind pleading guilty to that; removing him bodily after knocking him out was all right too, but calling it kidnapping *(sequestro di persona)* was a bit steep, especially as he had been told that he could get eight years only for that. But the *pièce de résistance* was the fourth and final charge: concealing the body by throwing it into the Tiber *(occultamento di cadavere)*. In other words, according to them, the lack of a corpse simply made his crime worse.

It was only when the preliminaries were over and the first witnesses were called that Mike discovered the unique point of court procedure that distinguished an Italian trial from the ones he had seen on the screen. There was no direct interrogation, no cross-examination by people like Perry Mason, no spectacular repartees. All questions and answers had to be addressed to the President of the Court, who rephrased them and passed them on in his own words to the person they were intended for, as if translating them into a foreign tongue. Thus, although perfectly audible both times, every single thing that was said had to be said twice, then a third time, more slowly, in a condensed and still further paraphrased form, when the President dictated it all over again to the *cancelliere* with red braid on his gown, who wrote down every word in careful longhand.

One whole morning was spent in this way, questioning people who had seen Mike striding up and down Via Veneto in the early hours of March twenty-second, while the *giudici popolari* were lulled into a comatose state by the woolly monotony of it all. By lunchtime they all had glazed looks on their faces, and when Mike noticed that one of them was wearing dark glasses to conceal his eyes, in case they happened to close, he gave up hope of their ever grasping the truth. The honest facts were sinking deeper every hour under an unending avalanche of triviality.

The tedium was suddenly relieved by the appearance of an unknown woman who came forward and claimed to have seen Mike trying to throttle somebody in Piazza Mattei during the night of April twenty-second of the previous year.

"That's not true!" he shouted, unable to keep quiet.

"We have photographs," said the prosecutor, and indeed he had—piles of them, including the one of Mike pulling Beppe out of the fountain by the scruff of the neck.

"But I didn't try to throttle him!" Mike protested. "And in any case it was a whole year before—" He stopped, realizing he was not doing himself any good.

"Before what?" the President asked him coldly.

Sora was already on his feet, raising his hand. Mike shook his head and sat down.

But the next witness was Leo Santi, the photographer whom Mike had punched in the nose outside Doney's, ages before Beppe came into his life at all, an episode that showed—according to the prosecutor—how Mike had always had a tendency to use his fists.

"What's this got to do with Beppe Palazzo?" Mike burst out. "You're just confusing the issue."

"Mind how you speak," the President warned him—and Mike saw that he had earned himself another black mark.

Avvocato Mellini did try, on one of his rare visits to the court, to raise an objection to this probing into Mike's past life. The objection was overruled on the grounds that the specific facts thus divulged were necessary to establish the character of the defendant in direct relation to the charge.

But that's not my character, Signor Presidente. You've got it all wrong. No, he couldn't shout that out, no matter how much he wanted to. He couldn't jump up every minute and say, "That's not true!" or, "That's beside the point!" It only got on the President's nerves, and did more harm than good.

So he listened in silence while Franco Bernabei was forced to admit that Mike had always hated Beppe's guts; and Nicola, of all people, not only confirmed this but, when pressed, embroidered on it by saying it was almost a persecution mania. Mike blamed Beppe for everything, he said, even his father's death.

"His father's death?" exclaimed the President. "How could that be?"

"Well, he thought—you see, his father died of a heart attack, and—well, you know, there *had* been some very nasty insinuations."

"No, I don't know," said the President. "What insinuations?"

Mike caught Sora's eye and signaled to him that this had to be stopped. But Sora merely patted the air and let it go on.

"That Mike was involved in the case of the girl on the beach." This provoked a murmur of comment, prompting Nicola to add quickly, "Which wasn't true!" But it was too late then. What he had said first had already made its impression; the judges had jumped to a conclusion that was entirely false.

"And what had these 'insinuations' to do with Palazzo?" the President asked.

"Who knows? Nothing, probably. But Mike thought he must

149

have slipped them to the press. I tell you, it was a kind of obsession he had, that's all."

Mike's heart sank. An obsession, that's all. In a minute they'd be saying he had killed Beppe while the balance of his mind was disturbed. Sora had already jumped up once and asked a witness if Mike had appeared to be in a state of intense anger, which meant he was planning to fall back on Article 62, Subsection 2, by virtue of which, if he could show that Mike's anger had been provoked by the unjust behavior of a third party, he could claim mitigation of the sentence.

"Why can't you just tell them I didn't do it? Period." Mike shouted at Sora as soon as he got a chance to see him alone. "There's been no murder! Nobody's dead!"

"Eh-eh," went Sora with a knowing nod and a gesture that meant that if Mike thought the law was as simple as that, he was in for a surprise.

In the end, Mike sat back and let them go muddling on. The wilder the testimony became, the more helpless he felt. And when the manager of the Diavolo Blu testified that he was convinced Beppe was already dead when Mike carried him away, he let it pass.

"What's happened, have you given up protesting?" Carlo Rolli asked him later, when the court had retired to discuss some point of procedure.

"Why can't someone else protest for a change? You, for instance. You were there. You know he wasn't dead."

"I couldn't swear to it, Mike. I don't think he was, but you know, when you're under oath, you have to—"

"Tell the truth? Well, thanks."

Mike was convinced that most of the lies were told in good faith. Massimo, for example, the boy whose megaphone he had snatched, gave a scrupulously accurate description of how he did it, but when the prosecutor asked him, "Did you see anyone in the car with the defendant that night?" he answered without hesitation, "No, he was alone." That was the kind of mistake people made every day of the week, but as a rule it did not matter so much.

150

They kept Robin's testimony until almost the end. When they had finished with her and she was allowed to join his other friends at last on the public benches, she looked paler and sadder than he had ever seen her. It was not surprising after what they had put her through.

"I should like to ask the witness," the prosecutor had begun in a speculative voice, "what kind of male friendships she was cultivating at that time."

Trembling, Robin had looked from the prosecutor to the President, as if hoping that the outrageous question would be withdrawn. But the President's version of it was cruder still:

"Which men did you know—intimately?" he inquired.

She had turned round in search of comfort from Mike, in the dock behind her back, and the President had snapped, "Look at *me*. And answer the question."

Avvocato Mellini was not there that day, and Sora's feeble objections were overruled. The morality of this witness was not merely relevant, he was told, it was the basis of the entire case. She had dodged and denied the truth of their allusions. But meanwhile that wretched copy of *Fandango* was being passed from hand to hand. When the President handed it to her, she turned it over nervously and shook her head. "It wasn't like that," she said. "The pictures have been tampered with." But a photograph is a photograph. What was the use of denying what everyone could see? In any case, it made no difference whether they had been tampered with or not. What mattered was the effect they had had on Mike. The newspaper vendor who had sold Mike that particular copy of *Fandango* in Via Veneto just before midnight on March twenty-first had already testified to how Mike had turned white when he caught sight of the cover, and snatched it up, leaving the change from a thousand lire behind.

"When he went out again, after midnight," the prosecutor asked Robin, "did he say that if he found Palazzo, he was going to kill him?"

Robin bit her lip and shook her head.

"May I remind the witness once again that she is under oath?"

"Signor Presidente!" Mike exploded, red in the face. "Even if I did say I was going to kill him, you don't think I meant it, do you? Nobody in their right mind would say that and then go and do it, would they?"

"But you weren't in your right mind!" shouted the prosecutor.

"*Silenzio!*" shouted the President at the top of his voice. He stood up and pointed at Mike. "If you say another word, I'll have you expelled from the court."

Mike shut his eyes and sat down.

"Signorina Lane, will you tell us now what the defendant said when he returned at five to three?"

"I don't—exactly remember."

"Is that so? What kind of mood was he in?"

"Calm. And tired. I think he just—went to sleep."

"Without a word? But surely you were very upset?"

"Well, I had been."

"And you weren't anymore? How was that?"

"Well, I think Mike said it was all right now."

"What was?"

"Everything. He'd settled whatever it was. I mean, he said Beppe wouldn't be bothering me any more."

The prosecutor arranged his notes, shrugged his gown back a little off his shoulders, pursed his lips, and set about running Mike down.

"Look at him, *signori della corte*, there he sits making fun of us all, a man used to a life of luxury—expensive cars, girls of doubtful virtue, money, fine clothes, success—there's no limit, I tell you, to his effrontery. He does not quail before the eyes of his victim's mother, he does not turn pale before her grief, he does not break down and weep and ask her forgiveness. Worse, he says this lady, this bereaved mother, who has sat with us and kept her head high throughout this trial, not only knows that her son is not dead, but helped him to get away, to escape from heaven knows what. For this slander alone, *signori della corte*, he deserves something like twenty-four years imprisonment. Not a word, not a tear, for an elderly widow left alone in the world by the murder of her only son."

This was only the beginning, naturally. The prosecutor talked for four hours without stopping, demolishing Mike's own version of the facts with such thoroughness and conviction that Mike sat listening to him without moving or protesting once, so amazed was he by the verisimilitude of untruth.

When this long harangue was over, Mike knew it was too late. What could the defense do now but repeat the arguments that the prosecution had already destroyed?

"You have no proof," cried Avvocato Mellini. "Nothing but suspicion." But his heartfelt tone sounded like empty rhetoric, which was exactly what it was. The judges had so much suspicion that they did not need any proof. They had only circumstantial evidence, but it all pointed one way.

"Have you anything to declare?" the President asked Mike when Mellini had finished.

"How can I make you believe that Beppe Palazzo's still alive?"

"The court will retire to deliberate."

The court was in the Camera di Consiglio for eighteen hours. They took Mike back to the prison and told him to try and get some sleep, but all he could do was smoke and look at his watch and think of all the mistakes that Sora had made, all the gaps that had been left in his defense, all the proof he had neglected to provide himself. His cellmates were sympathetic and discreet—too sympathetic and too discreet for comfort. It was easy to tell what they thought the verdict was going to be.

The *carabinieri* came for him at seven o'clock the next morning, and the courtroom, when they got there, was packed to overflowing. Even the corridors were crowded with people trying to push their way in.

Mike caught sight of Robin staring anxiously towards him. Her face was white, and it suddenly struck him that she looked very thin. Nicola, beside her, raised his hand in a vague salutation. Franco Bernabei was just behind them. Yes, they were all there, waiting. None of them had meant to do him the harm they had done.

There was a great silence when the judges filed in, looking haggard and irritable after their sleepless night. The President remained standing while they all took their places. Then he put on his spectacles and read out the verdict.

"In nome del popolo italiano . . ." he began. Out of the long rigmarole that followed, Mike caught only one word: *guilty*. He felt the two *carabinieri* grip his arms and, far away, he heard the sound of sobbing. Through a mist that must have been the tears clouding his own eyes, he saw Robin, with her hands over her face, half buried in Nicola's arms.

Then they put the handcuffs on him again and led him away.

Part 2

SEVENTEEN

Beppe's head was floating on the water like a football. Mike was punching at it, trying to push it under, but it kept bouncing back to the surface, a little bigger each time. Now it looked like an obscene, overinflated, pink balloon. Mike made a dive for it and grabbed it with both hands, but it slipped out of his grasp and refused to go under. Floundering out of his depth, exhausted and exasperated, Mike struck out at it as hard as he could, but in the water there was no strength in his arm and he could barely reach it with his fingertips. What they touched was repulsively soft, warm flesh, not Beppe's head at all, but Robin's swollen belly.

Mike screamed and woke, shaken and disorientated in the darkness of what he thought must be his cell—except that he smelled an unfamiliar fustiness, a faint odor of mothballs. It was only a matter of a second; then he remembered.

He switched on the lamp and fumbled for a cigarette. It was a drab little room, as frugal and impersonal as most rooms in small, cheap hotels. To wake in such a place on his first morning of freedom did not give him any particular feeling of joy. On the contrary, his first thought was of the men he had left behind, and as he lay back and slowly found his way to full awareness, all he felt was solitude.

He reached out for the tattered yellow paperback that Memmo had pressed upon him as a parting gift, and smiled at its lurid cover design illustrating the title *La Morte è Femmina*. Trust Memmo to have felt the impulse to give him something, anything, and to have snatched up the first thing that came to hand, unsuitable though it was. He had given him a quantity of advice as well—sound, practical advice about how to handle each stage of his plan, a matter in which Memmo felt deeply involved, having volunteered his services a long while back as a technical consultant. He had had a good laugh about it at first, the day he found out what Mike had in mind, but little by little he had become almost as obsessed with the plan as Mike was himself and, apprehensive of the trouble Mike might get himself into if he was not properly prepared, he had insisted on helping him work it all out, down to the last detail. He was a professional thief and as rough as they come, but he was a good friend, was Memmo, maybe the only real friend Mike had in the world; and since he had ten years more to serve, there was little chance they would ever meet again.

Mike looked at his watch. It was nearly half past five. He got up and opened the window and pushed back the shutters. Via della Vite was wonderfully silent. But two lamps were burning brightly outside the back entrance of the main post office, on the other side of the street, and the faint whistling of a tune inside the half-open door proclaimed that somebody was already at work in there. The swish of a bus passing the end of the road on its way down the Corso reminded him that Rome is a city of early risers. Still, it would be two hours before the real madness began. Now was the time to walk the streets.

It was still dark, but the sky had turned a rich indigo blue and the terra-cotta buildings of Piazza di Spagna seemed infinitely tranquil. In Via Babuino he met a *vigile notturno* wheeling his bicycle along the pavement on his last round of inspection, stopping at each shop to check the locks and leave his ticket. He threw a cursory glance at Mike, then mounted his bicycle and pedaled slowly away.

A young man came round a corner carrying a long ladder and a pail, and in a side street, a tiny old lady in a black dress, with a black kerchief tied tightly round her head, was stooping over a huge, old-fashioned broom, meticulously sweeping the cobbles outside her door. Bent double as she was with arthritis and old age, she seemed to be examining each cobblestone for dust.

In Piazza del Popolo, Canova's was as bright as day and swarming with men in blue overalls, furiously washing floors and windows and polishing every scrap of brass and steel.

Even at this hour the fountain was lit up and the four white lions were spitting their fan-shaped jets of liquid light at the foot of the sun god's obelisk, one of the oldest things in the world, a shaft of vivid pink against the ultramarine sky that was now rapidly turning paler behind the trees on the Pincio. Mike headed up the winding road in that direction.

There came a moment when the lightening sky tinged all the rooftops of Rome with blue. That brief and extraordinary moment was like a revelation, a fleeting glimpse of something he almost dared call hope. Morning after morning, Rome basked in this shifting light of dawn, regardless of the indifference of the human race, unaffected by its shallowness and its cruelty. He thought of all the vacant faces in the streets yesterday, all the people pushing one another out of the way, hurrying God knows where, obsessed with God knows what mirage; and he thought: You only have to climb up here just once and let yourself be embraced by the transient color of infinity to see how small man is, and perhaps be a little less afraid.

A moment later the blues gave way to grays and pinks. A bird began a cautious morning song. Mike could hear water trickling somewhere and, in the distance, a faint rumble of traffic.

At half past nine, Viale Mazzini was a sea of cars. Mike stood transfixed on the curb, watching them fume and hoot like angry monsters, creeping forward in turn, darting and dodging, flank to flank. He shuddered to think what it was going to be like to learn to drive again, which was vital to his plan of action; it was Item Number Two on his list of preparations. But it would have to be postponed, at least until he could get accustomed to this traffic. At the moment it was all he could do to cross the road.

He had an appointment at Sora's office first of all—to sort out his things, which Sora was impatient to be rid of. The rattle of a typewriter stopped as he entered the lobby. A girl with fuzzy hair peered out at him anxiously through an open door, and then hastily withdrew into an adjoining room.

"Your secretary looks as if she's seen a murderer," he said when Sora came out to greet him.

"Take no notice. She's a silly girl."

"Couldn't you have explained that I'm not?"

"She wouldn't understand. Some people don't. You may have to get used to that."

In the middle of a vacant room at the end of a corridor, four suitcases and three large wooden boxes stood waiting to be opened. "You'll find everything here," Sora told him. "Exactly as it was packed when we cleared your flat."

Left alone, Mike pushed back the shutters to let some light into the dreary room, which was cluttered with the black, pseudo-Renaissance furniture that Italian lawyers tend to favor. He had been looking forward to getting back his belongings; he thought they might help him find his old self. But when he delved into those musty cases full of the past, all he found was more bitterness. The tangible fragments of his lost life had been packed up more or less haphazardly, thrust into a cellar, and left to turn green with mildew. The luxurious clothes he had been so fond of were not only moldy but riddled with moth holes; anyway, they were out of fashion now. The shoes might be all right, if the green film they were covered with could ever be removed; the socks and the underwear might be wearable if they could be thoroughly bleached and did not disintegrate in the process; one or two other items might conceivably be retrieved by an exceptionally courageous laundress; but most of it was fit only for the dustbin. It depressed him to look at it.

He lifted the lid off one of the wooden boxes and began pulling things out of it and lining them up on the floor: kitchen gadgets, books, a leather toilet case he had never used, all kinds of expensive gewgaws that had presumably been presents, including five gold key rings still in their jeweler's boxes, and three watches that had not ticked for twenty years. He picked out a Piaget, wound it up, and put it on his wrist; he selected a few books that were old favorites; the rest of the stuff was too long forgotten to concern him in any way. He tumbled it all back into the box.

In the second one he found the papers from his desk: fan letters, business letters, offers, contracts, bank statements, and bills.

There were several large envelopes bulging with photographs and press cuttings, the script of *Povero Valentino*, and the last one Joe Mannino had offered him, which he had never had the time to read. This used to be me, he told himself. All of this was essential once. Not a scrap of it meant anything anymore.

He pulled the last few things out of the box: his electric razor, a camera he had never used, an unopened bottle of whisky and a half-empty one of Courvoisier, and the lab form with the result of Robin's pregnancy test, in a silver frame that had gone black. At the very bottom, wrapped in tissue paper that had turned brown and brittle with age, was the breakfast set for two that Robin had bought him after she fell downstairs with the tray, the morning she decided to surprise him with breakfast in bed. They had had a good laugh about that while they were scooping up the mess, and she had confessed that she was glad she had smashed it all, anyway; she had been a bit bothered by the idea of other women's lips on those cups. The next day she had brought him this teapot and jug, with the two cups and two plates to match, in the chunky, rough-glazed green pottery they make in Vietri, with a childish design of circles and blobs that were supposed to be flowers. And here they were, with their air of bright candor so typical of Robin herself, just the same as when he first saw them, twenty years ago, in Robin's hands. He could hear her voice saying, "Don't you dare use these for breakfast with anyone else," as he placed them carefully on the table, to keep. To keep for what, he had no idea. They were cumbersome things to carry around, but they brought Robin back to him more than any photograph ever could.

He picked up his old address book full of faded names, faceless ghosts that must once have played some part in his life, and leafed through it until, sandwiched between Oscar Lorenzi and the Lion Bookshop, he found the name Robin Lane, with the telephone number she had written in beside it in her own hand in the restaurant of Cinecittà, the number he had dialed innumerable times. He felt a ridiculous urge to dial it again now, certain that no voice could answer it but hers.

Pocketing the address book, he opened the third packing case and found his long-forgotten false noses in their old cardboard box. That made him smile. He took them out and fingered them lovingly, one by one, before putting them aside to keep, with the books and the breakfast set and the rolled-up poster of the clown, which he had also spotted at once on top of the third case. He found nothing else in it but books and pictures and a few more scripts. His British passport was not there.

He strode along the corridor to Sora's office. "My passport isn't there," he told him. Sora merely shrugged. "Well, where is it?" asked Mike.

"Are you sure you didn't have it on you when you were arrested?"

"Positive."

"Then you must have lost it. You'd better go to the Consulate and apply for a new one." With that, Sora considered that he had settled the matter of the passport, to which he attached very little importance. But Mike could not dismiss it so easily. He needed it for his plan, first of all, and he did not know how long it would take to get a new one; but apart from that, as he sat down to go over his accounts, there was a half-formed thought nagging at his brain that he could not yet quite define.

Sora had been holding Mike's money in trust all these years, and in this respect Mike had to admit that he had done his job well. He had sold what there was to sell after Mike's arrest—the Alfa Romeo and the only valuable painting Mike had possessed—and he had collected all the payments that had fallen due on the films Mike had made in Rome. These were modest sums compared with what stars earned now, but all the same there had been enough to cover Sora's fees and expenses and still leave a sum that would take care of Mike's immediate needs and tide him over until he could start earning again.

"That's the first pleasant surprise I've had for a long time," Mike said, when the financial business was settled. "Thanks, Sora." He stood up. "And on that joyful note I'll say goodbye."

"You are leaving?" Sora smiled hopefully. "You are going to England after all?"

"Sorry, no, I can't oblige. But don't worry, I won't give you any more trouble." He was already at the door.

"And your things? Shall I send them to your hotel?"

"No, I'll come back and fetch all I want to keep in a day or two. You can chuck the rest out. It's all moldy anyway."

"Moldy? I'm sorry."

"Oh, I don't blame you. Why should I blame you?"

In spite of himself, Sora blushed.

EIGHTEEN

Olga Palazzo had been the Contessa De Cleris for so long, and she had slipped so easily into the part, that she almost fancied she had been born an aristocrat. The Conte Gastone had proved a disappointment to her. His distinguished appearance had concealed a muddled mind. By the time she married him, his faithful administrator and a long stream of other people had been living off the fat of the land at his expense for a great many years, so that long before she could get her hands on his considerable property, it had dwindled to barely enough to live on in comfort, and only that as long as the Conte De Cleris was alive. When he died, the succession duties were so high that she had to sell it all in order to pay them, and the price she procured by selling in haste was far below its true value. When all the debts were settled there was not much left.

For the past twelve years she had lived in strict seclusion in Via Lazio, on the third floor of one of those gloomy, old-fashioned buildings round Via Veneto where the brass is highly polished but the porter looks sour, the cagelike lift will not work unless you put ten lire in the slot, and then it glides upward very slowly and stops with a loud rattle, as if shuddering at the effort it has made. There is little comfort in these turn-of-the-century buildings. The rooms are oblong and symmetrical, with gray stucco ceilings and wilting wallpaper. The bleakly spacious bathrooms have a dank smell no plumber can obliterate. There are no terraces and no view. As the rents in this area are exceedingly high, most of the apartments are used as offices or *pensioni*, while the rest are inhabited by their owners, the elderly survivors of decaying families, whose names are engraved on brass plates on massive, inhospitable front doors.

Mike had no difficulty in finding the address. There was no other De Cleris in the phone book, and he remembered hearing once that she had gone to live near Via Veneto.

He rang the bell. After a few minutes he heard a shuffling sound and the clink of a safety chain being inserted into its socket. A bolt scraped back, a key was turned in one of the two locks, and when the door finally opened as far as the chain would allow, the pallid face of a young girl peered out at him through the crack.

"I'd like to speak to the Contessa De Cleris," Mike said. "I'm an old friend of her son's."

The girl, who had clearly been told repeatedly to trust no one, screwed up her face with the effort of trying to discern whether Mike was a genuine friend or a foe. She decided in his favor, eventually, and removed the chain and let him into a dark hallway that smelled of age and furniture polish. She pushed open the glass door that led into the drawing room, and nodded to him to go in.

The drawing room had the stagnant elegance of a room that is rarely used. The windows were tightly shut to keep out the dust, the shutters held aslant by the catch to prevent them from blowing back and letting in the sun. Mike longed to release the catch and flood the room with daylight, as he had at Sora's, but he resisted the impulse and paced up and down while he waited, an old prison habit. He noticed that though there were some fine pieces of antique furniture and a lot of trinkets that were probably valuable, the sofa was faded and threadbare. On a small table near the middle of the room there was a large photograph of Beppe, grinning at him in a silver frame.

"Who are you?" asked a thin, angry voice behind him. The Contessa was now seventy-four, but her hair was dyed a stubborn blonde and her wizened cheeks were daubed with rouge. She held her small, frail body tenaciously upright, and before coming out to face the stranger who she had sensed could only be an enemy, she had taken pains to outline her eyes in black and shade them heavily with blue. She ignored Mike's conventional greeting and waited for him to answer her question.

"My name's Rossi. Roberto Rossi," he told her, conscious of the hostility of her tight lips. She raised her eyebrows but said nothing, nor did she offer him a chair. "Your son and I did some business together," he said, "many years ago."

"And so?" she snapped.

"I need to find him."

She stared at him coldly. "One moment," she said, and left the room.

Mike began to feel uneasy. He sat down on the sofa and stood up again. He walked to the window, opened it, and shut it again. She had been gone more than five minutes and he was deliberating whether to slip away when she came back carrying a large scrapbook.

"Signor Donato," she began, "I may be old, but I am not doddering. Did you really think I wouldn't know who you were?"

She placed the scrapbook on the marble coffee table and opened it. Mike stared down at it, defeated. It was full of press cuttings concerning his trial.

"That's you, isn't it?" she said, prodding one of the photographs with a pale, knobbly finger. "And that—and that! Oh, you've aged a lot, but you can't fool me. How dare you come into my house and tell me lies?"

"It's no lie that I want to see your son. It's thanks to him I've been in prison for twenty years. Do you have any idea what prison's like?"

"Mariella!"

The girl instantly poked a frightened face round the door, where she had evidently been crouching to eavesdrop.

"Go and stand beside the telephone. The minute I ring this bell, dial one-one-three for the police and say there is a murderer here."

The girl gasped. "Yes, Contessa!" She dashed away.

Mike stood watching the old woman as she seated herself in an armchair and placed her hand on the little table beside it, where the handbell was. What an evil old harpy she is, he thought to himself.

"Now," she said, "I give you one minute to tell me what you came to say. I presume you did come to say something."

"I came to find out where Beppe is."

"Beppe is dead. You killed him."

"You know that's not true. If you don't, then he cheated you as well as me. But if you let me be condemned for murder just to shield him, you've got a lot on your conscience."

"You are obviously mad." She took hold of the silver handbell and gave it a vigorous shake.

"All right, then I'll tell you something else. It ought not to frighten you if you think he's dead. According to Article Ninety of the Italian Penal Code, no man can be condemned twice for the same crime. So when I find Beppe, I'm going to kill him—and there's nothing anyone can do about it. Just tell him that from me."

He kept his eyes riveted on the old woman's face, endeavoring to detect some ripple of emotion. She refused to give herself away. Only when she spoke did he think that her voice was a trifle too carefully toneless:

"Will you go now," she said, "or wait for the police?"

Mike turned and made for the front door. Mariella darted out of the shadows and slammed it behind him.

He was in such a fury as he strode away down Via Lazio that he turned into Via Veneto without thinking. He had intended to avoid it by threading through the back streets, as he had when he came. He was afraid of running into old acquaintances who might or might not look him in the eye. He was not ready for that yet.

When he found himself outside what used to be Rosati's, he almost turned back and escaped. Then the past welled up inside him and the fascination of rediscovery led him on. It warmed him to see how little everything had changed: more cars, more neon signs, a few smart new awnings outside the cafés, where people were sitting and talking and staring, as they always had. Only there was something foreign about even the familiar things. There were no friends, no smiles. Nobody noticed him. It was not a place where he belonged anymore.

Two men were arguing on the corner in front of Doney's. He recognized one of them as an actor of sorts who had had a small part in *Un Bel Pasticcio,* and who now had all the self-conscious swagger of a star. He kept shrugging and gesticulating and shaking his handsome silver head, while the other man nodded and patted him persuasively on the arm. It's all still going on, Mike thought. Agents, actors, and producers—they're all still hard at it, making deals, squabbling over percentages and minimum guarantees and above-the-line and below-the-line and completion bonds. How remote it all seemed, how incredibly far away from what he had become.

Then an extraordinary thing happened. A car drove slowly out of Via Lombardia and stopped on the corner, by the newspaper kiosk. A woman jumped out of the car and ran to buy some papers, while the man at the wheel kept the engine running.

It was Robin.

She looked older, of course, but still youthful, in a way perhaps more beautiful than before, with an elegance that was new to him and short, extremely well cut hair.

Mike shot across the road without giving the traffic a thought. She was leaning over the bench where the magazines were displayed. He went up behind her and whispered, "Robin!"

She spun round. "Oh, my God!" she said.

"You look wonderful."

"Mike!" she murmured. She had turned very pale. "Have they—are you—?"

"Yes. They let me out."

"Oh, my God!" she said again.

They stared at each other for a second.

"That's my husband sitting there in the car," she said. "Don't look. He's probably watching us."

She turned to snatch up a couple of magazines, and while she was fishing in her purse for change, he said, "I'm at the Hotel Belvedere in Via della Vite. Room one-oh-seven."

She gave no indication of whether she had heard or not, simply paid the vendor, lightly touched Mike's hand, and murmured, "Goodbye."

She was gone. He watched her jump into the car and smile at the man at the wheel, a pleasant-looking man in his early fifties. The car drove away.

As he walked on down the hill, past the Café de Paris, it dawned on him that he had just condemned himself to sitting shut up in his room indefinitely. She might not call him for days, and if she never called at all, it would be hard not to go on waiting and hoping— instead of getting on with the all-important business of finding Beppe. Until then he had been resigned to the fact that Robin had nothing to do with him anymore, not out here in the world of reality, where she had been living without him for so long. It was years and years—fourteen, fifteen, he had lost count—since she had written to tell him she was getting married. A very tender letter it was, almost apologetic: "My dearest, dearest Mike," it said, "forgive me, please." As if he could have expected her to wait for him all her life. He had written torrents back, and most of it he never sent; nor did he send her any of the passionate letters he went on writing to her for ages afterwards. It helped a lot, pretending she was out there listening, caring what went on in his mind. Seeing her in the flesh was a different matter. This neat, composed, well-dressed woman with a smiling husband in a car was somebody else—and yet curiously, undeniably, still the same.

Everything was the same, that was the trouble, all just the same and all quite different. He stopped on the corner of Via Ludovisi and stared at the newspaper kiosk where he had bought that last, fatal copy of *Fandango*. He was not sure if it was the sameness or the difference that was beginning to stir in him now a kind of excitement, a longing to look up old friends and find out what everyone was up to nowadays. He put his hand in his pocket and fingered the old address book. Nicola, for instance. Supposing he still lived on the Aventino, supposing he was home now, ready and eager to welcome him back? There was a phone booth on the other side of the road.

"Mike!" cried Nicola. "Where are you? Where have you been?"

"Where have I *been*!"

"Oh, sorry. You know—it's been so long. One forgets."

"Oh, I know. One forgets."

"No, I didn't mean that, it's not true. Mike, if I stopped writing, it was only because—"

"You couldn't keep it up. I understand that too. Listen, I didn't call you to complain. I just found your old number and thought I'd give it a try. I hardly expected you'd still be there. I mean, you might have moved."

"Am I crazy? Where will I find an apartment like this one? So— tell me. When am I going to see you?"

"Now, if you want." Mike paused. "Or—whenever you say."

"Well, you know, I'm shooting this week. Let's make it Sunday, okay? In the morning my writer is coming to talk about the script, but—well, let's phone each other about lunchtime."

"Got a part for me in the film?"

There was a tiny pause before Nicola said, *"Oh Gesù!* You could have been Buck."

"Who's Buck?"

"A young bandit who becomes a revolutionary. Fantastic character."

"Nicola, I'm forty-eight."

"So what? You would have been perfect. *Che peccato!* Well, I have another script, even better—*ma certo.* That one has a part for you. A fantastic part. Exactly you."

"You haven't seen me for twenty years. You may get a shock."

"You're still younger than me. And *I* haven't changed. Much."

"But then you're a successful man."

"What's success? Only another kind of prison."

It was Mike's turn to pause a moment now, before saying quietly, "Let's not exaggerate."

"No, *sul serio,* what I would give to be back in the days when we made *Corriera*—remember? I didn't know a boom from a zoom, but we were happy then. Innocent. Know what I mean?"

"And now?"

"Oh, now I know everything—but I've forgotten what I wanted to say."

"The money you must have, though. You've been making one film after the other."

Nicola paused now. Then he said, "Tell me something, Mike— forgive me if I ask, but—you didn't really kill Beppe, did you?"

Mike felt his pores tingle. He said softly, "No."

"I'm sorry. But—you know, Beppe never was seen again. In the end, many people—"

"Said I *must* have killed him?"

"More or less."

"Well, that's life. And you talk of giving me a part."

"Why not? But have you talked to Franco? He's a big, big agent now—a whole organization, with offices even in Los Angeles."

"Good for him. Don't worry, I was joking. I don't want a part. I've got other things to do, besides making a comeback. Tell me, though, do you ever see Robin?"

"No. Not for years now."

"Where does she live, do you know?"

"No, I lost touch. You know how it is—when people get married."

"Are you married, Nico?"

"Yes and no. That's a long story."

There was a silence. Then Nicola said, "Mike, I'm so glad you're back. You call me Sunday, eh?"

"All right." The conversation was at an end.

"Goodbye, then."

"*Ciao.*"

Ciao, Nicola D'Angelo, old friend. But whatever happened to the Nico I used to know?

Mike pondered this all the way back to the hotel. The fact was that Nicola had not really changed, he was exactly the man he had always been. But it was easier to see through him now that Mike himself was so much older—much more than twenty years older, more like a hundred. He could see only too clearly now how Nicola had managed to get on in the world, with very little talent behind all that energetic *niceness*, simply by ignoring any form of unpleasantness that might have stood in his way.

I could have asked him for Franco's number, he thought—not that he was in such a hurry now to contact anyone else. They'll all be the same, he thought, they'll all be half apologetic and half scared—and bored to death with having to bother with me.

The hotel porter slammed down Mike's key without so much as a glance at him, and became intensely absorbed in the compilation of his football coupon. Here we go, Mike thought; and sure

171

enough, there was a newspaper lying on the desk with a photograph much in evidence, placed there deliberately, perhaps, to catch his eye. He picked it up.

So he was not completely forgotten after all. *Paese Sera* had published a picture of his old radiant, successful self, with the title: "Mike Donato Free." Underneath, little more than a caption: "Michele Donadio, alias Mike Donato, the actor who won fame in the fifties for his performances in such films as *Povero Valentino* and *Un Bel Pasticcio*, left Porto Azzurro on Thursday after serving twenty years' imprisonment for murder."

"Signor Donadio," said the manager's voice behind him, "or should I say Signor Donato?"

Mike turned to face him and shrugged. "Suit yourself," he said. He could tell what was coming next.

"I'm afraid we'll be needing your room tomorrow."

Wonderful how some bright reporter can scotch a man's existence with a single sentence.

"What, on account of this?" Mike said. He dropped the newspaper back onto the desk and jingled his key. "Let's discuss that tomorrow, shall we?" Who could tell? She might even phone tonight.

The manager thrust out a hand to bar his way. "There is nothing to discuss. This is a respectable hotel. I must ask you to leave your room tomorrow by midday."

Mike contemplated the man's smug pink nose and reflected that in the old days he would never have been able to resist flattening it out. But Sora was right; he would have to learn to put up with this kind of thing. "I'll leave when it suits me," he said, pushing past the manager to head for the stairs.

The manager's face turned a deep red. He began burbling some kind of thinly disguised threat, which Mike forced himself to ignore. He could not afford to let himself be provoked; he had to keep on walking, with all the dignity he could muster in the circumstances, up the stairs and along the corridor and into his room. Once safely inside, he locked and bolted the door and braced himself to withstand a state of siege.

He was hungry. At lunchtime he had not had the courage to go into a restaurant and sit down and order a meal. He had fancied they would all be looking at him, noticing his clumsiness and nudging one another and saying, "Look at him; you can see where he's just come from." He felt sure people could see the marks of prison on him. In the end he had found a *rosticceria* where, standing at the counter, he had self-consciously swallowed a plateful of greasy lasagne that must have been cooked a week before. It had descended like a load of lead into his defenseless stomach and settled there for the afternoon.

He would gladly have braved a restaurant now for the sake of some good hot food. But that would have to wait. He had made up his mind to give Robin at least three days and, hungry or not, he was determined to stick it out.

NINETEEN

All night long, Robin tossed and turned and thought of Mike. He had never been far below the surface of her mind. For years she had sent him parcels of food and books and gone to see him when she could get permission, though this had become more and more difficult after they moved him away from Rome. Viterbo was not so bad—she could get there in two hours—but Trento and Alessandria were far away up north, and when he was sent, finally, to Porto Azzurro, on the island of Elba, it meant changing trains and then catching the boat, and to be there in time for the visit she had to stop somewhere overnight. All for an agonizing half hour, with a wide table between them and a glass barrier in front of their faces, and babies howling and women weeping, in a room full of people shouting to make themselves heard. They were not allowed to talk softly or say incomprehensible things or kiss or exchange notes. At the most, when the guard was looking elsewhere, they would reach out over the glass to touch fingertips; and afterwards, that feathery moment of contact would burn in her mind and make her sick, physically sick with frustration. They were torture, those visits, worse than nothing, much worse, but she had to keep them up because they were the only visits he had, and in the end the strain of it drained the love away and left only searing pity. And guilt— the sense of guilt she had never been able to shake off. After she was married it became unbearably intense, because she deserted Mike then and never went back. She had to, of course, it was not her fault; though, to be honest, it was a relief. But still, sometimes, she would climb up the hill of the Gianicolo, as she used to when Mike was still in the Regina Coeli prison, on the bank of the

Tiber directly below, and, looking down at those terrible silent roofs, she would ask herself what happens to a man in such a place. True, it was a long while since she had done that. She had avoided the Gianicolo lately as much as she could; but there were always moments when she would stop what she was doing and say to herself: Here am I in this evening dress, drinking Barolo, and he's still there, he's still shut up in there.

It came as a shock to her every time, the recollection of his mute presence in a world where everybody had forgotten him, including, on occasion—no use denying it—herself.

And yet those few months she had spent with him stretched into infinity, beyond the limits of time. She knew the exact dates of the beginning and the end: the day they started shooting *Valentino* and the day of his arrest. But those were only figures on a calendar; they bore no relation to the crystalline happiness in between, when they were together, living the best part of their lives. Nothing else, before or after, was so real.

The first time she was unfaithful to him, it was terrible. Useless too. When she saw those alien eyes looking down at her, dark with excitement, the only thought in her head was: Mike—where are you? She hated that heavy breath on her cheeks, those greedy hands, but when the man said, "Don't you like it?" she said she did because it seemed rude to say no. It was a man she hardly knew; she was teaching him English at the time. "De geerl's pencil," he was saying. "Not de, the." "Ze geerl's—" "No, not geerl, girl." "Ze gul's—" "No, look—" She showed him the tip of her tongue between her teeth. "The. The girl's pencil. It's the Saxon genitive," she said, having learned this herself from a lady in cashmere who had learned all about it at school. In those days there were always ladies in cashmere and pearls, eager to brush up their notions of the *genitivo sassone* in the interests of culture. Not to mention lecherous males like this one, who showed more interest in her knees under the table than in the grammar book on top. "*Scusi?* Repeat again—*genitali sassoni?*" His hand went sneaking up her leg. "Geni*tive*," she snapped, fending off the invading hand.

175

Then she gave up bothering to stop him. It was a way of making herself believe that Mike was gone. I've got to make love with other men sometime, whether I want to or not, she told herself. But it made no sense at all; she found that out as soon as she was naked on the bed, feeling about as eager to kiss his wretched penis as to teach him the Saxon genitive.

"You English girls," he said afterwards.

"Sorry," she said, and went home to wash the sperm off her thighs and have a good cry. And think of Mike, with his strong young body that felt so right and natural joined to hers and gave her, more than just pleasure, a unique feeling of oneness— something she had never experienced with any other man.

There had been a particular joy, too, in talking the same language in a foreign country and catching little subtleties that went beyond words and became a secret form of mutual possession. She could never have explained to Nicola how, when Mike said "buttercups," it had in it all the tenderness of her childhood and his. Nor could she envisage sharing a poem with Luca, or laughing all the time, as she used to with Mike, about nothing and everything, whether it was tripping headlong with a loaded tray or trying to make toast over a blazing log in his bedroom; or his exclaiming "Oh, to be in England!" as he plunged his fork into a pile of spaghetti *alla carbonara* at Checco er Carrettiere. They had laughed till they cried that time, on account of the way he said it and the absurdity of the moment and mostly for no reason at all other than that they were foolishly, totally happy.

"Did Mike mind you not being a virgin?" Serena had asked her once, out of the blue.

"A *virgin*! Serena, honestly!"

Serena was a soft and tranquil woman a few years older than Robin, who had helped her through her blackest days after Mike was imprisoned. At that time she ran a secretarial agency where Robin worked off and on when there was no other way to make ends meet. They had very little in common; their conversation rarely went beyond clothes and recipes and shops where things cost a little less; but Robin had cherished Serena's friendship through the years because of the solidity of her kindness.

"Mike is Italian, I think," she had said in a quiet, firm tone.

"Not the way you mean," Robin had told her. "Not about that kind of thing. And anyway, I've met some Italian virgins. Home every night by nine o'clock and what they get up to in the afternoon is nobody's business—it's amazing what you can do without breaking the hymen. Thank God I was never like that."

"You are really proud of it, eh?" said Serena.

"Of not being a hypocrite? Yes."

"No, of doing *everything*, instead of, you know—half." Serena blushed. "As for the other, forgive me, but I think we are all hypocrites sometimes. Even you. Sometimes yes, and sometimes no. You are a mixture."

"I expect I've been in Italy too long."

"No, I think it is not good to be too frank. Men do not understand."

"Oh, I know. Sex is a battle of wits in Italy. If they can get you into bed, you're a *puttana*. If they can't, they talk about respecting you—which really means they despise you. But Mike grew up in England. It's different."

"And Luca?"

"Oh, Luca—I don't know. He's so sweet and forgiving, I could throttle him at times. Of course, it's Mike he forgives me for, Mike and the baby, and a few vague wild oats before I came to Rome. He thinks that's plenty, too. I can hear it grinding around in his head sometimes, and I almost wish he'd say something about it instead of fidgeting with his halo. Goodness knows what he'd do if he knew the whole story."

"So I *am* right. You are not always frank."

"Well, as you say, Luca might not understand."

He was a good husband, no question of that. He had always taken pains to see that she was well cared for and well dressed. He often bought her expensive presents. Oh, yes, he was exceptionally thoughtful and kind. All the same, when he introduced her as "my wife, Roberta," she sometimes had the impression that she was nobody anymore, just a thing of his own creation that he liked showing off. He was always telling people, "My wife is English!"—as if this made her somehow superior, like English tweed. But by choosing to call her Roberta, he had deliberately wiped out the girl she used to be, along with her unmentionable past. And somehow she had managed to adapt herself to his point of view, just as she had to the role of Signora Ferrero, a person fabricated by Luca and Luca's friends, perfectly respectable and only half alive.

He was the kind of big, protective man who makes you feel, when he holds you close, that everything is going to be all right, and he had turned up at a time in her life when everything was so far from all right that she was never tired of nestling in his arms. There was something comforting, too, about the very fact that he was an architect, absorbed in the practical problems of everyday life. She, who had never been domesticated, discovered in home-making a powerful drug. It was soothing to be in the hands of a man who knew exactly what texture he wanted on the walls and how wide a window ought to be. This new world of floors and doors was wonderfully solid and reassuring and quiet.

Their first home was fun: an attic he built himself on top of an old building near the Pantheon. That was the only apartment of theirs that she ever felt was hers as well. Not that she had been allowed much say in any of it, but at that stage in his career he was still making things with his own hands and telling her what he had in mind to do. They used to go out and buy gadgets together—he had a passion for gadgets—and if he did choose most of them himself, at least he told her why. He shed that kind of enthusiasm later and turned into a businessman. As he got richer, the apartments got bigger and more impersonal, and running them became a burden and a bore.

The one they lived in now was beautiful. But the carpet in the living room, which Luca had had dyed a unique emerald green, was a regular cause of friction with Adele, who hated the vacuum cleaner and held that carpets ought to be brushed by hand. Adele was a large, angular woman, who suffered from arthritis and talked hardly at all. She was honest and hardworking and unsmiling, and her lumbering daily presence ruffled Robin's nerves. She would purse her lips and scowl when dusting the steel-and-glass coffee table, which was laden with special glass shapes and was a devil to polish. She would grumble and sniff at the multicolored cushions on the deep leather sofa, which had to be scattered in a particular pattern, and which she persisted in lining up every day in a neat row. Robin was sick of rearranging them after she had gone. She was sick of all that tasteful, barren luxury, and cushions to plump and plants to pamper and Adele flumping around all the time.

Lying awake with Mike on her mind, she found herself reaching back, as she hadn't done for years, to her little place in Via della Scrofa, where the floor tiles were cracked, the bathroom smelled of gas, and if you switched the light on in the dark you usually surprised a cockroach or two skulking round the wall. That was part of the flavor of Rome in those enchanted days, when all her clothes fitted into two drawers plus the narrow space behind a curtain that she had rigged up on a string suspended between two nails.

She could vividly remember the first time she and Mike had made love there, how they burst in, laughing and breathless from running all the way up the stairs, and how suddenly their laughter stopped and, without bothering to find their way to the bed, they took possession of each other there and then, standing up in the dark just inside the door. And afterwards they had started laughing again, at their own impatience and excitement and joy.

She could even remember setting out the two plates for their first breakfast together, the next morning. They were the only two plates she had, white with a green line round the rim. There was no tablecloth; such objects had not yet found a place in her life, any more than saucepans or what she now called morals—which really only amounted to the fear of being devalued by making oneself cheap. It was Luca who had introduced her to that kind of mentality.

"If I have a wife," he had said only the other evening, when they were having dinner with an American client, "I expect certain moral qualities. If not, there is no purpose. She is just an appendix."

"A what?" asked the American, startled.

179

"An addition, useless. Pleasant, but no more."

"Ah," said the American, looking confused.

Robin had sat there and smiled. "Appendage" was the word he meant. She was an appendage to him. He believed in equality, or so he said; but if she was his wife, she must comply with his moral code.

It had taken her years to discover that she was supposed to be a woman he had redeemed, that he seriously believed he had been generous in making her his wife. Yet Luca was not noticeably straitlaced. He considered himself broad-minded and up to date. Ah, but that was the point. It was because he was broad-minded that he had married her. It had taken a bit of swallowing, that idea, but in the end she had learned to accept it, like everything else. Only rarely did she feel a slight bristling of rebellion. Luca was not rapture, certainly, but he was peace, calm affection, placid contentedness. It was comfortable to be protected and serene.

All the same, the sight of him cheerfully dipping bits of cake into his *caffelatte* made her feel oppressively hollow after her sleepless night. She had struggled through to the morning without calling Mike's hotel, but as she watched Luca dressing, her sense of guilt was accentuated by the combination of self-absorption and clumsiness with which he scattered ties and socks here and there in his search for the right ones, tossed yesterday's clothes all over the bedroom floor, considered his waistline in the mirror while fastening his belt, studied a wrinkle, and tried to flatten his bristling curls.

When he asked what she was doing today, she shrugged and said nothing, knowing it did not occur to him that she might do anything but go shopping or see Serena or stay home, none of which interested him as much as the profile of his new coat, which he was busy admiring in the glass. When he turned back to her it was to obtain her approval, as he always did when he had finished getting himself up as the fashionable architect he was supposed to be. He looked more like a teddy bear to her; and that tremulous smile of his meant that he was not really sure the coat fitted or that the tie matched his shirt. She gave him the appropriate nod and, reassured, he kissed her goodbye and left her to clean up the mess as a matter of course. She had been doing it for years without thinking any more of it than he did. This morning, though, it both enraged and disarmed her to see how much he took her for granted.

She sat down at her dressing table and took stock of her few, scarcely noticeable wrinkles. What effect would they have, she wondered, on someone who had last seen her when she had none? She patted on some tonic and tried foolishly to erase them with some cream. Oh, God, what was she doing? Had she, then, made up her mind? She screwed the stopper onto Luca's bottle of cologne and wondered what he would do if he knew she was thinking of phoning Mike and arranging to meet him. He would be amazed, that was sure—deeply hurt, probably. He would not understand.

She ought to have told him right away that she had seen Mike, the minute she got back into the car with the magazines, so that he could shield her from whatever was to come. Her deceitfulness frightened her; it left the door open to a kind of darkness. What was worse, she did not want to close that door.

She loved Luca, she really did. But Mike was something else. The sight of him had wrenched her back to a forgotten dimension of pain, and made her present state of lethargic luxury seem shamefully unreal. She did not want to deceive Luca; but she could not reject Mike. What had happened to him was too heavy a weight on her conscience.

TWENTY

There was a bell ringing somewhere. The alarm bell—that was it. Some poor devil trying to escape.

Ding. Ding. Diiinng!

Mike opened his eyes. The bell went on ringing. When he realized it was the telephone, he sprang up in a panic lest it should stop before he could reach it. In his excitement he knocked over the bedside lamp and had to fumble for the receiver in the dark. By the time he found it he was trembling.

"Pronto," he whispered.

"Mike. It's me." Of course it was her. He knew that long before he heard her voice. "You were asleep."

"No, not really. I was waiting for you to call."

"I tried not to."

"I knew you would."

"I don't even know what to say."

"When can I see you?"

"Oh, Mike."

"You don't want to?"

"How can I?"

"Because of your husband?"

"Well—yes."

"I see. Oh, well, never mind. Are you happy?"

"Yes."

"I'm glad."

There was a silence at the other end. After a moment he said, "Robin?"

"Yes."

"I thought you'd gone."

"I was thinking. Remember Porta San Pancrazio?"

Remember Porta San Pancrazio? How could he forget?

"Be there at eleven."

"But—"

She had hung up.

He retrieved the lamp from under the bed and switched it on. It was a quarter past three.

Robin sat at Luca's desk with her hand on the telephone, wondering what she had done. The voice on the phone was not the voice she remembered. Perhaps she had forgotten what Mike's voice was like. It aroused no emotion in her, only uneasiness.

She crept back to bed and lay still, staring into the night. Luca was a comfortable mound beside her. She reached out to touch his crisp gray hair. He was as trusting as a child.

But Porta San Pancrazio, of all places.

At about five o'clock, Mike gave up the attempt to sleep and went into the bathroom. He felt a compulsion to wash and wash again before meeting her, to try and rinse away the odor of twenty years; and as he watched the water dribble tepidly into the stained, old-fashioned tub, he saw that everything was lost and gone forever; nothing remained but this aching loneliness.

Robin, Robin—why did he long for her so ferociously, so illogically, now that he dreaded having to face her eyes? He looked into the mirror and saw what she would see: a fossil, deprived of fresh air and love, the flesh grown puffy, the skin parched, the eyes dulled by the scarcity of light. But still alive, damn it, still kicking, and that was a miracle in itself. He had survived twenty years without turning into a wall, and he wasn't going to give up fighting now just because freedom fell so far short of his hopes.

He was a fool to have shut himself up in here to nurse worn-out illusions; he had been telling himself that all night, and all yesterday too. Robin was Robin when she was his. She had been someone else's now for fourteen years. What did he want with her?

183

What did he hope she would have to give? He ought to have been out and about, getting on with his preparations, instead of lying around, letting the long wait sap what little confidence he had, with the pangs of hunger sharpening from hour to hour and the manager periodically knocking on the door.

He had made some attempt to reach out from his self-imposed solitary confinement and find someone who might know where Robin lived, but that had only made it worse. None of the numbers in his old book were of any use. All he got was a series of strangers telling him he had made a mistake. The only one who was still in the same place was Oscar Lorenzi. Mike had decided he might as well try phoning him too. Why not, after all? he had asked himself. He's probably dead anyway.

He was not dead, merely unavailable. The switchboard girl had put him through to a secretary, who put him through to an assistant, who politely took his number. But Lorenzi never called back—nor did Mike's name create any kind of stir either there or at Franco's office, which was now called Bernabei Associates. Mike had procured the number from Sora, but when he rang it, a crisply American female voice inquired who was calling and said Mr. Bernabei was in the States.

After that he had given up and lain still on the bed, dozing on and off until she called; and now here he was, with no emotion left except fear, scrubbing and scrubbing away at his skin as if soap and water could wash away the years. He was afraid, that was the truth: afraid of seeing her, afraid of the reality that was about to oust his dearest dreams, and afraid that after all she might not come and he would have lost his only point of contact with her, because once outside the hotel, he would never be allowed back in. He was afraid of leaving this nasty little room, which offered, like his prison cell, some form of protection—and afraid, above all, of facing up to the desolation outside.

When he was ready, he put his few belongings into his suitcase and carried it downstairs, saying he would be back later to collect it and pay the bill.

It was ridiculously early, not even half past six, but he was going to walk all the way to the Gianicolo and it would take him a long time. He could easily go by taxi, of course. It would be less tiring, but it would mean doing things that he could not trust himself to do properly: paying and tipping and collecting the change, with the taxi driver's eyes on him. A bus would be worse, with people pushing and staring at him, perhaps guessing who he was. No, he would make his way there slowly on his own two feet, after first finding a café where he could sit for a while and appease his empty stomach with hot coffee and buns.

By nine o'clock he was more than halfway up the Gianicolo, at the spot where he had parked between two plane trees and kissed Robin for the first time. There was a car there now with a man and a girl in it, only instead of kissing they were quarreling, and Mike resented their sulky usurpation of a place so dear to him. He turned his back on them and sat on the low wall that skirted the side of the hill.

He felt comforted, as he always had, by the sight of Rome stretching out beneath him, so patient and long-suffering and wise. And as he sat there, elatedly contemplating the city, recognizing cupola after cupola like long-lost friends, the air was pierced by a sustained, high-pitched wail:

"Niii . . . nooo . . ."

It was the voice of loneliness and despair, the hollow sound of helpless love.

"Niii . . . nooo . . ."

He could not see the woman. She was over to the left, near the lighthouse, perhaps in the orchard lower down. He could imagine her cupping her hands and straining to make her voice carry from the slopes of the Gianicolo to her man in the prison in Trastevere, below.

"Niii . . . nooo . . ."

For a while there was no answering cry from Regina Coeli, no sign of life behind the bleak rows of windows with their slatted iron screens known as "wolves' jaws" slanting up from the sills, to keep the sunlight from getting in and the men from looking out.

185

The woman was silent. Perhaps she had lost hope of being heard. Then a disembodied howl wafted up the hill from somewhere inside the prison walls.

"Ro . . . saaa . . ."

"Ni . . . no!" shrieked the woman. It was a mixture of joy and rage.

"Ro . . . sa!" The man's voice was a compound of frustration and delight. Mike knew exactly how he felt.

"*Co . . . me stai?*" yelled the woman called Rosa.

How are you? What could the man reply?

"*Be . . . ne! Sto bene! E tu?*"

I'm fine. And you?

"*Be . . . ne!*"

Fine!

All the misery of the woman's gutted life was contained in that one stoic word, that one brave lie. And yet Rome seemed to be smiling, in her placid way. She was accustomed to human pain.

Mike swung his legs off the wall and continued his climb up the hill, to the statue of Garibaldi. The big panoramic terrace was crowded with cars and buses and people and balloons. There was a new ice cream stand over on the left, but the Punch and Judy show beside it might have been the same one that was there in his day. He walked on.

Porta San Pancrazio—there it was. The little trattoria opposite was still there too, and the café next door to it. Nothing had changed except the number of cars streaming from all directions towards Via Aurelia Antica. Mike sat down on the stump in the middle of the archway to wait, suspended between the present and the past. By the time a small white car stopped in front of him, he was lost in a forest of melancholy thoughts.

She leaned out of the window and said, "Hello."

He stood up and smiled. "Hello," he said. He felt completely blank. She opened the car door and he walked round and climbed in. But everything was strange, wrong. It was she who started the car and drove slowly round the Porta San Pancrazio—she, who used not to know how to drive. She was the one who had her feet on

186

the pedals, her hand resting easily on the gearshift, while he, the reckless driver who had scared her once by racing round this very gateway, was now a helpless passenger, crushed by the present day. It would have been better if he had kept his dreams intact and left his memories of them both as they used to be.

Robin had always had a gift for looking cool when her heart fluttered most. She was smiling now, intent on her driving; it was something her hands and feet and part of her mind could do on their own, even if the rest of her was numbed by the shock of Mike's unnatural presence in her little car, the everyday car that was usually filled with bags of food from the supermarket and flowerpots for the terrace and supplies of detergent for the washing machine. Yet this stranger beside her was a lost part of herself.

"Oh, Mike!" she said.

He could not find the strength to say anything at first. Then he murmured, "Where are we going?"

"I don't know," she said. She was driving automatically down the hill. "Where *shall* we go?" She stopped the car. All he wanted was to get out.

"Let's walk," he said.

"Walk?" The idea seemed to alarm her.

"Yes. Or sit somewhere. There, for example." He pointed at the iron rail round the Fontana Paolina. Robin stared at it dubiously, and frowned. Noticing her glance nervously at a passing car, Mike realized that she was afraid of being seen.

"Let's go into the park," she said. "There's Villa Pamphili just up the road."

They found a bench in the shade of a giant cedar, where the long damp grass was dappled bright green with sunlight.

"I don't know where to start," she said at last.

"I know. It's difficult." He turned away and watched a little girl walk by with a puppy on a lead. "It's nice here," he said.

He had never been into Villa Pamphili before; it was not open to the public in his day. He was glad they had come here, where there were no memories, only a distant echo of his childhood in the muted cries of some boys kicking a ball about, and the special quietness that all parks have. It was a good place to sit beside this person who was not really Robin, yet who might have Robin hidden somewhere underneath the new veneer.

"I want to ask how you are," she said. "But even that sounds stupid."

"Tell me about yourself. You haven't changed much, you know. Just—this elegance. That's new. No shortage of money, I see."

"No."

"Do you love him, your husband?"

"Yes."

"That doesn't sound too convincing." He turned to look at her. "Or are you trying to be nice to me?"

"No. I do love Luca. I really do. But it's nothing like it was with us. I'm not just saying that. You know it, don't you? What we had was—"

"So long ago. Wasn't it?"

"Mike, I never forgot you, I swear. Never, never. I'd have waited if—"

"Of course you couldn't wait. There was no question of that. I'm glad you're happy. Honestly."

There was an awkward silence.

"Oh, God, this is awful," Robin blurted out. "It's so hard to talk."

"We don't know each other anymore, do we? I'm not the man you remember. And you're not my Robin. Everything's different. The world is a different place."

"What are you going to do?"

"I have a plan."

"Work, you mean? As an actor?"

"God, no. Are you crazy? Who do you think wants an actor who's been labeled 'murderer'? That's a label that sticks. By now everyone seems convinced I did it, even Sora. Even Beppe's mother, and God knows *she* ought to know better."

"Beppe's *mother*?"

"Yes, I went to see her. The bereaved mother. She keeps it up, too. Not a crack in the armor anywhere."

"Mike, perhaps he *is* dead."

"You, too?" He was shocked.

"No, I don't mean you killed him—of course not, but—"

"You think maybe he died of the plague or something? Or killed himself—to spite me?"

"But how can a man just vanish?"

"That's precisely what everyone has been saying all along. He can't have vanished; I must have killed him. That's the kind of logic that put me in jail for twenty years. But the fact is he *did* vanish. And the only way to prove it is to find him. I've got to find him. Understand?"

"And if you do—what then?"

"I told you, I have a plan."

"What kind of plan?"

"Let's say, to get even. Set the record straight. A kind of poetic justice, if you like."

"Oh, Mike—whatever are you going to do?"

"If I told you, you'd probably say I'm crazy. But don't worry, I know what I'm doing."

"But—after all these years—you can't mean to—"

"What's this? Defending Beppe? Don't you think he deserves to be punished?"

"Not by you."

"Well, anyway, what counts is to find him first."

Sometimes an unexpected image will spring up like a jack-in-the-box out of nowhere, triggered by some devious mechanism in the brain. So it was that the image of Beppe getting ducked in the fountain flashed across Robin's mind, with the same sense of shock it had given her when they showed her the newspaper in the lobby at Alba Films. The other man in the picture, the one who had baptized Beppe the *bacherozzo*, had been anonymous then. At least she had never identified him consciously as Mike, who at that time was still no more to her than a name. Deep down, though, she must always have known it was Mike. Otherwise she could not now have envisaged him—as she did, with terrifying clarity—holding up Beppe's head.

Stop dreaming. That was what he had to do. Stop remembering. Stop mourning what was gone. Even now, after leaving Robin, if only he had still had a room he could shut himself into, he would have lain there for days, clutching at what was left of those threadbare memories, like a child clinging to the ragged remnant of a comforting shawl. It was lucky for him that he could not go back to his room at the Belvedere. It forced him to move, find a new hotel, fetch his suitcase, pay his bill. Practical things, all of them, to help him wake up and come back to life. He had to eat, too, and he was not going to eat in a squalid *rosticceria* or a bar. He was going to walk into a restaurant and order a proper meal. He decided to do that first of all. He was exceedingly hungry and he was walking past La Campana, where the food was good.

A waiter pointed out a place at the far end of the crowded room, and he had to walk the gauntlet down the long aisle between the tables, where, at any moment, someone might point him out or whisper a comment or stare and nudge. No one did. They were all too busy eating and talking to care about him. He sat down and shut his eyes, waiting for his pulse to ease before scanning the room with a certain pride. No one knew who he was. He picked up the menu and ordered *tonnarelli* and some wine. He had taken the first hurdle; now it would not be so hard.

Robin had dropped him off at the traffic lights on the corner of Via Zanardelli, and the first thing he had done was to take out his old address book and cross out Robin Lane. It hurt, but he did it deliberately, to force it into his head that Robin Lane was not at that old number any more, nor at the new number she had scribbled for him on a page torn from her diary, which belonged to a person called Ferrero, a married woman who had been reluctant to give it to him, not sure he could be trusted to use it with discretion and ashamed to ask him not to use it at all.

"It's only so I know where you are," he had said, to reassure her. "I promise not to put my foot in it."

She had agreed, after some hesitation, to meet him again in two days, and had felt obliged to give him a lift back into town, but she had hated every minute of it. He had been conscious of her unconfessed anxiety, especially in the heavy traffic along the river, with all those faces peering out of all those cars, perhaps recognizing her and noticing him. Robin, Robin, he could never have expected this. He had been afraid to find her aged, and she had aged so little that he was all the more shocked by those small things that showed how she had changed: the immaculate shoe on the accelerator, the well-manicured hand. What distressed him most was not the touch of gray in her hair or the barely perceptible wrinkles round her eyes, but the immeasurable gap between them, and the silence.

When he raised his eyes after she had gone, he found himself staring straight across the river at the old Palazzo di Giustizia, the ornately cumbersome building where he had been sentenced to extinction as a man. Even then it was known to be sinking into the ground an inch and a half each year, and now, he heard, it was falling down altogether under its own excessive weight. Robin must have passed it so many times that she no longer connected it with him. It was the nearest point to his hotel on her way home, and she had dropped him there without considering what effect the sight of it would have on him, without remembering, either, that the shortest route from that point to Via della Vite would take him through Via della Scrofa, past her old door. Evidently she did not understand how sore these old wounds still were.

It was up to him to stop brooding and come to grips with the many things he had to do here and now: learn how to drive again, for one, and get a new passport.

The new British Embassy was a frightening place. There were iron bars all round it, and massive gates, all locked except one, which was guarded. There were lavish fountains and well-kept paths, and arrows pointing the way to the scintillatingly modern building, which Mike could only stare at through the railings and hate with all his heart. The old Consulate near Babington's Tea Rooms in Piazza di Spagna was just a small door and a modest room. He would not have minded strolling in there and telling anyone he found inside that he had come about the passport he had lost. But before he could make himself walk through this guarded gate, he had been hovering outside long enough to attract the

191

attention of the gatekeeper, who he imagined was loath to let him in.

The man was not really unkind. His voice was firm but quite soft. It was his job to intercept people at the gate and write their names down on a pass, the stub of which remained on record in his book. He could not know that this kind of thing made Mike turn hot and cold, and that he had to dig his nails into his palms before he could force himself to say "Michele Donadio." It was silly of him, utterly silly, but the fear was ingrained.

He was quickly soothed, though, by the Englishness of the Consular Section, all light wood and sunshine, with a rosy picture of the Queen on the wall and a lot of notices on a board. People often lost their passports, apparently. It was only when he said he had lost his twenty years ago that the girl looked up and blinked. The application form she was handing him stopped in midair.

"Did you report the loss at the time?" she asked.

"No. I've been in jail," he explained.

"Oh, I see," she said pleasantly. It was none of her business where he had been. "Well, you must report it, you know. We need a statement from the police to say you've done so."

"The police?"

"Yes."

"But it was twenty years ago. What do they care?"

"It's their job to look for it."

"You must be joking. They never even bothered to look for the man they said I'd killed."

"I beg your pardon?"

"Never mind. You mean if I don't go to the police, I can't have a new passport?"

She looked puzzled. "It's quite straightforward," she said. There were other people waiting to be attended to. A small white-haired lady with beige kid gloves was tapping her passport irritably on the counter. The girl began to look harassed.

"Forget it," said Mike.

He sat down at one of the tables to study the application form, and saw at once that it would not be an easy form to fill in. "Occupation", for instance. What should he put? "Actor"—or "murderer"? "Ex-convict"—or simply "unemployed"? "Residence" was a word that meant nothing to him any more. He had forgotten what his height was in feet and inches; and as for "Visible peculiarities," which seemed to call for an answer in the plural, it had only the shortest of lines beside it, just enough space for a word like "squint" or "harelip." He was tempted to write down "fossilized" or "ghostly" or even "dead," but he restrained himself and moved on to "Countries to be visited." It said in the Notes for Guidance, "It is to your advantage to state the countries you propose to visit. By doing so you will enable us to advise you about passport problems which may arise in certain countries." His heart warmed to this friendly and explicit style, but he thought it might be unwise to ask which countries had no extradition treaties with Italy. He had no idea when the "Date of departure" would be, and he feared that "escape" might not go down too well as the "Purpose of journey."

"I don't know any of this," he said to the girl, after waiting for her to finish with the people at the counter. This time she gave him a look that said, You again?

"What is it you don't know?" she asked politely.

" 'Passport number.' 'Issued at.' 'Place and date of loss.' 'Circumstances in which . . . etcetera.' I told you, it was twenty years ago."

"Well now, let's see," she said. She was being remarkably patient. "Perhaps it would help if you could remember when you last had it."

"I know it would help if I could remember. The trouble is, I—"

He broke off. His eye had caught the row of marriage banns on the notice board; a vivid recollection sprang to mind. He saw himself and Robin, laughing and happy, walking into the old British Consulate in Piazza di Spagna and slapping down their passports side by side on the counter.

"Hold everything—I've just had an amazing thought." He snatched up the form and told the girl, "There's something I've got to check. Something that might explain everything." Her courteous smile now looked about to crack. "Don't worry," he said. "I'll be back."

TWENTY-ONE

Colors, smells, haphazard snatches of the past kept darting out at Robin throughout the following day, and it was hard to keep going as if nothing had happened, with all kinds of disquieting thoughts crowding in, all kinds of guilt and doubt.

So Mike was back, Mike was actually back; and he meant nothing to her at all. She could not believe that the quiet, sad, middle-aged stranger who had sat beside her in the park yesterday and muttered vague schemes for revenge was the man whose child she had conceived—that distant October day on the beach at Sabaudia. The thought of it brought back memories of the sand on her sunburned skin, and the scratched record of *Les Feuilles Mortes* that had haunted her lonely evenings, later, for years. *Et la mer efface sur le sable les pas des amants désunis désunis désunis dèsunis*—the scratch seemed to have put itself there on purpose to make the record more particularly, painfully hers.

But many years had passed since then, and it was horrible to start lying to Luca now for the sake of a man she no longer loved, no longer knew, after what seemed like a lifetime of harmonious sincerity. No, it was madness: she was jeopardizing her marriage for nothing. She must tell Mike plainly that it wasn't right for her to go on meeting him behind her husband's back. It was too dishonest, and what was more, it wasn't fair to Mike. She had nothing to give him now. The past was the past; he must be made to realize that.

The simplest way was not to go tomorrow. It would be unkind, but it would make him understand. He would know she couldn't have phoned him because he had changed hotels. Yes, but then he

194

would phone *her*. Oh, dear, she couldn't risk that. In any case, the idea of him sitting there waiting all alone appalled her. There was no way out. She would have to go once more and explain it to him, but that must be the end of it.

She parked her car outside the gate of Villa Pamphili and started up the long avenue. She could see him at the far end, on the bench under the cedar tree, and all the way she kept trying to think how to word what she had to say; but she had no sooner sat down than, to her consternation, she discovered there was not a hope of saying it. Mike already took her for granted as much as Luca did. He was looking livelier today and he greeted her eagerly, impatient to spring a question he had obviously been keeping bottled up until she came.

"Do you remember the day we went to the Consulate?" he asked. "Not the first time, for the oath, but the second time, when we got the *nulla osta*, after the banns had been up for three weeks."

She looked at him, disconcerted. The *nulla osta*, the oath, the banns: it all came back instantly, like a splash of sunlight, but the last thing she was prepared for just then was to be plunged once more into the past.

"Don't you remember?" he insisted impatiently.

"Yes," she said. The aura of that day was indelible. She remembered the laughter, the loose yellow corduroy jacket she had on, their passports on the counter, even the piece of paper with the declaration on it to say there was no impediment to their wedding. She knew she had come close to being Mike's wife that day. But all the rest of it was gone.

"It was that day, wasn't it?" Mike was asking her. "It was that very night. What a fool I am not to have thought of it before."

"You know I haven't the faintest idea what you're talking about."

"My passport. It's disappeared. Everything else is there, but not that. Sora swears it can't have been in the flat. What I'm getting at is this. I had it that day, didn't I? I must have, right?" She nodded, mystified. "I couldn't have left it behind at the consulate, could I?"

She shrugged, still unable to grasp what he meant. "I got mine back, so I suppose you did too."

"Right. I put it in my pocket, I'm sure I did. This pocket here." He stood up and thrust his arms into the sleeves of the mac he had been clutching on his lap. "This is what I had on that day, remember?"

He turned up the collar and grinned at her excitedly, and suddenly there he was in front of her, just the way he used to be— in his English riding mac. It looked grayish now, but it had once been a light cream, and it had looked fantastic on him then, with the collar turned up like that, and a silk foulard. It was the ultimate chic in Rome in those days, which was reason enough for paying through the nose for it in Via Condotti when it would have cost a fraction of the price at home.

"Remember?" he said again, because she still had not answered. She was gazing up at the memory of him holding it round her like a cloak as she waded down the Spanish Steps.

"Yes," she said. "I remember it very well."

"Right. I had it on when I was arrested, too. No doubt about that—I had it with me when they let me out. So if I put the passport into this pocket at the Consulate and didn't take it out again in the flat, it ought to have still been in the pocket when I got to Regina Coeli. But it wasn't. They turned everything out and put it on the table in front of me. In the state I was in, I never gave it a thought; and later on I assumed I'd left it at home. However, the night before, the famous night when I went off to look for you-know-who, I must have picked the mac up automatically on the way out, because I distinctly remember throwing it over the back of the seat beside me in the car. And who was in that car later on?"

Robin gasped. "You mean—Beppe?"

"Do you get it now? Remember the fuss they made about Beppe's passport being found under lock and key in his desk? Of course, they said, he *could* have got a false one, but that takes time, and the point was, he vanished into thin air that very night.

But supposing he pinched mine and left his own at home on purpose, to prove he was dead?"

"He wasn't a bit like you."

"Photographs can be changed. It's passports that are hard to come by. You do admit it's quite a coincidence?"

"If it *was* the same night."

"That's why I've got to find out. That's why I need your help. Memory plays funny tricks; you get things twisted round sometimes in your mind. But between the two of us, we ought to be able to reconstruct it, bit by bit."

Robin sat very still for a moment and said nothing. I can't stand this, she thought. To reconstruct it, bit by bit. To reconstruct the torture of twenty years ago, now that, mercifully, she had shaken most of it out of her mind.

"What's the matter?" he asked, with a touch of bitterness. "Am I asking too much?"

"No, of course not. Only—could you tell me just one thing?"

"What's that?"

"Why?"

"*Why?*" Mike laughed and covered his face with his hands. "Oh, my God! Why? Why do I want to find out?"

"I mean, what's the point of going over and over these little things? What difference does it make now, if he took your passport or not?"

"Well, I'm glad you can't understand. I'm glad you don't know what it's like being in prison for twenty years, asking yourself that same endless question. Why? Why am I here? Why won't anyone believe me? Why can't someone find out the truth? Why? For twenty years. Twenty multiplied by three hundred and sixty-five is seven thousand three hundred days, which, multiplied by twenty-four, means one hundred and seventy-five thousand, two hundred hours. Do you want to know how many minutes that is?"

"No! I'm sorry."

"I don't want you to be sorry. I want you to try and imagine what it's like. You can't, I know. No one can who hasn't been through it. But if I tell you there are men who swallow razor blades to put an end to it, it might give you some idea. Twenty years without a woman. Know what that means? Violence. Violence pounding away inside your brain and violence all around you, in the very air you breathe. All that pent-up male energy—do you realize the hatred that comes out? I've seen things I don't want to remember, things you don't even imagine could exist. There's only two ways to survive in all that. Either you switch off and turn into a vegetable, or you find somewhere for that energy to go. A lot of men turn to politics, and they're the lucky ones, the ones that find something to cling to, something to carry them forward. I used to envy them; they had a kind of light inside them. I used to wish I could believe what they believed. But all I could think of was you, and the child, and the fantastic, enchanted life I'd lost and how Beppe had robbed me of it all. And the more I thought about what he'd done to me, the more I swore I'd have my revenge on him one day. And all the time I kept thinking—how, how did he do it? How did he manage to beetle off like that and leave me looking like a mur-derer? I've spent the greater part of a hundred and seventy-five thousand, two hundred hours trying to think how the devil he got away with it, and how I am going to *prove* how he got away with it. It's a funny thing, you know, but even now that I'm 'free' and I can walk about the streets and eat in a restaurant, I still want people to know that they should never have put me inside."

"Please, Mike, stop. Don't you think that's what I want too? Of course I'll help you if I can."

It took him a moment to calm himself. Then he said, "While we're at it, there's one question I'd like to ask you. Just one, no more."

She turned, stung by his tone; but his eyes remained fixed on a young woman who was slowly wheeling a pram along the gravel path. "The baby," he said. "It *was* mine, wasn't it?"

"Mike, how could you ask?"

"I *am* asking. I'd like a straight answer."

"It was yours, I promise you. Of course it was."

"And all that stuff Beppe said?"

"What stuff?"

"You know what stuff."

She flushed. "Mike, for heaven's sake! After twenty years!"

"About time I knew, don't you think?" He closed his eyes, as if dreading her answer. Instinctively she placed her hand upon his, which remained tense, unresponsive to her touch. "Listen," he said, "I've got to know. Did he fuck you or didn't he?"

There. He had come out with it at last, and the brutality of the question shocked them both. Had she had Beppe's penis inside her vagina or not? That was what it boiled down to in the end, and it sickened her to think anything so irrelevant could have decided the course of their lives.

"Do we have to rake up all that wretched old dirt again?" She tried hard not to let her voice sound strained, but it was no use; being evasive was the same as answering yes.

"I'd been hoping there was no dirt to rake up."

"I don't know what you mean by dirt."

"It was you who called it that."

"I think we must be very old-fashioned. No one sets any store by things like that these days."

"Oh, I know I'm twenty years behind the times. And I always was a romantic fool, it seems."

"Don't say that, please!"

"What do you want me to say—'pazienza'? When the one girl in my life I believed in turns out to have been lying to me all along?"

"Mike, that's not fair! You knew perfectly well you weren't the first."

"No, nor the second, nor the third, was I?"

"Look, I'm sorry, but you just can't start nagging me about morals after twenty years. You always knew I'd been in and out of a good many beds, and you never asked whose."

"Not Beppe's. You pretended you'd never heard of him."

"I know I wasn't quite honest with you about that, but I wasn't really dishonest, I swear! There was nothing between us, less than nothing."

"No. Just that when he announced he'd been screwing you, he was telling the plain truth."

"Now you're being beastly."

"Yes, the truth *is* beastly, isn't it? It *is* beastly to look the facts in the face."

"These things are never as simple as they sound. Look, I couldn't tell you about Beppe, honestly. I couldn't bear even to mention his name. Besides, what difference did it make?"

"None, I suppose. Except that what I loved about you most was the fact that you were clean. Clean inside."

"Can you blame me for not wanting you to think I wasn't?"

"No. But I can't help seeing that you weren't the girl I thought you were."

"Just because I'd had Beppe on top of me once or twice?"

"Oh, God! I can't bear to think of it."

"After all these years? Doesn't that just go to show I was right? If you'd known, you might not have loved me."

She knew as she said it that this was exactly the point. He ought to have had the right not to love her; if he hadn't loved her, he wouldn't have spent twenty years in jail.

"I expect I'd have loved you just the same, but I might not have—"

"What?"

He caught her startled look and gave her a bitter smile. "I might not have behaved the way I did," he said.

There was a long silence. Mike stretched out his legs in front of the bench and thought: It's funny, but I still can't believe it, not even now she's told me in so many words. It just doesn't make sense.

Robin eventually found voice enough to ask, "Mike, how *did* you behave?"

"Christ! Are we back to that?"

"I know I shouldn't ask, I shouldn't even wonder, but—there are some things I never did get straight."

"Such as?"

"Well, for instance, after you knocked him out, why on earth did you pick him up and cart him away?"

"Heaven only knows. I was in such a rage, I don't think I knew what I was doing. Talk about seeing red. I saw sky-blue pink, purple, orange, and black. Mostly black. Still, I suppose the main idea was to get a retraction out of him somehow."

"But—if you kind of blacked out like that, couldn't you have—?"

"Killed him?"

"Without even realizing it."

"Oh, for God's sake! I didn't really black out—not to that extent. Christ! You'll have *me* thinking I did it before long!"

"But what did you do with him? Dozens of people saw you blazing down Via Veneto with the megaphone, but not one of them caught a glimpse of Beppe."

"Where do you think he was, then?"

"I know he must have been in the car, but—"

"He wasn't dead, if that's what you mean. I gave him a lift home, dammit! And I'll tell you another thing. As I turned right into Via Venti Settembre, a police car came tearing round the corner in the opposite direction, and I said to him, "Hello! They're in a hurry! Bet they're off to the Diavolo Blu to give me what-for.""

"And what did *he* say?"

"I think he gave a sort of grunt or something."

"Mike, you're making it up. You can't remember him making a sound."

"All right, so he just sat there and kept mum. Having a good hard think, I shouldn't wonder. I'd just been shouting to the four heavens that he was up to his neck in God knows what, so if it was true, he was in a hell of a spot. And as he was lying there racking his brains for a quick way to get out of it, lo and behold, what should he see but my passport sticking out of the pocket of my mac, right in front of his nose."

"If it *was* the same night."

"It was, I'm sure it was."

"How can you be sure, after all this time?"

"Look, let's think for a minute. Let's see how much we can reconstruct. For example, the baby was kicking more than usual that night, wasn't it? I remember you saying it was a *bimbo vivace*."

It came back to her suddenly: Mike rushing to her side and saying, "What is it?" "Only Pan," she had told him, "kicking me black and blue." "With fury, probably," he had said, his own fury rising again. Yes, it was that night, she was sure.

"You're right," she said. "It was the doctor who'd said that, about the *bimbo vivace*. And do you know what I told him when he said it? I can hear myself now. Of course! It was that same afternoon because I said, 'I expect he's glad his mother's getting married. They gave us the *nulla osta* today.' "

Mike turned to her and grinned. "There. See how easy it is when there's two of you?" Now it was he who put his hand on hers. It was a possessive hand, and for a moment it bewildered her, though she didn't have the heart to remove her own.

"Even so," she said, pretending not to notice, "what does it prove?"

"Nothing yet—except to me. But they're going to have to start checking now. And if that passport ever turns up, I want to see what they'll say."

"But still—he'd have had to think pretty fast, wouldn't he? To have staged all that in so little time?"

"Oh, he always was a fast thinker, Beppe was. Must have had it all worked out in no time. Because when we got to the Island, he said, cool as a cucumber, 'You can drop me off here, if you like. Save you going all round.' "

"Oh, Mike, he couldn't have."

"He certainly did. He even muttered *'buona notte,'* the little rat. Slunk off across the bridge—with his tail between his legs, so I thought. Oh, he certainly pulled a fast one on me that night."

TWENTY-TWO

A bicycle bell woke Mike to a strong smell of coffee. He could hear shuffling feet on cobbles, and voices, and cars—all the daytime noises of a small Roman street. For a moment he lay floating in space, not knowing where he was, in the present or the past. Then he propped himself up and saw his suitcase on the bench, and on the table a bag of cherries with the remains of some bread and cheese and prosciutto he had bought last night. He remembered moving to the Albergo Girasole, which was remarkably similar to the Hotel Belvedere, except that the bathroom was a little less antiquated and the room a little more agreeable—or at least he felt disposed to find it so. He had slept late for the first time. For some reason that still escaped him, he felt good.

But of course! He had found the key to Beppe's disappearance. And to think it had been there as plain as porridge all the time.

He got up and stretched and leaned out of the window. It was not yet eight, but Via Mario de' Fiori was already wide awake. The smell of coffee came from a bar across the road, full of people clamoring for espressos and cappuccinos on their way to work. There was a tang of fresh bread in the air too. He saw a baker's boy go by with a huge basket on his head piled high with rolls, and it stirred in him a sensation he had not felt for many years: the germ of a new taste for life.

He sat down at the table and smoothed the crumbs off the application form he had brought away from the Embassy. He had started trying to fill it in last night and found himself stumped by a bit on the very first page: "Please enter below details of next of kin or other person to be notified in the event of an accident."

Who should be notified? Who would give a damn if he died? Robin? Hard to tell. Memmo? Perhaps. Dear Memmo, I hereby name you next of kin. *"Cazzo!"* he'd say. That was what Memmo said to most things, good or bad. One terse, masculine, five-letter word. Obscenity was his armor, it was his way of staving off tears. He couldn't stand the way men cried in prison, he said. That thought reminded Mike that the address of the prison would not look too good on the first page of the form.

So who was left? His relatives in Anticoli? Uncle Gino and Uncle Vito and Aunt Rosa and Aunt Pasqualina and all those nameless, faceless cousins of his who had screamed "Michele!" and wept tears of joy when he first arrived? They had long since wrapped themselves in a shroud of family shame, believing every word in the newspapers they painstakingly read out loud to each other, taking the verdict of the court for gospel truth. Mike had written to them swearing that they had nothing to be ashamed of other than the callous indifference of their fellow men, but such words were lost on them. Uncle Gino had done his duty by visiting him a few times at the beginning, but after he was sent away from Rome to another prison, he never saw or heard of any of them again, except for a brief note to tell him his mother had died.

He was a kind man, Uncle Gino, but he lacked imagination. His conception of prison was an abstract one, like so many other people's, limited to the just and proper removal of dangerous criminals from everyday life. He had never for a moment tried to picture to himself the anguish of four walls perennially enclosing the existence of a man who was more or less the same kind of animal as himself. If he had, he might have asked someone more skilled than himself with a pen to tell Mike in gentler words that his mother was dead, or at least to tell him a little more.

Nothing had made Mike feel more helpless, more unutterably trapped and confined, than the thought of that lonely, ignorant woman being faced with the news that her son was a murderer. He had done his best to explain in a letter what had happened, but in her reply, if reply it could be called, she made no reference to what he had said; he never knew whether she understood it or not, whether she accepted or rejected his word. All her letters were disappointments. She was even less literate than Uncle Gino, and the few straggling sentences she managed to write down told him nothing. *"Caro Michele, spero che mangi abbastanza. Chi ti lava la biancheria? Hai una buona maglia di lana?"* Did he have enough food? Clean underwear? Warm woollies? These were her worries, the things that came within her scope of comprehension. Between the lines, he thought he could see her desperately trying to grasp what kind of place he was in, and who was with him, and whether he had a proper blanket on his bed. The rest was too black and unimaginable for her to contemplate. What he had done, what had been done to him—she closed her mind to all that, so as not to be annihilated by the weight of it.

Uncle Gino had no idea how cruel it was to be inarticulate. When Mike wrote to him, begging to be told how his mother had died, the letter he received in reply was even briefer than the first: *"Povera Elsa. E' morta di crepacuore."* Was it true? Had she really died of a broken heart? Or of a heart attack? Or had she, like one of her plaintive, useless little candles, gone on burning down and down in a long, unheard prayer until she quietly guttered out?

It was years ago, all that. For the moment what counted was that to all intents and purposes he had no next of kin. So, underneath "next of kin or other person to be notified in the event of an accident," he wrote: "Robin Lane Ferrero." Under "Relationship (if any)," he wrote: "Love."

Then, turning to page four, under "Circumstances in which passport was lost," he wrote: "Stolen from my coat pocket by Beppe Palazzo." And under "Place and date of loss," he wrote: "In Alfa Romeo owned by Michele Donadio. While driving from Via Veneto to Isola Tiberina," followed by the exact date and hour.

You can't be more accurate than that, he thought. Now let's see what the police are going to do.

He had to brace himself to cross the threshold. There was something about the dust on the floor, the stains on the walls, the bleakness of the rooms that brought a sudden flush of sweat to his hands and face. But his heart gradually stopped thumping once he had made himself say *buon giorno* to the first policeman he met inside, and obtained a civil *buon giorno* in reply. The policemen in the room he entered were all young. When he gave his name it made no impression on them, and to his relief no one asked to see his identity card. Indeed there was no reason why they should, since he introduced himself as a British subject who had lost his passport. The only trouble that arose was in connection with the date. He must mean—

"No, I mean what I say. But if you think it sounds silly, let's forget the date and say it's lost and that's all."

"How come you didn't report it earlier?"

"I've only just found out."

He sounded so casual that the men were floored. They could all see that what he was saying made no sense, but for the moment none of them could think what was wrong with it.

"It was stolen, actually. And if any of you want a chance to deserve promotion, here's a case it might be worth your while to solve."

"You mean you expect us to find it? After twenty years?"

"Not it. Him. The man who stole it. Or don't you care?"

The men looked at each other and raised their eyebrows.

"All right, forget it. I was told to report it and I have. Okay?"

"**R**elationship (if any): Love."

The girl at the Embassy frowned when she read this. Her pencil hovered over the word "Love."

"Mr., Mrs., or Miss?" she inquired, perhaps to gain time.

"Mrs.

She inserted this in brackets before Robin's name.

"*Not* a relative, I take it?"

"No."

She crossed out the word "Love" and replaced it with "None."

"Why did you do that?"

"Because you say she's not a relative. There is no relationship between you." She spoke carefully, as if to someone whose grasp of English was poor.

"Oh, yes, there is. Exactly what I put. A very deep relationship of love."

At least there was. Where had it gone? he wondered. Where did love go to? Where did the present go to when it turned into the past? And solid facts when they turned out to be fantasies, and memories that turned inside out?

The girl behind the counter was staring at him in alarm. Meeting his eyes, she hastily averted hers to the application form, catching sight, as she did so, of "Purpose of journey," beside which he had written in the word "Fun." Her pencil wavered disapprovingly for a second; then she decided to dismiss this frivolity with a shrug. Nor did she make any comment on what he had written under "Circumstances in which passport was lost or destroyed"; and since she was by then inured to his extravagance, her face remained impassive while she read what he had written under "Supplementary information":

"Beppe Palazzo vanished that night and was never seen again. Police say he's dead, killed by me. I say he stole my passport and used it. Ergo, missing passport is vital clue. *Kindly take steps to track it down!*"

She may have blinked after reading this. She certainly glanced round the room to make sure she was not alone. Comforted by the serenity of an African priest quietly filling in a form by the window, she briskly clipped the photographs to his form and said, "Right." She even managed a kindly smile.

"You will try and find the old one, won't you?"

"Well, I'm afraid I—"

"Now listen, this happens to mean a great deal to me. Look, I've written it all down here."

Perhaps he had raised his voice a little, or allowed a shade of menace to creep into his tone. The girl dropped her smile as sharply as her pencil.

"I think you'd better talk to someone else," she said in an altogether harsher voice. She retreated hastily through a door at the back of the room, and Mike heard some whispering outside. Then a pleasant voice said:

"Would you like to come this way, Mr. Donadio?"

The owner of the voice was extremely sympathetic. He took Mike into his private office and listened gravely to the grim tale he had to tell.

"I see what you mean," he told Mike in the end. "Yes, I do quite see what you mean. But as for trying to track it down, at this stage—" He shook his head.

"Isn't there a record somewhere of the passports issued?"

"Indeed there is. At the Foreign Office. But as you didn't report the loss, all they'll have on yours is that it's expired. Unless—"

"Unless?"

"Unless it has been renewed by someone else." He smiled. "That's hardly likely, is it? Even assuming that your theory is correct."

"You never know. Anything's possible. Supposing he did try—to renew it, I mean. What were the chances of his getting away with it?"

"In theory, very slight. But as you say, anything's possible."

"So all you've got to do then is ask the Foreign Office."

"We can check, certainly. But frankly, I—"

"*If* it was renewed," Mike cut in, brushing aside the man's doubts. "If, and above all where. That's what I need to know. Where he went."

"Let's hope he's not too far away," Memmo had said. "Be expensive if he is." Complicated, too. To make his plan really work, Mike needed Beppe here, in Italy, which meant that if he was somewhere else, as was more than probable, he would first have to be brought back. According to Memmo, it wouldn't be hard to make an arrangement with some "friends," so that one dark night Beppe got a bonk on the head and ended up in a box on a plane. It had been done loads of times. "Remember that Israeli spy they nearly shipped off to Cairo in a trunk?"

" 'Nearly' is the word," Mike had objected. "Didn't he wake up and start shouting for help before they even got the trunk on the plane?"

"We'll make sure your chap doesn't."

"I don't want him turning up dead. That would spoil everything."

"All right, we'll find another way. There are plenty of ways. Let's just hope he's not in South America, that's all. Cost you a fortune, that. In fact, it'd pay you to go and fetch him yourself."

"How about a cable: 'MOTHER DYING COME AT ONCE'? Don't you think that would bring him back fast on his own two healthy legs?"

Memmo had looked shocked. *La mamma* was sacred even in his book of rules, and such treachery would never have entered his head. He preferred to ignore the idea entirely and quickly suggested something else: a coffin, for instance—that was a well-tried method that always worked.

Mike let him talk. Who could stop him, anyway? He came up with new idea every day, and they all had the same drawback: they depended entirely on the help of "friends," which was the kind of help Mike was determined not to use. There was going to have to be one exception, he knew, one service he could not do without. But apart from that, he had no intention of falling into the oldest trap of all, getting help from the wrong people and landing straight back inside.

So far, he had avoided looking them up, those old friends from Porto Azzurro and Regina Coeli and Trento and all the other places of punishment he had been shuttled round to over the years. He had not even kept his promise to go and see Memmo's wife. He felt like a louse about that, but he knew too well what the dangers were. At Porto Azzurro, Memmo had been his one stalwart companion, but to take up that relationship outside was a commitment in itself.

In any case, he had his own ideas about how to get Beppe back. What counted most was to be ready when that moment came. It was time to get moving, for God's sake, to start coping with all the things he had been putting off, like learning to drive again; he felt ready for that now. When he came out of the Embassy, he walked straight across the road and enrolled for lessons at a driving school.

It was only after that, when, in the fading light, he set off slowly along Via Venti Settembre with nothing but a lonely evening ahead, that he found he could no longer keep his mind off yesterday's talk with Robin, nor stop himself from wondering what the admission she had made was going to mean to him.

It had struck him hard then and there, but like the shock of a cudgel on a man in armor, it had had no real effect. The Robin he had loved was too firm a fixture in his consciousness for him to reverse his conception of her overnight, no matter what she had done or said or left unsaid.

What did confuse him was what she had become. He had no idea what went on in her mind nowadays, not even whether she wanted to see him or not, and if not, why she did see him. Out of pity, was it? Or guilt? Or the plain inability to say no?

People change when you're not there to watch them. You think you've got them trapped in your mind and they slip away out of reach and turn up different, and then you wonder: Are they different now from the way they were, or did I never know what they were really like? Or were they always changing even before, like actors first in one role, then in another?

It was the hardest thing to get used to again, the fluidity of things in this free, living world. In there, in the sheltered nowhere land that had been his habitat for so long, you could fix your memories the way you wanted them, invent your own past, establish the facts to suit yourself and keep them constant that way in your mind. You had to, to survive. Because reality got lost in the end, and the only consolation was that the pseudo-reality you created to replace it had a permanence that was dangerously lacking outside, where the truth was forever slipping and turning and eluding your grasp.

TWENTY-THREE

They were having supper at La Maiella. Three tidy couples talking about the usual old stuff. Food, mostly. The relative merits of crêpes *alla ricotta* and spaghetti *alle vongole* and such ill effects as these and other delicacies might have upon the liver, bowels and blood. Serena gently pointed out that *vongole* are bad for hemorrhoids; and her husband, Alberto, who knew this perfectly well, pouted at his craving for their forbidden succulence and muttered a skeptical *"Mah!"* as he stared wistfully at the menu. Luca turned to Robin, who was far away from all this, more than twenty years away.

"Roberta?"

"Oh, anything. The same as you."

Against the cheerful racket from the other tables she heard the list of dishes rolling off his tongue: *tonnarelli* and *risotto* and *piselli* and *carciofi* and *melanzane* and *abbacchio* and *capretto* and *mazzancolle* and . . . Can they really want all that food? she thought. Are they really that hungry?

"What's *lattonzolo*?" she asked when he had finished.

"Suckling pig."

"Ugh!"

Serena and Elena had put their heads together for a session about domestic help and schooling. That was all they ever seemed to talk about. That and the price of meat and skirt lengths and heels and hair. The men, meanwhile, were discussing cars or some such tedious thing, and Robin began to float in a sea of reflections of her own.

Her last talk with Mike had had a curious effect on her, as if she had shaken a kaleidoscope and watched the particles settle back into a different shape. Since then she had felt her values shifting slightly; blurred images were crystallizing in her mind. There was a new image too, the one that Mike had evoked of Beppe slinking off with his tail between his legs after being knocked about and made a fool of, which reminded her, for some reason she could not fathom, that Beppe used to send her flowers. She thought of him smiling at her in his black hairnet and calling her his darling. And she wondered why she had loathed him so much.

Above all, as she crumbled bits of bread on the orange table-cloth between sips of Pinot Grigio, she was trying to think what was wrong with Mike's theory of the passport. She knew it had all been thrashed out at the trial; there had been all sorts of reasons for presuming that Beppe must be dead—one in particular. What was it?

All at once the men raised their voices in that way they had, as if they were all about to stand up and hit each other, when in fact they were having a peaceful discussion about the price of a house Enrico could not afford to buy.

"Non posso firmare cambiali, io!" Enrico shouted. *"Lavoro in banca, io!"*

In banca—that was it! The headline sprang out at her from the past: *Il Conto in Banca.* What it meant was not so much "the bank account" as "the final proof."

She stood up and said, "I'm cold. I think I'll get my coat," and slipped away towards the cloakroom before any chivalrous man could offer to fetch it for her. The telephone was in the cloakroom. She put her coat over her shoulders before asking for a *gettone* and hurriedly looking up the number of Mike's hotel.

"Ciao," she said, turning her back to the door in case anyone came in.

"Robin!"

"I want to ask you something. What was it the bank manager said at the trial about Beppe's money?"

The question took him by surprise. He paused before asking, "You mean about it all being left in the bank?"

Yes, that was it. No substantial sum had been withdrawn near the time he disappeared. Either before or after.

"And there was something about the checkbooks too."

"They were all found in his desk. Intact."

"Are you going to be there for a bit?" she asked.

"All night." He laughed.

"I'll call you back."

When she returned to the table, no one took any interest in the length of her absence. They were all intent on the second course.

"Enrico," she said in a casual tone, "if you leave a pile of money in the bank when you die, what happens to it?"

They all turned to look at her in astonishment.

"Why do you ask that?" asked Luca, not pleased.

"Oh, nothing. It was in a book I was reading—it just struck me, that's all, the fact that Enrico works in a bank and would know."

Enrico was delighted to show off his expertise. "If there's no will," he said, "eventually it will go to the heirs."

"What heirs? Who?"

"Sons, brothers, sisters, wife, mother—"

Mother. But of course!

A plate of suckling pig appeared in front of her.

"Oh," she said. "I'm not really hungry." Luca was watching her with concern. She looked up at him and asked, "Would you mind if I went home?"

"Home?"

"I've got such a headache. I think it must be flu."

The others stopped arguing to turn and look at her again.

"Do you want me to take you?"

"No. I'll get a cab."

Luca was too surprised to reply. She had never done anything of the kind before, and it amazed her how easily she got away with it. Looking suitably wan, she said good night—without kissing any-one, in case it was flu—sauntered round the corner to the taxi stand in front of Passetto's, and gave the name of Mike's hotel.

It was an extraordinary thing to do, in the circumstances. When she came to her senses briefly in the taxi, she perceived that she was diving headlong into every kind of trouble—and for almost no reason except that some demon seemed to have crept up behind her and given her a push.

So here she was, slipping the night porter a ten-thousand-lire note to let her go upstairs with no questions asked. It was melodramatic and exhilarating, but silly beyond belief.

She was not sure herself what she wanted, really, except perhaps to find out if she was still alive. But it was true that the dullness of the evening she had left behind, the crass mediocrity of the innumerable evenings exactly like it that stretched behind her into an inconceivable number of years, had all at once made Mike seem more important than anyone else. In a way, of course, it was the same old guilt thing again, the feeling that Mike had to be helped, whether it suited her or not, even if it meant flying to him at this most unsuitable of moments, risking discovery and an unholy row, knocking at his bedroom door after ten at night, and unintentionally giving him all the wrong ideas.

He peered out suspiciously through the crack in the door, still buttoning the trousers he had evidently just pulled on. She had caught him in his undershirt—a dingy one at that—and he looked more embarrassed than pleased.

"Robin!" That was all he could say at first. He did not even move when she walked in past him.

"I know it's mad," she apologized. "I just had to see you." Oh, God! she thought. Mad is the word.

The room was awful, and she saw at a glance, from the dent in the rumpled bed strewn with books, the shoes and socks on the floor, and the shirt dangling from a chair, that she had barged into the full squalor of his solitude. He must have felt exposed.

Then he had his arms round her and her face was pressed tightly against his chest, and as she said to herself quite coldly, This is idiotic, he asked, "What about your husband?"

His fingers were tense on her back, reluctant or perhaps afraid to move.

She murmured, "Don't worry. He won't be home for an hour at least." And thought: Oh, Lord! That sounds as if I mean we've got an hour for you know what. Nothing was further from her thoughts.

Physically, she had rarely felt more detached than she did at that moment, or less inclined to be unfaithful to her husband. But the room was small and she could not help being uncomfortably aware of the bed. Now what have I got myself into? she asked herself. And she went on holding him because it seemed to be the only thing to do—just to stay where she was and see what happened next.

They stood and held each other like that for some minutes. But there was no rapture, only the alien texture of unfamiliar skin. Mike told himself: I've got her in my arms. But she did not arouse him. She was a comfortable thing to hold on to; it was good to inhale her scented warmth; but she was too crisp and glossy to be his. Or perhaps there was nothing left in his parched body to be aroused.

"We're still the same people," she said, after a while. Which was exactly the opposite of what she was thinking.

"I'm not," he said, and drew away from her.

She turned aside as he started putting on his shirt. The bed was not three feet away, sordid as only a cheap hotel bed can be, and to disguise her awkwardness at the sight of it, she picked up the book he had left face down on the pillow. It was *Il Mestiere di Vivere* by Cesare Pavese, of all things. They had bought it together, that winter; and they had found something in it that applied to them, as they always did in everything, even in Pavese's gloom. She had scribbled a translation of it on the flyleaf, and there it was still, in her own candid handwriting, like an omen:

> Nothing is like the rest, the past. We start again all
> the time.

Was it a good omen, or bad?

"I found that at Sora's," he said, "with a lot of other relics. Like this." He picked up her breakfast cup and pulled off the tissue paper to show it to her.

"Oh," she said, transfixed by its innocence. "I'd forgotten that."

He stared at her in her black silk blouse adorned with a long gold chain, and thought of the barefoot, laughing girl whom he had

215

rolled on the floor and recited poems to, in front of the fire.

She had sat down on the edge of his bed and seemed to be expecting him to make love to her, as if the years in between had left no trace, as if it were all as easy and translucent as before. He wondered if he ought to tell her bluntly that it was no use.

"I never did get to have breakfast with anyone else," he said. "You did, though."

"Not the same kind. We don't have any stairs to fall down. Nor even a fireplace."

"You have a bed, though, I daresay."

"Yes." A very expensive bed, as a matter of fact, made of leather, with an equally expensive cover of patchwork fur. "Rather a horrid one, actually," she said.

He smiled. "You'll be telling me you don't make love with your husband next. But you do, I suppose?"

"Sometimes. Not that often. And you know, when you've been married for years, you—"

"What?"

"You just do it. Like cleaning your teeth. I can't remember what it used to be like."

"I can."

"Oh, Mike—it was another world we lived in then. And who-ever wakes in England—remember?—sees one morning unaware, that the something bough is in tiny leaf and the something—oh, dear, you see? I've forgotten everything."

> " 'Sees, some morning, unaware
> That the lowest boughs and the brushwood sheaf
> Round the elm-tree bole are in tiny leaf,
> While the chaffinch sings on the orchard bough
> In England—now!' "

"You remember every word."

"Yes."

She held out her hands spontaneously then, and he moved towards her because it was only natural that he should.

It was only natural, too, that he should fail.

"I'm sorry," he said in the end. "I ought to have known."

"It doesn't matter. That wasn't what I came for, you know."

Mike lifted his head to look at her. "Wasn't it?"

Oh, God, she thought, was it?

It was easy to say it was not this she had wanted, not this clumsy, embarrassed tumble on a sordid, untidy bed, but if she had not wanted *anything*, would she have run the risk of coming here in this breathtakingly unreasonable way?

He had dropped back onto the pillow and was staring at the ceiling. Impulsively she turned on her side and reached out to stroke the light crop of hair on his chest, the hair that was once beautifully black and had now turned gray.

"Recite me something, like you used to," she said. "Let me hear your voice."

"Eh, my voice," he said, with a wry smile.

"You know how I used to love it," she said. "Your voice and this." She ran a finger gently over his sex, which refused to stir.

"Well, leave that alone now," he said, pushing her hand aside. "It's no good any more."

"Don't say that. It's too soon, that's all. We're close again, that's what counts. Come on, recite me something special. I'll have to go in a minute."

He caught hold of her hand and kissed it.

" 'Thou art so true,' " he murmured, turning towards her:

" 'that thoughts of thee suffice
To make dreams truths and fables histories;
Enter these arms, for since thou thought'st it best
Not to dream all my dream, let's act the rest.' "

Smiling, he opened his arms wide, and before she knew it, she had thrown herself into them. Inexplicably, she found she had tears in her eyes.

"You're still the same," she whispered.

"If only I were."

"Doesn't it make you feel kind of tranquil, to know I can touch you here and we don't mind if nothing happens?"

"*You* don't mind."

"I don't mind at all. This is what matters, just being here like this. Not, you know—"

"Fucking?"

"Yes. Honestly." He gave a kind of snort. "There, you'll laugh in a minute. Then I'll really know it's you." She pulled herself up and glanced at her watch. "Oh, damn! Now I must go or I'll be found out."

She kissed his forehead quickly and got up, straightening her clothes. He propped himself on his elbow and watched her run a comb through her hair. All at once he badly wanted her to stay.

"Will you come back another day?"

"Yes." She turned back towards him and, to her surprise, the way he was looking at her made her, too, wish she could stay. But she knew she had been there much too long as it was.

"I almost forgot to tell you what I came for," she said.

"What was that?"

"Something I've just found out. About Beppe's money. It was the money thing that clinched it, wasn't it? More than the passport?"

"There was a lot of fuss about it, but I never could see why. A chap like Beppe was bound to have funds in Switzerland or somewhere."

"Still, to go off and leave all that money behind—that made a big impression. There was a lot, wasn't there?"

"Apparently. They wouldn't say how much, of course."

"And people said no one would just go off and leave it like that. Well, the point is that if Beppe was dead, I mean if he was supposed to be dead, all his money would have gone to his mother in the end. He didn't need to take it out of the bank. He could have got it from her."

Mike was stunned—above all, by the fact that he had never thought of this himself.

"What made you suddenly think of that?"

"There was someone having supper with us who works in a bank, and all at once it went click. It's so obvious, isn't it? It's amazing the way things escape you when they're right under your nose."

"The old bitch. Of course, she was in it up to her neck."

"Isn't there some way to find out if she transferred any money abroad?"

"Like asking every bank in turn?"

"The police could find out, couldn't they?"

"A fat lot they care. They'll look pretty silly if Beppe turns up now."

"What happened to her husband?"

"He died, years ago. It was in the *Messaggero*. I always kept an eye on the deaths."

"Just think, though, all these years, pretending Beppe's dead. How can she keep it up?"

"She's got to, hasn't she?"

"She must know where he is, too."

"You bet your life she does. But she's not letting on."

"We'll have to watch her, that's all."

"We?"

"Yes, yes, I'm in this too. Of course I am. But I must dash now, really."

She had reached the door and he still had not moved. She darted back to the bed and kissed him quickly, and ran a hand through his gray hair. "Oh, Mike, it is you, isn't it? Say 'buttercups.' "

"Buttercups."

She laughed. "I'll phone you tomorrow."

TWENTY-FOUR

It was almost midnight when Robin reached home, and by then she was breathless with panic lest Luca had arrived there first. She had been racking her brain all the way to think of an explanation that sounded remotely plausible, and when she opened the front door and found blessed darkness inside, she could have shouted with relief. But she had barely had time to scramble into bed and switch off the light before he came in, and she was still trembling when he bent over and whispered, "How do you feel?"

"Better, thank you," she told him, and it was the truth. She felt better in every way once he was there beside her again and she could dismiss the madness of the previous hour from her mind. Mike's buttercups were ephemeral compared with Luca's weight in the bed. Comfortable, solid, monotonous Luca—the last thing in the world she wanted to do was hurt him. But when you have a duty to two people, you're bound to be a bit dishonest with one of them. Or both. Thank goodness, though, she had not been unfaithful, not to Luca anyway. That was one comfort at least, even if she did know she had no call to pat herself on the back for it, and that in any case it was not what mattered most. The real betrayal was meeting Mike in secret and deciding to leave Luca in the dark. But then, after all, she had never really stopped being Mike's.

It was a puzzle, this duplicity of hers; she was still grappling with it when she fell asleep at last, and when she woke, it was to the certainty that she had been split in two.

There were all the usual morning chores to be done: pulling up shutters, boiling milk, sewing a button on Luca's coat. Safe, boring little chores that should have meant life was going on the same as before—when it wasn't. Nothing was the same as before.

Her imitation of a dutiful housewife was nothing but deceit—which she accentuated still further by pretending to take two tablets of Novalgina Chinina and telling Luca that it was probably the two she had taken the night before that had stopped the flu from developing, if flu it was. "It may have been something I ate," she added, not wanting to have to go on taking the tablets for days. "I'm really quite all right today."

"Stay in bed anyway. I won't be in for lunch, so you can take it easy."

"*Va bene*," she said, liar that she now was.

Instead, that very morning, she started watching the Contessa, an enterprise that turned out to be harder than it looked in films. There is a limit to the number of times one can walk up and down a short stretch of road without attracting attention; especially when it is populated only by legitimate idlers, such as a little old man in a yachting cap, minding parked cars, and a *portiere* lolling expectantly in a doorway. About the sixth time round, Robin became aware of their inquisitive eyes and tried to cover up by taking an intense interest in Spagnoli's window full of knitwear on the corner—very pretty too, she might have thought it, if she had not had her head full of the old woman behind the closed shutters across the way, barricaded in with her precious knowledge of where her son was to be found.

Beppe had shown Robin a photograph of his parents once: his mother small and plain, stiffly self-assertive; his father, Umberto Palazzo, a lanky soldier about to embark for Eritrea, where he was killed. Beppe was ten at the time. His mother, left penniless but unflinching, had had to find ways to earn money enough to keep them both. Robin recalled the glow of adoration in his voice when he told how she had taken a humble job in a dress shop and fought her way up to the management of a high-class boutique. As if no other woman had ever gone out to work for a living, or put up with hardship during the war. To listen to Beppe, you would have thought the war was just one woman's fight to protect her child. Nothing mattered to her but him: how to feed him and keep him safe from the Germans and the Fascists and the Communists and the Allies alike—which she did, triumphantly, by keeping him dressed as a monk for the greater part of the time and hiding him, when the need arose, on the roof.

Beppe had told Robin all this, as far as she recalled, in bed, and since it did not interest her much, she had flicked it straight to the back of her mind. If only it had thrust its way to the fore again at the time of Beppe's disappearance, it might have offered a vital clue to the Contessa's role.

Robin remembered her sitting there, tight-lipped and tense, at the trial—so convincing a picture of a mother whose son had been killed that she was taken to represent the living proof of Beppe's death. A bereaved mother is a holy thing in Italy. Her hatred of the murderer smoldered in her visibly, day in and day out. No one dared suspect her of conspiracy. No one dared suspect that her bereavement was faked; indeed, in a way, it was not. Beppe was gone and could never come back, so, dead or alive, she had lost him all the same, and it was Mike she had to thank for that. No wonder she had seemed to hate him. Robin could see her now, a woman as powerful as she was petite, determined to do battle with every man, woman, and thing that threatened her son, ready to live in seclusion for twenty years to prove that he was dead. One thing was sure: unless he really was dead, she must keep in touch with him somehow.

Robin's gaze must have clouded over in her reverie and aroused the suspicion of the people inside the shop, who—she realized with a jolt—were peering out at her in some alarm, as if wondering whether she was planning a smash-and-grab. She quickly pulled herself together and crossed the street to throw a desultory glance at a shop on the other side. Feeling too conspicuous by then to go on loitering in Via Lazio, she went round the corner into Via Veneto and sat down to order a coffee at one of the tables outside Carpano. This is hopeless, she thought, standing up after a while and strolling to the corner to take a peek. I could hang round here for a week and she might never go out. Come to that, how can I be sure she's in?

There was a public telephone in the café. Robin looked up the number in the book, and dialed.

"Pronto?" said a voice too imperious to be the maid's.

Robin replaced the receiver, imagining, as she did so, the click at the other end, and the Contessa's pique. Which brought to mind another image—of herself, left holding the receiver in the same way. How many times it had happened when she was alone in Via della Scrofa, after Mike's arrest. Someone had called and hung up, exactly as she had done now—to check, or to gloat, or just to hear her voice—who could tell? It was Beppe she had suspected then. He was a great one for hanging up, anonymously or otherwise, and of course he would have had to be anonymous then, since he was supposed to be dead.

She stood by the telephone, gradually registering the implications of something in the Contessa's tone. Something more than the high-handedness, which was perhaps only a form of self-defense. She was on her guard, that was it; she was anxious, even afraid. Still, that was hardly surprising. Now that Mike was free, she had plenty of reason to feel nervous, and in any case, anonymous phone calls are always a bit frightening. Robin used to hate them herself, and an old woman living alone was entitled to be afraid of a hidden, hostile presence that might easily be a thief, if nothing else. Yet there was more to it than that. There was expectancy, there was—Robin checked herself. Was she running on too fast? Was it likely that such a fierce old harridan as the Contessa De Cleris, who had successfully kept her secret for twenty years, was going to give herself away with a single *pronto*? Likely or not, she had. That was all there was to it. That half-haughty, half-fearful *pronto* had in it an unmistakable note of hopefulness, the pathetic hopefulness of a lonely old woman waiting to hear a beloved voice. Beppe's. The association was inevitable. The telephone—that was it. That was how they kept in touch. How else?

The telephone place was all marble and steel, uninvitingly aseptic and bare. Robin spotted her quarry at once. Filing cabinets, row upon row of them, reaching from floor to ceiling, filled the whole vast room beyond the counter that kept the public at bay. It must be in those cabinets that they kept the long-distance charge cards, with all the towns and phone numbers and even names of people who had been called scribbled on them in pencil. And on one of them, charged to the account of the Contessa De Cleris, might be the phone number of Beppe Palazzo.

Robin approached one of the two young men behind the counter. "I'm the Contessa De Cleris's secretary," she began. The young man instantly smiled, though he had no idea who the Contessa De Cleris might be. "She told me to ask for the long-distance cards, so that she can check her last bill."

"Have you brought the bill with you?" he asked in a breezy tone.

"That's the trouble." She placed on the counter a folder with "phone bills" written on it, and opened it to reveal its emptiness. "I had them all in here, and they must have dropped out on the way." She looked up helplessly at the only one who now had it in his power to come to the rescue. He stared down dubiously at the empty folder.

"I'm sorry. In that case—"

"Oh, please don't say no. She'll be furious. And I need the job so badly. I thought if I could only get the details to give her, she might never find out I'd lost the bills."

"Impossible. It's against the rules."

"I know it is. I hoped you'd be kind and help me."

The young man shook his head sternly and proclaimed in a loud voice, "I'm sorry, but there's nothing I can do."

"Oh, dear!"

"She's lost all the phone bills," the young man explained to his colleague, who had approached, attracted by her distress. He shrugged and said, "*Eh, beh*—" a sound that, in Italian, means, "In that case, alas, there is nothing anyone can do."

"Thanks all the same," said Robin, and she was about to move sadly away when, to her surprise, the first young man jerked his head towards a secluded corner at the far end of the counter.

"You understand that there is no way I can help you," he said softly. "What you want is strictly against the rules."

"Yes, I do know that."

"All I can say is this. If an attractive woman asks me for such a

224

thing, I might risk breaking the rules, if she offers me something sexual in exchange."

His bluntness took her breath away. It was so unexpected that for a moment she could find no words, and he took her failure to protest as a sign that she was amenable. "It's a risk for me, you see," he went on. "I couldn't do it for nothing, could I? But if I stand to get something out of it that interests me, then I might say I'll bring the documents you want to your home—tonight, if you like. What do you say?"

"Oh! Well. It's—" She faltered, trying to decide whether there was any way she could go on bluffing this out.

"No?"

"Oh, no—I mean, yes. I mean—"

"Where do you live?" he asked, getting out a pencil to write it down.

"Via della Scrofa," she blurted out, mentally kicking herself for not having foreseen this in time to decide what address she could give. But how could she possibly have foreseen anything like this? She'd lost her chance now, anyway. By giving her old address— funny how it had popped out—she had botched all hope of getting what she wanted out of him. Presumably he would insist on gaining access to a bed before handing over his part of the deal. Mean- while he was waiting for her to say what number in Via della Scrofa.

"I'm sorry," she said. "I really can't make a deal like that." He put his pencil away and shrugged. "I mean—I'll have to think about it a bit. Do you mind?" He smiled—lasciviously, she thought. He was quite handsome, actually. "What's your name?" she asked.

"Never mind my name. If you want to talk business, you'll find me here every day, from nine till two." He gave her a little wink and turned briskly on his heel, heading for the first of several customers who were now vying for his attention.

"So that's the way they do it nowadays, eh?" Mike laughed. But it was the rest of what she had told him that enthralled him: the prospect of finding out where Beppe was with such unhoped-for ease. And what pleased him just as much as this was the fact that she had gone and tried to pull it off for him on her own. Small wonder that as he sat turning it all over in his head, he was positively beaming with delight.

They were in Robin's little white car, driving up over the hill of the Gianicolo towards Villa Pamphili. She had picked him up at Castel Sant'Angelo this time. She was getting reckless, she realized that; it was a sensation she found she enjoyed.

"It's so obvious too," he said. "It's so easy you could scream."

"*Easy?*"

"Well, God! Just think—there's a card sitting there with his number on it. And you got bloody near it first time round."

"So near and yet so far."

"Don't tell me you plan to leave it at that?"

She laughed. "What do you want me to do? Invite the man home?"

But just then Mike noticed they were driving past the place with the plane trees, the special place where he had paused on his way up the hill the other day. Instead of answering her, he said, "Stop here a minute."

She knew what he meant at once, and without a word, without a second thought, she turned left and parked the car between two trees. "Remember?" he said. She nodded, and gazed out at the familiar roofs and cupolas and towers. Did I really have to go and park the car here? she thought, belatedly aware that she was sitting beside Mike again in the most hackneyed lovers' spot in Rome. Giving him hopes she had no right to give. She reached out quickly to start the engine and escape, and it was then that he said,

"I know! We can book into a hotel."

"We?"

"Yes, Signor Donadio and Signora. You and me."

"Come on, I can't do that."

"Why not? It's so simple. All you need is a suitcase and a free afternoon. Say we book in about three or four, and give your chap an appointment a bit later. Fix it with the porter so he can walk right in—nothing immoral about that, if there's two of us. Only I won't be in the room when he arrives. I'll be up the stairs or somewhere, ready to come pounding in and do an Othello on you in the nick of time."

"Mike, honestly! You can't be serious."

He was; and soon he had talked her into conceding that it might be worth a try. So excited was he at the idea of actually getting his hands on Beppe's number that even if the chances of success were no more than fifty-fifty, she had not the heart to dampen his spirits. True, there were a number of points that hardly bore thinking about from her angle—like the risk of encountering a familiar face just as, suitcase in hand, she was walking into some crummy hotel with Mike; and the improbable moment when the young man knocked on the door and stepped in to collect something sexual from her as arranged. She couldn't believe she meant to let herself in for quite that much. But by now Mike was past such small considerations; he was euphoric.

"Why don't we go and fix it now?" he asked.

"What, *now?*"

The young man spotted her straightaway when she entered the telephone place the second time. She herself was almost too frightened to see, and it took her a minute or two to distinguish him from the other young men behind the counter and perceive that he was not only staring at her with a particularly quizzical smile, but was also making covert signs to her to join him, as before, at the far end. She gained the impression, vaguely, that his colleagues had noticed all this too, and that knowing looks were being exchanged all round, but that may have been her imagination.

"I was thinking" she began. "What you said the other time—"

"Ah?" He raised his eyebrows slightly. "So?"

"So all right," she said lamely.

He looked her over then, a good hard look at the merchandise in hand. "Tell me," he said, producing a memo pad and pretending to note something down. "Do you like making love?"

Oh, hell! she thought. "What's that got to do with it? I understood it was strictly a deal."

"Ah, it's like that, is it? Look, I will tell you frankly—you interest me sexually, even if you are older than me." She glared at him and he gave her a nice, titillating smile. Or rather, *he* thought it was nice; *she* thought it was the limit. "It can be very pleasant, if you want," he said. "But if for you it is exclusively a deal, then, as I am honest, I must say no."

Well, for God's sake, she thought, this chap is really too much!

"You see," he went on, with a very slight change of tone. "After you went away before, I looked up the cards of De Cleris."

Could he, by any wonderful chance, have decided that she was too old to bother with? Could he be about to hand over the lowdown without demanding her bit in exchange?

"That was very kind," she said.

"No. I was curious."

"And so?"

"So now I am more curious still. Why did you tell me you had to check the long-distance calls on the phone bill of the Contessa De Cleris?"

"Why not? Most people check their long-distance calls, don't they?"

"Yes, if they've made any. But the Contessa De Cleris has made none. And very few local calls either."

His look was coolly speculative now. Robin felt goose pimples on the top of her head. She couldn't think of a single clever thing to say.

"And another thing," he said. "I phoned her number and asked to speak to her secretary. Do you know what I was told?"

"Yes. She hasn't one."

"Right. You know I could call the police."

"I don't think I would, if I were you."

"Want to have supper and explain?"

"No, thank you, I don't think I will. Oh, well, sorry about the sex. Some other time, maybe."

She had the suspicion her face was on fire, but at that point she didn't mind about being found out. It merely added a bit of extra fizz to the sensation of relief that had made her suddenly cool as she slid away towards the door.

Mike was as disappointed as might be expected when she told him what the young man had said. Disappointed and puzzled, because it was curious, to say the least, that the Contessa never telephoned anybody outside Rome.

"I hate to say it," said Robin, "but it's beginning to look as if he really is dead."

"Of course he's not dead," Mike snapped. But his voice carried less conviction than before.

"All right then, he's alive and she just doesn't phone him. Perhaps he's in America and it costs too much. Or perhaps he does the phoning himself, to save her paying the bill. That's natural enough, I suppose. We'll have to concentrate on the mail, that's all. She may not phone, but she's bound to write to him, isn't she?"

"What do you want to do next? Go to bed with the postman?"

"No, use my wits, if you don't mind. You men have all got bed on the brain."

TWENTY-FIVE

"There's a lady from the Italian Orphans' Fund," Mariella announced breathlessly one day. "She wants to know if you could let her have any used stamps."

"What do orphans want with used stamps?" snapped the Contessa, her fingertips tingling at the smell of danger. What would *anyone* want with used stamps, for that matter?

"She says they sell them to raise money for food."

"Do they now? Well, you tell her to find something better to sell, and leave respectable citizens in peace."

Shocked by such a blatant lack of charity, Mariella opened her mouth and remained where she was.

"Don't stand there. Do as you're told. And don't open that front door again unless it's somebody you know."

Mariella shut her mouth and disappeared. She was easily bullied, but this time she was not convinced. She knew the old woman was stingy, but orphans are orphans, and what harm could there be in raking up a few old stamps? She made her way back to the front door and whispered through it, *"Un momento!"* Then she tiptoed quickly to the kitchen, pulled out from under the sink a plastic bag full of wastepaper, and rummaged in it for a wad of old envelopes she had stuffed in there herself the day before, after spring-cleaning the Contessa's room. She hurried back to the front door and, without removing the chain, opened it quietly and pushed the envelopes through the crack with an unceremonious "Psst!" The lady outside was evidently surprised by such uncalled-for secrecy, for it took another "Psst!" to make her catch this furtive offering before Mariella shut the door again, only just missing the lady's

230

hand. Not soon enough, however, to escape being caught. The Contessa had opened her own door a crack, not having heard Mariella say what she had been told to say, and she was just in time to see a handful of assorted envelopes disappear into the unknown.

"Mariella!" she hissed furiously. "What have you done?"

The lady outside, who was none other than Serena, stood for a moment in some bewilderment, clutching a handful of crumpled envelopes and listening to the startling torrent of recrimination that the donation of them had unleashed on the other side of the door. She glanced at them to see if any banknotes had inadvertently been left inside. No, they were all empty and, as far as she could see, devoid of value; even the stamps on them were quite ordinary. She nearly rang the bell and handed them back. But on the whole it was easier to beat a retreat; so she hurried away down the stairs and headed for Via Veneto, where Robin was waiting for her outside Carpano.

"What is this story?" she asked, handing Robin the booty and sitting down. "I go there, I do as you say, I get from the maid this treasure of *carta straccia*. Now please I want to know why you ask me to do this stupid thing. And why the lady was so angry about it."

"She was?" Robin looked up from her scrutiny of the envelopes.

"She was screaming at the maid for giving them to me. It's crazy."

Robin studied the envelopes with fresh interest, unspectacular though they were, with typed addresses and Italian stamps, most of them, and postmarks that showed some of them were a year or two old. There was one American stamp, on an envelope of the type used for greeting cards, and one, only one, that was different from the rest, an airmail envelope with a smudged postmark and a Lebanese stamp. And the handwriting—but no, she was letting her imagination run away with her; she could not possibly remember what Beppe's handwriting was like. These silly scraps of wastepaper probably had nothing to do with the Contessa's shouting at the maid. She might have been angry because she had been awakened by the doorbell or disliked the way the floor had been cleaned. Still, it *could* be Beppe's writing. Those elegantly looped and rounded characters were the sort they teach in Italian schools. Pity she couldn't make out the date of the postmark.

"Well? Tell me! What does it mean?"

Serena was displeased, no doubt about that. She was looking at Robin with prim, pursed lips. Robin realized that enlisting Serena's help was as rash as any of the foolish things she had done in the last few days. "I'm off to do something a bit crazy," she had told her. "Want to come?" And Serena, in her good-natured, indolent way, had said, "All right, if you like," and allowed herself to be whipped off to Via Veneto, sat down at Carpano, and persuaded to go round the corner and do what she had just done.

But now she expected an explanation. "Well?" she said again, in a quiet but unusually firm tone. For once she did not intend to let her docility be abused.

"The lady in Via Lazio, the Contessa De Cleris, is Beppe Palazzo's mother."

Serena gasped. It took her some time to get out—a mere murmur—the word "What?"

Robin told her then that Mike was back and that she had been meeting him in secret. She needed to tell someone this, and that was probably why she had brought Serena along, more than because she needed her help to procure some useless old stamps. But relief though it was to let it out, she knew it was unwise of her to put it into words. As long as nobody knew she was meeting Mike, she could go back to being Luca's wife each time without any serious pangs of guilt. True, she did occasionally stop in her tracks with some kind of a twinge, when it occurred to her that she had lain on Mike's bed and fingered his naked sex. But as long as nobody else knew this, she could take a deep breath and dismiss such folly from her brain, and go back to plumping cushions or watering plants or whatever she happened to be doing, and even convince herself that cushions and plants and Luca's socks filled her life the way they had a week before. But when you say these things to another person—even a person you are certain you can trust—you fix them as facts that, afterwards, will always be there to face you, facts that get out into the open air and slip away beyond your control.

How could she be sure that Serena would not tell Alberto, after swearing him to secrecy and trusting him as much as Robin trusted her? Alberto might think it his duty to tell Luca, in some heavy-handed, moral way. Or Luca might ask Serena outright why Robin was so strange these days, and Serena might blush and tell some clumsy tale without looking him in the eye. And supposing later there were developments that Robin would not wish to tell Serena? It would become more and more difficult then to know what to say and what not to. And the very thought of this startled her, because it meant that unconsciously she was considering the possibility of their doing what they had not done the other time. It meant that deep down she knew that if Mike overcame his present state of impotence and wanted her to make love, she probably would not say no.

Yet all the time she was thinking how much better it would be to keep all this to herself, she went on pouring it out, and Serena sat and listened and occasionally muttered, *"Oh, Gesù!"* and finally, when Robin had finished, she asked apprehensively, *"E allora?"*

Robin shrugged. *"Allora*—we've got to find Beppe. Don't you see? To prove that Mike is innocent. He's got nobody to help him except me. I can't let him down."

"Yes, but—"

"You're going to tell me that if Luca finds out, he won't understand. I know. That's why he mustn't find out. I hate being dishonest about it, but there's no other way. I've got a duty to Mike, too. And after all, I'm not doing anything wrong."

Serena looked skeptical. She disapproves, Robin thought, averting her eyes in embarrassment, cross with herself for blurting it all out; and as she turned, she saw a most unexpected thing.

A small upright figure in a purple coat was standing at the bus stop twenty yards up the road, beyond Via Lazio. Robin had not seen her for twenty years and she was shocked to see how grotesquely she had aged, but there was no mistaking the regal bearing, the haughty tilt of the head. When the Number 55 bus arrived, the step up to the back door was too steep for her; two of the passengers had to stoop down and give her their hands so that she could clamber up. Only then, too late, did Robin cry out, "There she goes!"

"Who?" All this agitation was too much for Serena.

"The Contessa De Cleris! Beppe's mother! Oh, my God, I mustn't let her get away."

"Ma sei impazzita?"

The bus was sailing slowly past them on its way down the hill. Robin thrust her car keys into Serena's hand.

"You get the car and go home—or try and follow me if you want—and pay the bill, will you? See you later—*ciao!*"

Serena had no time to object before Robin was off, sprinting down the road after the Number 55 bus, trying to keep in sight the speck of purple inside it that was all she could see now of the Contessa De Cleris. On the corner of Via Lombardia she leaped into a taxi that someone else had just vacated, and breathlessly told the driver, "Follow that bus!"

The driver did not move, did not respond in any way for a moment. Then he turned slowly round to give Robin a long, disdainful look.

"Please!" she said. "Don't let it get away!"

He let out a long breath through puckered lips, and then slowly turned back to start the engine, and slithered round the corner into the traffic in Via Veneto, which was at a standstill. He ended up with his front bumper almost touching the back of the bus.

"Va bene così?" he asked sarcastically. She felt a bit foolish then, and twisted her head round to see if there was any sign of Serena in the car. There was not. When the taxi driver asked how far she planned to follow the bus, she replied rather sharply that she did not know. Whereupon he launched into a diatribe about people taking taxis when buses would do, and added—somewhat illogically, she thought—a warning to the effect that it was not worth his while to take on a fare for a short run.

"Look, I'm sorry to have disturbed you," she told him. "But it happens to be very important to me not to lose sight of that bus."

"Cost you less to get into it. No?"

"I can't do that. And I might miss it if I tried."

It must have been the slowest car chase ever. The only place where they picked up any kind of speed was on the one-way run down Via Nazionale, but they churned to a halt again at the end, where another jam blocked the approach to Piazza Venezia. At every bus stop she opened the door of the taxi and put her head out to watch the bus doors open and shut, to make sure the Contessa did not give her the slip. Eventually, when the driver's growling had wound down to a grumpy silence, she started feeling giggly. She had given chase without a moment's thought, but where did she honestly imagine the Contessa was going? It would be funny, after all this melodrama, if it turned out she was off to buy a new hat.

The Contessa alighted from the bus at Piazza Argentina and set off briskly along Corso Vittorio. Robin paid the taxi driver and followed on foot at a cautious distance, so cautious that when the old lady turned right at Piazza San Pantaleo, Robin had to run like mad for fear of losing her. There were two roads leading out of Piazza San Pantaleo, and it was only luck that Robin chose Via della Cuccagna, for it was not until she reached Piazza Navona that she caught another glimpse of purple, on the right-hand side of the square. And just as she was thinking, Now she's going to go and have an ice cream or something equally stupid, she stopped short, seeing the old lady come to a halt and ring one of the bells beside a door with a street intercom. After a moment she pushed open the door and went in. The heavy door clicked shut.

"We can't really stick our noses in everywhere she goes, can we?" Robin said to Mike when she saw him next.

"Why not?"

"Because it's ridiculous. She's probably got a canasta crony in there, or something. Or a fortune-teller. Or just a friend."

"Or a son."

"Now come on, Mike. Is that likely? Oh, by the way, how about this, though?" She fumbled in her bag and pulled out the envelope with the Lebanese stamp.

They were strolling through the gardens of Villa Sciarra, along a path shaded by a vaulted roof of foliage, past the young mothers who sat knitting beside parked prams.

" 'N.D. Olga Contessa De Cleris,' " Mike read, examining the envelope as he walked. He turned to look at her, intrigued. "How did you get it?"

"It wasn't hard. But is it any use? Can you remember what Beppe's writing was like?"

Mike shrugged and shook his head. "Didn't even know he could write." He turned the envelope over and tried to decipher the postmark. "It's an Italian, anyway. Only an Italian would put 'N.D.' like that, for *Nobil Donna*. And Lebanon would have been a good place for him to go. It's a thing to bear in mind, anyway."

It was one of those fine April days that are better than summer, when the smell of damp grass is in the air and all the leaves are young. At the end of the cool, green, silent tunnel, they came out into a sunlit space where there were *au pairs* chattering and children squealing, old men dozing and white doves cooing in the blossom-covered branches of a tree inside the aviary they shared with an assortment of geese, hens, pigeons, and peacocks.

A wide-eyed child of about three was staring in through the mesh with a face halfway between awe and hostility, while his father complacently ordered the male peacock to open its tail: *"Pavone, fa la ruota! Pavone, fa la ruota!"*

The peacock paid him no attention, but continued to pick his disconsolate way round the gravel, with two yellow goslings nibbling at his bedraggled old tail, which the peacock was too bored to open for the benefit of any child, any more than for the emerald-necked female wistfully waiting nearby. And when he had walked all round the cage and found nothing to interest him, he subsided in a heap to make the most of the sun-warm stones, and nibbled at himself, as the two goslings were now nibbling at each other, because there was nothing else to do.

"Alas! Poor peacocks!" said Mike. "They ought to be on a lawn. Isn't that where they used to be? Strutting about the emerald grass in the sun—that's how I pictured them. Among the lilies and the lotus flowers."

"I'm sure there have never been any of those round here."

"All right then, among the daisies and the daffodils. And the gaudy melon flowers."

"What, with that open gate over there? Come on, if it wasn't for the cage, they'd have been off down to Trastevere before you could say 'roast peacock.' I wonder if it's all like that, what we remember. If any of it ever was the way we imagine."

"Do you mean if we were ever young and happy and wild?"

"No, we were, I know. But was it as marvelous as it seems to us now? I remember some things with nostalgia that weren't marvelous at all."

"Like what?"

"My place in Via della Scrofa. I even think back lovingly of that. But it was a dreadful little hole, wasn't it?"

"It's not the four walls and the floor that you're nostalgic for. It's—I don't know—the air, the light, the hopefulness of those days. That squeaky old bed—remember? An awful bed, as beds go. But touched with whatever it was—magic, if you like—that was in us. It was unique. Uncomfortable as hell. But also holy."

But I made love on it with Beppe as well, she thought.

"Supposing we'd been married and had the baby and—"

"Lived unhappily ever after, like everyone else?"

"Well, the shine does wear off, you know, after a while. With anyone."

"That's time, not marriage," Mike said. "Look at the poor old peacock. When he was young, somebody told him peacocks are the proudest birds in the world, and he thought, 'I'm a fantastic peacock; when I show off my tail the ladies will swoon and everybody will go "Ah!" ' They do, too. When he spreads his tail they all go 'Ah!' But then they turn their backs and forget all about him, so what's the use? As for trying to impress the ladies, he got over that long ago. So here he is, no better off for all his grandeur

237

than that silly little gosling there. But at least a gosling doesn't expect any more out of life than growing up to be a goose."

Robin laughed, or pretended to laugh; for some stupid reason she had tears in her eyes.

"When I was up there in the hospital—for the baby," she said, steering him away from the aviary and down the steps to the lower level of the garden, "I used to hear them cry out in the night. At least I think it was them. Do peacocks cry out? I'm not sure if I really heard them or if it was only a horrid dream I had—about a huge bird, a mixture of a peacock and an eagle, that swooped down from the trees outside on to a little kitten that was mewing in the grass. The mewing and the cry of the bird were real, I think. And when I woke up I decided it must have been the peacocks."

"What a bad dream."

"I used to have a lot of them. I was always dreaming I'd left the baby somewhere in a parcel and forgotten it. Or thrown it away in the rubbish bin by mistake. I suppose that kitten was the baby too, come to think of it."

"What made you want to come here? If it brings back such horrible memories?"

"I'd forgotten all about it till now. I just thought it would be a nice place to come to, for a change. I'd forgotten the peacocks."

And the baby.

"Did I ever tell you it was a girl?" She was staring at a rather pretty *au pair* who was reading under a tree, holding on to a toddler by his harness strap. She would have been about as old as that girl by now. "The nuns christened her Grazia."

"*Christened* her? But—do they christen a miscarriage?"

"It wasn't a miscarriage, Mike. She died in the womb. I had to go to the Anagrafe, you know, and register the birth and the death. Grazia Lane. They wouldn't let me give her your name."

Mike said nothing. He was trying to assimilate these strange new facts. A daughter called Grazia. Born and christened and dead. Who, if she had lived, would now be twenty years old, and look like Robin. Or him. Or a little of both. He had never thought of the child as real. Little Pan was a fantasy.

"Why on earth didn't you tell me all this at the time?"

"You'd only just been arrested. I thought I'd wait and tell you when you were freed. And when they finally let me see you—"

"You just said you'd lost it. I didn't realize—"

"You had trouble enough, without me upsetting you still more."

Mike paused a moment before asking, "Have you—had other children?"

"No. There was something wrong. I never did quite understand what—doctors are so vague. If I'd really wanted to, I could have gone to Switzerland or somewhere and got myself put right, but—"

"It's not too late, is it?"

"Too late for what?"

"To have a—"

"A child? You mean—?"

"Us."

"Oh, Mike, what are you saying? I'm forty-five. Among other things."

"You wouldn't anyway, would you?"

"Leave Luca? Mike, I couldn't."

"Sorry. It was a silly thought. Let's change the subject. I'm having lunch at Nicola's tomorrow. Want to come?"

"Don't be silly."

"Of course—it's Sunday. Luca's home."

"I couldn't go with you anyway, you know that."

Yes, he did. It was silly of him to ask. He was getting a lot of silly ideas today, what with the smell of spring and the two of them feeling so much more relaxed.

"Besides, I haven't seen Nicola for so long, it wouldn't make any sense." Mike looked at her, detecting, he thought, a faint sourness in her tone.

"What happened between you two? Did you quarrel?"

"Oh, no. He was always very nice, just—a bit of a coward, I suppose. He was scared stiff of getting stuck with me. And on top of that—well, none of us were particularly proud of the way we'd behaved."

"Why, how did you behave?"

"We just didn't do enough. For you, I mean. Well, did we?"

"I didn't do enough for myself, if it comes to that."

"I saw him last summer, actually, in Piazza Navona. I was having an ice cream with Luca and some other people, and he walked right past without seeing me."

She had wanted to call out "Nicola!" and see his face; but Luca was there, and you never knew with Luca. So she had simply sat and stared and said to herself: You were once naked in bed with that man. She couldn't believe it, though. He was as remote as his name on the screen when they went to see his films.

"Funny how you lose touch with people," she said.

"That's what he said. You'd lost touch. I thought I had too, when I phoned him first. I was supposed to see him the Sunday after that, but I couldn't face it—you know, that vacuum. Then I thought, Oh, hell—I want to see the bastard anyhow. And when I called him again he was quite different, as if he'd realized who I was and who I used to be. He's asked Franco to come too."

"Franco! Is he still around? I always think of him when I'm offered *zuppa inglese* for dessert. Remember?"

"*Zuppa inglese!* God, yes!" He laughed. "Franco's English soup. That night we tried to make peace with Nicola."

She had volunteered to cook an English meal, a task she would have found formidable now, but approached without a qualm in those carefree days when she had never cooked a meal of any kind in her life. She recalled a dishful of oily rocks that were supposed to be potatoes, and an object that the butcher had sworn was "rosbif," though it had shriveled up in the oven until it resembled a sausage more than a roast. Franco had turned up at Via Gregoriana with a round confectioner's box dangling on a string.

"English soup!" he had announced, proud of himself for finding just the thing.

" 'What sort of soup?' I said, and you said, 'Sweet and creamy. Like a sort of a trifle, only more so.' "

"And when you tasted it you said, 'Ever such a lot more so.' "

"And Nicola got cross because we couldn't translate."

"And we started giggling like a couple of nincompoops, and he went off the deep end."

"He couldn't stand being left out of things."

"And the supper was supposed to be for him."

"My God, that supper! How could I ever have had the nerve? I didn't even know how to make the gravy."

"I sloshed my whisky into it, remember?"

"And then in came Franco's wife and covered everything in béchamel. That awful Luisa was there too."

"That's right. She'd attached herself to Nico in a big way."

"What happened to her, I wonder."

"Nothing good, I shouldn't think."

They had walked all the way round the garden and come back to stop at the gate. A brilliant splash of pink almond blossom caught Mike's eye and he stared at it absently as he asked, "Do you think we're all like the peacocks now? With moth-eaten tails, and nowhere to fly to?"

"Perhaps we just don't know how to fly."

He turned to look at her, hopeful again. "Shall I tell Nicola I've seen you?"

"No," she said. "Don't tell anyone. Please."

TWENTY-SIX

"Well, so what's it like being back?" asked Franco Bernabei.

"Not easy," said Mike. "Not yet." How could he explain what it was like walking into Nicola's flat and finding thick carpets where once there was parquet, textured silk and a wealth of modern paintings on what were once austere white walls, finding the flat full of strangers, all talking about things he had never heard of, in just the same easy, bantering way he used to talk himself when he was as much at home there as they evidently were now? Who would understand what it was like coming in on the tail end of an argument about the effectiveness of a certain dialogue change, and seeing scripts lying open on the coffee table, and yellow pads covered with scrawled notes that had nothing to do with him? How could he describe what it felt like when he embraced Nicola, and they went on laughing and laughing over each other's shoulders because they were both afraid to stand back and see what the other had become? When, finally, they did let go of each other, they laughed nervously again, to hide the unexpected moisture in their eyes. Franco, standing by, had said, "Good to see you, Mike," as casually as if he had just breezed in from New York. But a conventional lie like "you haven't changed" could not be coaxed off any of their tongues.

Nicola was the one who, at first glance, appeared to have changed least. His skin was coarser and the lines on his forehead more deeply carved, and his white hair looked more natural than it used to, but it was chiefly in his manner that his age showed, in his self-assurance and a certain droopiness that came from having everything—except the stimulus of making an effort once in a while.

Franco, who was sixty now, had a paunch and a gravity he never had before. His attitude towards Mike was one of professional kindness and his opening question over the lunch table mere conversation, but his practiced smile did seem to denote genuine concern, and Mike clutched at that smile in the wilderness of chatter he could take no part in.

There was an English script girl named Jean sitting on Mike's right, and on his left a beautiful black girl who, when he arrived, had kissed him on both cheeks and said, "I'm Terry." A new young Italian actor known as Steve had appropriated the chair at the head of the table and started on about the script again with the writer, a crusty old hand called Renzo, sitting opposite Mike, between Steve's girlfriend, Valeria, and Franco, who leaned across and poured Mike some wine before asking, "So what are your plans?"

"My plans?" Mike paused and gave a dry little laugh. Should he tell them what his plan was? Shake them up a bit? No, better not. Not yet. "Well," he said, and shrugged, "that's a long story. The main thing is to get going. Find out how to *do* things again. You'd be surprised how much you find you've forgotten." Even how to help yourself to spaghetti, he thought grimly, finding himself confronted with the dishful that a manservant was gracefully handing round.

"Hey, Stelvio, *un momento!*" Terry called out, noticing the meager spoonful on Mike's plate as the manservant moved on. Stelvio turned back and she served Mike a large extra dollop. "What's the matter?" she asked. "You shy or something?"

"Thanks," he said, still intent on getting across to Franco, who, though now busy eating, appeared to be willing to go on listening as well. "You know," Mike told him, "after twenty years, you're used to being—protected, told what to do and where to go and when. It comes as a shock when all of a sudden you're on your own. There was an old man at Porto Azzurro. He was in for life, but he was sixty-seven and he had cancer, so they told him he could go. Well, he wouldn't. He'd been in for twenty-eight years and he couldn't face the world outside. They had to give him a job as a gardener and let him stay. You see, inside there is a kind of peace. When you come out, after such a long time, you haven't got anything. Or anybody. Even your dearest friends have—moved on."

The silence was stone cold. He realized too late that he had said too much; he had committed the unforgivable sin of telling the truth, his truth, which was unpalatable, and which they had all been doing their damnedest to keep covered up. He was in time to catch a lightning exchange of looks between his one-time dearest friends, see Valeria drop her eyes into her plate, notice at last the film of indifference that veiled Franco's eyes in spite of the smile that still hovered mechanically about his lips, before they all started talking about something else with such alacrity that for a moment they were all talking at once.

Random remarks, questions, compliments were bandied back and forth to relieve the tension. The main thing was to blot out what they did not want to know, blot Mike out as far as they could from their midst, while he alone sat silent and wondered what could have made him think they would want to be faced with the harsh facts of his life. How could he have failed to observe the ennui in Franco's face, the complacency on Nicola's, the nervous embarrassment that had prevented Valeria and Jean from ever once looking him in the eye? The last thing any of them wanted to hear was what it felt like to have been twenty years in jail. I ought to have gone along with the small talk, he thought, and left it at that. Well, I can always try again.

"Are you Nicola's agent now?" he asked Franco.

"No, I'm Steve's."

Touché.

Just for the hell of it, Mike asked, "How about a job for me?"

Another bad moment. You could almost hear Franco gulp. "Why not?" he said. "If you change your name."

"Bad as that, is it? And when I've changed it, what if people recognize me?"

"I don't suppose they will, do you?"

"They don't seem to, I admit. No one recognizes anyone, if you ask me. Would any of you recognize Beppe Palazzo, if you happened to pass him in the street?"

"Beppe Palazzo?" They stared at him in dismay.

"What's the matter? Aren't I supposed to mention his name?"

At that moment, luckily, there was a diversion, in the shape of Stelvio's entrance with the second course, a huge earthenware pot of what looked like stew.

"Here comes my burgoo!" said Terry.

"Che cos'è?" Steve asked suspiciously.

"Non è male," Nicola reassured him. *"Una specie di spezzatino."*

"Hey, what do you mean, *spezzatino?*" protested Terry. "It's Kentucky burgoo."

"Yes, yes, my darling." Nicola took her hand and kissed it. "Isn't she beautiful?" he said to Mike. "We are to be married soon, you know."

"Maybe," said Terry.

"Mamma mia, come sei acida! You know divorce was impossible in Italy till now."

"Sure, honey, I know. *Que serà serà.* When in Rome, relax." She turned to Mike. "Don't you agree?"

"Absolutely," he said. "It's that feeling of permanence. Have you ever watched the sunrise from the Pincio?"

"No!" she laughed, not catching his train of thought but giving him nonetheless a curiously sparkling smile. "I bet it's beautiful."

"Yes, it is."

"When you live in Rome you never see anything," she said. "You think it's all going to be out there when you want it—the sunrise and the sunset and the Colosseum, and the friend you've been meaning to call for the past five years."

"And in the meantime," said Jean, "the plane trees are dying. Can you believe that? I read it in the paper."

Renzo nodded. *"Sì, è vero. Dicono che stanno morendo, i platani al Gianicolo."*

The plane trees on the Gianicolo. Oh, no, they couldn't die.

"I had a canary once that died," said Mike. "They let me keep it in my cell at one time. Cocò, I called it."

They were all looking at him again in acute discomfort, but he was too engrossed in what he was remembering to notice.

"Ever held a canary on your hand?" he asked Terry. "Its claws are very light and tender and diffident. You have to stay very still, but if you're patient enough, after a good long time it may move sideways up your arm a little, and you don't know how good it feels to have those little bird feet clinging to you, making you into a friend. Specially when it's the only contact your hand has with a living thing."

He stopped, suddenly aware of the chilled hush his words had caused.

"And it died?" Terry asked gently. Perhaps she was the only one who understood.

"Yes. Just went flop on the floor of the cage, I don't know why. That lively little singing, hopping, seed-crunching person was nothing but a cold yellow ball that I had to wrap up in a bit of paper and throw out with the rubbish. When you think how we talk and struggle and dream. All you have to do is snip a vein and it's gone."

Terry was frowning at him anxiously. The rest were staring in undisguised horror.

"What's wrong?" he burst out. "Aren't I supposed to mention death, either? Because of Beppe, is that it? You really think I killed him, don't you? Well, I've got news for you. I didn't. Not yet. I will when I find him, though. You can count on that." He suddenly threw down his napkin and stood up. "You'll have to excuse me, but I've had enough. Listen"—he pointed at Steve— "what happened to me could have happened to you, my friend. I had a lot to lose and I lost it all. I thought you knew that, Franco. Everybody makes mistakes, even judges and juries and lawyers and policemen. It could happen to anyone, understand? So thanks for the lunch, Signor D'Angelo, nice to have met you all, and goodbye!"

They sat petrified, listening. He was out of the room before they had recovered from the shock. Nicola leaped to his feet and rushed after him, followed by Terry.

"Come on, Mike," said Nicola. "Don't be a fool!"

"I *am* a fool," said Mike. "I was a fool to come and I'd be a bigger fool to stay." He turned back at the door to kiss Terry's cheek and give her a gentle pat on the head. "Sorry about this—you're a sweet girl. I just don't fit in here anymore." Nicola grabbed his arm and tried to hold him. Mike took his hand and pressed it. "No, Nico, don't insist. I knew when I talked to you the first time that it was no good. Nothing is ever like the past. You have to move on and forget. Thanks all the same."

He plunged on out and shut the door behind him. He was free. He had refused to take it. He had stood up and walked out, and he didn't care if he never saw any of them again. He had more important things to get on with now.

He had planned originally to rent the car he was going to need for Operation Beppe. "*Rent* a car?" Memmo had scoffed, shocked at the very thought. And he was right: the car-rental people all wanted huge deposits and made a habit of checking identity cards. But then, according to Memmo, there was only one way to procure a car you needed for a job, and if Mike was not up to that himself, there were plenty of friends who would do it for him. It was no use trying to explain that he must on no account commit any crimes for which he had not already been condemned—murder was all right, but theft was out—this was an argument that left Memmo stumped.

"But can't you see? That's what this whole thing is about?" Mike had told him. "It's all there in that blessed Article Ninety. If I kill Beppe they can't touch me, as long as I do it the same way I'm supposed to have done it before."

"But you said you weren't going to kill him."

"That's not the point. What counts is that I can *say* I'm going to; I can put it in the papers, tell the police, shout it on the radio or the television or what have you, and nobody can do a bloody thing to stop me."

Memmo looked very skeptical indeed, and began shaking his head. "Hey, Mike, come on now—don't tell me you believe that. You think you can tell the police you're going to kill somebody and they aren't going to lift a finger to stop you? Since when?"

"I'm not saying I'm killing just anybody. I'm saying I'm killing somebody who's dead."

"Shit! Now you've got me all screwed up. You told me what you were going to do was—"

"What I'm going to do is something else altogether. What I'm trying to say is, I must be extra careful not to get caught for something silly. Understand? I can't go stealing cars or picking locks or any other stuff like that. It's all got to be absolutely legal. Okay?"

"If you say so." Memmo shrugged. "*I* say if you've got friends, you use them. But you do what you like."

Instead of stealing, Mike had decided to try the dumps where unsaleable, broken-down cars ended their days as melancholy carcasses, stripped of their wheels and windows and piled one on top of the other like skulls in a Capuchin cemetery. He found nothing at the first two of these places he inspected, but when he walked into the third and saw the red Alfa Romeo Spyder, he loved it instantly, much more than was sensible, in spite of its main drawback, which was that, like all two-seaters, it was designed for youth rather than for creaking, middle-aged bones. Apart from that, it was exactly what he wanted: a car that would be noticed, recognized, and remembered, battered but still jaunty, more or less intact, and his for a song.

His luck had changed: he was sure of that now. And as if to confirm it, he found a message at the hotel telling him to call the British Embassy without delay. The news he received from the vice-consul sent him hunting for the scrap of paper torn from Robin's diary, with the phone number on it he was not supposed to use.

"**I**s it all right?" he asked, when she answered the phone at last. "Can you talk?"

"Yes, but—heavens! You shouldn't be ringing now."

"I know I shouldn't, but I've been trying all afternoon and I just had to tell you. They've found my passport! I mean, they've found out it's been renewed—in Beirut, eighteen years ago. When I was in Regina Coeli! If that's not proof, I'd like to know what is."

"Proof of what?"

She couldn't help sounding a bit cool. She had just returned from the hairdresser's, and it was after half past seven. Hearing the phone ringing as she opened the front door, she was expecting to hear Luca's voice wanting to know where she had been, as he often did these days, rather querulously too, sometimes. She was running short of explanations, and the feebler they became, the more irritated she felt with Luca, not only for not believing them, but also and above all for expecting her to account to him every time she went out, as if she had no right to do anything without informing him. What she certainly did not need, however, was Mike phoning at a time like this, when Luca might easily have been there and when he was liable to come in at any moment. In any case it struck her as nonsensical, all this excitement over a passport, lost or found. Anyone would think it was the key to everything. Mike evidently thought it was.

"Proof of *what*?" he said. "Why, that Beppe's alive, that's what. The envelope with the Lebanese stamp did come from him. He must have skipped off to Beirut with my passport, pretending he was me."

"How do you know it was Beppe?"

"Well, for God's sake, who else? Who else but Beppe would have the unutterable nerve to walk into the British Embassy and get it renewed? He must have stuck his own photo in it, instead of mine, and had the dry stamp on it forged. It would have had to be a perfect job, they said, or he'd never have got away with it. No flies on him, I'm telling you. Picked the right place too. There's no extradition from Lebanon to Italy, so even if he'd been caught out, he'd still have been safe. But he didn't get caught, not him. Just quietly turned himself into me. Went round calling himself Michele Donadio, the little creep! Can you beat that?"

"So now what are you going to do, go to Beirut?"

"Oh, I don't suppose he's there now; why should he be? The passport was only valid for another five years. He'd have had to move on before it expired, and if you ask me, the most likely place is here. It's so easy. I've been reading about whatsisname, that Mafia bloke they found in Milan. He'd been wanted for years—everybody knew that—and all the time he was comfortably established in a middle-class suburb, with a wife who hadn't a clue who he was."

She could hear in his voice the need to talk, the need to keep her on the line as long as he could, and it crossed her mind that when she hung up he was going to be left all alone in his nasty little room, and there was nothing she could do about it.

"Mike, listen," she said, "I can't stay on the phone now. I'll see you tomorrow, if you want."

"I'll be in Via Lazio tomorrow. All day and every day from now on, until I get a bite. La Contessa, she's the answer. She's bloody well got to be."

TWENTY-SEVEN

La mamma, that was it. In Italy *la mamma* is everything, everybody knows that. Especially this *mamma* here, locked up indoors waiting for the phone to ring, and yet never making a long-distance call.

It had struck Mike as natural, at first, that she should go on playing the part she had played all along. It had seemed logical to suppose she would be endangering her son if she went to join him—in Lebanon, or South America, or wherever he was. But that was when Mike still believed in absolutes, when he thought missing people were inevitably spotted in the streets, and that it all still mattered as much as it used to matter to them, in the old days. If there was one thing manifestly certain now, it was that no one any longer gave a damn about Beppe Palazzo and his mother. There could be only one reason, therefore, for her living all alone in Rome: namely, that Beppe was not far away. The old lady was the link, no question of that. All Mike had to do was persist.

Having reached that conclusion, he parked his red Spyder outside the house in Via Lazio and sat in it all day long, provoking considerable grumbling from the old man in the yachting cap, who had to be plied with hundreds of lire to leave him in peace. It was no joke sitting cramped up for so many hours at a time, not when prison had left you full of rheumatism, with chronically stiff joints. He had to get out and stretch his legs from time to time, and flex his arms and take a few deep breaths; but he was determined not to give up, even if he had to stay there for a month.

He watched the Contessa's door relentlessly for three whole days—without the slightest result. Each morning he saw Mariella sally forth and return with bags full of groceries and greens, but the Contessa never set foot outside; and so curious was he to know what went on up there, inside that shuttered and inviolable flat, that for two pins he would have applied to one of the less reputable private detectives who were known to go in for phone tapping when required. But no, he must not do anything illegal. He could not afford to get into trouble now that he was out.

By the fourth day it had become impossible to keep his eyes focused constantly on the Contessa's door, and he had grown so accustomed to her failure to appear that he almost missed her when she did. He lost a few more minutes debating what to do with the car, before deciding to leave it where it was and hurry after her on foot, by which time she had turned the corner into Via Veneto. She was not in any hurry, however, and he soon spotted her purple coat again, at the kiosk on the corner of Via Lombardia, where she bought some magazines and a couple of paperbacks before retracing her steps up the road. She paused to look in the window of a dress shop, and again to survey Spagnoli's knitwear; then she proceeded to take a seat outside Harry's Bar, where she drank a cup of tea.

Mike watched her for the greater part of an hour, as he paced up and down outside the Hotel Flora on the other side of the road, alternately scanning the street and consulting his watch, pretending to wait for someone who never came. She stood up at last, shook her skirts straight, and headed for home, and it dawned on Mike then that this afternoon stroll must have been the highlight of her week. All it amounted to, the result of that whole day's spying, was a breath of fresh air for an old woman who was still vain, but desperately alone.

Two days went by without another peep. But then, one fine morning, she came out at twenty past nine, set off briskly down the road—and disappeared into Riccardo's, a hairdresser in Via Veneto. Mike had followed her in the car this time, for the simple reason that he had not found anywhere to park, and now he was stuck alongside the cars already parked in front of the hairdresser's. He had no intention of budging until he was satisfied she was going to stay inside, regardless of the horn-tooting and gesturing and rude words such behavior provoked. Within five minutes he had caused a sizeable obstruction and was forced to move on, but though he circled round and round the block, there was not a space to be seen. In despair he returned to Via Lazio, handed the keys over to the old man in the yachting cap, and left the car to him. A good half hour had passed by the time he sat down outside the Café de Paris, where he could keep an eye on Riccardo's door, but nearly two hours more went by before the Contessa came out, resplendent with glitteringly set and freshly peroxided hair. Fantastic, thought Mike. Six days gone, and I finally know where she has her hair done.

It did occur to him, however, that an old lady who goes to so much trouble to look her best must intend to be seen by someone other than Mariella; and sure enough, instead of turning left, towards Via Lazio, she turned right, downhill, past the Café de Paris and into the bank. Mike glanced in through the door and saw her waiting to be attended to at a crowded counter. After a few moments' indecision, he set off at a gallop up the road to fetch the car again, then drove around the back way so that he could stop on the corner of Via Ludovisi and be ready for action, in the event that today something actually might be about to take place.

She came out five minutes later and raised an imperious arm at a newly vacated taxi by the traffic lights. "I knew it," Mike muttered. "This time she's going somewhere."

She was indeed. Her destination was Standa, a large, popular store in Via Cola di Rienzo. Not exactly exciting as destinations go, not interesting at all, really, and what was more, another devilishly hard place to park. Once again he had to wait alongside the parked cars, more or less in the middle of the road—always a busy one, crammed with shoppers—and more than once a policeman told him sharply to move on. He kept moving on a bit and then backing up again; luckily for him, the policeman was being kept so busy by other people doing worse things than that, that he managed to escape being fined or arrested or carted away by a crane. After about three quarters of an hour, the Contessa came out laden with plastic bags. Evidently she had been doing her weekly shopping at the supermarket in the basement of the store. But that in itself was odd; what about all the bags he had seen Mariella carting home each day? For only two people, they seemed to require an inordinate quantity of food.

The old lady put the bags down on the pavement and began searching for a taxi. Once or twice she called out in vain, and she had begun to look a little harassed when one finally pulled in to the curb. She climbed in and drove away, with Mike in pursuit.

The taxi swung right, as was to be expected. It was the only way to go back towards Via Veneto, since there was no left turn for the whole length of the street. To his surprise, though, instead of continuing down the parallel road as far as the river, the cab turned right again at Via Marco Colonna and headed straight across towards Piazza Cavour. So she was not going home; she was going out to lunch, shopping and all. Curiouser and curiouser. Could it be that he was onto something at last?

In any event, he was getting a tremendous kick out of doing a car chase through the busy lunch-hour traffic in his nifty little Spyder, which he was beginning to handle with some degree of confidence now, after a whole course of rather painful driving lessons and the odd bit of practice he had been able to fit in between his long bouts of sleuthing. And in the meantime, here they were back at the old Palazzo di Giustizia, heading across Ponte Umberto towards—hey! Mike grinned. She wouldn't be going *there* by any chance? She would. She was. She paid off the taxi in Corso Rinascimento and walked off round the corner into Piazza Navona.

Hell! Somewhere to park, quick! The only space in sight was far too small, but he squeezed the Spyder in obliquely, one wheel on the pavement. If they fined him, he'd pay, that was all. He leaped out and charged after her, rounding the corner just in time to see her vanish through the door of Number 112.

"This time I'm *sure* we've struck gold," Mike said to Robin when she called him later on. The Contessa had spent nearly three hours inside Number 112 and come out minus the shopping bags. "I mean, she wouldn't go doing a week's shopping just for anyone, now would she? It must be somebody pretty special in there."

"You really think it's—Beppe? What, in Piazza Navona?"

"Well, what do *you* think that was, her good deed for the day?"

"But Mike, he's never been seen—by anyone. Not for twenty years."

"Tell you what—why don't you go and ring all the bells on that door in turn, and see who answers?"

"Why me?"

"Because you look so beautifully respectable. No one could take you for a burglar, if you ring their bell and ask if the Contessa De Cleris is there. And just see how each one reacts."

The idea made her feel extremely nervous. She could not deny that this madness of playing sleuth excited her, but that did not prevent her hand from trembling as she approached Number 112 two days later and reached out for the first bell.

Mike was right, though; it was easy. The first person who answered let her into the building without a qualm, but knew nothing of the Contessa. Nor was there any sign of Beppe behind any of the other doors inside, one or two of which were opened by maids, who went off to inquire and came back shaking their heads. One was an office. The only tough customer was a certain Signora Pizzi, who looked astonished at being asked if the Contessa De Cleris had paid her a visit. "La Contessa De Cleris?" she said, frowning as if unable to believe her ears.

Whereupon, blushing scarlet, Robin launched into a garbled explanation about the Contessa being a friend of her mother's, who had told her to come and fetch her there, but had forgotten to mention the name of the friend she was having tea with.

"Really?" said the lady, in a tone that could not have been more skeptical, backing away slightly, as if to view Robin through an invisible lorgnette.

"Oh, well, it doesn't matter. I'm so sorry I bothered you." Robin made a dive for the stairs, conscious of the lady's sharp and speculative eyes on her back.

One thing was clear if nothing else. The Contessa De Cleris was unknown in every flat in the building, except the flat at the top, the door of which remained resolutely closed, though she rang and rang. Max Molinari—that was the name on the bell—was evidently not at home.

There was another door too, on the top landing. The key was in the lock, so she opened it and found that it led to the kind of communal terrace where all the occupants of a building hang out their washing. Evidently some workmen had been busy out there that day; the floor was scattered with tools and gritty with loose cement, and a ladder had been left propped against the wall. Probably it was the workmen who had left the key, which Robin, quite to her own surprise, quietly removed and slipped into her bag. As if electrified by her own petty larceny, she suddenly darted out on to the terrace and climbed up the ladder to peer over the top.

She did not know what made her do it, nor what she hoped to see; all she saw, in fact, was a large group of chimneys and the sloping tiled roof of the fifth-floor flat, only the tip of which was visible from the ground. Once she was safely back down in the piazza again, and her heart had stopped thumping under her elegant silk blouse, she pointed it out to Mike.

"It's a modern penthouse that's been added on, by the look of it," she told him. "A bit like the one Luca built for us when we were first married—all crazy, sloping ceilings to keep it out of sight, because nobody ever seems to know if it's legal. Hardly the old lady's cup of tea, I shouldn't think."

"What a place for him, though, eh? A flat that's practically invisible. He could be sitting up there watching us now, and we wouldn't know. Look, shield your eyes and look up. Supposing he was there, leaning right over that railing—what would you see? Only a shadow against the sky."

A photographer, that was what he needed—a paparazzo, as they called them nowadays. There was certainly no shortage of them around. But the one who, in his view, was more suitable than any other was Leo Santi, whom he had once knocked flat in the gutter for the sake of a silly *principessa*, and who subsequently testified in court that Mike was known for his violent temper and pugnacious ways. Leo owed him a fat favor for that, Mike reckoned, and he went to great pains to track him down.

There were two and a half columns of Santis in the phone book, without a single Leopoldo. The old phone number yielded nothing, nor did any inquiries at various magazines. But he finally found a bunch of paparazzi lying in wait for someone outside the Grand Hotel, and one of them had been around long enough to remember Leo from the old days.

"Haven't seen him for years," he said. "Heard he's been ill. Heart, poor devil. Had to give all this up."

"So where is he?"

The paparazzo shrugged. "I can inquire."

He had opened a shop, it turned out, in a remote and rather seedy suburb, a tiny shop full of spectacles and cameras, with the back room rigged up as a studio for passport photos. Leo was sitting behind the counter, reading a newspaper. Business did not appear to be too good.

He had put on a lot of weight and aged far beyond his years. His hair was long at the back to make up for its thinning on top, and he had bushy white sidewhiskers and a walrus mustache. I hope I don't look as bad as that, Mike thought, as he stepped up to the counter and said, "*Salve!* Remember me?"

Leo stood up quickly with an obliging smile, eager for a customer, anxious to give no offense.

"I once punched you on the nose," Mike said.

"*Santo Cielo!*" Leo exclaimed, clapping his hands. "Mike Donato! I can't believe it!"

So then they thumped each other on the back like the long-lost friends they never were, and asked after each other's health and took stock of each other's state of deterioration.

"How would you like to do something a bit crazy?" Mike asked. "Take a holiday from all this and be a devil, just for once."

Leo laughed. "How crazy?" he asked.

That he agreed to do what Mike proposed was a fair measure of his boredom, and of the squalor of doing nothing but passport photos in the little back room—he who had ambushed Humphrey Bogart and Gary Cooper, and chased King Farouk and his girlfriends through the sweet nights of Rome.

"What if he has a heart attack up there?" said Robin, after Leo had disappeared into Number 112 with the key to the communal terrace in his pocket and his gear draped round his neck, telephoto lens and all. He had rung the office bell and had himself let into the building easily.

"What happens if I get caught?" Leo had said himself. But it was only an afterthought; when Mike shrugged, he had shrugged too and, chuckling, off he had gone.

Mike and Robin went into the Tre Scalini café, opposite, and sat at a table by the window in the deserted room upstairs. It was not altogether prudent, but prudence was becoming a dreadful bore and, all things considered, as long as they stayed indoors, the risk was not too great. It was a fine day, and what customers there were at that hour were taking advantage of the spring sunshine outside; and if anyone did come upstairs, they would hear them coming in time to separate until they saw who it was.

From the little balcony behind their table, they had a clear view of the door of Number 112 and more of the roof than you could see from the piazza, as well as the balustrade of what appeared to be Signor Molinari's terrace, with a cactus in a big round pot at one end. No sign of Leo, though; evidently Robin had been right when she said she thought that behind those chimneys would be the perfect place for him to hide. They only hoped it would not be too long before Signor Molinari chose to show himself on the terrace.

At twelve o'clock Robin went home. Luca would be there for lunch that day. She had to go and get him a meal and look normal. Business as usual and life going on as drably as before.

Oh, those damn lunches—what a pest they were, especially today, when she had so much else on her mind that she had forgotten to buy anything, even fresh bread. Luckily she found the remains of some roast veal in the fridge, and a few of the artichokes Adele had cooked the day before. Luca would grumble if there was no pasta to start with, but she was too late getting back to bother with making sauce. She measured out a liter of water and unearthed a packet of dehydrated vegetable soup—rather a joyless kind of thing, but it would have to do. "Simmer for twenty minutes," the instructions said. She turned the gas down low and went off to dump the rest of the stuff on the table.

Something was brewing inside her; she was not sure exactly what. She felt trapped every time she came back to that apartment, and yet, how could she just walk out on something she had spent fourteen years putting together? Could she ever go back, now, to having no pillows and no tablecloth, not much money and no little white car? And what would happen to helpless Luca, forever searching the wrong drawers for his socks? Besides, she really did have a deep affection for Luca, a genuine need for his gentle, sheltering arms. Even when he exasperated her by playing the tyrant, he still inspired tenderness of a kind—yes, even today, coming in and sitting down the way he was doing now, as if it were her natural duty to wait on him, eyeing his reconstituted soup with long-suffering distaste, an expression of his that always drove her wild, especially when she knew quite well she could not blame him. But poor Luca, she had nothing against being his wife, if only he would let her breathe and be herself. The trouble was, he wouldn't. He expected allegiance, more than love. Never in a thousand years could he conceive of an autonomous wife.

Still, this was her home. Looking around her, she could see a lot of things she would be sorry to have to do without. There would be a certain sadness even about abandoning some of the plants that had given her so much trouble. It was silly how attached you became to the things that enslaved you, even to the monotonous safety of these four walls.

She took the soup plates away and sat down again to serve Luca his veal.

You grew lazy, that was the trouble. You started getting

rheumatism and feeling less and less like struggling out of bed in the morning. You knew life was still going on out there somewhere, but you couldn't be bothered to go out and join in. It was that laziness that kept a marriage going when the pleasure had all seeped away. It was one of the tricks nature played on you, to stop you from gallivanting off after new partners when you were past the age of reproduction. Your body tricked your mind into thinking that all you wanted was to keep quiet and stay put. Stability began to appear more desirable than love, and boredom synonymous with happiness.

It wasn't—she knew that now. What exactly she was going to do about it, she had no definite idea, only a vague yearning to venture forth in search of the things that mattered, the lost treasures she had scattered behind her along the way—those rare and fleeting moments of exhilaration when she had felt that, if she tried, she might stretch out her arms far enough to touch all the world.

"What's wrong?" Luca asked, watching her tinker listlessly with her artichoke.

"Nothing," she said, with a guilty smile. "Just thinking."

"Thinking what?"

"Oh, nothing special." It came home to her then that she did not know what to say. What did they generally say to each other over lunch? They must be in the habit of saying something as a rule, or he would not have noticed that she was abnormally quiet.

Supposing he knows, she thought. Supposing he's known all along that Mike was back. No reason why he shouldn't; it was in the papers. Oh, but he'd have made a scene. He might not have, though. Luca had a theory that if you talked about things, you only made them worse. Their quarrels generally took the form of morose silences, which lasted until he decided to forgive her for whatever he considered she had done to incur his reproach. Whereupon he would begin speaking to her again, in a kindly, condescending tone. Infuriating as this was, she had long since given up trying to argue about who was really in the wrong; the only effect that had was to prolong the silence. Luca's a wonderful husband on the whole, she would tell herself. You have to take the rough with the smooth. But oh, dear, those silences; they were the death of everything.

Maybe he's waiting to see what I'll do, she thought, and then— oh, come off it. If he knew, he would say so, in no uncertain terms. Knew what, anyway? There was nothing to know. Much.

"I think I'll go and lie down," she said. "I feel a bit tired." You liar, she thought.

"Yes, you look a little pale," he said. "It's the spring, perhaps. In any case, I must go. I have an appointment at half past three."

Supposing he waits outside and follows me, she thought. The situation was clearly getting out of hand. It would be better to tell him the truth and be done with it. There was nothing to be ashamed of, after all. Except having kept it from him so far. Which he might not understand. Or forgive.

After he had gone, she quickly cleared the table, shoved everything into the dishwasher, and set out again herself, looking round rather carefully as she emerged from the street door, to make sure there was no sign of Luca, or Luca's car. There wasn't, and as far as she could make out in such a sea of traffic, nobody followed her back to Piazza Navona.

Mike was still where she had left him.

"No news?" she said.

"Not a peep. Hope to God he's all right."

"Poor Leo, he must be famished. Supposing whoever it is never goes out on the terrace at all? They may be away, for all we know. Perhaps that's why they don't answer the bell."

"Wait here," Mike said suddenly. "I've got an idea."

He hurried downstairs to the telephone, and snatched up the directory for M–Z. There it was: *Molinari Max, 112 Piazza Navona*. What a fool he was not to have thought of that before.

The voice that said *pronto* was Beppe's voice, he felt sure. Beppe had always had that particular, half-furtive way of saying *pronto*, as if expecting God knows what kind of conspiratorial call. Now that he heard it, Mike realized it was unmistakable. Funny how one could forget a little detail like that.

"Pronto," said Mike. "Signor Molinari? This is Police Officer

Rossi speaking. We've received a complaint regarding a flowerpot on your terrace, which appears to be dangerously insecure. If it falls, it may kill someone. So I suggest you take steps immediately to see that it doesn't."

"What?" said the voice—baffled, more than anything else. "What steps?"

"A piece of wire, firmly tied, might be sufficient for the moment. Failing that, rope. Otherwise you should immediately remove the pot from the parapet and put it on the ground."

Mike replaced the receiver and rushed back up the stairs and straight through the first-floor room to the window. "Quick, come and look," he told Robin.

A moment later a male figure appeared on the top terrace of Number 112 and walked slowly to the end to examine the flowerpot on the corner, which was, of course, perfectly secure. Now what was he doing? Scratching his head? Looking down at the piazza? Looking puzzled, one might surmise from what little one could see. With a shrug, he turned round and disappeared from view.

"Come on," said Mike, setting off ahead down the stairs and out across the piazza. It was not long before the door of Number 112 opened and Leo emerged. He made a face when he saw them, and stretched his aching joints.

"*Gesù, Gesù!*" he muttered. "I'm not so nimble on the rooftops as I used to be. Didn't have arthritis in the old days."

"Did you get it?"

"Got something. God knows what."

What he had was a series of blurred photographs of a plump, middle-aged person with a balding head and a big, bushy mustache. The three of them pored over them in Leo's shop. It could have been Beppe. It could have been anybody. But then Mike had heard the voice on the phone.

"It's him!" he cried. "I know it's him."

Leo shrugged. Robin looked frankly skeptical.

"You'll need more than this," she said.

"All right, so now we get down to business," said Mike. "We'll get hold of some old photos and look at things like the ears. We'll get to work on the Contessa. Leave no room for doubt. You're right. I don't want anyone saying it might be him and it might not. But it's him, all right, believe me. I feel ten years younger already. How about you, Leo? Feel in the mood for a bit more fun?"

Leo grinned and put a hand on his back. "Preferably not on any more rooftops. My back will never be the same again."

"No, this time it's a nice, respectable landing. You'll have to dodge an old sourpuss of a *portiere*, that's all, not to mention various elderly tenants. I mean I don't want anyone to notice you sitting outside the Contessa De Cleris's front door. It'll be a game of skill this time, more than acrobatics."

"Well, I won't say no to a bit of excitement. It's better than sitting here."

"Right," said Mike. "I hereby appoint you Official Paparazzo for the Identification of Palazzo. Top secret, mind. Not a word to anyone. Okay?"

"Okay."

"What now?" Robin asked.

"Now we go to town. You'll see."

TWENTY-EIGHT

Back there in his cell, lying awake in the snoring, groaning nights that reeked of dying masculinity and wasted sperm, revenge was the only thing he could think of at times. And it was not just Beppe he had in mind, not in the early days; it was the judge and the *giudici popolari* and the examining magistrate and all the blind, deaf, and invisible men of authority who had conspired together to steal his soul and trap his body within those excruciating four walls. Sometimes, in the helplessness of his rage, he would dream of lining them all up against the wall like a row of faceless dummies on a shooting range, and mowing them down with one long, relentless crackle of machine-gun fire. But in the course of the years his mind had come to focus exclusively on Beppe, and his plan to get even had gradually become an end in itself— something to occupy his mind and keep his faculties in trim, and help him believe there was such a thing as the future, when he felt like packing it in.

It had done him a world of good too, right after his release, to have to get busy on his preparations for the day when he would translate this long-cherished fantasy into fact. Having something precise to do had helped speed up his return to the normal world. Things were different now, though, very different, from when he had first stepped out of jail. Robin was once again a reality on which he dared set some hope; and the plan was turning into a game. They had begun to enjoy themselves, he and Robin and Leo, as if what they were perpetrating was a colossal practical joke.

It was not a joke; it was still revenge, though the other two did

264

not seem to grasp it. And even if revenge was no longer the one thing in life he most desired, he was still determined to carry his plan through. It was a good plan, a perfect plan for perfect justice, and his mind had been full of it too long for him to realize he was not angry enough now for it to make any kind of sense.

It was going to cost him a great deal, too, this masterpiece of poetic justice. It would prove his innocence, but to make it work, he would have to leave Rome for good; and as he stood in Piazza di Spagna, feasting his eyes on the quiet majesty of the Spanish Steps, topped by the twin towers of Trinità dei Monti, he found it hard to believe he was never going to see it again.

Crossing the road, he began slowly mounting the steps, not consciously heading for the old flat, but drawn to it irresistibly, as he had been ever since his return. When he saw the splash of vermilion down there on the left, it was somehow not really a surprise. Those brightly colored cards meant only one of two things: To Let or For Sale; and this one was—yes, it was up on the door of Number 49. But of course! The flat was to let. He must always have known it would be, sooner or later; that was what had brought him back past the door again and again. When he was near enough to read the magical word AFFITTASI, with the even more magical *Attico* scrawled underneath, his only immediate thought was: I wonder how much it costs. For one wild moment he pictured himself taking the flat again and settling back into his old life, with everything the way it used to be; as if four walls could bring back the youth and laughter and love they once contained.

The daydream was short-lived, mercifully. Yet even after common sense had been restored, the desire to revisit the flat remained. He went back the next day, intending to ask the *portiere* to let him go up and have a look, but the *portiere* was standing right in the doorway, and when Mike saw that it was the same one as before, he balked. In the old days Luigi was generously tipped and rather over obsequious, but who could tell what his attitude would be now? If he started looking down his nose, Mike was liable to explode. Better not risk it. No. He walked on past.

But by now he was obsessed with the idea of stepping back

inside the memory, of taking one deep breath of the halcyon past before plunging into an uncertain future.

When he put it to Robin, she agreed at once. If she heard a voice murmuring in her mind that of all the reckless things she had been doing, this was the most dangerous, she chose to ignore it. She was much too intrigued to say no.

It was easy for her to ask Luigi for the key. A respectable married woman had a perfect right to go and look at a vacant flat and to be left undisturbed while doing so, especially after slipping Luigi ten thousand lire for the privilege. Luigi did not appear to notice Mike waiting on the other side of the road and following her into the building, but whether he did or not, ten thousand lire was ample reason for him to keep his mouth shut.

All the same, when Mike turned the key in the lock and pushed open the door, for a moment they both wished ardently they had not come. Probably neither of them knew exactly what they had been hoping to find in there, but what met their eyes was dereliction. Everything had gone—even the light, it seemed, though this was certainly an illusion. It had never been a well-lit flat—there were not enough windows—though, admittedly, when it was furnished it had looked a good deal less gray.

"Cor!" Mike murmured. He could find no other words. The carpet was dirty, impregnated with dust, studded with the imprints of vanished furniture; the walls were covered with a film of grime, accentuated by the pale squares where other people's pictures had lately hung. At the far end of the el, the alcove was starkly empty, with grease marks on the wall where the headboard of the bed had been. The telephone had been left stranded on the floor. Mike opened the bathroom door.

"Bathtub's still there, anyway." Same blue and gold tiles too, same neon light. "Hello, they've left a bit of firewood." In the same place, behind the bathroom door, but in a basket—that was new. It would have been hard to say just then which was worse, the things that were new, or the things that were still the same—their things, like the fireplace, where other people had been callously lighting fires for twenty years. Like the kitchen, which was

266

practically unchanged, with the same built-in cupboards, painted brown now instead of green.

"Is that our old stove?" Mike said.

"Oh, it couldn't be."

It was the same little kitchen, though, where they had giggled together over her terrible cooking, where they had sat chatting time and again, and drinking cups of tea, on the two high stools that had now gone. That was the same old-fashioned, porcelain sink where she used to wash the dishes, but the smallness of it surprised her; she had forgotten it was like that, after all the other sinks there had been in the meantime.

She turned, half expecting to see the breakfast tray propped up against the wall, with the tea caddy in front of it. There was nothing there now but someone's old bottle that smelled of kerosene. Mike gave it a sniff and said, "Not everyone uses Courvoisier to light their fires."

It was odd how all these little things brought them together, how the forgotten minutiae of their life in common still belonged to them both. Like the hook on the kitchen door that Robin had stuck there herself to hang up the apron she invariably forgot to put on, and that ugly window, too high up to clean, that she was always saying she would cover with a curtain one of these days. The things they had meant to do and never done. Find a place to put the baby, for instance. Their golden boy that never was.

"Let's have a look upstairs," Mike said.

The living room was rectangular, with an attractive tiled floor that made it look more cheerful than the rest. It wasn't as big as Mike had thought it was, but the tiles were astonishingly familiar. He opened the shutters and stepped out onto the little terrace, resplendent with greenery now, as it never was in their day.

"Oh, Mike, look. Do you think those are my nasturtiums?" What she called her nasturtiums were some seedlings someone had brought them by way of a hint that terraces are supposed to have flowers on them. Robin had watered them vaguely, on and off, when she remembered to, and greeted their first flowers at the beginning of March as a prodigy of her gardening skill, leaving

267

them nonetheless to languish in the tiny pots they had been brought in. But who was to say that these, this great pot full of them in lush scarlet bloom, were not the descendants of her own frail little half-starved flowers, which had been growing and proliferating ever since. Something of theirs that was still here, alive.

"Do you believe in ghosts?" Robin asked.

"Of course I do," said Mike. "I am one."

"Perhaps I am too. Perhaps we both are. And that's what we're doing here. Haunting."

"Or searching. Isn't that what ghosts do?"

"Searching for what?"

"Themselves—life—whatever it is they've lost."

Perhaps it was just that sense of loss that made them embrace, or the discovery of something they had suddenly found. Perhaps it was to hide in each others' arms from the place as it was now, and feel their way back somehow to the cloudless past. Whatever it was, something had changed. When she felt his sex rise, all Robin knew was that she was completely out of her depth.

"What, *here*?" she said.

"Where else?" He held her at arm's length and smiled at her bewilderment. He was a man again, self-assured. This was his place and nobody else's. She was his girl. All at once he felt capable of cleaning up the flat and putting back the furniture and living the way he had lived when he was here before. And making love the way he used to, long ago. "I know," he said, "let's go and make a fire." He took her hand and led her towards the stairs.

They found an old newspaper in one of the kitchen cupboards and built the fire in the hearth downstairs together, with the bits of wood left in the basket in the bathroom. When he touched a match to the paper, they crouched side by side to watch it flare up. "That's better, eh?" he said. That's the wise thrush, she thought. He sings each song twice over . . .

Mike walked quickly to the door and slipped the bolt.

But no, it wasn't rapture any more. It was a strange mixture of sensations, not all of them good. The fustiness of the air, the dust on the floor, the slightly heavy odor of his breath, as if his whole body had somehow gone sour. She remembered the fragrance of it in the old days, how touch and taste and smell used to fuse into one as she melted in his arms and lost all consciousness of where or what she was. In the old days, not now. I suppose I'm not as sexy as I was then, she thought. Got out of the habit. Or got past it, or something. All those thoughts getting in the way, thoughts that had no business to be there, like: What's he been doing for sex all these years? and What will it feel like with Luca afterwards? and Why am I doing it if I'm not enjoying it? and What if someone knocks on the door? She wasn't going to come, that was obvious, and there was something a bit sordid about it all, in spite of the blazing fire and their desperate desire to pretend they were back where they used to be, full of hope and confidence and light. Hark, where my blossom'd pear-tree in the hedge leans to the field and scatters on the clover blossoms and dewdrops . . . But she was still the same person, and Mike was still Mike, in spite of everything. She was giving him back something that was his by right—his manhood, perhaps his very self. It wasn't rapture, certainly—more like a struggle for his life. When he cried out, it was a cry of anguish more than love. She felt him die in her arms and come to life again, and by some miracle his arms, clutching her, suffused her with warmth and joy. As he subsided on her breast, spent with fatigue, her own arms tightened round him in tranquility. "Robin!" he gasped. "Oh, Robin."

A little later, lying peacefully back on the dusty carpet, he opened his eyes and smiled. Reaching out his hand to touch her, he said, "You're mine, aren't you? You always have been."

She placed her hand on his and thought, with the faintest touch of bitterness: Do I have to be somebody's? Can't I just be me? Could it be that she wasn't anybody, wasn't a person at all, except in relation to somebody else—some man?

"I think we'd better be going," she said, reaching for her clothes.

"I suppose so." Mike sat up and took a last, fond look round. "Either we take the flat or we go."

"Mike, do get dressed. Supposing someone comes?"

"No one will come. You gave him ten thousand, didn't you?"

She remembered Luigi's shifty smile and thought: My God, he'd tell on me like a shot if anyone asked. Once again it crossed her mind that Luca might know all the time what was going on. He might have followed her here, for all she knew, or put one of those horrid *investigatori privati* on her tail. But no, she thought, Luca wouldn't do a thing like that to me. Not any more than I'd do a thing like this to him. She picked up the empty wood basket and carried it back into the bathroom in a vague and futile attempt to remove the evidence. The fire had burned down.

"Do you think we ought to throw some water on that?" she asked.

"Why? Let it burn as long as it can."

When they were both dressed and ready to go, she asked, "Do I look all right?" What she meant was, Does it show, what I've just done? She flicked some imaginary specks of dirt off her dress.

"Stop fussing. And come here."

He pulled her to him and held her close for a moment. Then he kissed her forehead and her nose and said, "Old Robin Rednose," and laughed. That was what he used to call her when her nose went pink after being in the sun. "Remember that bit you translated from the Pavese book?" he asked.

" 'Nothing is like the rest, the past?' "

"You got it wrong, you know. I looked up the Italian. It's *'Nulla si assomma al resto, al passato,'* not *'si assomiglia.'* What Pavese really meant was that nothing can just be added to the past. We must always start all over again. Makes more sense that way too. For us, I mean."

She smiled a little uncomfortably, and said nothing.

"I'm going away very soon," he said. "Will you come?"

"Going away? Where to?"

"I don't know yet. Somewhere far away."

"I thought you loved Rome so much."

"I do, but Rome doesn't love me anymore. Let's start all over again, shall we? Somewhere else?"

"It's not nearly as easy as you seem to think."

"I don't think it's easy. I just think it's right. You don't belong here, with him. It's all false, the way you're living now. Those clothes aren't you. Having money to burn isn't you. By the way"—he pulled a ten-thousand-lire note out of his pocket—"I don't want Luca paying for Luigi's bribe." She took it from him and frowned. He was right. The thought had crossed her own mind. But it made her feel a little worse just then. "You've forgotten all the poetry. You've almost forgotten how to laugh. And when you make love, you just do it—you told me so yourself. That's not you, my love, not my Robin. He may be very kind. He may call it looking after you. I call it suffocation. I want you to wake up and start living again. Before it's too late."

"You mean just run away, without knowing where to?"

"It doesn't really matter where to, does it?"

Come live with me and be my love, and we shall all the pleasures prove—yes, and before you know where you are, you're washing his underpants. At least there was Adele to do that at home.

"Well? Can you look me straight in the eye now and tell me you love Luca?"

"But I *do* love Luca!"

"What were you doing just now, then? Mucking around?"

"No!"

"Don't tell me you're going to go back to him as if nothing had happened—and maybe make love with him again tonight?"

"No, it's not like that at all. That's not the point."

"What is the point, then? Have you been unfaithful to him before?"

"Never. Honestly." Since her marriage she had felt no inclination to run after other men and, enclosed as she was on all sides by Luca's presence, no man had tried to run after her. She had been glad; it made life much simpler. Till now she could have sworn she was happy with Luca. Even now she was not sure it would not be a relief if Mike just went away.

"When are you going?" she asked.

"That depends."

TWENTY-NINE

Carlo Rolli had done well for himself. He was one of Italy's most prominent journalists now, and a well-known face on television too. Once a week, on Friday nights, he probed some of Italy's sorest spots in a controversial program called "Telescopio," which Mike had always made a point of watching whenever he could, at Porto Azzurro. It was not hard to track him down, and the prompt alertness in his voice on the phone, when Mike told him who he was, suggested the pricking up of professional ears.

"I won't beat about the bush," Mike said, when they had gone through the ritual well-wells and how-are-yous. "I've got a proposal to make. Can we meet?"

"Why not? I live in Via Sistina. Want to come over?"

He was waiting in the doorway at the top of the stairs, a tall, scrawny figure silhouetted against the light. He must have been over fifty, but he looked astonishingly young, one of the few that life had enhanced, instead of damping down. His hair—still brown, barely spattered with gray—tended to stand up on end from his forehead, and when he smiled, the crow's-feet round his eyes stretched down towards his pointed and vivacious chin, which rose in a curve to meet his beaklike nose. When he was young, that scragginess had made him a not particularly handsome man, but now it gave his face a peculiar charm and stamped him as a strikingly forceful personality.

He took Mike into a large studio room, full of books and newspapers and muddle. There was a typewriter on a desk scattered with notes, where he had evidently been working when Mike came.

"I won't ask the obvious questions," he said. "You're here, that is the main thing. And you look well, considering."

"I could be worse. I could also be better, if none of it had ever happened. And you know, if no one else does, that it shouldn't have." Carlo said nothing to that. He became doubly attentive, but a little wary. "That's why no one is more qualified than you to present the truth to the world."

"Ah. And what is the truth?"

"That Beppe is alive, as I've said all along. Alive and well and living in Rome." Carlo still said nothing—simply smiled and waited for more. "You wouldn't say no to the chance to unmask him on your program, would you?"

"Sounds great, but I'd want to know more."

"I brought you these, to go on with." Mike handed him Leo Santi's rooftop photographs of the so-called Signor Molinari, which Carlo took over to his desk and examined under the lamp. *"Mah!"* he muttered finally, raising his eyebrows skeptically. "Is that all?"

"Don't worry, it's him, all right. I brought you these too, so you can check."

Mike tipped a pile of old photographs of Beppe out of an envelope onto the desk. They were the fruit of days spent in the press section of the National Library, scouring the back numbers of newspapers, especially those dating from the time of the trial, when they had all had their pictures in the paper day after day. From time to time he had had to stop, enchanted by a photograph of pale, anguished Robin, or fascinated by some journalist's imaginative account of what Mike or Robin or Nicola had said in court; and he could have gone on for weeks, poring over those great, musty volumes full of vanished days, if he had not felt obliged to drag himself away and make use of the library facilities to obtain copies of all the closeups of Beppe he had found. There were more than enough to illustrate his point.

Signor Molinari's photograph might be a bit blurred. Signor Molinari himself might be too plump and too bald. The bushy mustache changed the look of the mouth. But he had the same hairline, what there was left of it; he had the same ears and the

273

same nose. Even Robin and Leo were convinced of that by now. Carlo, however, refrained from committing himself.

"Look," said Mike, "I can prove it, I swear. If you say you want to do it, I'll tell you where he lives."

"I imagine you have something more in mind than what you've said so far."

"Oh, yes. A lot more."

"Why don't you explain, then? Whisky?" There was a bottle on the desk, half buried in papers. Carlo took two glasses off the shelf behind him and poured some out and handed it over, neat. "There's ice in the kitchen, if you insist," he said. "But they told me in Edinburgh I must drink it like this—which is easier, don't you think? So, what is it you want? To prove that you were always innocent?"

"That too."

Carlo shrugged. "You know, Mike, it's very sad, but a miscarriage of justice is not of much interest in itself today. There are so many worse things around of a different dimension altogether: tortures, massacres, violence everywhere you turn. People know it and shut their minds to it. How else can they go on? They have reached—what do you call it?—saturation. They don't care anymore, or they care a little, for a little while, and then something else comes along and distracts them. Your case has many other aspects that could be of interest, but just to tell me that Beppe is still alive—to *you* it seems like a major scandal. To the public, I'm afraid, it is worth no more than a shrug. *"Poveretto!"* they'll say. *"Ma guarda un po'!"* They are too tired to bother more than that. Remember the Gallo case? The man who got life for murdering his brother—who was found alive after seven years? It was in the papers, oh, yes. For a few days it was on the front page. And in a few weeks it was forgotten. They let Salvatore Gallo out on parole, but there was some legal problem that made it impossible to annul the verdict. He received a pardon, I think, in the end, from the President of the Republic. You see? I don't even remember."

"I do, because his case was so similar to mine. Up till then, no one had ever imagined that you could be condemned for killing a

274

man who was not even dead. There was no provision for it in the Penal Code, and they didn't know what to do. They couldn't just say, 'Oh, sorry, we made a mistake,' and wipe the crime off his slate. It took him years to get another hearing in a court of appeal, and even then they didn't let him off; they sentenced him to four and a half years for doing his brother bodily harm. It was true he had hit him, you see. They found blood on the ground—two liters of it, someone said at the trial, and though someone else said there were only fourteen drops, the judge chose to believe the two-liter version and expressed the opinion that two liters of blood was as good as a corpse. He was the first to be shocked, I think, when the mistake came to light. But as he said himself, a judge is only a man, not the Holy Ghost; he has to believe what people tell him, and if they tell him lies, how is he to know? One good thing did come out of that case, though, in the end. Four years later, in 1965, they reformed the law. So now, if the man you're supposed to have killed turns up alive, you're entitled to a new trial. Fantastic, eh? But I don't want a new trial. What's the use? Those twenty years are gone and they won't come back. No. There's only one way I can see to make it all fair and square, and that's to kill Beppe Palazzo."

"You're not serious. You can't be."

"Why can't I? I've paid for that murder, so I've got a right to commit it. And I want to tell the world why—on your program. What do you say?"

"I say you need a psychiatrist."

"Maybe I do. But the fact remains, no one can stop me from killing a dead man. And I'll tell you another thing. No one can make me pay for it all over again." Mike pulled out a pocket edition of the Penal Code. "Here you are, see for yourself—page one-seventy-two, Article Ninety. Nobody can be tried twice for the same crime. Fair enough, don't you think?"

"You don't expect me to believe such nonsense?"

"All right, don't. I don't care—as long as you let me say my little piece. After all, it ought to be pretty good for the ratings. Just think of the dust it'll raise."

Carlo was walking up and down, rubbing his long, hooked nose.

275

"What proof have you, apart from these"—he waved at the photographs on his desk—"to show that Beppe is alive?"

"His mother."

Carlo stopped. "His *mother*?"

"Listen, I promised you proof, okay? All you need is some film equipment and a little patience."

Massimo Fabbri, the boy Mike snatched the megaphone from that famous night, was now a producer. His handsome baby face had sunk complacently into a double chin, and he had all the air of a sleek wheeler-dealer. His office in Via Panama was small but elegant, and he kept Mike waiting only a quarter of an hour—just enough to point out who stood where. After that, he received Mike with a fairly good grace, showed him a copy of *Variety*, where a film of his was listed among the fifty top grossers, and looked frankly amused to hear that he owed Mike a favor.

"How's that?" he said. "I thought it was the other way round. Something about a—"

"A megaphone. Quite right. Shall I buy you a new one?"

"Heavens, no. I don't use the things any more. It belonged to the production anyway."

"All right, I'll buy you a drink, or send you some flowers, or something. Now let's come to what you owe me. Your evidence really fixed me—do you realize that?"

"No. What did I say?"

"You said I was alone in the car, and that was what put the lid on it."

"But you *were* alone in the car."

"I wasn't, but never mind. All I want now is a helping hand, if it's not too much to ask."

Massimo stared at him. "What kind of a helping hand?" he asked, on his guard.

"Not money, don't worry. Not even a job. Just a permit to shoot a scene with a car in it in Piazza Navona, and one reliable person to help. Any smart young fellow will do. And needless to say, I'll pay whatever it costs."

"What are you going to shoot?" Massimo asked, curious now.

"Something for TV," Mike said. "Something with a good part in it for a broken-down, middle-aged character like me. Put myself back on the map, maybe. You never know."

A look of scorn crept into Massimo's eye. An Italian television film for an aging, forgotten star? Hmmm. No dice, for his money. *Povero illuso*, he seemed to be thinking, what are you hoping to pull off?

If you only knew, Mike chuckled to himself.

It was around lunchtime on a Thursday when Mike informed the management of the Albergo Girasole that he would be leaving early the following day, and sent the porter to bring down two large suitcases and a box full of his books from Porto Azzurro, which he said he was going to send on as advance luggage.

He had been sorting and packing his things for weeks, patiently polishing moldy shoes and wading through old papers, which little by little he had torn up into shreds and taken out himself to deposit, bit by bit, in the anonymous rubbish bins of the neighboring streets. A superfluous labor, that, a touch of voodoo almost, to be sure the old identity was well and truly wiped out and not picked up in scraps and harbored by some inquisitive member of the hotel staff. Before bringing the two suitcases away from Sora's, he had filled them with his old clothes. Moldy and moth-eaten as they were, they had appeared irretrievable at first sight, but after a glance at the prices in the shops, Mike had begun to look at them with different eyes. Everything that seemed still to deserve it had been dry-cleaned, all the shirts and underwear fiercely laundered. Those that had not survived rehabilitation had been destroyed and, like the papers, thrown into other people's bins.

A number of recent purchases were already in the car: a large cushion wrapped in brown paper, and a plastic bag containing a pair of gloves, a bathing cap, a small, watertight pouch, a sharp kitchen knife, some cotton wool, and a length of sturdy rope. There was also a small new suitcase containing his basic needs for two or three days, along with an airline ticket, and a false passport and a driving license, both in the name of Danilo De Michele, which he had obtained from an old prison acquaintance and paid for handsomely in cash. The photograph in both of these documents was not recognizably his own; it was the result of many evenings spent searching for a new identity, sticking on improbable mustachios in front of the mirror and trying out false noses until, carried away with that heady sensation he used to love, he was off again, back in the land of long ago, turning himself from Cyrano into Mr. Puff and from Mr. Puff into a melancholy, white-faced clown. All nonsense, of course; the disguise had to be foolproof in the daytime, and greasepaint just wasn't any good. Nor were false noses and, to be realistic, a beard took much too long to apply. In the end he had settled for a good dark brown wig, heavy tortoiseshell spectacles, and a mustache he could slip quickly on and off. He had packed these into the leather toilet case he had found at Sora's, and placed it on top of the small suitcase that was already in the car.

Nothing was left in his room now but the other small suitcase, the one he had brought with him from the prison, in which he had packed a second set of basic essentials, differing from the first only in that they were older and tattier, all things he could happily do without. He had tucked his British passport into the pocket on the inside of the lid.

He opened the canvas top of the Spyder to make more room, and with the box balanced precariously on the passenger seat and the suitcases squeezed into the space behind, he set off through the town, across the river, and up over the Gianicolo. It had taken him a long time to find the ideal spot for the operation he was about to embark on. The place he had chosen was Via della Nocetta, a narrow road off Via Aurelia Antica, enclosed between two high walls, with a turn to the right about a hundred yards down, and another to the left some twenty yards farther on. It was there, in the crook of the first bend, by a disused gateway into Villa Pamphili, that he stopped the car and got out. From that point he could spot any other car approaching long before the driver was near enough to see him.

Another car was parked there already, a dilapidated old gray Fiat 1400 from the same car dump where he had bought the Spyder. He had picked this one up for almost nothing—who would ever want a 1400 these days, especially with an engine that was on its last legs? But it happened to suit his purposes exactly, with that capacious trunk, to which he at once transferred the two large suitcases and the box of books. He threw the small suitcase onto the front seat and left the plastic bag and the parcel in the Spyder, which he closed and locked. That was Mike's car. The gray one belonged to Danilo De Michele. He intended to be meticulous about keeping the two characters distinct, even to the extent of not driving Dan's car while wearing Mike's clothes.

"You can't be too careful," Memmo had told him time and again. "Suppose you run into a roadblock, say, on the way out, or just some fussy cop who wants to see your license, and then the same one happens to stop you again the next day in the same car, and there you are with your wig and your whatnot and your license in a different name. Take a bit of explaining, wouldn't it?"

A car came round the corner and Mike buried his head in the open trunk of the Fiat until it had passed. Now I'm overdoing it, he thought, enjoying the drama of it and grinning at his own mounting excitement. He had placed a shirt and tie ready on top of one of the suitcases, together with one of his most successfully rehabilitated old suits. He dodged round behind the car and quickly changed into these, which he called Dan's clothes—as opposed to Mike's, which he had taken off and placed on the back seat.

Now for the disguise. Climbing into the front to open the small suitcase, he took out the wig, pulled it on, and smoothed it down. Speed was essential, and he had rehearsed all this till he had it pat. He slapped on the mustache, then the spectacles, and checked the effect in the mirror from the toilet case. He rather fancied himself, as a matter of fact. He looked younger.

"Vastly well, sir! Vastly well!" he said out loud. "And now, egad, here we go!"

He drove back along Via Aurelia Antica to Porta San Pancrazio, which he saluted in his way by circling round it a couple of times before continuing on down the hill, stopping for a few minutes by San Pietro in Montorio to take a long last look at Rome. Oh, no, he thought, this won't do. If I start getting sentimental now, I'll never go through with this. He pulled himself away from the parapet and got back into the car, then drove on down Via Garibaldi to the river and along it past the Island, past Piazza dei Ponziani, across the Ponte Rotto and past the Anagrafe. Ghosts everywhere you turn, he thought. If it's not Garibaldi, it's Beppe; and if it's not Beppe or Queen Christina, it's Robin and me. On past the Forum, past the Colosseum, past the Baths of Caracalla to Via Appia Antica, and then on out of Rome, past Ciampino Airport and off to the left, up Via dei Laghi till he reached Nemi. He did not turn into the town, however; he drove straight on along the road that overlooks the famous volcanic lake from the top of the ridge that encircles it. He had made a number of trips out here before to make sure he had everything right, so he knew exactly where he was going to park the car.

Once there, he changed back into Mike's clothes, left Dan's clothes in readiness on top of the suitcase together with some underwear, removed his disguise, and replaced it in the toilet case, which he locked up in the trunk with the small suitcase and the rest of the luggage. Let's hope it doesn't get stolen, he thought, pocketing the car keys and heading down the road on foot towards the local bus stop. He had to wait half an hour for the bus to Rome, which left him at San Giovanni. He took a taxi from there to Via Aurelia Antica and walked round the corner into Via della Nocetta, where he had left the Spyder. So far, so good.

THIRTY

A pigeon sat drowsing on the head of Bernini's Triton; a couple more were resting on the arms. They looked very much at home there, Robin thought. She had never noticed before how many pigeons there were in Piazza Navona; they flew round and round with a great flapping of wings whenever a motorbike revved up or a balloon went bang. The rest of the time they kept busy on the ground, mostly in front of Ristorante Mastrostefano, where a great horde of them were pecking at bits of bread.

Robin was sitting on one of the stone benches trying to think and in fact doing nothing but listen to the quietness—the water rushing from the fountains and the soft scuffing of shoes on the cobblestones. A youth in a poncho, with a red cap perched on long, bushy black hair, strolled past with a monkey on a leash. A little boy of about four pedaled gleefully by on his tricycle. There were young mothers wheeling prams, and dogs of all sorts romping in and out among the strollers, and no traffic. Cars were not allowed in, only taxis and an occasional police car circling slowly round, looking for trouble and finding none. The air was thick with the smell of marijuana, but it was all marvelously peaceful. Robin wished she could go on sitting there, like that boy on the fountain railings, quietly smoking and enjoying the beauty, without having to go through with what she was about to do.

Beppe had phoned her a few days before. *"Ciao, amore,"* he had said, as naturally as if he had been talking to her every day.

"Who's that?" she had asked, instantly trembling, for she knew very well who it was, right away. No one else would have said, *"Ciao, amore,"* like that.

He had laughed then. "Don't you know?" he had said. "Can't you guess?"

"All right, then. I can guess."

281

"You wanted to find me, no? So—here I am."

"How did you know my phone number?"

"I know everything."

"But how? How could you know we were looking for you?"

"That's easy. Mike told my mother. He told her another thing, also. Something that frightened her."

"What do you mean?"

"You don't know? Really? Oh, I hope that is true."

Robin fell silent, thinking uneasily of Mike's hints at a diabolical plan for revenge.

"But why don't you come and see me?" Beppe was saying. "I want to talk with you seriously. Come and have tea."

"Come and have *tea*?"

"What is so strange? You came already, no? You rang the bell. Mike sent you, I suppose, to see if the person here was me. So— this time I will open the door, and we will talk."

She would never have dreamed of going if Mike had not insisted. It was he who had fixed the time: half past one, on Friday.

"That'll be perfect," he had said.

"Perfect for what?"

"I'm not going to tell you. I don't want you involved. Just trust me, will you? Just go, that's all."

She didn't like it. She didn't like it one bit. It was hard to say which made her most nervous: being left in the dark about Mike's mysterious plan, or the feeling that there must be a catch somewhere, a motive for Beppe's sudden decision to come out into the open after all these years. She wished she had not given in and agreed to come.

There was a spy-hole she hadn't noticed before in the door of Beppe's flat; so that was why he didn't open up the other time. She half hoped he wouldn't this time, either.

He did. He flung the door wide and smiled. *"Ciao,"* he said.

He was utterly different—bigger, broader, balder, sadder— well, no, not sad exactly, more sober, that was it, more serious, and yes, in some indefinable way, improved. Perhaps it was the mustache that helped to give him substance, or merely the weight of twenty years that they all had on their shoulders, the weight of twenty years thrown away.

"Come in," he said.

She walked past him straight into the living room—there was no hall—and what she noticed first were the paintings, the very ones he had had on the walls at Piazza dei Ponziani; and as if this were not enough to make her feel strange, surely that was the table under which she had once found herself in an ignominious state of undress, with him in his pale blue underwear. She stared at it, dazed by the way a thing like that could spring up and hit her.

"I'm so happy you came" he said, watching her walk round the room. "It was a big surprise, you know, to see you standing outside my door, that day you rang the bell."

The spyhole, she thought—of course.

"But it was also a shock to see I had been found. I became used to the idea only later, some days later. Then I thought, if she comes again, I will let her in; and I began to hope that you would. But please sit down, no? Shall I call the restaurant and tell them to bring us lunch?"

"*Lunch?*"

"Why not? It is the time, I think, no?"

"You said you wanted to talk," she said, terribly embarrassed now, not knowing what attitude to take.

"We can talk and eat. That is what people usually do."

"For heaven's sake, how can you be so casual? Anybody'd think it was quite natural for me to come paying you a visit like this."

He winced, and she realized his cheerful manner was nothing but a front. "Will you drink something, at least?" he said.

"No, thank you."

She perched herself awkwardly on the edge of the sofa. It was, she felt certain, the same sofa he had before, but it was brand-new then and glamorously white, whereas now it was full of dust, with a drab cover that was threadbare on the arms. The whole place was shabby. It had the cluttered, dingy look of bachelor digs gone to seed. Could he really have been cooped up in here alone all this time?

"Still afraid to drink, eh?" he said, pouring himself a Scotch

283

and watching her out of the corner of his eye. "Don't worry. I gave up seducing English girls long ago." He sat down in the armchair facing her. "Mike was quick to find me, I must say. But it was not difficult; I have become lazy about hiding. You can't hide forever, you know. In the end, you half want to be found."

Could this be that awful, slimy Beppe? This quiet, mellow, middle-aged man?

"Well?" he said. "Shall I order lunch?"

"I'm not hungry, honestly."

"*Va bene.*" He shrugged and got up to fetch a packet of popcorn that was lying, already opened, on the table. He tipped it out into an empty bowl and began munching. "You look well," he said. "No one would guess you were forty-five." He laughed, seeing the way she bristled. "We can't fool each other, can we? I know you are only two years younger than me. But you look less, and I look more. *Mah! C'est la vie.*"

One of the buttons of his coat was hanging loose, and she had to suppress an idiotic urge to offer to sew it more securely in place. "But—" She faltered, not knowing what to say. "Do you stay in here all the time—by yourself?"

He laughed again. "Are you afraid for my sex life, perhaps? Don't worry, my dear. That is one problem I always was able to solve."

"But what do you *do*?"

"For sex, you mean?"

"No! For a living."

"Oh, *mi arangio. Come si dice?* I manage. I am good at managing. In Beirut, I was quite successful buying and selling films. Now I deal in—what shall we say? Girls."

"*What?*"

"Nice girls for lonely businessmen to have dinner with—" He caught the look on her face and added quickly, "No, no—it is all completely respectable. They are interpreters, babysitters, guides—an agency, nothing more. You worked in an agency yourself at one time, no?"

"But that was plain, hard typing. And anyway, how do you know that?"

"Vera told me. Remember Vera, the telephone girl at Alba Films? A nice girl, very helpful."

"You talked to Vera? What, after everyone thought you were dead?"

"With a different voice. I was good at making different voices. I used the telephone a lot, always. It was my secret weapon. *Dring-dring!* and you're inside somebody's house."

"So it *was* you, then. All those beastly anonymous phone calls I used to get."

"Beastly!" he laughed. "Just because I wanted to hear your voice?"

"How did you find out where I live now?"

"I've always known where you were. That's not difficult, in Rome." He smiled, observing her reaction. "When you live as a hermit, as I do, it is like being blind. You feel things that you cannot see. You understand things that people think you cannot know. I have followed everything, all these years."

"And to think I'd really begun to believe you were dead."

"Even you? You thought Mike had killed me? That is strange."

"No, no—of course I didn't think that. I just couldn't imagine you'd have sat back and let Mike be condemned. Not if you knew."

"You're a funny girl, you know. You have funny thoughts sometimes. Did it make you sad, a little, to think I was dead?"

A sudden wave of anger swept over her, the same kind of anger he always used to provoke, even when she did not know why. He might look a lot different, but he was Beppe all right. There was no mistaking that now. He was leaning back in the armchair, sipping his whisky and smiling at her in exactly his old lubricious way.

"Don't you feel sorry at all for what you did to Mike?"

"What I did to Mike? How about what Mike did to *me*? Make no mistake. He ruined my life."

"*He* ruined *your* life? When you deliberately staged a murder and left him looking like the one who did it?"

"It was not a murder that I—staged, as you say; just my own death. And it was Mike's fault, anyway. I was in a panic, thanks to him."

"Why? Because of all that shouting he did about your being

mixed up in whatever it was—girls, drugs, dirt—I never did quite get it straight."

"Drugs! Who told you that?" He laughed. "It seems funny now, the little bit I used to do. But no, I was not afraid of being arrested. It was the other thing."

"What other thing?"

"No, it's better I don't tell you. It is still dangerous to know about that."

"Heavens, what is it?"

"A secret. Which I only wish I didn't know. That was why I ran away, my dear—why I wanted everyone to think I was dead. If I had stayed—" He shrugged. "Remember Mitzi?"

"That Austrian girl? The one who killed herself?"

"She was killed, stupid girl. She had got into things that were too big, but she was too greedy to run away. Worse, she tried to use what she knew. It was not my fault, what happened to her, but what was terrible was that I knew the truth also about that. And Mike took a megaphone and told everyone in Rome that I knew."

"And you were afraid that—my God, do people really get killed like that—in *Rome*?"

"People get killed everywhere—when the stakes are very high."

"So you disappeared. But how?"

"It wasn't difficult. No one ever really tried to find me."

"You just left everything behind and went?"

"Not everything. There were certain things I could not leave— my address book, for one." He laughed.

"So you did go home. But the cleaning woman said—"

"Do you imagine the cleaning woman knew how many socks I had? Naturally, I left everything tidy, but do you think I went without my clothes? Naked? I left the suit I was wearing that night on the riverbank."

"That's one thing I always thought was a bit funny. Why should a murderer take off your clothes?"

"A murderer, no. A suicide, maybe. All I cared was to show it was me, dead. But the fuss they made of that suit—you would think it was a body. I followed it all, you know, in the newspapers.

It seems they wanted to believe I was murdered. They looked so clever, arresting Mike so fast. And they didn't need a body; they had my passport. Remember? They said if I left that in my desk, I *must* be dead. As if I could never have got another one."

"You took Mike's."

"Yes, but even if I hadn't, the police know false passports are easy to buy."

"But come on now, it wasn't only the passport. The way you'd staged it, they couldn't help thinking it was murder."

"With no dead body? I promise, I never thought they could condemn Mike without a body. And when they did, what could I do? Come back and say, 'Sorry, I was joking'?"

"Yes! You should have."

"Oh, my dear, I'm not such a hero. And do you think they would have let Mike out even if I did?"

"Of course they would. They'd have had to."

"Who knows? What is sure is that they would have put me in. I could have got twenty years for—what was the word?—staging that crime. *Calunnia*, they call it in Italian, when you stage a crime so that someone innocent is condemned. And when it's a serious crime like murder, they give the maximum penalty."

"Well, that's only fair. If one of you had to do twenty years, you at least did deserve it."

"Now wait—who created all that melodrama, me? You think he's innocent. But I got beaten up, and that's six months he deserved. At least."

"But not twenty years!"

"And how about *sequestro di persona*? He knocked me unconscious and carried me away. That's a fact. That's called kidnapping, isn't it?"

"Oh, come on, now!"

"*Sequestro di persona* in Italian law is the act of depriving someone of his personal liberty. And the penalty is from six months to eight years."

"You don't suppose they'd have given him eight years?"

"Then there is *ingiuria*," he went on, brushing aside her objection. "Anyone who offends the honor and decorum of a person gets six months, which becomes one year if it refers to a specific fact and is increased if the offense is committed in front of a number of people. Oh, I know it all by heart, I assure you. Anyone who offends the reputation of a person is guilty of *diffamazione* and gets one year. Two if it refers to a specific thing, three if it is done in the press or through any other means of publicity—how about a megaphone in Via Veneto, eh? So you see we have already reached about twelve years just with what he really did."

"Are you trying to tell me that Mike was guilty and deserved what he got?"

"I'm trying to tell you that he was not so innocent as you think. And I was not so wicked, either." He leaned forward and lightly touched her hand, which was resting on her knee. "I am not really a villain at all, you know. Just a man who has had to make the best of what he could get."

"You'll be telling me next you never did anything bad."

"If I did, I have paid for it."

Sadness caught up with him momentarily and he fell silent.

"Why did you call me?" Robin asked. "You must have had a reason."

"No. Only a little nostalgia—and a great desire to see you. And as I said, in a way it was a relief to be found."

"But from what you've told me, you can't afford to be found."

"No. You're right. The temptation was too great, but it was very foolish. I'll have to run away again when you've gone."

If you're not too late, she thought, remembering, with a shudder, that Mike was even now plotting some obscure and intricate scheme for revenge.

"And you, *amore*, what has life done for you?" he asked with the brightest smile he could muster. "Do you like being a signora and living in Parioli? Are you happy, huh?"

"Very," she said, a little too sharply. Seeing his smile turn skeptical, she hastily changed the subject by asking, "So where *did* you go that night? You still haven't told me."

"That famous night? To the Via Appia Antica." He laughed. "I walked all the way—imagine. I was afraid even to take a taxi. But

I knew a place there where no one would find me—one of those ruined Roman tombs that is like a little house. I spent two days in there. Then my mother took me to a villa that my stepfather had in Toscana, where I lived for nearly three months, till the fuss was over. Then I went to Beirut."

"With Mike's passport?"

"Yes. I had the photograph changed, and by then I had a beard and a mustache. No one even looked at me."

"Incredible."

"No. The incredible thing is that we think it would be different. Do you know how many people there are in the world? How can anyone check everyone who passes by to see if he is one of the ones that is lost? How can the police find out who is guilty and who is not? Mitzi killed herself, they said. Why should they go beyond that? It sounded true, it looked true, everyone was very happy to believe it was true. And in a way it *was* true. Those silly girls always do kill themselves—with their own stupidity. There was no one at her funeral, you know. I went to see who would come. No one did. No one cared. It's quite easy, you see, to get away with murder. Sometimes."

He scooped up a handful of popcorn and began tossing it into his mouth. A middle-aged man dejectedly munching popcorn—so this was the prey she had cheerfully helped Mike run to ground. Why had she done it? she wondered. Why had she let Mike lead her on this far without telling her what he intended to do when he found him? Why had she closed her mind to everything but the excitement of the hunt? Glancing from the worn-out sofa to the pictures on the walls, and back to that strangely familiar table, all the silent witnesses to the darkest side of her sexuality, it occurred to her that what she had perhaps been searching for was the proof that she had once dared to be much more dangerously alive.

But watching Beppe now, she felt so deflated that she could find nothing more to say.

Mike had left Carlo and his crew to finish their lunch at a trattoria round the corner from Piazza Navona, with instructions to move in and be ready by a quarter past two.

It only took him a minute or two to make sure that Massimo's nephew, Piero, a pale, callow youth fired with the consuming desire to work in films, was ready with a couple of wooden barricades on the corner of the road leading out of the piazza at the north end. Leo Santi, too, had arrived and was stationed with his camera in front of Number 112.

"*Pronti?*" Mike asked him.

"*Prontissimi!*" Leo assured him with enthusiasm.

"And the door?"

"All fixed. Whoever's in that office opens up at the slightest buzz. And I've slipped the catch so it won't lock, the way you said."

"Perfect." Mike handed him the shooting permit he had procured with Massimo's help. "You hang on to this," he said. "I'll go and fetch the car."

It was exactly one-fifty-six.

The next stop was a phone booth in Corso Rinascimento, which he stepped into at two minutes to two. He placed a *gettone* in the slot and let another minute pass before dialing the Contessa's number.

"Contessa De Cleris?" he asked, putting on an exotic accent.

"Who's that?" she demanded.

"I am speaking for your son. He needs urgent help."

"My son is dead," she snapped.

"Naturally, yes. But even the dead have troubles."

"Who are you? What do you want?"

"I am a friend of Max's from Beirut. He asked me to tell you he must get away—at once. Mike Donato has found him. Every minute counts, every second. You know what the danger is, don't you?"

"My son is dead."

"I know. I am referring to Max Molinari, who lives in Piazza Navona. He would phone you himself, but his phone is bugged. And he has no money with him to get away. He says please, *please* go there at once—now—immediately! Don't let him down."

Mike heard a click. The Contessa evidently thought she had

heard enough. It was two o'clock. He quickly dialed Beppe's number, before she had time to do it first. When Beppe said *pronto*, Mike said nothing. He could not help relishing the anxiety in the second *pronto* and the note of panic that crept into the third, but the purpose of this phone call was not to torture his victim, only to isolate Beppe's phone and prevent the Contessa from getting through. When with a muttered obscenity, Beppe finally slammed down the receiver, Mike left the one in the phone booth off its hook, which he plugged with a little wedge of folded paper to delay the release of Beppe's line still more.

When he set off towards Piazza San Pantaleo, where he had left the red Spyder, it was one minute after two. It would take fifteen minutes at least from Via Lazio to Piazza Navona by taxi—he had timed it twice, with traffic and without—plus the time for the Contessa to get dressed and go downstairs to the street, after trying Beppe's number a few more times. Unless she was very lucky, it would take time to find a taxi, too. Her reckoned he had until two-twenty-five, at the very least.

The anonymous phone call seemed to have jangled Beppe's nerves. Robin watched him pour himself another drink and walk thoughtfully across the room with it, nibbling his nails.

"Now you know what it's like," she said. But he ignored her remark and, after a moment, turned back towards her with a smile.

"I loved you, you know. I really loved you. Perhaps I was the only one who did."

"Oh, come *on!*"

"You think Mike was the one, don't you? But Mike loved you, not for what you are, but for what he wanted you to be, which was quite different. Why did he hate me? Because I showed up a side of you he could not accept. He pretended to be a modern, cosmopolitan man, but in his heart he was a *contadino* like his parents, impregnated with the old, old idea that whores can do anything they want, but the woman he loves has to be pure. I never cared if you were pure or not. Half of you was, I think; the other half, who knows? I loved that inconsistency of yours, that mixture of truth and lies in your head, and specially—specially—the way you became excited, you who looked so cool and virginal when you were not in bed. Yes, you were quite a special girl, I think. And now this Luca Ferrero, this bourgeois husband, has turned you into a rich and respectable lady, or thinks he has, because I'm sure you are still telling lies all the same, your own kind of half-innocent lies. Which Luca Ferrero cannot even imagine, because he doesn't know who you are and he doesn't want to know. You are part of his career, like his valuable apartment and his expensive car. He gives you a lot of money, I think, no? And elegant clothes, I see, and jewels and a very expensive watch. Why? To show the world he is a successful man. Am I right or not?"

"No."

"You don't like the truth, do you? You never did. And yet here I am, in the state you see, because of you. I could have been rich and successful too, like your Luca. Much more, probably. *Ma non importa*. I love you all the same. Yes, in a certain way I think I love you still, in spite of everything, even in spite of the kind of man I am—or was. In a way, you have changed me. Isn't that funny? Here, drink a little. To us!"

She let him press a glass into her hand and, stunned by what he had said, lifted the glass mechanically to touch his. He stood up abruptly and opened the French windows, beckoning to her to follow him as he went outside onto the terrace. "Come and see," he said. They stood by the balustrade, looking down towards the *Tre Scalini*.

"It was funny, you know," he said, "looking down from my terrace in the evenings and seeing you all taking it easy in Piazza Navona."

"You saw us—*me*?"

"Everyone goes to Piazza Navona sometimes. You too, no? It gave me a good feeling. And sometimes I went down too, and had an ice cream like everyone else."

"You sat in Piazza Navona and ate an ice cream? I don't believe it."

"Why not? Who would know? Does anyone recognize Mike? Of course not. Nobody cares. Will you understand that? Fundamentally, nobody cares." He stared at her for a moment, and in spite of herself she stared back, into unexpectedly doleful eyes, which seemed to be peering out at her from an inner wasteland of relinquished aspirations and unappeased desires, of lonely nights and desolate days and guilt. "For a long time I was afraid to go out. I handled all my business on the telephone, or through a secretary who came up here to work. But my office is very near, in Corso Rinascimento, and now, when I need to go there, I go."

The doorbell rang.

Beppe jumped and said, "What's that?" and darted away inside to peep through the spy-hole in the door.

He gasped at the sight of a huge, balloonlike nose, which was pressed grotesquely close to the eyepiece. "*Chi è?*" he called out nervously.

The soft wail of a banshee was the only reply: "*Woooooo—*"

"*Chi è?*" Beppe repeated, though by this time he knew very well.

"*Wooooo!* Beppe! It's me—I've come to get you."

"What do you want?" Beppe asked hoarsely.

"I want to kill you, Beppe. I've got a right to, don't you think?"

"Go away or I'll call the police."

"You call them. I'll tell them who you are."

Beppe paused, thinking hard, before saying, "Robin's here, so—"

"I know. I'm not going to kill you now. But don't think I'll let you off, because I won't. I've paid for this murder and I want my money's worth. You'd better start saying your prayers."

But Beppe was no longer by the door. He had tiptoed away towards the terrace, where Robin was leaning over the balustrade, gazing down at the piazza.

"It's Mike," he whispered. "He's come to kill me."

"Oh, don't be ridiculous."

"That's what he told my mother he would do. I think he's crazy."

Why did she have goose pimples suddenly? What was that

thumping in her chest? Mike couldn't have been deceiving her, could he?

"You can't believe he meant it."

"What does he want, then? Tell me."

"To prove he didn't kill you, of course. To show you're still alive. That's all."

"That's *all*? That's the same as killing me."

"What do you mean?"

The bell rang again.

"*Oh, Dio! Dio!* What shall I do?"

"Don't get hysterical. Ask him what he wants. Or shall I?"

"Yes, you!" he said, struck by an idea. He paused to make a rapid calculation. "I know what I'll do. I'll go over the roof—yes, that's it. You open the door and keep him in here talking—will you? Will you do that for me? And I, in the meantime, will climb over the roof and escape. Quick, where did I put the key?"

He was rummaging through drawers, stuffing things into his pockets—documents, keys, money, passport—and hunting feverishly for the terrace key.

"You're just getting in a state about nothing," she told him, but he was too busy pulling a stepladder out of the broom closet to hear.

"Come, quickly," he whispered, staggering out through the French windows with the ladder, "so I will tell you when to let him in."

He went bustling up the ladder like a frightened hen, and it was hard not to giggle at the sight of him scrambling on all fours over the slippery, sloping tiles. Before vanishing over the top, he turned and hissed, "Go!" And the silliest part of it was that when she went back to let Mike in, Mike was not there.

Beppe sat down on the cornice above the communal terrace and allowed himself a moment to recover his breath. He was not used to all this exertion, and as for the jump that was now his only way out, he saw no hope of tackling it without breaking at least a leg. The sight of a ladder, propped tauntingly out of reach against the far wall, made him even more nervous. What he did not expect, though, when he lowered himself agonizingly to hang from the edge and shut his eyes and finally let go, was to be caught in midair and gripped by two firm hands from behind. All he managed was one startled wriggle before his hoarse shout of *"Aiuto!"* was smothered by the gauze pad that Mike pressed over his face and held there until he went limp.

"Mike!" cried Robin, transfixed in the doorway. "What have you done to him?"

"Nothing. A spot of chloroform, that's all. Close that door, will you? Till I make sure he's gone."

She pulled the door shut and went on staring.

"Don't look at me like that," Mike said.

"What do you want me to look like? You never said you were going to do anything like this. You made me come here so I could—Mike, you tricked me!"

"No, I didn't, I promise. It's all right."

"But what does it mean? What are you doing?"

"Look, I can't explain now. There just isn't time."

"Why didn't you explain *before*?"

"I told you, I didn't want you involved."

"But I *am* involved."

"Sorry, I can't stop to argue." He had gripped Beppe by the armpits and was dragging him across the terrace. "Open the door for me now, will you?"

"Not unless you tell me what you're going to do."

"All right then, don't. I can manage."

If she had had more presence of mind, she could have darted back inside and locked him out on the terrace until he explained, but she didn't think of that until later. At the time, she was too stunned to do anything but trail after him, helplessly nibbling her thumb, as he dragged Beppe towards the lift.

"He's not dead, is he?" she whispered.

"Of course not."

"Mike, you've got to tell me, you've got to."

"Sshh! Want to get me arrested?" He smiled. "I'll tell you this much. No matter what you hear, it won't be true. Remember that." He opened the lift gate and hauled Beppe inside; then he stepped out again and kissed Robin quickly, on the mouth, on the forehead, and on the tip of her nose. *"Coraggio!"* he whispered. "I'll be in touch as soon as I can."

He stepped back through the gate and clanged it shut. The lift sank instantly out of reach.

Patience was not Carlo Rolli's strong point. Sitting around having lunch made him nervous, with material still to be edited for the evening program and no clear idea what would come of Mike's promise of a scoop. When he and his crew joined Leo Santi outside the door of Number 112, he had not yet made up his mind whether Mike was completely sane. All he knew was that even if Beppe turned out to be as dead as everyone supposed, and Mike's "little piece" was nothing but the rambling of a man driven demented by long imprisonment, the story would be a matter of controversy all the same, because what happens to men in prison always is, particularly when the result can be proved bad.

But when the door of Number 112 was thrown open and Mike staggered out into the sunlight with a cry of "Shoot!" carrying what appeared to be a dead body on his shoulder, Carlo could only groan, "Oh, no!" This looked like the kind of scoop he couldn't even use.

"Behold the immortal Beppe Bacherozzo!" Mike proclaimed dramatically, turning round to show Beppe's bald head dangling down his back. Leo Santi started jumping about, taking shots from every angle like a paparazzo half his age, but even he looked surprised to see Beppe unconscious.

"What happened?" he whispered, plunging forward for a close-up.

"Nothing," Mike told him, heading for the Spyder, which was parked by the curb with the key in the ignition and both doors open. "Everything's under control."

"So what does it mean?" Carlo cut in coldly. He was waiting to see if he would have to call the police, and though he had signaled to his cameraman to pan with Mike to the car, he was in no mood to waste much more valuable time.

"It means he's dead," said Mike, lowering Beppe onto the passenger seat.

Leo abruptly stopped clicking and leaned forward with a doubtful frown to touch Beppe's lolling head.

"If you go to the Anagrafe and check," said Mike, "you'll find he's legally dead and buried. So the way I see it, he's got no right to be alive. Because if he is, what about me?"

He smiled and walked round the car to the driver's side, and Carlo nodded to the cameraman to carry on. He had decided to let Mike have his way for a bit, in spite of the looks of consternation he was getting from his crew. In the meantime a number of people had stopped to stare, and Carlo Rolli's name was being whispered in awe as others gathered round to watch the shooting of what they took to be a film.

Mike turned to stare gravely at the camera, with one hand on the car door. "How are you going to give me back the woman I loved, who went and married someone else?" he said. "Or the child that was born dead because I wasn't there to see it born alive? Or the Oscars I never won? Or just those twenty years of plain, old-fashioned, happy, or unhappy, everyday life? Do you think I ought to say *pazienza, non fa niente*, to err is human and what's done is done? Well, I'm sorry, I can't. To forgive may be divine, but I'm not God. So by the time you see this, Beppe Palazzo really will be dead. And you can all say I only got what I deserved. And so did he."

With that, he leaped into the car and started the engine, at the same time snatching a manila envelope from the ledge under the dashboard and tossing it to Carlo. "Here's the rest of the proof you wanted. Pictures of his mother, then and now. She'll be here any minute, so scram out of sight quick. Leo'll tell you what to do next. Goodbye!"

"Hey, wait a minute," Carlo protested. "Where are you going?"

"To kill Beppe—where do you think?" Mike laughed and drove off—straight through a sea of pigeons, who flew up and flapped indignantly round and round.

Robin burst out of Number 112 in time to see him go, and with his last words ringing in her ears, she found herself, to her intense embarrassment, face to face with Leo.

"Oh!" she exclaimed, looking askance first at Leo's camera and then at the microphone and the movie camera in the hands of Carlo's men.

"*Presto! Seguitelo!*" Carlo shouted.

One of the men made a dash for the van marked RAI–RADIO-TELEVISIONE, but by the time he had started it, the Spyder had vanished round the corner at the north end of the long, oval-shaped piazza.

"What's going on?" Robin asked Leo, nervously watching that last glint of red.

"Wish I knew," he told her. An anxious smile flickered on and off his face. "Did you hear what Mike just said?"

"He was pulling Carlo's leg," she said firmly. *No matter what you hear, it won't be true.*

"Yes," said Leo, with a dry, uncertain laugh. "But then, how come Beppe was unconscious?"

She stared at him, a sense of panic rising in her throat and no answer to give.

A screech of brakes made them turn and see that the television van had skidded to a halt in front of the wooden barricades that now blocked the only way out of the piazza at the north end. The man in the van was shouting abuse at someone, evidently the person who had blocked his way after letting Mike pass. And Robin's instinctive fear turned into a kind of dread as she perceived that this arrangement, too, must be part of Mike's plan. Oh, God! she thought, and then, Oh, Mike—*no!*

When Leo turned to scrutinize an approaching taxi, she slipped away with a breathless "*Ciao!*" and raced off through a pedestrian alleyway to Corso Rinascimento, in case, by some miraculous chance, there might still be a glimmer of red to be seen somewhere. There was not; it was much too late by then. She ought to have run downstairs after Mike the minute he shut the lift gate, instead of dashing back into Beppe's flat first for her bag, and then uselessly stopping to lock the communal terrace door, pocketing the key as if it were some kind of guilty clue. Clue to what, for heaven's sake? Even if it *was* the one she had stolen herself, what would that prove? What was she thinking Mike was going to do? She couldn't honestly imagine he had meant what he had just jokingly called out—could she? Still she went on running, the whole length of Corso Rinascimento, unable to make herself give up until she was certain there was no sign of Mike round the corner at the end. Surely there was a chance, a tiny chance, that he might have been stopped by a policeman, or bumped into another car, or blown a tire. Only when she had run all round the block and reached the corner of the street at the north end of Piazza Navona where she had seen the little red car disappear, did it come home to her how much more sensible it would have been to stay and ask Leo more about what he knew of Mike's plans; and although she was quite out of breath, she started running again, back through the piazza to Number 112. But by then Leo and the others had vanished too.

The Contessa De Cleris was extremely nervous. When the taxi entered Piazza Navona, she sat forward, bolt upright on the edge of the seat, her sharp eyes darting everywhere for signs of some trick. There was a police car circling round the piazza ahead of them. That was not unusual these days, with the kind of people who generally filled the square, but after alighting and paying the fare with shaking hands, she waited until it had completed its round and driven on out of the piazza before letting herself into Number 112. Her heart was pounding as she entered the lift, and it was an old heart. Twenty years ago she was like a rock in the face of such perils, but now she was not sure it might not prove too much for her. She was trembling all over—not just her old, frail, withered hands, but the whole of her being. She knew something terrible was about to happen. It was not even a premonition. After a phone call so obviously false as the one she had received, and the impossibility of getting through to Beppe on the phone afterwards, it was only common sense. Mike Donato had told her what he intended to do. He knew as well as she did that there was no way she could prevent it. But why did he want her to come here now? She knew instinctively that it was a trap, and yet how could she fail to go? Supposing the message was real and Beppe was genuinely in need of her help?

She rang Beppe's bell and waited. No one came. What could that mean? Where was he? She rang again, and knocked on the door. Nothing. She had a key to the flat, which, as a matter of respect for his privacy, she rarely used. She burrowed in her handbag for it now, and after a moment's pause, she fitted it into the lock and pushed open the door.

"Are you there?" she called out. *"Ci sei?"* Silence.

She walked unsteadily into the flat. "Max?" she called out in a quaky and almost breathless voice. She hated going into the bedroom, expecting always to find him in it with some girl, but she pushed that door open too now, and found nothing. She noticed the two glasses on the coffee table. One of them had lipstick on it, not that that meant anything. The door to the terrace was open. She went over to it and called out, "Beppe! Where are you?"

She heard a strange whirring sound behind her, and spun round. The front door had been pushed wide open, allowing a clear view of the room from the landing outside, and framed in the doorway was a movie camera. That was what was whirring. She gasped. There were men there too, but she could hardly see them. Her mind was numb with the shock. She had no idea who they could be or what they could want.

"Contessa De Cleris?" said Carlo in a courteous tone, from the darkness on the landing.

"Sì?" she said, trying to see who it was.

Then she realized, and with a howl of rage, she rushed forward and slammed the door.

THIRTY-ONE

Mike's timing had taken into account the lull in the traffic that generally occurred around half past two; so he was able to sail smoothly out of town, stopping only once, in a deserted road, to lift Beppe up out of the passenger seat, which offered no support for his dangling head, and heave him into the narrow space behind, where he could just be made to fit, with his knees bent up and the cushion bought especially for this purpose wedged under his head. Having relieved him of his shoes, Mike took the added precaution of securing his wrists and ankles with a piece of rope, before closing the hood of the car and proceeding on his way.

When he reached Nemi, it was twenty past three, and he went scorching through the narrow, winding main street at a speed that caused the inhabitants to jump out of his way and glare after him in disgust as he swooped out of sight again, under a tall archway and down a long, winding road towards the lake.

By then Beppe's eyes had been open for a quarter of an hour, but he had not uttered a sound nor made any attempt to move until now, when he suddenly started up and subsided again, finding his ankles tied and his body so tightly wedged he could hardly move.

"What's happening?" he muttered. "Where are we going?"

"Down to the lake," said Mike. "So I can chuck you in."

"What?"

They had turned into a narrow, cobbled road that led straight to the water's edge, between long, ghostly, plastic greenhouses full of tulips and carnations and lilies. The dark volcanic lake exuded an atmosphere of menace, wrapped in a strange silence, as if there were not a living soul for miles around.

Mike drove clockwise round the lake, close to the water's edge, until the asphalt road came to an end. The place he had chosen for the scene of his crime was twenty yards beyond that, a muddy clearing reached only by a bumpy, slippery path lined on either side by thick brambles and barely wide enough for the Spyder to pass.

When he reached the clearing, he stopped the car with its nose facing down the slope towards the gray water, dappled briefly with a splash of late sunlight among the reeds. Elsewhere it was a fine afternoon, but the ring of hills round the lake was almost black against the sky. There was not a sound except the croaking of toads and the intermittent calls of birds.

"Well, here we are," Mike said. "The famous volcanic lake of Nemi. Where things sink without trace, and people too, when they drown. Ideal place for a murder, eh?"

"You're joking."

"Joking?" said Mike, putting on the gloves out of the plastic bag he had left in the car the day before. "Well, I suppose it is quite funny. Go to jail first and do the murder afterwards. Glad it makes you laugh." He started taking off his clothes.

"What are you doing that for?" Beppe asked.

"Thought I'd go for a swim. Afterwards." He had on a pair of bathing trunks underneath.

He took the keys of the old gray Fiat out of his coat pocket and put them into the watertight pouch from the plastic bag, together with a thick wad of banknotes, which was all the money Sora had been holding for him, all the money he now possessed. He slipped his new identity card in the name of Michele Donadio into the glove compartment and made sure his old driving license was in there too, before cramming his bare feet into Beppe's shoes (which were a size too small for him), and stepping out of the car to go around and squeeze his own shoes and clothes into the small suitcase in the trunk. Returning to the driver's seat, he delved into the plastic bag again and took out the small, sharp kitchen knife.

"What's that?" said Beppe, his eyes widening in alarm.

"What does it look like?" Mike lifted the knife theatrically, like a dagger.

"N-now listen, Mike, l-let's talk this over, eh?"

"Talk what over? Whether or not I've got a right to kill you? Or whether or not I actually will?"

"If you were going to kill me, you would not give me a pillow for my head, I think."

So that was why he'd been keeping so bloody quiet back there. He'd been sitting tight and having a good hard think, like the other time.

"Not bad," Mike said, lowering the knife. "Still got a brain that ticks, I see. And quite right, of course. I never did mean to kill you. Murder's not really my line. But justice, poetic justice, now that's different. An eye for an eye—that's all I want."

Kneeling up on the seat, holding the knife, he lurched suddenly towards Beppe, who cringed and instinctively shielded his face with his arms. Mike laughed and pressed the handle into Beppe's roped and gloveless hand. "Relax. You're still all in one piece," he said, smiling as he retrieved the knife, taking care not to smudge Beppe's fingerprints. He rolled back his glove and, bracing himself to the pain, plunged the tip of the knife into his own hand, drawing copious blood, some of which he allowed to drip onto the car seat, and some of which he daubed on Beppe's clothes. Beppe's baffled expression slowly turned to dismay as he began to suspect what Mike had in mind. *Et voilà!*" said Mike, slashing the rope that bound Beppe's ankles and wrists. After smearing some more of his own blood on the blade, he tossed the knife out into the mud, narrowly missing a toad, which hopped into a clump of bright green weeds and blinked.

"Well, that's fixed you," he said. "You can run away now, if you want." But as Beppe painfully pulled himself up, Mike added, "I warn you, though, there's no way out of here but the way we came, so you'll probably run slap into the police."

"The police?" Beppe's hand stopped in midair as he stretched out shakily for the door. He was still groggy from the chloroform.

"They should be here any minute now. Be a bit awkward, that, won't it? What with my blood all over you, and your fingerprints on the gory knife."

"I don't understand. First you say you will kill me, and then—"

"And then—whoops! *You* kill *me*. And how did you do that, I wonder, if you're dead?"

"I think you are completely crazy."

"Oh, no, Beppe dear, just busy—getting a lot of public attention fast and showing that you're alive and I'm innocent and leaving you with a murder charge—all in one go. *And* giving you a chance to plead self-defense—which I think is pretty big of me, considering. As you see, I've thought of everything. When the police come, I'll have disappeared, and if they catch you running away, it'll be obvious—won't it?—that you did me in with my own knife."

"And you think you can escape by swimming? But they will find your footsteps."

"No—only yours. Your shoes are over here, by the way." Beppe cast a dazed glance at his stockinged feet. "Don't go without them. I hate to think what would happen to your socks in this mud."

"And how is it the police are coming?" asked Beppe, skepticism dawning as the befuddling effect of the chloroform wore off. "You can't have called them."

"I left a message—in reliable hands. Oh, they'll come, don't worry. In about"—he consulted his watch—"ten minutes, I should think. Just in time to find my car in the water, with a suitcase full of my stuff—including my British passport—for them to fish out and gawk at in lieu of a corpse. Because of course there'll be no corpse this time, either; but then everyone knows the tricks these volcanic lakes play. So I reckon you'll have a hard job making them believe the story you're going to tell. But don't worry. If it's self-defense, you'll get off with much less than they gave me."

He could hear himself talking too fast and too loud, as if it were a part he had learned but not properly rehearsed, and he was hamming it up like a beginner, as if he were back on the stage at the "Q" theatre, overdoing it for the sake of his father, who was watching him from the back of the stalls. Only it wasn't his father; it was Beppe Palazzo who was staring gravely at him now. He had propped himself up with the cushion, and this time, when he spoke, his tone was unexpectedly reasonable and quiet.

"I don't believe it. You can't be that vindictive. You can't hate me that much, not now."

What stunned Mike was the instant realization that Beppe was right. In prison he had seemed to hate someone that much, but it was not this man here, not this plump, aging person with melancholy eyes.

Beppe was watching him anxiously. He was sweating, Mike noticed, and it struck him then that he must have been out of his mind to think he'd be capable, in cold blood, of inflicting what he had been through on any real, live human being. Fantasy was one thing, human reality quite something else. The truth was, he had put so much energy into his plan that he had been carried along with it on sheer inertia, irresistibly impelled to go through with it to the end. But for a long time now, it had had nothing to do with hatred; the rage had burnt itself out.

He stared back at Beppe, thrown quite off balance, while everything he had been planning for so long dissolved, in a moment, into nothingness. What was worse, the police would be there any minute, and he had set the stage with such care that he could see no way out.

"I think there is something you don't know," Beppe said, reassured a little by Mike's silence. "It is not a question of an eye for an eye—though you forget that if they find me, I could get twenty years just for *calunnia*. But the danger for me is much more than that, if certain people discover I am alive. Why do you think I ran away, twenty years ago?"

"You were afraid of being arrested, no?"

"*Gesù*! It was you who did all that shouting. Do you mean to say you didn't even know what it was about?"

"Mitzi?"

"Mitzi was killed. You know that—and you know why. It was you who told *her* to run away, no?"

"And she said she couldn't because you had her money."

"She was a liar. What money? She said everyone owed her money."

"And she knew all about the girl on the beach. Right?"

"*Ma certo*. But Mike, I know much more than Mitzi. Can't you see now why I had to pretend to be dead? It was my only chance to stay alive."

Mike paused. In all these years, that was one aspect of the story that had never occurred to him. "But that's all over and done with now. Filed and forgotten."

Beppe shook his head. "How can it be? The case was never solved. Even now, from time to time, some clever journalist pulls it out. And the people who were important then are much more important today. I have to stay dead, Mike. I have to."

A thin little long-forgotten voice wafted to the surface of Mike's mind—Mitzi's voice saying, "Mike, I am afraid." With his eyes riveted on the blood he had daubed grotesquely over Beppe's shirt, he recalled the blue veins in her pale, scraggy wrists, the veins the newspapers said she had slashed. And here was Beppe—slippery, bumptious Beppe—with the same look in his eyes that Mitzi had that time, as if he too were pleading, "Mike, I am afraid."

His plan, his revenge, suddenly seemed like a hollow joke. Poetic justice, indeed—he had had no idea what he was doing. One step more and he would have condemned Beppe to death.

"I'm a fool," he said. "I should have realized."

He peeled off his gloves and tucked them into his trunks, trying to think as quickly as he could what to do. He looked at his watch. It was two minutes to four.

"The trouble is, I've already proved you're alive. It'll be on Carlo Rolli's TV program tonight."

"On television! What?"

"Everything. The whole story, complete with shots of me carting you away, and your mother turning up and finding you gone."

"My *mother*?"

"I tricked her into going—at least I think I did. Now don't you look at me like that. I had to establish the link with her, to prove it really was you."

"But they will arrest her for *favoreggiamento*."

"Oh, they wouldn't do that. Mothers are allowed to help their sons, surely."

La mamma è sempre la mamma. Yes, but the law is the law. And what this *mamma* had been doing for the past twenty years was not called "helping," but "aiding and abetting"—*favoreggiamento*, that is, in Italian—since her son was guilty of several crimes, of which pretending to be dead and living under a false name were only two of the ones that counted least. Mike remembered the tilt of her head and the fire in her old, bloodshot eyes and the tremor of anxiety, so quickly suppressed, in her voice on the phone. A game old bird if ever there was one, he thought; and all at once he was appalled at the idea of her going to jail.

"She's got five hours. Time to get clean away."

"At seventy-four? And where to?"

"I might try calling Carlo to see if—"

"If he will leave her out of it? Or maybe drop the whole thing?" Beppe laughed. "An old journalist like him is going to kill a story like that just because you say 'please be nice'? Anyway, how can you call anyone now?"

"Christ! What a mess!" Mike muttered.

He stepped out of the car and into Beppe's shoes again, and strained his eyes in the direction of Nemi. A whitish speck was gliding down the winding road towards the lake. Whether it was a blue and white police car, it was impossible to say, and if it had a siren wailing, it was too far away to be heard. Still, he did think he could see the faint flashing of a blue light.

"We've got five or six minutes," he said, getting back into the car.

"*Per la miseria!* Let me out!" Beppe clambered clumsily over the back of the passenger seat.

Mike grabbed his arm. "Don't be an idiot. There's nowhere to go. I told you, this is a dead end."

"I'll hide."

"Oh, no, you won't. If I stay, you stay."

He knew as he said it that he could no more stay and wait for the police than he could hand Beppe over to them in cold blood. His hands were suddenly moist with fear—the illogical, icy fear of being made to give his name and answer questions that, ten to one, would land him back behind bars.

307

Beppe ripped off his jacket. "So we'll both go, together," he said. "Your idea was to swim, no? Okay, I'll swim too."

Beppe's torso, now shirtless, was flabby and pale. Mike eyed it with distaste. "*Can* you swim?" he said.

"No. But there is no other way." Having wriggled out of his trousers, Beppe stuffed his socks into the pockets and opened the car door.

"Here, wait a minute," said Mike. "We can't just jump in the lake. There's a knife down there with blood on it."

"*Bellissimo.* You killed me and escaped. You have that part already planned, I think, no?" He pointed at the watertight pouch in Mike's hand.

"The idea was to prove my innocence and leave you to face the music. Not to get left looking like a murderer all over again."

"So what do you want, then? To see me dead, really?"

"Ssshh!" Mike turned his head to listen to the faint sounds of the lake: a soft ripple lapping at the reeds, a dog barking somewhere far away—and yes, there it was again, a moan, the unmistakable, swooping moan of a police siren. All at once it grew louder; it was threateningly close. There were only two or three minutes left.

He snatched off his watch and slipped it into the watertight pouch before placing this inside a bathing cap—the last item in the plastic bag.

"One minute," said Beppe, pulling off his own watch and fumbling for his passport in the pockets of his coat. "And these?"

"Oh, damn you, all right," Mike said impatiently, taking them from him and squeezing them into the pouch. He paused to stare at the roll of banknotes—mostly dollars, he noticed—that Beppe was holding out to him. And here I was, asking *mamma* to hurry over with some cash, he thought. She must have known he always kept a little nest egg handy, in case he had to do a sudden flit.

Mike inserted the now very bulky pouch into the bathing cap, which he carefully fitted on his head. "Don't forget they're your fingerprints on the knife, not mine," he said.

"Fingerprints? In that mud?" Beppe shrugged. "And anyway, if they don't catch me, how can they know?"

"And all the other clues? My clothes, my documents, my British passport sunk with the car in the lake? It was all supposed to point to your killing me. It doesn't make any sense the other way round."

"Maybe they'll think you killed me and committed suicide. Or we killed each other—*pum! pum!*—like in a Western. Listen, let them think what they like. Just let's go."

"Here. Put your clothes in this. They'll get wet, but it's the best I can do." Mike tossed Beppe the empty plastic bag. "But dammit," he said, "I don't want people thinking that when I said I was going to kill you, I actually meant it all along. That leaves me looking like a real bloodthirsty bastard."

"Why do you care so much what people think? If it's Robin you mean, we'll tell her the truth."

"How? If *I* tell her, she might not believe me."

"That will be the test, no?"

But the siren was now very loud indeed; the police car must almost have reached the end of the road. There was no more time left to talk. Mike slipped Beppe's muddy shoes in on top of the plastic bag and helped him tie as tight a knot as he could.

"Slip the loop over your arm and hope for the best," he told Beppe, starting the car and releasing the handbrake. "Keep the door open and hold on to it. Now—be ready to jump. God! I hope I know what I'm doing."

The car began gliding slowly towards the water as the siren petered out with one last, eerie wail.

The two men who leaped out of the police car were in time to see the red Spyder slip smoothly into the lake beyond the reeds, and sink.

They started running at once, slithering and stumbling in the mud, but when they reached the clearing at the far end, there was nothing left. They stood and stared at the smooth surface of the lake. A few bubbles, then nothing more. The car had disappeared.

There were thick bramble bushes all round, and beyond them, a high chain-link fence enclosing someone's private property. The only way out of the clearing was the path they had taken to reach it themselves; and the only sound was the rhythmic croaking of the toads.

Only a few yards away, concealed behind a thick clump of reeds that jutted out into the water, Mike and Beppe were clinging to the muddy edge of the bank, trying not to make the slightest sound. Neither of them was in particularly good shape, and though they had had to swim only three or four yards, it had winded them badly, especially Beppe, who had begun spluttering and floundering in the ice-cold water, and had to be tugged frantically to safety. But there was no time to hang about. Mike heaved himself up onto the bank and hauled Beppe out after him. It took them a moment or two to recover their breath before Mike helped Beppe to his feet and they set off, two dripping and naked skulkers, heading for a flight of thickly overgrown stone steps.

They were in private grounds now, the extensive garden of some privileged person's summer residence. Mike was counting on the fact that, as far as he had been able to ascertain in his surveys of the area, there was no other way up to the road above on that side of the lake. Nor could the police enter the grounds from below— except by boat—because the chain-link fence shut them out. The only way for them to reach the upper road, where the old gray Fiat was parked, was to go back the way they had come, through Nemi itself—a good fifteen minutes' drive.

On the way up, Beppe opened the plastic bag and, with a series of little hops, stops, and runs, managed to struggle into his sodden clothes as he went, without getting left too far behind. At the top of the steps he stopped and squeezed his feet into the waterlogged shoes, which squelched and weighed him down as he walked.

Luckily there was no one about. At that time of year the house was still shuttered and uninhabited. They strolled past it as casually as they could, and clambered out over the railings into the road where the Fiat was waiting. Mike peeled off his bathing cap, fished the car key out of the pouch, and made a dive for the clothes and the wig and the mustache he had left ready in the suitcase in the trunk.

By the time he had it all on and they both tumbled into the car, the excitement of the escape had swept all else out of their minds. They collapsed, panting and laughing with relief, like two little boys who had just missed being caught after gobbling stolen apples on an orchard wall. All that mattered just then was that they had run away. But from what? The police? Imprisonment? The shadow of death? Or just themselves, and the tangle of mistakes that lay behind?

THIRTY-TWO

The long, winding road to Nemi crept uphill through a thick forest, and to Leo Santi, in his battered little Fiat cinquecento, with its engine rattling fit to burst from the strain, it seemed that he would never reach the top. *"Oh, Dio! Oh, Dio!"* he moaned, honking his horn ferociously at every car that blocked his way, as one after another did, chugging slowly up the hill, carrying day-trippers enjoying the view. He had long since lost sight of Carlo Rolli's van, which had raced on ahead and had probably reached Nemi by now.

"What's the time?" he asked Piero, Massimo Fabbri's young nephew, who was perched nervously on the seat beside him.

Piero looked at his watch for the umpteenth time and said, "Four twenty-five."

"Four twenty-five!" Leo echoed in despair. "But why—*why* couldn't you give me the note sooner?"

"Because Mike told me to give it to you at half past three, that's why. How many times do I have to tell you?"

"And when he told you to block the road so no one could follow him, couldn't you have *guessed* there was something wrong with that?"

"How? I thought it was a joke or something. Maybe it is."

"A joke, yes—very funny. That's what we all said—ha ha! But you don't tell people to call the police for a joke."

"How was I to know that was what it said?"

"Oh, *Maria Santissima!*" Leo cried, jamming on his brakes in front of a flock of sheep that was lumbering tranquilly across the road with a gentle jingling of bells, followed by a young, rosy-

312

cheeked shepherd. The turnoff to Nemi was only a few yards ahead of them on the right, but another two minutes passed before they could drive on.

Mike had sketched a map of the lake on the note he had left with Piero, to show Leo where to send the police. "Phone them the minute you get this," he had written, "and then drive on up here yourself. Beppe'll be dead by the time you arrive, but that'll double the value of any extra shots you can get, and you deserve a nice scoop like that."

At the end of the asphalt road round the lake, there were two police cars now, as well as Carlo's van and a young policeman, who did his best to stop Leo from charging past him down the muddy path, and succeeded only in holding back Piero. But not even Leo could get past the much heftier policeman who made it his business to prevent him from entering the clearing, where quite a scuffle was going on between two other officers and Carlo's crew, who were being pushed forcibly back towards the path. One policeman was thrashing about among the brambles, cursing every time he got scratched as he tried to find a gap in the chain-link fence, while another was examining what was left of the tire marks after the mud had been churned up by a dozen pairs of feet.

"What's happened?" Leo shouted. "What's that?" He pointed at the knife a plainclothesman was holding, carefully wrapped in a handkerchief. The plainclothesman only shook his head and shrugged.

"Car fell in the lake," said the policeman nearest to Leo.

"A red sports car," Carlo added pointedly, as he was forced back onto the muddy path beside him.

"In the lake? Oh, no!" Leo moaned. "Why don't you do something?" he cried out, looking from one policeman to the other.

"It's half an hour now," said the hefty man near him.

The plainclothesman just held up the knife in his hand, as if that alone were sufficient reason to do no more.

Carlo signaled to his crew and they all turned and hurried back to their van.

"Why can't someone dive in and look for them?" Leo insisted.

"Them?" said the man in plain clothes, moving closer.

"Mike Donato and Beppe Palazzo," Leo blurted out, unable to contain himself. "Where are they? What's happened to them?"

"You seem to know more than we do," said the plainclothesman. "I think we'd better go and have a talk."

After losing sight of Leo in Piazza Navona, Robin had raced straight home in the hope that Mike might phone. "I'll be in touch as soon as I can," he had told her. But what did he mean? In an hour or two, or tomorrow, or next week? And in the meantime, how was she going to stand it, limply puttering about as if nothing had happened, in the well-carpeted silence of that claustrophobic flat? What was she doing there, rearranging the ornaments on the steel-and-glass coffee table, and the cushions that Adele had tidied into a straight row, and watering the plants and nibbling her fingers and staring helplessly at the phone, with Mike off God knows where, up to heaven knows what?

Leo was the only person she could think of who might have some idea where he had gone, but she had dialed his two numbers again and again, and there was never any answer, which began to seem strange after four o'clock, when the shop should have reopened.

At five, the phone rang. Startled, she rushed to snatch it up. But it was only Serena, who asked in a hoarsely furtive voice, "Did you hear?"

"What?"

"Open the radio, quick!" She hung up without saying what program, but of course she meant the news, which was half over by the time Robin could switch it on.

". . . All we know at present is that it was a red sports car," the newscaster was saying, "presumably Mike Donato's Alfa Romeo Spyder, and it sank so fast that he may have been trapped inside."

Robin stared at the radio, numb with horror, trying to tame the thumping in her chest by repeating to herself: No matter what you hear, it won't be true.

". . . One of the many disquieting aspects of this mysterious affair is that Donato himself appears to have taken elaborate steps

314

to be sure the police would be on the spot in time to see the car sink, which tends to rule out the possibility of an accident."

It couldn't be true. It made absolutely no sense. Whatever you hear, he had said, trust me. But supposing something had gone wrong? A blown tire, a skid. When the phone rang again, she jumped.

"What do you think? He is dead?" Serena asked in a conspiratorial whisper.

"No."

"How, no?"

"No, that's all. No! He can't be. It's a mistake."

"Why? You know something?"

"No. I don't know anything. I just—well, what *did* they say? Can you tell me? They don't know either, do they?"

"You want that I come round?"

"No! Oh, sorry. I didn't mean to—look, I'll call you tomorrow. *Va bene?*"

"*Va bene, va bene. Ciao.*"

Serena hung up, offended, and Robin moved away from the phone, thinking: Oh, God, is that it, then? Is this my life forever now? Cushions and ornaments and clothes and food, and Serena and Alberto after supper? She stared out at the dull, flat countryside beyond Piazza delle Muse, trying to imagine what it would mean, Mike's being really and truly gone. A sense of blank dismay came over her at the idea that there would be no more meetings under the cedar tree in Villa Pamphili, no more peacocks in Villa Sciarra, and no more of the other thing, which had not seemed so good at the time, but which had since acquired immense importance in her mind.

But it wasn't true, it wasn't. Mike had been quite definite: "No matter what you hear, it won't be true . . . I'll be in touch as soon as I can."

She dialed Leo's number again—still no answer. Not knowing what else to do, she looked up Max Molinari in the phone book and dialed that number too. If only Beppe's voice would answer and say, "*Ciao, amore,*" as if nothing had happened. But nothing *had* happened—he was just out, she told herself when the phone went on ringing and ringing in his flat, like that other time, years ago, when she had tried phoning him from Nicola's. It had the same ghostly feeling to it that it had had then. But he wasn't dead then. Everyone thought he was, but he wasn't. Why should he be dead now? Oh, Lord, her hands were getting shaky, just at the idea.

She rushed to the television set and switched it on, in case there might be some news. There wasn't—only a little girl singing a silly song. She turned down the sound and began meandering restlessly about the room, keeping one eye on the silent images flickering on the screen and feeling more frantic every minute.

When she heard Luca's key in the lock, her first impulse was to run and tell him the whole story, a frame of mind that was reversed in an instant when he asked in a somber tone:

"Where were you at one o'clock?"

"What's the matter? Aren't I allowed to go out?"

"I wanted to have lunch at home."

"Well, I'm sorry, but as you said you wouldn't, I took the liberty of not being in attendance."

"Why do you speak like that? What is wrong with you?"

"Nothing. I'm just sick of being expected to be on tap all the time."

"You have not told me where you were."

"I went and had lunch out, imagine! I went and sat outside the Café de Paris all by myself and ate chicken salad and ice cream."

All she needed was a smile or an outstretched hand, and she would have broken down and made a clean breast of everything. But instead of smiling, he stared at her with a sort of blank solemnity she could not fathom. It might have been sad accusation, or regret for having been suspicious. It could have been disbelief in what she had just said, or even knowledge of what she had really been doing. Perhaps he knows everything, she thought. Perhaps he knows every move I've made during all these weeks. Anger at his lack of faith in her easily outweighed any sense of guilt she might have had. For a moment she really believed she had been to the Café de Paris, and she resented his failure to believe her tale. His hostility struck her as insufferable when she was so badly in need of moral support. She wanted to say, "Please, Luca, *please* don't be like this!" But no, without another word, she stumped back into the living room and turned up the sound of the television set.

She was not prepared for the sight of Mike's little red car, spitting and spluttering water as they hauled it up out of the lake on the end of a long cable. The program had changed to the news while she was out of the room, and a commentator was saying:

"No bodies have so far been found, and it is still not clear what happened to the second man in the car."

It was not so easy to keep on repeating, No matter what you hear, it won't be true, while watching Mike's belongings being taken out of his suitcase, all sopping wet, and spread on a table at the police station. A close shot of his sodden identity card, with its ugly, unflattering photograph, made the blood rush to her head, and when a man with a microphone asked a police officer, "Whose body are you actually expecting to find?" she stood mesmerized, hardly able to breathe.

The police officer gave the viewers a sphinxlike smile and said, "As far as we know, the only person missing is Mike Donato."

"But," pressed the interviewer, "supposing Donato were to be found alive?"

"At present, that appears unlikely."

"And supposing you had proof that Beppe Palazzo was alive this afternoon—"

"Supposing, supposing—" The police officer's tone turned a shade testy.

"Supposing, only supposing," the man with the microphone insisted, "you had proof that it was Beppe Palazzo in the car with Donato, and all the evidence were to indicate that Mike Donato had killed him today. What would you do—if you found Donato alive?"

"Arrest him." The police officer seemed amused at being asked anything so obvious, though he added at once, "Naturally, we are speaking of a simple hypothesis."

"But Mike Donato was convicted of that same murder years ago. Do you mean it's not true that no man can be tried twice for the same thing?"

"That's for the courts to decide, not us. If a murder's been committed, we arrest the murderer. But all this is mere theory. Let us return to hard facts." He held up Mike's British passport. "A man who leaves his passport behind would not appear to have escaped alive."

With her eyes riveted to the screen, Robin recalled Mike's excitement at the discovery that this very same passport had been renewed while he was in jail. To him it represented the proof that Beppe was alive, and now it was supposed to prove that Mike himself was dead.

"Oh, Mike!" she murmured, cupping her hands to her cheeks. "Oh, my God—Mike!"

"So he's dead," said Luca. She heard him take in a deep breath behind her. "Ah, well—perhaps it is better."

"Better!" She spun to face him. "How can it be better for a man to be dead?"

"It can be better for you, and for me."

"How can you say that?" she shouted. "How can you say anything so—horrible?" She turned away quickly to try and stop the tears, but they flooded her eyes and turned the images on the screen watery, though she dimly perceived that there were boats out there now, and divers dragging the lake, and hordes of policemen sifting the mud, or something.

"You are crying?" Luca said. "For this man? This murderer?"

"Mike's not a murderer!" she retorted, turning angrily to face him again.

"My dear, you cannot change facts to please yourself."

"What facts? You don't know anything about it."

"Ssh! Sit down and look—and listen to what they are saying."

She turned back and subsided into an armchair facing the television, in time to see Leo Santi facing the man with the microphone by the lake, looking profoundly embarrassed and upset.

"So who *was* this other man with him in the car?" the interviewer asked him.

"I've told you—Beppe Palazzo."

"Alive?"

"Alive! *Cristo!* Will you get that into your heads? Mike's done twenty years for killing a man who's alive!"

"Let's say he *was* alive at—when was it? Two-thirty? But a lot of people heard Donato declare that no one could stop him from killing Palazzo any more, because he'd paid for the crime in advance."

"He was joking!" Leo protested. "Mike wouldn't hurt a fly."

"Now wait a minute," said the man with the microphone. "He's just done twenty years for murder."

Leo gave a howl of exasperation. "But that's what I'm saying! If he did kill Beppe twenty years ago, he couldn't have done it today, now could he? And if Beppe's still alive, Mike's got a right to prove it. No?"

"How do you explain the knife with blood on the blade?"

"I can't. Can you?"

"It looks to me as if someone got killed with that knife."

"All right, then—who? You tell me!"

Luca turned away from the television to look sternly at Robin. "So?" he said. "Do you consider it pleasant to be involved in this affair?"

"What do you mean?"

"Roberta, I am not a fool. Do you think I have not noticed how you have changed since he returned?"

She felt herself blush; so he did know, then.

"I said nothing because it is better to say nothing of such things. But I can be patient so much and no more. *Adesso basta.*"

He had decided. Enough was enough.

"You don't seem to understand," she said. "It's Mike they're looking for in that lake out there. Not just anyone—Mike! They think he's dead. And I love him."

"Perhaps you did once, or thought you did. Now you are just a little confused."

"No!"

"You can't love a man who has been in prison for twenty years. For murder!"

"All the more reason, don't you think—if he was innocent all along?"

"Ah, so that is it—just pity."

"No, it's *not* pity! It's—it's—"

"Love?" His tone was deeply sarcastic, even contemptuous. "Or simply a foolish desire to run away from reality and pretend to be young again? Such cases are very common at your age."

"Oh, you can be nasty when you want to, can't you? Such cases, indeed! You think of everything in terms of clichés. It all has to fit the rules—your rules. Well, Mike doesn't, and I'm not going to either, anymore. You can't just say *adesso basta* and turn me back into a thing."

"A thing?"

"Yes, a thing, a thing! One of the many things you own. But I'm not a thing. I'm *me*."

"*Ah! Ma sei isterica!*"

"Oh, I'm hysterical, am I? If I say I want to be me?"

"Calm yourself, please."

"Luca, tell me. Who am I?"

"What do you mean? You are my wife."

That was it. She wasn't anybody. Just his wife. An appendage, nothing more.

"Oh, Luca. Couldn't you have said 'Robin'?"

"Listen, I can't speak to you anymore. You are upset—you do not realize. Why don't you take some *camomilla* and go to sleep?"

Take some *camomilla* and go to sleep—ye gods! I've been asleep for fourteen years, she thought. It's about time I woke up.

At that moment the phone rang, and she rushed to get it before Luca could. "*Pronto?*" she whispered, breathless with hope.

"Signora Ferrero?" said an old woman's voice, the last voice she expected to hear.

"Yes," she murmured, with a glance at Luca, who was standing watching her. "Who's that?"

320

"I am the Contessa De Cleris. I have a message for you. But I was told to be sure you are alone. Are you?"

"No."

"*Chi è?*" said Luca.

"A lady I know," she told him, adding into the telephone, "Hold on—I'll take it in another room." Luca's forehead creased into a deep, incredulous frown as she replaced the receiver and turned to run down the corridor. At the bedroom door, she glanced back and saw him staring after her, which made her shut the door behind her and, after a second's hesitation, turn the key in the lock.

Throwing herself down on the bed, she lifted the receiver beside it to whisper, "I'm alone now. What is the message?"

"First, nobody must know what I'm going to tell you. Is that clear?"

"Yes, yes."

"Second, I was to say, '*E' finita la notte*'—which I was told you would understand."

The night is over. Oh, God, yes, she knew what that meant. It was from a poem of Pavese's they used to love, called "In the Morning You Always Come Back." It meant that Mike was all right, first of all.

"Yes," she whispered, weak with relief; and again, faintly, "Yes?"

"He has to leave the country tonight. If you want to go with him, he says you must come at once."

"At *once?*"

"If you want to. It's for you to decide."

"Where?"

"He says there are two special plane trees on the Gianicolo. He was certain you would know which ones he meant."

"Yes."

"Can you be there at eight o'clock?"

"Eight o'clock? But it's twenty to seven now. And I—I have things to settle here."

"He said eight o'clock. And to remember to bring your passport. Am I to tell him yes or no?"

321

Robin heard herself utter a very faint, "Yes," though where the decision had come from she could not think; perhaps she had made it long ago. All she knew now was that she had no choice. She could not stay with Luca and let Mike go.

"Remember, no one must know where you are going. No one must follow you. Is that clear?"

"Yes," said Robin. It was the only word that kept coming out. Replacing the receiver, she realized she had forgotten to ask about Beppe; but if his mother was phoning her, he must be all right. How very extraordinary, though. She looked at her watch again; it was six-forty-two. She had just over an hour in which to turn her life upside down.

Stunned, she looked round the room, wondering where to begin. She pulled a suitcase out of the wardrobe, but it was a leather suitcase and very expensive; on second thoughts, she pushed it back in again, unlocked the door, and sprinted down the corridor to the kitchen to collect a few plastic supermarket bags instead. She left these on a chair in the hall while she slipped quietly into the living room to fetch her passport. Luca was still staring at the television and appeared not to notice her opening the drawer of the desk behind him. But as she closed it again, he stood up and turned to face her with an air of belligerence.

"Who was that on the telephone?" he demanded, his face strangely pale.

"A lady. Signora Caruso," Robin told him, picking a name at random. "She wants an English teacher for her granddaughter." Lies were two a penny, once you got started.

"And it is to talk of English teachers that you lock the door?"

"Look, it's none of your business."

"Ah, no? And this?" Luca waved at the television. "Is this none of my business also?"

Robin glanced at the television and froze at the sight of herself with her great pregnant belly, flashing on and off the screen alternately with that old, fatal photograph of her kissing Beppe and various shots of Mike punching paparazzi. Offscreen, she heard Carlo Rolli's voice saying, "They called it the mystery of the child

322

with two fathers, and a mystery it still remains. What kind of man was—or is—Mike Donato? And is Beppe Palazzo alive or dead? We'll try to find all that out on 'Telescopio' tonight at nine-thirty."

"*Che figura!*" said Luca.

"Oh, Christ! Is that all you can think of—*la brutta figura*? Yes, it is shocking, isn't it? Your wife mixed up in a scandal, imagine! Pregnant by a murderer. What a terrible figure you'll cut. That's all you're going to say now when I leave you—'*che figura!*' I don't believe you'll miss me at all, actually. You'll just be worried silly about what people will think."

Luca straightened up and tightened his jaw and drew in his breath. She hated it when he looked hurt like that.

"What are you saying?" he said.

"I'm going, Luca. I'm going to leave you. Now."

"What does it mean, now?"

"Now. *Adesso*. As soon as I've put a few things together."

"*Ma sei impazzita?*"

"No. I'm just coming back to life again. I suppose that is a pretty insane thing to do by your standards, but you see, I've had all I can take of your standards. *Adesso basta*. I'm sorry, Luca, really, but I can't help it. I've got to go."

"Where?"

"Away. I don't know where."

His face began slowly to turn a very deep shade of red. "This is very strange," he said. "First a mysterious telephone call. Then suddenly you decide to run away. In a great hurry. Can it be, perhaps, that your precious Mike is not so dead after all?"

"Why? Don't you think I'm capable of going away on my own?"

"Frankly, no. I think a woman does not leave a good husband and a good home except for another man."

"Well, I'm sorry if you think that, but there's nothing I can do about it."

She turned and ran out of the room, snatching up the plastic bags on her way back down the corridor to the bedroom, where she began pulling things out of drawers in handfuls and stuffing them into the bags. She picked out a few dresses and skirts and coats from the wardrobe and lay them on the bed, still on their hangers. She left all the jewels, everything of any real value except her watch, which she needed for the moment. Anyway, damn it, he had given it to her for her birthday; it was hers, not his.

Looking up, she saw him standing in the doorway, watching her. He was very, very angry. Angry, not upset.

"Roberta," he managed to say at last. But it was an admonition, not a plea.

"What's the matter?" she snapped. "Aren't I allowed to take my clothes? Do you consider *them* yours, too? No, that's not fair." She ran to him and put her arms round his big, solid chest. "You've always been very generous, I know. I'm sorry, Luca, honestly I'm sorry. You've been a wonderful husband in your way and I do love you, really, but—" She broke off. He had remained rigid, a rock of respectable marital indignation.

"You have a strange idea of love," he said.

She bit her lip and backed away. "Oh, hell!" she burst out, turning to gather up the things on the bed.

"If you go like this, you will not come back," he said. "You will not be my wife anymore."

"No, I'll be Robin again. Won't that be fantastic?" She turned back, ready to go, three bulging plastic bags looped over one arm and the pile of clothes on their hangers over the other. "Oh, Luca," she said, "this is horrible. Give me a kiss or something, please."

"A kiss?" he said, his face almost purple.

"Oh, damn! Never mind. Goodbye."

She blundered past him with her unwieldy burden, straight on down the corridor to the front door. He did not move. He did not turn. He did not say another word. As she shut the door behind her, she thought: Oh, my God! I've done it now.

The false passport felt like a bomb in his pocket the minute Mike walked into Fiumicino airport and saw that it was teeming with policemen. That was the worst of these spur-of-the-moment changes: they made you lose your grip on things. The way he had planned it, no one would have been on the lookout for runaway murderers. The police would already have had Beppe under lock and key, and the only place they would have been looking for Mike Donato was at the bottom of the lake. But now, anything could happen; and here he was, an ex-convict, walking round with a wig on and a silly, phony mustache. He had always known it wasn't much of a disguise, but he felt so conspicuous wheeling his luggage through the crowded airport that he expected some bright policeman to pounce on him any minute. He was tempted to let go of the baggage cart and make a dash for the bathroom, to peel it all off, tear up the passport, and flush the lot down the drain. Just for the passport, he could get another two or three years. Steady on, he told himself. Don't be a bloody fool—you need that passport like bread, now that you've gone and dumped your real one in the lake. Just keep your head and look casual, and no one'll ever notice you're there.

Of all the places to attract attention, the airport really took the biscuit. He had surprised even himself when he agreed to drive Beppe there; he could just as well have found the blighter a taxi. Anybody'd think he owed him something. Well, perhaps he did. Anyway, he had come; for some reason he couldn't explain, he hadn't been able to help himself.

It was nearly six o'clock by the time they reached the airport. Chugging along at about fifty miles an hour, which was the most he had dared ask the old Fiat to do, getting stopped again and again in the dense traffic of several small towns along the way, it had taken them an hour and twenty minutes; and during all that time they had churned over and over the various risks they both ran as things now stood, coming back every time to the inevitable conclusion that the only way to be safe was to leave Rome that night.

Mike himself was already booked on a late plane for Madrid, where he could pick up a connection for Mexico City the next day. It would have suited Beppe very nicely to go with him as far as Madrid, but it was obviously unwise for them to travel together. In any case, Beppe did not much care where he went that night, as long as it was somewhere out of reach, not too far away, where he could sit and quietly await developments. All he was worried about at the moment was getting through passport control, without anyone taking it into his head to stop him.

"Why should they stop you?" Mike had said. "No one's looking for Max Molinari."

"But they can be looking extra carefully at passports."

"Crikey! So they can."

That was when Mike had started having serious misgivings about his own, and kicking himself for sinking his British one in the lake; but it was too late then to turn back, too late to do anything much except hope for the best and take what precautions they could, such as keeping discreetly apart, once they were inside. Beppe had gone bustling off ahead to see what flight he could find at that hour, while Mike fetched a baggage cart and unloaded his baggage, which he had decided to leave at the airport till he came back in a few hours to check in himself.

They had agreed to meet again behind the newspaper kiosk. There was a narrow space between this and the glass front of the airport, where they were concealed by other kiosks and various concrete pillars, to one of which was attached a public telephone. When Mike arrived, Beppe was already there, whispering into the receiver with his hand cupped over his mouth and his face buried in the eggshaped plexiglass hood of the phone. He was saying goodbye to his mother, presumably, but so passionate were the movements of his head as he tried to set her mind at rest, that a casual observer would certainly have supposed him to be talking to a lover. Glancing round, he caught sight of Mike and held up the airline ticket he had just procured, waving his hand to show that time was short, before turning back quickly to the phone and, after a moment, hanging up.

"*Ah, la mamma, la mamma,*" he said, shaking his head.

"What will she do—without you?" Mike asked him.

"She will wait, and hope I come back, like before."

"But she is seventy-four now; it's a bit different."

"It's a little late, no, to remember that? Ah, well—" Beppe sighed. "I gave her your message, to phone Robin. You will know

326

the answer when you go to see her. You *will* go, no? As we said? She is taking a taxi immediately to Piazza Navona to pack up all the things she can and take them home with her, so she can ship them to me when I tell her where. I told her she must go this evening. If the whole story appears on television tonight, who knows what will happen after that? She saw something about it on the news already, but not much—she said they seemed to know almost nothing. So tonight I think it is still all right. Tomorrow, though, it would be too dangerous. If the police know the address, they may watch the house."

"I'm not sure it's exactly safe, even now. Who knows what Leo may have told them?"

"Nothing is exactly safe anymore. But quick, I must leave. There is no time."

"Where are you going?"

"Athens tonight. Tomorrow—who knows? Maybe we all come back. Or maybe you will like it in Mexico more than in Rome, and one day—I could even join you there."

"What, in Mexico?" Mike looked shocked.

Beppe laughed. "That would be funny, eh? Maybe I could launch you on a new career over there. I have a great talent for such things, you know. We could be a fantastic pair."

But in spite of Beppe's perky smile, as he said it, Mike felt him trembling—with the vulnerable hopefulness of a man who has no real hope.

"Twenty years ago, we both had great talent in our various ways," Mike said. "But now it'll take all the talent we've got just to survive."

"And if I don't go quickly, I will miss the plane. Well, *ciao*."

"You know," Mike said thoughtfully, when Beppe had already turned to go, "there is one incredibly easy way out of all this."

Beppe turned back to look at him. "What's that?"

"I simply stand up and confess that I killed you twenty years ago." Beppe stood staring at him in astonishment. "That way you couldn't be Beppe Palazzo, could you?" Mike went on. "Beppe Palazzo couldn't be alive. They couldn't accuse me of killing you

327

today. And your mother couldn't be guilty of *favoreggiamento*."

"And the television? She said they filmed her in my apartment."

"But we've found an explanation for that. Isn't that what I'm going to see her about?"

"And the photographs they took of me?"

"That was Max Molinari, a friend of mine who looks a bit like you would now, if you were still around. Even Leo was only half convinced it was you."

For a moment Beppe remained hesitant, half wanting to believe it might work. Then he laughed.

"You really want to stay, don't you?"

"Well, for God's sake, why not? I haven't done a damn thing."

"You hadn't the other time, either, and look what happened then."

"That was twenty years ago. Things are different now."

"I wouldn't count on that. Listen, you do what you want. The police might even believe you—or find it convenient to pretend to. But there are other people—remember?—who might not. For myself, *caro* Mike, I cannot stay one minute more. So, give my love to Robin. And—*arriverderci*."

He ran off through the crowds, towards passport control. Mike followed slowly and stopped some distance off to watch him hand over the passport in the name of Max Molinari and strain himself to look relaxed while the policeman in the glass booth carefully checked it, page by page. Mike could not tear himself away at that point, though he knew it was lunacy to go on standing there. But Beppe retrieved the passport without a hitch and walked on a few steps, past the metal detector, before turning back to grin, and signal thumbs up, and wave. Then he was gone, leaving Mike alone with the unsettling thought that he had just waved Beppe Palazzo goodbye. And the hope that he had not made a terrible mistake.

The Contessa looked older, ten years older, than when Mike had seen her last. The cold, dry hand she proffered was tremulous, her breathing labored, and she wore no makeup on her parched, sallow skin. It was as if she had shed her armor and thrown down her arms. All that was for Beppe, Mike thought, the rouge and the peroxide and the fire in her eyes; now that he had gone, she seemed to have shrunk. Beppe's phone call from the airport must have been the last straw, after the shock of her encounter with Carlo Rolli. She ought to have been resting in the safe comfort of her room, yet she had rallied to Beppe's parting request and summoned the strength to come and deal with his things at the flat. He found her there when he reached Piazza Navona at half past seven. She opened the door and stood before him, trembling but still erect.

"Come in, then," she said in a tired voice, turning her back on him and walking away. Mike followed her into the bedroom, where she was busy filling a huge suitcase with Beppe's clothes.

"I phoned Signora Ferrero," she said, taking a pile of shirts out of a drawer and placing them on the bed. "The answer is yes."

"Yes! She's coming? She'll be there at eight?"

"I imagine so," the Contessa said dryly, packing a layer of shirts into the case.

"Oh, my God—thank you!" In his joy, he reached out impetuously for her hand. He would have embraced her if she had let him. But she turned sharply away to fetch a jacket from the wardrobe. "So?" she said, without looking at him. "What is it you came to tell me?"

"Can't you leave that a minute? I haven't got much time."

"You can talk while I finish it," she said, folding the jacket carefully and fitting it in with shaky but determined hands. "It's nearly done."

"No, please, come in here," he said, walking back into the living room. "I must turn the television on, just in case."

She straightened up then and turned to follow him with her eyes. "In case what?" she asked.

"In case they say anything about us that makes it too dangerous to be here."

"Dangerous?" she murmured from the bedroom doorway.

"It all depends on what the police think happened at the lake,

329

and if they change their minds about Beppe being dead. The point is, you see, Contessa, I've done my damnedest to prove he's alive, and we won't know if I succeeded until 'Telescopio' comes on at half past nine tonight. By which time I should be at the airport, getting ready to board a plane. And you may possibly find yourself in the soup."

She stared at him, resting one hand on the doorjamb as if she feared her strength might be about to fail; then she made her way across the room and sat on the sofa. A moment or two elapsed before she said, "What do you mean?"

Mike sat down in the armchair facing her. He had switched on the television and turned down the sound so that he could keep an eye on it while they talked. "Beppe said they caught you here this afternoon."

"Unfortunately, yes."

"Did you use your key?"

She nodded, seeing what he meant. "I don't know if they saw me open the door, those—"

"Television people. From 'Telescopio.' That's what I'm talking about. Apart from the key, was there anything you did that might prove Beppe is alive?"

She took a deep breath and drew herself up. "I'm afraid I did call out 'Beppe.' I am more careful as a rule, but I was extremely nervous. Finding him gone like that—at my age such things take their toll."

"All right, now listen. The main point at the moment is that if it comes out that Beppe was still alive this afternoon, you stand to be arrested for aiding and abetting him—"

"*I?*"

"Yes, you. You could get up to four years. And I risk being accused of murdering him today."

"Wasn't that what you wanted to do?"

"No, never—I swear. All that talk about Article Ninety was only for effect. What I had in mind was quite a different kind of revenge; but that was when I thought black was black and white was white. It's a bit late now, I know, to find out things aren't that simple—but what can I do?"

The old woman remained silent for a while. She leaned forward, shaking her head reflectively, and examined the bowl Beppe had left on the coffee table with a few stale bits of popcorn in it.

"I shall never see him again," she said. For the first time, her shoulders sagged. She looked exhausted and very tiny, sunk in the cushions of the sofa.

"Of course you will—if you do what I say. Now listen. If the police, or any other people, come to question you, what you must say is that someone called at your house, claiming to have proof that your son was alive. He told you to go to Piazza Navona, gave you the key to the flat, and said that if you went in, you would find Beppe living there under the name of Max. You knew it was nonsense, but what mother could resist the temptation to go and make sure? The whole thing was a hoax, understand? A hoax organized by me. And you were tricked into making it look real. But as for this Max Molinari, you never heard of him till today. If we can make that stick, we'll be all right."

"And how am I to handle Beppe's business, if no one is to know of any link between him and me? How am I to close down his office and pay everyone off?"

"But don't you see? If the police accept the fact that he's Max Molinari, he can come back. And I don't see why they shouldn't, if you play it right. Do you think they're that keen to find out Beppe's alive? Do you think anyone is?"

She gave him a long, mournful look and sighed. "Possibly not."

"The other people are the dangerous ones, though, aren't they?" Mike blurted out on an impulse.

"The other people?" Her eyes flickered for a moment in surprise, but noticing the watchfulness in his eyes, she stared at him warily and instantly recomposed her expression. "It is best not to think about that," she said, getting to her feet as she added, "Let me finish the packing."

"There's no time now to do any more," Mike told her. But she ignored him and set off back to the bedroom. "Look, I must be out of here in two minutes," he said, following her.

"Go—go," she said, surveying the wardrobe like a general counting the ammunition.

"Don't tell me you can lift this by yourself. Come on, just get it shut and I'll give you a hand with it down to the street." Mike picked up the remaining shirts on the bed and threw them in on top.

"There's no need—I can manage," she said coldly, opening the drawer of the bedside table and staring at the jumble of things inside. For a moment she seemed to have lost her bearings. Mike pulled the whole drawer out and emptied the contents into the suitcase, before pressing the lid down and with some difficulty getting it fastened.

"But there are so many other things," she protested, watching him stagger with the suitcase to the front door.

"Never mind. I must go now, and so must you. Don't worry—if I know Beppe, he'll manage, with or without his favorite shoes. I'll leave this downstairs and send you a taxi. You just go home and get some rest. And remember, if anyone comes asking questions, play the bereaved mother for all you're worth. You're a fine actress, Contessa. You almost fooled *me*.

It was well after eight and nearly dark when Mike reached the place on the Gianicolo where Robin was waiting for him in her little white car. She jumped out, her face radiant with relief, as he swung the old Fiat off the road and parked in the space between the two plane trees on her left.

"I thought I'd missed you," she cried out. "I was beginning to think I'd arrived too late." She stopped in surprise, peering in through the car window. "My goodness, you look so different."

He put his finger to his lips and leaned over to open the car door for her. When she climbed in, he put his arm round her and tried to draw her close, but she held back.

"What's the wig for?" she asked, with a nervous laugh.

"What are disguises usually for? I'm in a bit of a mess, to tell you the truth. I'm still trying to decide if I'm alive or dead."

"On television they as good as said you'd drowned. I've been going out of my mind the whole afternoon."

"So tell me, quick, what did they say?"

"Not a lot, really, except that if you turned up alive, they'd arrest you. Well, no, that's not right; it was all 'ifs' and 'supposings'; they would if they thought you'd killed Beppe—today, I mean."

"But they didn't, right? Did they think it was him with me, or someone else?"

"I don't know. They were all terribly evasive. The television man was trying to get some police chappy to say it's not true, then, that you can't be tried twice for the same thing. But all he'd say was, 'That's for the courts to decide, not us. If a murder's been committed, we arrest the murderer.' "

"Oh, great. And if they don't know whether a murder's been committed or not, they haul you in anyway on the good old principle, 'Arrest the man first and think about it later—*con calma—molto calma*—while he's left to rot in solitary confinement.' So much for Article Ninety. I told you I was in trouble. Or rather, I will be if I show up now and Beppe doesn't."

"Mike—where *is* Beppe?"

"Gone. That's the awkward part."

"Gone? Where?"

"I put him on a plane to Athens a couple of hours ago."

"You *what*? Oh, come on! I saw you with my own eyes, chloroforming him and carrying him off like a sack of potatoes."

"Well, I'll tell you one thing—Beppe is no potato. I've a strong suspicion he may be the biggest con man of all time."

"For heaven's sake, what happened?"

"Just when I'd got him right where I wanted him, he knocked me sideways with a sad story about why he had had to pretend he was dead. Made it all sound so reasonable that it broke my heart. Now that I think about it, I'm not so sure. I have a sneaking feeling I've been had all over again."

"But he told me that story too. About the Austrian girl, no? And how he was afraid of being killed like her. It didn't sound like a yarn to me."

"We'll never know. You have to hand it to him—at his own slippery game, he's a master, is Beppe. I even quite got to like the bastard in the end. And to think I spent twenty years working out how to get his skin."

"What actually was it you wanted to do?"

"Very simple. I just wanted the police to catch him and think he'd killed me, the same way they caught me and thought I'd killed him. How would that have been for poetic justice, eh? And you should have seen the way I had it staged. A bloody masterpiece, that's what it was—except that I hadn't the heart to go through with it when it came to the point."

"I'm glad you didn't. I wouldn't have liked to think you'd done something cruel. It would have been cruel, you know, no matter what he did to you. I'm glad he made you change your mind."

"Yes, but now what?"

"Now I'm here." She smiled. "You do realize I've left Luca? I mean completely, finally."

"Oh, my God—Robin." He put his arms round her and she let her hands cling to his back while she fought the disquietude she felt. So they stayed for a while, holding each other fast, fighting the strangeness that surrounded them, clinging to the certainty that if they held on long enough, they would find peace. "Is it true?" he asked finally, running his hand through her hair. "Is it really true?"

She pulled back a little to smile at him and take his hand in hers. "So? Where are we going?"

"I'm booked on a plane for Mexico, and so are you, if you feel like coming. But we don't have to be at the airport till ten. That's why I wanted to meet you here, so we could talk a bit, quietly, and I could give you a fair chance to change your mind."

"This is a good place, too, to start again."

They stopped talking to look down at the darkening city beneath them. Here and there a glow of amber appeared as, one by one, certain special buildings were lit up; a string of lights marked the course of the Tiber from Castel Sant'Angelo to the Island, and another shimmered faintly on the Pincio, close to the skyline on the far side of the town. Down on their left, the white giant of the old Palazzo di Giustizia glowed palely in the darkness.

"Tell me something," Robin said. "How come you had Beppe's mother phone me? You couldn't have been counting on that, if you were aiming to see that Beppe got caught."

"No, I was planning to phone you myself, from one of the places you go through on the way back from Nemi. It would have been about half past four, maybe five, and I'd reckoned that Luca wouldn't be home at that time. But then, having Beppe with me and not knowing exactly what I was going to do—I left it too late, and if Luca *had* been there, it would have been too dangerous."

"What if I'd been out?"

"I'd have phoned from Madrid—or Mexico. Don't worry, I'd have reached you somehow. I wasn't going to run away and leave you, if that's what you're thinking."

"I still don't understand why you didn't tell me before. Didn't you trust me?"

"Oh, my love, of course. But I don't trust Luca, and without meaning to, you might have—"

"God!" she cried. "Luca! Supposing he's called the police?"

"Don't tell me you told him?"

"No, but—he may have guessed. Mike—the car! He could have given them the number."

"Accused you of stealing it, you mean?"

"He can't do that—it's in my name. But he can tell them to look for me, can't he? He can tell them he thinks you're with me. I mean, it said on the news they were looking for you."

"So we won't use your car. We'll leave it somewhere for Luca to come and fetch."

"And supposing he tells them to watch the airport? He'll have seen that my passport's gone."

"He wouldn't do that, would he?"

"I don't know. He was so livid, he might."

For a moment Mike stared at her in stunned silence. Then he forced a laugh. "For God's sake," he burst out, "what's the panic? We haven't done anything wrong."

"You're the nervous one," she said. "Look at you—in disguise."

"You try getting twenty years for nothing, and you'll see how nervous you feel once you're out."

"Are we going to be scared for the rest of our lives? Mike, that's crazy! I think we'd better calm down and come to grips with this right away. It seems to me you've got things all out of proportion. Just because there was one enormous, scandalous mistake twenty years ago, it doesn't mean everybody makes that same kind of mistake every day of the week."

"No, but that mistake didn't go away. It stuck to me. It's still there. It colors everything people think about me."

"But it's not going to make anyone make the same mistake again today. They said you killed Beppe then. They can't say you did the same thing again today. Beppe is still alive, isn't he?"

"Yes, but I can't prove it."

"You can; it's just that you don't want to now, because it would get him into trouble, maybe worse trouble than you. But you can, don't forget that. If you have to, you can. You have photographs of him. Carlo Rolli filmed him. I'm here as a witness. And there's his mother. If you want to prove he's alive, you can, Mike. No one can say you've killed him anymore."

"And how do I explain what I was doing down at the lake? Ever heard of *simulazione di reato*? Staging a crime?"

"Beppe was telling me about that today. He called it *calunnia*."

"That's one stage worse. Making an innocent person look guilty. That's what he did to me."

"And what you were intending to do to him."

"That's right—you've got it. I might get out of it and I might not. I can say I was trying out an idea I had for a film, and the hand brake came unstuck and the car slid bonk into the lake. I can say it—but will they believe it? It's a risk, and I just don't feel like running that risk. It's not that I want to go away; I don't. Less than ever, now there's no point in it anymore, but I just can't face up to the risk of getting put back inside. I want to get away from all that—far, far away—start all over again, somewhere else. The idea of Mexico is exciting, no? We can have a fantastic holiday there and forget everything and everyone—have the honeymoon we never managed to have before."

"And then?"

"And then I don't know. We can go somewhere else, or stay there, if we like it."

"Doing what? Living how? I don't know how much money you've

got, but I've got almost none. I spent nearly all I had in my wallet to buy a cheap suitcase on the way here. I didn't feel like taking one of Luca's snazzy ones. I didn't feel like taking anything much. None of it seemed to be mine, somehow. I felt like a thief coming away myself. Can you imagine that? Not seeming to belong to yourself? But when I was halfway here, it suddenly struck me that I could hardly leave the country with an armful of tatty plastic bags, so I stopped and got the cheapest suitcase I could find, which nearly cleaned me out. I can sell my watch, I suppose, but that's about it. And just the ticket alone to Mexico must cost the earth. I mean, are you being realistic?"

"No. No, I'm quite sure I'm not being realistic. I don't think I want to be. I feel like going somewhere extraordinary and doing something extraordinary, like—like—learning to be a clown—why not? Wouldn't that be the answer, eh? Nobody'd ever know what I really looked like or who I was—I wouldn't even have to know the language—and I might even get famous all over again, with a white face and a red nose and a name like . . . Pan."

"And what passport? I know they fished your British one out of the lake."

"I've got a false one, in the name of Danilo De Michele."

"But Mike, if you leave the country with a false passport—"

"I know. I could never come back."

"You'd be an outlaw forever—all for the sake of running away from the fear of injustice. Does that make sense?"

"No. But I can't help it."

"When Beppe disappeared, he was much cleverer than that. He waited till the fuss had died down. If you go tonight, you risk being caught. You know that, don't you?"

"Yes."

"Beppe waited three months—in a house in the country. When everyone had forgotten him, he left. But he *had* to leave. Maybe we don't. We could go to a hotel tonight, and see what the police say tomorrow. And I think it's about time you saw a first-class lawyer and found out where you really stand. And after that, if you ask me, you should go straight back to the British Embassy and apply for another new passport."

"Again? They'll say, 'Here, what's this? Making a habit of it, are you?' "

"Never mind. They'll still have to give it to you. And while you're at it, you can ask them, too, what you ought to do. You're a British subject; you were innocent in the first place and you can prove it. Why should you live in terror under a false name for the rest of your life?"

"Mike Donato's a false name too, if it comes to that."

"All right, so's Robin. So's Max Molinari. We're all phonies, if you like. But Danilo De Michele is just a piece of nonsense."

"Robin De Michele suits you down to the ground. Mike's little Robin. Mike's bird." He laughed and leaned over to kiss the tip of her nose. "So what are we going to do, then? Cancel our bookings?"

"For tonight, yes. Mexico won't go away. But I'd rather you left with a proper passport and your own proper name."

"Shall we get married, do you think, in the end?"

"Not until we're very old. Not for ages yet. I'm off marriage, quite honestly. Living in sin's much more my line."

"And tonight?"

"Tonight we'll go to some seedy little hotel. Like all self-respecting illicit couples."

"And tomorrow we can come up here again and see the dawn."

"You can see the dawn. I'm having breakfast in bed."

"Oh, God, Robin! I'm going to burst! Shall we see if we can afford the old flat in Via Gregoriana?"

"No, that would be silly."

"I feel like being silly."

"No, my love. You've been living in a dream for too long. Reality's better. Different, but better. Just because we're staying in Rome another night doesn't mean we're staying forever. There's a whole world out there waiting. The main thing is not to leave in a way that would mean you couldn't ever come back."

"You know, I really couldn't stand the idea of going away for good." He laughed and threw his arms round her. "Oh, I love you, I love you."

338

"Me—or Rome?"

"You, you. Rome can be a proper bitch. Look down there— 'Dost thou not perceive that Rome is but a wilderness of tigers?' Not bad, eh, for someone who never set foot in the place?"

"Who's that?"

"Shakespeare. I plowed right through the complete works when I was in prison, and that bit—out of *Titus Andronicus*—hit me right in the eye. I translated it for Memmo once, and he just sat and gaped and said, 'How did he know?' "

"Who's Memmo?"

"Oh, Memmo's quite a person. A brick, as you might say. Couldn't put two words together without one of them being obscene, but there was a kind of poetry even in that. Thank God, if I decide I'm not dead, I can write and tell him. That's good. He'd have been upset if I hadn't."

"If Rome was a wilderness, I don't think you'd be so keen to stay."

"That's because it's enchanted. Once you're in it, you can't get out. And you love it even though you know it's arid. You know it's full of tigers and you don't care. They're part of the scenery, you tell yourself, and if they kill you and eat you up, you say *pazienza*, that's life."

"Talking of eating, how about having some supper at our little trattoria?"

"The one at Porta San Pancrazio? It's still there, did you see? Fantastic. Then we'll be right back at the beginning again."

"And after supper, we'll find somewhere to sleep."

"*Sleep?*" He laughed and put his arm round her and drew her closer. They fell silent suddenly, struck by a new sense of tranquility as they gazed down at the sighing, twinkling lights of the town, a town full of ghosts, and demons disguised as crows, and hungry tigers on the prowl, a wilderness of irresistible beauty, where the plane trees are dying and nothing is certain—except the compassion of ancient stones that have witnessed all the humanity and the inhumanity on earth.